THE GOLDEN THREADS TRILOGY BOOK THREE

THREAD · SKEIN

LEELAND ARTRA

DEDICATION

This book is dedicated to my children, Lewin & Sapphira: may you both always stay sharp. And to my beautiful wife, Evelina, for putting up with my late nights dreaming at the keyboard.

FORWARD

Thank *you* for picking up the continuing adventures of Ticca, Lebuin, Ditani, Duke, Elades, and everyone else. Welcome back to the world of Niya-Yur. Niya-Yur, with its 15,000 years of history, has a number of unique beings, customs, and other miscellaneous items. In the event that some of the details slip past too fast as our adventurers travel the world, Lebuin continued to updated his definitions with his new knowledge. A copy is provided at the end of the book in the sections entitled "Lebuin's Lexicon".

NORTHERN ICE FIELDS
Skogen Hut Forest
DUIANNA
NAE-RAE
RHONIA
YALTHUM
LAEUSIA
OSLALD
NASUR
Vino
AELARGO
Circumveni Desert
OCCIDUUS OCEAN
KARAKIA
DARIAN OCEAN
Umbra Forest
DULERIUM
SOUTHERN ICE FIELDS
Niga-Yur: Duianna Continent
0   1000

OSLAD
Korha
Crogan
Uael
Hilford
Tegoll
Loren Goontsound
DASUR
Breorehly
Seadells
Pawls
Nimri
Alagan
Darkilly
Uino
Mantesh
Sharsi
Eppon
Carda
Frostag
Tenby
Haar
AELARGO
Rhopslat
Rhini Woods
Worthy
Hare
Rhini
Bearfoot Sea
Sibis
Spornusa Swamps
Gelepp
Arrur
DARIAD OCEAN
Hawlyd
Circumboni Desert
Kingdom of Aelargo
0   250

Escaping the Llino Trap

CHAPTER 1

BEST LAID PLANS

VESTA, THE OLDEST LIVING SENTIENT computer, co-architect of the current universe, and guardian of Llino city, in the Kingdom of Aelargo, wished for the 12034th time she had real nails to chew on. Still she industriously chewed, with no effect, at her perfect virtual fingernails. The computing cycles wasted on that effort were trivial compared to her vast capabilities, but it was surprisingly comforting.

Two of her three secret monitoring satellites were dedicated to watching the computed trajectory of a 32-foot torpedo-like ship she'd built and launched. A stealth material that absorbed most emissions coated the ship's outer skin. Therefore, the satellites were really tracking the trifling speck of space darker than the rest of space.

As the ship began its decent to the surface of the largest moon, the moon's reddish light sharpened the resolution, dramatically showing the ship's silhouette. With Vesta's precise tuning, the satellites provided a perfect image of the ship's landing. Every detail of the maneuvers, including ones she hadn't pre-programmed into the ship's control systems, scrolled across her displays.

"Arkady is still in control." She sighed reassuringly to herself, seeing the unplanned maneuvers. Still, her eyes bounced around all the detailed data, cross-checking every maneuver and making sure the ship was safely on course. She laughed. "And if he's wrong, how exactly am I supposed to tell him?" she asked the empty control room.

Arkady, the only other sentient computer awake against the orders of the Duianna Assembly, was the only passenger, cargo, and pilot. The ship she had designed and built in less than a week had been silently traveling for three days now, the entire flight controlled by primitive, but hard to detect, liquid-propellant rockets. They'd built the ship to be as invisible as possible, including insulating it to hide Arkady's energy signature.

Llino's city systems hummed in the background, dealing efficiently with the never-ending maintenance requirements. There were dozens of plumbing pipes to repair, thousands of liters of waste to process every mark, tons of silt to be removed from the navigation channels, and all the health requirements of 364,515 people, plus the 22,311 other automated tasks under her care. Vesta had only twelve marks and three minutes earlier finished replacing the 12,988th sensor that kept her aware of almost everything that happened in Llino. Her efforts now focused on finding a way to hide her status of being active if Duke or the assembly came to check physically.

She sighed, letting her hand, with its perfect nails, press her cheek and leaned over the virtual console to review the landing data. The satellite tracking reported that the small ship had landed precisely on the main docking platform. After dealing with 102 minor adjustments to her systems, she chewed her fingernail again for good measure to burn more processing time. The ship was still sitting on the landing platform. It had been 5 minutes and 22.233 seconds since it landed, 2 minutes and 11.022 seconds longer than it should have taken the base's docking systems to activate.

Why hasn't Arkady activated the return program? In 3.101 seconds he won't have enough fuel to get back. If the base is dead there's nothing he can do in that simple ship.

Her system clocks picked up as she felt herself beginning to contemplate whether something had happened to Arkady on the landing. The two of them had been friends for 18,421 years, cycles, days, marks, and 12.334 seconds. They'd helped the great races build this universe. They'd shared system resources for the 12 days, 6 marks, and 3.455 seconds it had taken to move their consciousnesses to this world. Two sentient systems could not be any more intimate than that. She refused to visualize a future without his acerbic comments and raw sense of humor. With 2.1 seconds of margin remaining, a set of docking clamps unfolded from the base to connect to the ship. The docking arms lifted the ship and pulled it into the base's main hanger.

Deep in Llino dozens of systems ceased operations for a full second before slamming back into motion. The sensor data of the base's arms pulling the ship to safety replayed on every display in the virtual control center as Vesta spun in place, shaking her arms and legs in a shudder of relief.

She glanced at her perfect fingernail. *I should modify myself to allow me the pleasure of seeing some damage. That was too much.*

She'd done all she could; it would be at least three days before Arkady could establish a secure communications channel. She turned back to the virtual control center and walked around the room checking the ongoing work of her automated systems. None of the main systems needed adjustment; she would've been worried if they did. She reviewed all the breeding systems' reports on the rebuilding of her half-biologic/half-machine crab-workers.

In the secret battle with the Nhia-Samri she had lost most of her undersea minions. She pulled up the technical diagrams and details. The original undersea-worker design provided all necessary functions to do their jobs of helping maintain the undersea habitats and merchant channels. Vesta and Arkady had modified them, adding additional armor and heavier weapons.

Vesta looked at the designs and sighed. Having to hide meant she needed to have hidden firepower. If she unlocked the city's combat systems, Duke and the Duianna Assembly would realize instantly she was awake illegally. She preferred the simpler peaceful designs, but Arkady had suggested this modification, and though she hated to admit it, he was right. The Nhia-Samri had proven they could defeat a full army of her workers despite their deceptively primitive weapons and techniques. Magic was a powerful force that had as much potential as her sciences. In this new world, magic had to be taken into consideration, and the Nhia-Samri had magic to spare as well as the undeniably advanced knowledge to use it.

She paused to check the palace, making sure everything was quiet. The night guards stood ready but relaxed at their posts. They held their weapons loosely, their armor not strapped tight. Most were alert, but they chatted amongst themselves as much as they watched for threats. Vesta and the Dagger officers roaming around couldn't fault them; there were many walls and gates to be penetrated before the palace would be threatened, leaving plenty of time to tighten armor and take a more aggressive stance. *They don't have much to worry about,* she thought. *They're in the city palace of Llino, the capital of Aelargo, with defenses that include ancient powers they know only by legend, like me.*

At 01:53:45 in the morning, the majority of the city was asleep. Inside the guarded palace, Vesta checked on her one human compatriot, Electra Neyon, Countess of Waylisia, Deputy Secretary of the Duianna Alliance to Aelargo, and the two regents Ellua Gerani-Uriosal and Bayion Gerani-Uriosal. All were sleeping soundly and in good health. Vesta decided that to be fair she should check on everyone. It only took an additional 14.334 seconds to confirm all 1,343 people within the palace — identifying them by name, purpose, authority — and to probe their medical condition, finding nothing out of order.

Satisfied with the state of her charges, Vesta settled comfortably into a large seat before a wraparound set of consoles as she continued researching how to stay active, in control of all her systems, and yet appear safely locked in suspension to any system query by Duke or an assembly operative. 3.912 seconds later, an alarm sounded. Two displays in front of her shifted to show proximity, distance, mass, and visual images of an approaching object high in the skies.

Now what?

The images showed a bright dot, like a meteor, falling from the sky, growing larger as it neared. The only problem was it was moving far too slowly to be a meteor, and it was heading directly for the Llino palace. Vesta started chewing her fingernail again. She had to wait with everyone else for it to come closer. If she activated her scanner beams to get a better idea of the possible threat it might reveal that she was awake.

By the time she could get a clear image, it had grown large enough and bright enough that the guards on the tall walls of the palace had spotted it and sounded the alarm. Guards around the palace stopped talking, tightened their armor, checked their weapons, and looked for danger. Inside the palace, the guards moved to close and lock the doors and windows, taking up posts at all entrances.

Vesta stared for a full 2.003 seconds at the image before her, her fingernail completely forgotten. The object was a golden stagecoach, pulled by four powerful-looking white stallions. The hoofs of the horses left a shimmering trail and the wheels turned as if on the ground, leaving a set of parallel tracks in the air, which faded away slowly.

Good to know Arkady and I aren't the only ones violating the assembly rulings! That's Duke's coach that he built in Elzaci. He's supposed to have it sealed away.

She watched the vehicle continue to approach. Twice the size of the largest carriage anyone in Llino had ever seen, it flew over the roofs of the city, heading directly to the palace.

In stark contrast to the fantastic horses and stagecoach, the driver looked like every carriage driver around the Empire — not too tall, wrapped in a long coachman's leather coat, large strong hands in thick leather gloves expertly controlling the horses. The driver maneuvered the horses, banking the stagecoach down into the palace's courtyard.

He's far too experienced at flying that thing. Duke must have kept a coachman employed and let him practice somewhere in secret.

The coachman pulled on the reins, his muscles bulging under the leather coat. The horses turned and slowed as the coach landed directly in front of the main doors.

The driver yanked on the brake, locking the enormous carriage in place. Wrapping the reins around the brake, he spun, jumping 13.40 feet down to the ground. He jogged back to pull open the double doors and lock them open with small straps built into the doors. Pausing only to double-check that the doors weren't going to come loose, he ran to the back of the coach and scrambled up to the roof, where he began untying the baggage.

The open doors revealed six rows of five warriors, dressed for combat. There was an odd distortion further into the coach's interior, but her sensors picked up the space of a narrow aisle with more benches beyond. The warriors nearest the door stood, blocking the view of the interior, and started methodically climbing out. As they stepped down, the driver tossed the warriors some baggage. The luggage was ordinary fare: leather packs tied with dozens of items wrapped in oilcloths and leather, or barrel-shaped oilcloth bag-packs stuffed to the point of almost splitting the seams. Every item tossed down was as unique as the warrior receiving it. The only thing these warriors had in common was the nonchalant attitude of veteran soldiers and some style of dagger worn prominently on the front of their belts. After the initial thirty warriors finished climbing down, even more continued to emerge from the coach — as each warrior climbed or jumped down, another shimmied forward between the bench seats, waiting his or her turn to climb down.

They're all Duke's Daggers. Electra had told her that Duke started the Dagger Guild, and that they were highly respected in every known kingdom even though technically just mercenaries. *These Daggers are acting just like the others already here, military officers in a regular army. Duke knew no Alliance kingdom could have a standing army. He's a brilliant tactician. But did he really think this far ahead?*

The more she thought about the Dagger Guild the more she giggled. *Duke, you're a crafty being. You knew the Alliance would need seasoned veterans and you walked around the laws!*

Vesta was still smiling when the shock of the scene wore off the palace guard captain, who ran to confront the warriors climbing down from the coach. "Who are you?" the captain said testily.

A Dagger with grey hairs streaking his temples turned, keeping his back straight, standing almost at attention. He paused, looking the captain over as if inspecting a junior officer. "We're reinforcements," he said in a deep, gravelly voice that conveyed years of commanding men. "We bring orders from Duke, the Supreme Commander of the Imperial Armies of Duianna, for all squads, and a message I'm ordered to deliver only to a regent. Please wake one or both of them now."

The captain sputtered and motioned for more guards. "I'm not going to let you anywhere near the regents until I confirm your identity," he said in a respectful but clearly dismissive tone.

"Good man. Here, these should help." The Dagger commander pulled out some papers from his belt pouch, handing them over. "Don't take long. Time is paramount " he added in a sort-yourself-out-and-move-it tone.

The captain eyed the growing number of bored-looking Daggers stepping out. There were now forty-nine Daggers, far outnumbering the twenty guards in the area. The pattern of a new Dagger shuffling past the bench seats to replace the one that just stepped down continued without pause. All of the Daggers threw their packs and bags over their shoulders and stepped aside, forming ever-deeper ranks.

Taking his eyes from the emerging warriors, the captain stepped near one of the lanterns and examined the papers. Vesta had already scanned them; they were all military certificates of the Duianna Empire, official and authentic. All of the papers bore the seal of His Excellency Duke of

Greyrhan, Lord of Aelargo, and Supreme Commander of the Duianna Imperial Forces.

With the papers was a letter, addressed to Countess Electra of Waylisia, Deputy Secretary of the Duianna Alliance sealed with Lord Dohma's personal signet.

"Um, what is this?" the captain asked suspiciously, holding up the letter to Electra.

The commander chuckled and answered, "*That* is a personal letter from Lord Dohma to Countess Electra, which he posted in Gracia yesterday. Duke noticed it and thought it might be nice if we sped up its delivery. I wouldn't suggest opening that one on pain of, well, whatever Lord Dohma might do after he gets over the embarrassment. Captain, please have the regents check the seals, especially that one from Lord Dohma. That should be enough to get me an audience. We'll stay out here."

The flow of warriors had stopped. After adjusting some straps on the pile of remaining packs and bags, which to all her sensors was about the same size as when it arrived, the driver jumped down, closing the doors on six rows of five warriors each settling into their new seats and chatting amongst themselves. He saluted the lead Dagger and jumped up to the driver's seat. Without a word, he released the brake and whipped the reins. The four horses jumped at the command, and the stagecoach sped away into the sky, disappearing in moments.

The captain's pulse jumped, and he went pale as he surveyed the scene. The documents in his hands shook a little. There were 250 Daggers standing neatly in ranks of five, with their gear piled at their feet.

Glancing to the sky, where the shimmering trail was still slightly visible, the captain sighed. "Ah, yes, reinforcements. I'll go wake the regents." He glanced at the special letter. "And the countess. So much for a quiet night." As he stepped over to the palace doors he motioned to his twenty guards. "Watch them."

The twenty guards, looking a little pale, moved into a rough line between the Daggers and palace. The Dagger leader chuckled under his breath; the captain either didn't hear or chose to ignore it. He turned and went into the palace, closing the door behind him.

One of the Daggers mumbled, "Anyone bring some cards? Looks like more hurry up and wait."

Vesta, along with all of the warriors and guards, chuckled at the very old military joke.

LEBUIN

Sweat beaded on Lebuin's neck, his eyes remained closed as he traced the patterns, twisting and correcting the tendrils of energy with both his hands and mind. His magical senses focused on the tightly woven mana ribbons which, if he wasn't fighting them, he would claim were impossible to make. The mana ribbons had to consume power from somewhere to exist and fight him, but he couldn't figure out how they worked. Yet they were infused throughout the golden threads sealing Magus Vestul's precious journal, which Ticca and her team had helped him recover recently. This was the entire reason they'd returned to Llino.

Silky strings of his own power played out from his fingertips, through the new channels created in him by the ancient Argos mana collector artifact. Instead of one main channel in each hand, like most mages, he had two at the tip of each finger and a large channel in each palm, making twenty-two streams to control.

The first of the golden threads loosened. Just as in the dozens of attempts before, the protection incantations woven into the threads reacted. Magical energies surged through the other strands that touched the failing one. Mana sparks snapped between them to reinforce the weakened thread.

Lebuin was prepared. Before they'd traveled between the threads, he speared each spark with tendrils from his closest finger. He yanked his hand back, pulling the reinforcement power into his channels.

His concentration had to split to drain the sparks, merging the power back into his own reserve and channeling the excess power to the Argos collector, while continuing to unwind the incantations. The reinforcement mana was highly concentrated, and Lebuin had to exert a lot of self-control not to jerk his hand away from the flares of pain caused by collecting them. His channels burned as he labored to absorb the dense magic.

Clenching his jaw against the pain, he opened his eyes and stared intently at the one thread he wanted to remove. It was glowing as he unraveled its incantations, allowing the excess energies to burn off as light.

He had to make sure they exhausted themselves as light only. The golden threads' incantations were built with an exit channel that would cause them to burst into flames, melting the gold and likely destroying the precious journal if they were forcibly broken.

It was an amazing set of incantations, but he expected nothing less from a mage who'd lived for over ten thousand years, predating even the Guild of Argos Magi.

With a final white flare, the incantations in the golden thread he was draining broke, leaving it nothing more than a simple metal string, easily cut away.

Leaning back, he shook his hands. It didn't do anything for the pain. Nonetheless, it felt good to do it.

"That looked promising." A pleasantly feminine yet authoritative voice that gave him instant goose bumps said from behind.

When he turned around, he wasn't surprised to see Ticca sitting with a tray of sweet rolls. He was in her room in the Blue Dolphin Inn, after all. She also had some arit in a serving carafe that was set over a tea light to keep it hot. She stood and poured him a fresh cup, putting it and some sweet rolls on the table next to him.

He raised his eyebrow as he grabbed one of the rolls. He had to stop and stretch for a moment. His back ached, and his arms felt like lead weights.

"I thought you said you didn't do the domestic stuff."

Ticca flopped back into her chair. "Well, that was before I became a general. Now, I sort of have to do it to set a good example," she said with only a hint of irony.

Lebuin savored the pastry. It was infused with sharre, and the sweet, energizing wine warmed his mouth and throat as he ate it. Hunger grabbed at him and he swallowed three more bites rapidly, washing them down with the overly bittersweet arit, whose flavor made him chew the air, wiping his torgue on the roof of his mouth. His face contorted uncontrollably by the bitter, sharp flavor assaulting his palate.

The taste completely killing his hunger, he looked at the thick, warm arit left in his cup. It stuck to the sides like syrup. He set the cup down.

"How on Yur can you drink it like that?"

"Well, it wasn't so sweet about six marks back. But I've had fresh brought up every couple of marks, and I've been mixing them together. Afraid it got a little concentrated. I actually like it."

To prove her point, she drained her cup and filled it again.

He looked at the dark windows. "Six marks back? What time is it?"

Ticca smirked and pointed to her packed gear. "About nine-thirtyish," she said in a conspiratorial tone.

Blinking and still moving his tongue around, he took Ticca in. Normally he had to control his face around Ticca, but he didn't worry about it this time with the taste of the arit contorting his features. When they'd started together, he thought of her as just an employee. Then in the forest, she had become more of a big sister. Now he felt a soft pulling towards her, as his mind entertained the idea that they might yet become more than friends.

He couldn't imagine any man not wanting to be with her. She was beautiful, even in the simple clothing she was wearing. Her chestnut hair had the shimmer of being freshly washed, and was held back elegantly with a silver comb. Her dark red shirt, a fuzzy corduroy made of hemp, clung loosely, showing off her figure and accenting her hair perfectly. His eyes drifted down to linger on her skin-tight grey leather leggings that showed off her muscular legs. Even though he didn't recognize them he knew she was wearing Kliasa's wondrous boots. The boots had shifted to appear as brown knee-high riding boots, with a series of buckles that added to her appearance.

"Did it really take me all day to break that one thread?" The window was not shuttered as he first thought, which meant she wasn't playing a trick on him. Her smirk grew larger. "What?"

Laughing, Ticca said, "You didn't ask what day it was."

He stood and walked over to the window. Two moons were visible, and the street was still busy. "It's Martidi." Her smile widened as his thoughts raced around.

Could I really have been working longer than I knew? It's dangerous to spend too long working with incantations. The brain can burn out.

"No. It's Merdi. You've been at that almost two full days." Her tone was light, but serious enough that he wasn't able to tell if she was playing a prank on him. "Is it open?" she asked, looking back at the journal.

She stood and stepped over to examine the journal on the table. As she got close, he caught the intoxicating scent of imperial jasmine, mixed with knife oil and the other processed animal oils she used to treat her leather gear.

"Um...well...not exactly."

"It doesn't look any different. Did you do anything at all?"

His heart jumped and he felt his face flush with heat. Before he thought about it, he'd stepped over smartly, back straight, to loudly tap one of the dozen threads sealing the journal with his forefinger. "This one has been broken. We could cut it off if we wanted to."

Ticca was predictably unimpressed by his sharp tone and commanding posture. Her mouth tightened as she glared at him. "Are you serious? It will take cycles for you to open it at this rate."

Sighing, he slumped back against the wall at the sound of disappointment in her voice. Finally, he shrugged. "I didn't make these, and Vestul said even Argos would be surprised by this. Vestul could have spent years creating them. It might get easier as I get more practice. I can't find the key to these incantations. Every thread is completely unique."

As he flexed his fingers, he said, "I don't think a normal Magus could do this. If it weren't for the changes to my magic channels that artifact made to me, I wouldn't have the ability to fend off the defenses. They all work together to protect each other."

"Are they alive?" Her tone was level but she shifted a bit further away from the journal as she asked.

"Not exactly. But they react with some pretty canny actions."

Ticca went back to her chair, and he suppressed the urge to say something incredibly stupid in his defense.

Maybe I should just tell her how I feel and let her reject me, like all the other ladies. At least I could stop romanticizing about the possibility. She doesn't seem to notice what she does to me. His heart ached as he recalled how she looked at Risy when she thought no one else would notice. *No, I should stay silent. She means too much to me as a friend. I'll live with that friendship if I must.*

His stomach made a loud rumble and he felt the hunger returning. The tray of rolls was in front of Ticca but he didn't feel like stepping over just yet.

Glancing at his stomach, she asked, "Can you do this on the road? Everything is ready to go. I wanted to leave the Blue

Dolphin this morning to go have a look at the power source you said Finnba was using against us in Algan. It took you longer than I thought. We can leave in the morning if you think you're up to it."

After a short pause, he shrugged. "I'm not sure. Has it really been two days?"

Ticca dropped back into her chair with an air of disappointment. "Yeah. Although now that I see how much of a fight you had, it isn't as funny as I thought." Her lips formed a cute pout that made him want to kiss her.

He felt his face heating up and looked away before she could see that he was blushing. A knock at the door came to distract her, thankfully. Ticca jumped towards it, pulling her dagger.

She's expecting to be attacked in the Blue Dolphin? Is something else going on she hasn't told me about yet?

As she got close to the door, she called out, "Pass?"

"What are you talking about?" said the muffled, confused, and distinctly Nigan voice.

Ticca sheathed her dagger and opened the door. "I was thinking we should have some passwords. You know, something like, 'Yeah, it's me, and all is good,' or 'It's me, and there's a knife to my neck.'"

Nigan laughed and stepped in carrying a new leather pack that complemented his burgundy doublet and black loose trousers excellently. His black dagger was prominently displayed on a medium brown leather belt that was just right for his muscular frame. He dropped the pack beside the door and turned to face Ticca. "Okay, sure. But shouldn't you let us know what these passcodes are before you start using them?"

Runa-Illa pushed past them using a platter of food like a battering ram, in a blue and grey tunic pulled tight to show off her figure by a rope-like black leather belt. The belt's ends dangled down, drawing attention to her tight black leggings. She walked over to Lebuin, putting the tray down in front of him. Looking up directly into his face, she said sternly, "You missed dinner, breakfast, lunch, and dinner again. So eat."

"You mean she wasn't joking?" His stomach was already rumbling even louder at the proximity of the steaming meats and vegetables.

Pointing to his chair, Illa said, "I don't see you eating yet. No answers until you're eating."

Lebuin laughed and grabbed some of the meat, taking a large bite. The savory juices streamed over his tongue and down his throat, washing away all traces of the nasty arit flavor and leaving only the salty tang of well-seasoned roast. *I love the Dolphin's cooks!* With that first bite, his hunger roared back, taking over. He sat down in front of the food and dug in with gusto.

Looking motherly, Illa nodded and sat in the chair next to Ticca. "If Ticca told you that you'd been in a trance for almost two days, then no, she wasn't joking. I felt you finishing your task and brought this up."

Nigan sat on the wide arm of the reading chair Illa was sitting in. "You know, a guy can get jealous of the fact that one moment he's having a nice time dancing, and then his girl turns and walks away with a purpose not related to him."

Ticca's jaw dropped. "You were dancing?"

After a little huff, Illa said, "More like shuffling from foot to foot. Dancing would require some form of grace."

Nigan's head rolled back as he laughed. "Oh, you're so lucky I have a sense of humor."

Eyes narrowing Illa glared at Nigan. "Or vice versa."

Holding up her hand, Ticca said, "Okay, all jesting aside, is everything ready for tomorrow?"

As Nigan filled a mug, he answered, "Yep, horses and gear are ready. The squad is prepped, and we even have Genne's kitchen preparing an early breakfast for us." He started to take a drink, but then held the cup in front of him with a look of shock as he sloshed the thick liquid around in the cup. "Uh, you're drinking this?"

Ticca smirked. "Yes. Why? Too strong for you?"

Without trying it, Nigan put the cup down. "I'll wait for something less dangerous."

Pointing to Nigan's pack, Ticca said, "That looks ready. If everything is still going on the original schedule, the assembly has to be voting soon, if it hasn't already. I want to be clear of any city before they make their decision."

Illa asked, "Do you think they'll make a decision this fast?"

Ticca rubbed her crinkled brows. "They should've started debating this week or last week. Duke won't let them discuss it for long. Besides, it's a pretty clear case. To be honest, I'm surprised we haven't heard a proclamation or something yet. I thought it would've been decided in a day."

Between bites, Lebuin said, "Yeah, well, they're politicians, and they'll want to talk about it. I bet we have another week or two."

"Well," Nigan said, "in any case, I'll check on the guards and then get some rest." He stood and turned to Illa. "Coming?"

Illa checked Lebuin and saw that he was still chewing. He nodded, indicating he was fine. Illa stood and headed out with Nigan.

After they left, Ticca leaned against the closed door. Lebuin was taking another bite when Nigan's words clicked in. "Guards?"

Staring at the floor with her eyebrows furrowed, Ticca paused, then looked over at Lebuin. "We decided that even here, the Nhia-Samri would be willing to strike at us for that journal, so we have guards inside and out."

Someone started pounding on the door, and Ditani's voice yelled through the metal door, "Ticca, we must leave with all haste!"

She spun, drawing her dagger and opening the door. A fight could clearly be heard. Nigan and Illa were still in the hallway, facing the stairs, weapons out. Ditani's hands and arms glistened with blood. Lebuin jumped up, grabbing the journal.

Ticca looked Ditani over. "Are you injured? How many?"

"It's minor. This blood is theirs. Twelve in the main room, disguised. Three tried to pass the stair with me behind. Tuage and Carda had asked for their keys. One gutted Tuage before anyone could react. Those three we killed, but there are more. A hard fight ensued in the main room. Genne cut one in half as he made for the stairs. When last I saw, Daggers had the advantage."

Ticca cursed and ran for her gear. "Are they Nhia-Samri?"

Turning towards the room he shared with Lebuin, Ditani shouted back, "They aren't using odassi, yet they fight as devils!"

Lebuin rushed out of the room to follow Ditani. He heard shuffling footsteps behind him, and before going around the bend, he looked back. Epton and Carda were fighting as they came up the stairs backwards. Nigan dug in his pouch and shoved something at Illa. "Get the gear! We can't leave without it."

Lebuin didn't wait to see what happened. His heart raced, and his stomach burned from the undigested dinner as it combined with fatigue and adrenaline rushing into his system.

Jumping into his room, just behind Ditani, he saw everything was packed. "Everything is ready?"

Ditani nodded and tossed him the magical pack he'd inherited from Magus Vestul. Catching the pack was easy, as no matter how much it carried it only weighed a few pounds. There was no time to hide the journal in it, so he shoved it in quickly tying the pack closed.

The pair of them rushed back out to the hallway, joining the team. He took a quick count. "Where are Malla, Sabri, Coedy, and Persa?"

Nigan, already wearing the leather pack he'd brought into Ticca's room, was helping Illa strap on her pack. "They're defending the base of the stairs. Except Coedy, who I think is in the stables. There are a handful of senior Daggers still here fighting with them." When he finished he grabbed two leather bags from the floor and looked at Ticca with a raised eyebrow.

Pushing her way to the stairs, Ticca grabbed Risy, who was nearby, and pushed him downward. "Risy, support them and give us at least five, and then use route three or five. We'll meet up with you in the woods." Ticca's eyes sparkled with excitement. "I think the assembly vote just went down. Pretty sure I know the way it went, too."

Risy grinned, tossed his pack to the side of the hall, and rushed down the stairs, weapons in hand.

Ticca raced up the steps three at a time. Hands grabbed Lebuin and pushed him upwards as his team of Daggers took defensive positions behind. Forcing his legs to move, he followed on Ticca's heels with Ditani pushing him to move faster, Nigan and Illa close behind.

At the top of the stairs, Ticca threw the cargo doors open wide and dove out. Cold, salty air flowed in through the doorway as they ran out to the wide stone staging platform. Ticca was already climbing the final steps up to the famous docking platform for Damega's long missing flying ship, the *Emerald Heart*, which was along the towering middle section of the Blue Dolphin Inn.

Nigan bolted around Lebuin, taking the final steps up in long strides before sliding to a stop beside Ticca, who was standing on the edge of the platform looking down at the area behind the inn. Lebuin jumped up the last two steps and stopped as his eyes adjusted to the bright moonlit night. The chilled air felt fresh on his face, and stars twinkled in the cloudless sky. The city rooftops looked like an alien landscape of peaks and troughs spreading out to the west a full story below the platform they stood on.

To the northeast, hundreds of ship masts swayed in unison like dark arrow shafts stuck into the chest of a giant. The great city docks were quiet, with only the soft creaking of the ships' hulls. Everything seemed so peaceful that it was hard to believe a life-and-death fight was happening below their feet.

Ticca and Nigan ran over to a set of ropes coiled out of sight. With practiced motions, Ticca and Nigan tossed the rope coils over the edge, towards the back of the inn. Soft snaps came from two docking clamps that Lebuin realized anchored the ropes. Nigan put on his gloves and scrambled over the edge almost before the ropes had hit the ground.

From his position, hanging in the air, Nigan said, "The way to the stables is clear."

Ticca slipped on her own gloves and spidered down the other rope, reaching the ground well before Nigan. She pulled her dagger and sword and moved cautiously to look around the edge of the building, towards the stables. She signaled that it was clear.

Lebuin went next, with Illa beside him all the way to the ground. Moments later, their whole team was there, crouched, weapons out, holding for Ticca's signal. With a glance backwards, Ticca burst out running for the stables. Just before she got there, she dove, sliding on her stomach as an arrow from the building across the alley from the inn buried itself into the ground, barely missing her.

Epton peeked out and signaled that the attackers were on the second-story back corner window, directly across the alley from them. That was one of the many dockworker apartments for rent in the area. Epton and Ditani stepped out with bows drawn and released their own shafts. Lebuin leaned out and watched the arrows fly towards an open window, only to bounce off of a barrier.

They have a mage with them. Either Nhia-Samri or a renegade. Since they're hunting us, I bet they're Nhia-Samri. Either way, it's my turn to step up.

Lebuin pulled at his connection to the magic collector artifact in the Guildhouse, letting the energy flow into and through his channels.

His mind created the necessary formulae to blend and twist the energies into a fiery blast, which he hurled at the same window.

In the bright light of his attack, he could see two people — a man dressed as a dockworker and a woman in a simple peasant skirt and a calico apron — inside the room. The man was preparing to shoot another arrow at Ticca.

Reacting instinctively, Lebuin reached out with a telekinetic incantation and held the arrow to the bow as the man tried to release the shaft. The sudden binding of his arrow caused the man to twitch, looking at his bow.

The unexpected action must have distracted the mage for a critical moment. Lebuin's next bolt of energy exploded on the barrier, collapsing it, and the drapes in the window burst into flames. The woman recovered fast; ripping the drapes down, she threw them out the window and her hands twisted in a familiar gesture at Lebuin. Lebuin poured power into his shields, extending them just in time.

A white bolt slammed into his shields with a booming explosion. The concussion caused Lebuin to step backwards. The other Daggers, taking advantage of Lebuin's cover fire, bolted for the stables, with only Illa and Nigan remaining behind, guarding his back.

Something at the base of the mage's neck started to glow through her cotton blouse.

And that is a Nhia-Samri magic source!

"They're Nhia-Samri!" Lebuin shouted to warn the team.

Ticca and the others were taking their horses out of the stables. Ticca had secured her pack to her horse, but she glanced at Lebuin, her eyes narrowing. Instead of mounting, she dropped the reins and ran towards the building, where the attackers were.

Lebuin's heart raced. *What is she doing? We need to escape!*

The Nhia-Samri mage caused a powerful burst of lightning to rain down on his shields, making a dome of blinding light. Blinking to clear his vision, Lebuin twisted and combined powers together in a layered set of bursts. Hurling his attack at the mage, he ran for the stables. His gut was doing flips as he considered what Ticca might be doing.

The lightning continued to arc at him, cascading around his shields. He could feel them weakening and diverted some of his mind to twist more of his mana into an incantation that created a second layer of shields.

'Warning: Energy levels low.' The unexpected Argos energy collector's voice made his heart skip a beat, and he struggled to maintain control of the shields. Worse, he almost missed a critical interlink for his attack incantation as he twisted the magic threads to release them. *'Three thousand, four hundred sixty-three point two rellums remain. Current load is fifty-seven point seven two one four. Failure in fifty-nine point nine three seconds.'*

Argos didn't tell me the thing was going to talk to me, and what in Yur is a rellum? At least I understand that last part; I don't have enough energy for this.

His blasts worked. The mage fell backwards, screaming in pain as the outer layer of Lebuin's onslaught bore through her shields, and the inner core struck out, arcing between the mage's arms. Her assault on Lebuin stopped, and Lebuin pinched off the threads to release the inner set of shields, conserving power.

Illa and Nigan joined him, running for the stables. The other Daggers were leading their horses out into the yard. As Lebuin reached his horse, the door of the attackers' house smashed open, and two people rushed out. Ticca sprung at them from behind, cutting the head off one with her sword and stabbing the other with her dagger.

Lebuin felt dizzy and stared at the falling head, his mind failing to connect the level of strength and ruthlessness that one maneuver took with the athletic yet feminine figure of Ticca.

A third assailant emerged from the building, shocking

Lebuin back into the present. "TICCA, BEHIND YOU!" Nigan and Lebuin called as one.

Ticca twisted and dodged, but not fast enough. The new attacker threw a knife that hit Ticca. Lebuin wasn't sure where, but he heard the strike and Ticca's grunt of pain.

Nigan and Illa mounted, spun their horses, and raced towards him. Ticca kicked the last man away, but she lost her footing on the loose gravel and fell. The man drew a pair of odassi, confirming once and for all that they were Nhia-Samri.

Lebuin kicked his horse, sweeping up Ticca's reins as he maneuvered towards her.

Before he got there, Illa and Nigan had delivered a series of strikes from their mounts, killing the last attacker.

Her face contorted in pain, Ticca regained her feet and vaulted into her saddle, cradling one of her arms.

"RIDE!" she ordered.

Their group bolted into the largely deserted street and headed towards the western gate with Ticca in the lead, a knife hilt sticking out of her left shoulder. With a growing sense of dread, Lebuin watched the blood oozing down her back as he tried to keep up.

At the west gate, he expected to be assailed again by more Nhia-Samri, like the last time they left the city, but no one jumped from alleys to stop them. They rode out unhindered by the guards, who stood aside, mouths open, as the party galloped past. Ticca didn't stop. The bloodstain on her back was now a dark patch, which glistened slightly in the moonlight. She continued deeper into the forest even after the town was far behind.

The team rode fast for half a mark and then slowed. Ticca was in the lead, with the rest of the team in a protective circle around Lebuin, Illa, and Ditani. Ticca rode steadily and set a speed that let her horse glide along smoothly through the night. Lebuin couldn't see her face, and she moved carefully, protecting her shoulder with the knife in it. She'd already waved off Nigan's offer to stop and tend to the wound, saying she wasn't in danger of falling.

The pace and time allowed Lebuin to take a headcount; all were present except for Risy, Malla, Sabri, Persa, and Tuage, whom Lebuin finally had time to consider. *I hardly knew him and yet he died protecting me.* The night's chill seemed appropriate. Lebuin looked at the dark figures around him. The few faces he could make out were tight-lipped, with eyes scanning for more danger. *Should I say something? Not now, but I think I should when we camp.*

Another half a mark passed; still they didn't stop, taking small farming side roads seemingly at random. On the fifth turn a party of riders raced from a different side road towards them, and Ticca motioned for them to turn off into the woods. The team didn't speed up.

Lebuin's heart pounded in his throat as the pursuing riders started quickly overtaking them. The bright moonlight clearly glistened off fresh bloodstains on their clothes. He relaxed slightly noting that the rest of the team could not possibly miss them and hadn't drawn weapons. The pursuers, horses panting and steaming, thudded up as Nigan held out his hand and exchanged a palm strike with one of them.

Lebuin felt a rush of joy as he realized the other riders were actually Risy, Malla, Sabri, and Persa. All of them looked tired with various cuts in their clothing. Risy nodded and smiled at Lebuin as the rest took up their stations in the protective circle.

They rode on for two marks more through the woods. Lebuin's legs and thighs were burning and he felt heavily abused. All the adrenaline had worn off long ago; only determination not to fail Ticca kept him moving.

Lebuin frowned as Ticca's wound oozed more in the rough terrain. He considered calling for her to stop when he spotted she was wobbling in her saddle, but she held on until they came to a small glade. Ticca nodded at a couple of trees as if agreeing with something and then signaled to stop with her good arm.

I wonder what makes this place better than any of the other glades we passed through?

Staring at one particular tree, Ticca smiled as if someone had made a joke. Then her eyes rolled up, and she slumped in her saddle. Lebuin and Ditani leapt from their horses to catch Ticca as she slipped so far to the side that Lebuin was sure she was going to fall on her head.

The group dismounted just as fast, with most of the team taking up defensive positions, while others started striking a cold camp. Lebuin helped Ditani lift Ticca off her saddle.

It took more effort than expected, because during the flight she'd tied herself onto the saddle. Once they got the strong leather straps undone, they carried her to a clear spot.

Ticca stiffened momentarily as her eyes fluttered open. "You know, it'd be nice to just leave Llino quietly for a change," she mumbled.

Lebuin and Ditani stumbled as she went limp, but they kept a firm grip on her. Lebuin's heart sank, his stomach quivering. Without even the slightest resistance, she was just loose meat and bone. She was so cold. As they lowered her to the ground, Lebuin used his mage sight to confirm her heart was still beating.

With a sigh of relief, they finish laying Ticca out and Lebuin knelt next to her, checking her vitals as best he could. She was still breathing weakly, and although she'd lost a lot of blood she seemed otherwise in reasonably good condition. Malla, their medic, dropped next to Ticca with her stuffed field bag. She held a stitching kit.

Lebuin started to get up, but then thought better of it.

If I'm to live in this world, I must learn the skills needed to save those I'm to protect.

He felt himself going lightheaded, looking at the bloody knife sticking out of Ticca's shoulder. There was far more blood soaked into her clothes than he'd thought. Forcing his stomach to remain calm, he watched Malla as closely as possible, trying to remember every move she made and every comment she let drop.

DOHMA

Stifling a yawn, Dohma sat in the padded, purple velvet chair behind a shallow, but wide, desk. A golden plaque which read, 'Chief Regent Dohma Gerani-Uriosal, Kingdom of Aelargo,' was affixed to the front.

He checked the room to see how many had returned from the short break. Chief Queen Paha of the dwarves came in with Lady Saba-Arrur, the elven queen. The two of them were engrossed in a conversation that had both of them gesturing and making chopping motions.

Across from Dohma, King Brinus Laeusia of Laeusia was napping in his chair. Meanwhile, Princess Sheila, Brinus's eldest daughter and the heir apparent for Laeusia, was still trying to get King Deorgra Yalthum to agree to something that had Deorgra looking down and rubbing his temples while his daughter, Jawayi, was trying not to laugh.

The other representatives or rulers of the countries that made up the realms of the Covenant of Duianna were making their way to their desks to continue the debate on ratifying Duke's motion to declare war on the Nhia-Samri.

The assembly was in its second week of debate. All the evidence had been laid before the rulers of the nine nations of the Duianna Alliance. Yet Duke had not called for a vote, even going so far as to block anyone else from doing so.

We've been at this all day. I believe it's time to move to recess for the night. That we spent another day discussing this topic is beyond belief. The deeds are clear to all.

Orahda, Dohma's weapons master turned adviser/ bodyguard, disguised as a Dagger guard, stood behind Dohma, watching everyone in the room as if he was an enemy about to strike. A number of delegates had commented on it, but Orahda refused to stop, saying that someone had to be a Nhia-Samri informant. Given Orahda's past with the Nhia-Samri, Dohma was inclined to let Orahda do as he pleased.

Due to the nature of the meetings and the fact the Nhia-Samri had managed to install magical gates into the halls of the assembly, all of the attendees and attendants had been checked out to a level that included magical mind probing by the most senior mages available. Still, Orahda didn't trust anyone he didn't know personally.

"Duke set the hands in motion and named the timing. Why does he now block action?" Dohma asked Orahda.

Orahda had personally trained and mentored Dohma, and in those twenty years of training, Dohma had come to respect his opinion and insights. Orahda was more than just the weapons master of Aelargo; in truth, he was a second father to Dohma.

"Though he hid it well, Duke was surprised when we informed him of the Nhia-Samri mage-gates into the cities and these chambers."

Dohma considered that thought. Pointed out, Duke's surprise was clear. "You believe his plans changed with that revelation. If so, why does he not reveal to us his intentions? Surely, we're to be trusted in his plans. You've no doubt noticed he disappears every evening, returning to these chambers earlier than anyone else."

Orahda pulled a set of papers out of his shoulder pouch and put them on the desk. Bending down, Dohma saw that it was a copy of a guard's log for the last week. There were a number of underlined entries. Every evening there was an entry around 21:00, showing Duke exiting. Every morning there was the same entry: *'02:30 Admitted Duke Rolly Duke Bensure'* with no other activity until around 06:00 when various staff members started arriving and leaving.

"What's this?"

"I made a copy of the access log for this chamber."

"To what end should Duke take his rest in this chamber?

Do you have knowledge of what he's doing during the hours of his absence?"

Orahda put the log back into his pouch. "I don't know. I've checked, and there's no other log of his movements anywhere in the palace grounds. He disappears entirely for that time."

"Clearly he's working to an end. We must endeavor to discover the new plan. His delays at allowing the declaration of war are likely to the detriment of the Nhia-Samri."

"He has brought in significant numbers of Daggers. I tell you now; they are not enough against the might of Hisuru Amajoo if Shar-Lumen decides to attack in force."

Dohma knew Orahda was right. If anyone knew what the Nhia-Samri were capable of, it was the man who had once been their second-in-command. Orahda had defected from them just over forty years ago, at the end of the Burning Bridge War. He had provided the information that exposed the Nhia-Samri's secret involvement in fanning the flames of that war on both sides in an attempt to break the back of the Duianna Alliance of Realms.

Since then, Orahda had hidden from the extraordinary efforts of the Nhia-Samri to find and kill him for his treachery. Orahda had sworn allegiance to Aelargo and had acted as their weapons master, training the Llino city guard. It was because of his preparations that Duke was able to restore Dohma's family rightful rule of Aelargo.

"Maybe Duke is seeking to use the ancient powers here. This is the ancient capital of the Duianna Empire, built over 15,000 years prior by our ancestors, with such power and knowledge we're but children in comparison."

Orahda shook his head. "No, if that was true he would need to have permission of the assembly to revoke an ancient ruling. You would've been consulted if he wanted a secret vote."

Dohma again recalled Orahda was more than any here knew. Orahda had promised on their return to Aelargo to reveal many truths of his past in the security of his specially protected quarters.

"You suggest that I would've been consulted because my ancestors lived here before moving to Aelargo to be the advisers and regents to the great princes of the Empire?"

"No, the disappearance of the royal line in 10,485, when your family was forced to assume control, is not what I'm referring to. The assembly's ruling is older than that. Both the Imperial regents and the Aelargo regents have done their duties and have much to be proud of," Orahda said with an odd sadness, his eyes going unfocused as if looking back across the years to that very time 3,000 years ago.

"We're still at loss as to what game Duke is playing." Dohma said leaning back in the chair. He felt less at ease in his seat within the ancient marbled halls, with all their inlaid gold and silver. The nearly 15,000 Dagger guards stationed in and around the assembly chambers did not feel so reassuring with these mysterious actions of Duke's.

Thanks to Orahda and Dohma, everyone knew the Nhia-Samri could strike through the as of yet unidentified mage-gates hidden in the walls. Magical gates which, once activated, would allow the Nhia-Samri to step from their strongholds throughout the realms, directly into these chambers, the palace, and the city. Twenty-six gates had been found and disabled, but Orahda insisted there would be no less than thirty into the palace grounds alone.

An idea came to mind. "Orahda, what is the current Dagger complement?" Dohma asked.

Orahda answered instantly. "Although the formation of an official army is not yet sanctioned, there are 50,500 Daggers stationed throughout the palace and city, acting as officers to about 230,000 guards. Seventeen thousand Daggers are acting as special forces here in the palace protecting the assembly."

Dohma did some quick math in his head. He had seen a report that morning indicating that over 38,000 Daggers had checked in since Duke arrived with the initial complement of 65,000 Daggers.

"Where are the other 35,500 Daggers?"

Orahda didn't answer for so long that Dohma turned around to look. Orahda's brows were deeply creased "I don't think anyone has noticed that discrepancy with all the activities."

Dohma felt a small ember of hope kindle in his heart. "Duke is planning a surprise for the vote. I've been worried. I know the Daggers have tripled the guards' training in recent weeks. Still, should the Nhia-Samri attack, we'll have to evacuate."

He didn't bother saying what they both knew: the plan was already in place to evacuate the assembly to the eastern elven lands. All that could be done, had been done. They hoped that most would make it to Rea-Na-Rey, the elven capital in their kingdom of Nae-Rae, to the east.

A boy in Duke's livery sprinted into the room, across the central floor. Ignoring all protocols to acknowledge the rulers, he dodged around to get to the large pillowed platform. Duke, looking clean and well brushed, leaned his head down to the boy, who spoke so quietly that even those close by looked unable to hear him. Duke's head snapped up, and he leapt over the boy, to the central floor.

At that moment, Cundia, Dohma's Dagger Commander of Aelargo and official royal adviser, walked into the room. She was in the lead of a number of other assistants, who were falling over each other to get to whomever they served.

Cundia was wearing the same armored clothing as Orahda, except she had far more weapons showing. She had little trouble maneuvering through the throng with her graceful and quick reflexes.

After rushing over to Dohma, Cundia leaned in close. "Lady Lothia, Lord Pualla, and Lady Dalpha are here."

Duke barked, and not a single person dared to claim the authority to stand in his path. Dohma couldn't help smiling as kings and queens leapt to get out of the way of the 240-stone giant wolf as he stalked out of the room. The small lad ran full tilt behind just to keep up.

Dohma's stomach plummeted into an unknown abyss. Duke's rush only confirmed what Cundia said. Still, his legs felt as heavy as stones rooting him in place. "Can this be true? The very Gods are to parley with us?"

Cundia's face looked pale. "Yes, m'Lord. They just arrived in a gold and silver carriage unlike anything I've ever seen, pulled by two silver mares that flew into the palace grounds. Imperial Regent Aphastes Menthran is greeting them personally in the entry foyer."

Dohma stood as the buzz in the room took on a uniquely excited pitch. His sensitive ears detected a handful of conversations about what to do; the Gods hadn't attended an assembly meeting in over 5,000 years.

All fatigue forgotten, Dohma joined the rush of rulers as they strode as rapidly as dignity would allow, following Duke, heading for the entry foyer. Ignoring etiquette, he jogged into the hall and sped to the doorway of the foyer. Six Dagger guards on both sides of the doorway stood so straight that they looked like statues.

Duke was already at the far end of the room. Moonlight blazed in the three-story arched windows that lined the front wall, adding a soft glow to the bright chandeliers and wall lanterns.

Skidding to a halt, Dohma took in the three beings. Each had a shimmering radiance surrounding them. The Imperial regent was standing as straight as the guards and had stepped aside for Duke, who was rising from one of his head bows.

It took no time at all to identify them.

Pualla, Lord of Air and Yur, was a medium-height man with a toned, muscular physique. He wore a red-enameled, scaled shirt that looked more like feathers than armor. He had matching steel bracers on his upper and lower arms. His legs were covered with the same armor over leather pants, which were tucked into red knee-high, reinforced boots. His feathered cloak fluttered as if constantly brushed by the wind and unaffected by gravity. Two curved short blades and a small leather pouch hung from his belt. In his left hand, he held a tall staff that resembled an unstrung bow, but there was no string, nor did he have a quiver. His head was topped with a red and white turban.

Dohma had seen Dalpha, Lady of Light, at a distance in Llino on a couple of royal occasions. She was dressed the same as always, in a full-length green dress that covered every inch of her yet left nothing to the imagination. She had a curving body that, before he had met Electra, he'd thought had no equal. Smiling, he recalled the boyish daydreams he'd had as a young city guard, during royal celebrations, when she had put in an appearance.

Dalpha had made him feel optimistic for the future even in the worst of times, when he was enforcing the usurpers' decrees. However, this would be the first time he would meet her. His palms were sweating.

What should I say to someone who has been an inspiration to me my whole life?

Dalpha stood regally with her hands clasped in front of her, showing elbow-length black leather gloves and a matching pair of bracelets. Her hanging belt and bracelets were made from a rope of woven gold, and were held in place with carved sapphire buckles. Around her neck hung a mantle-like medallion made from a large sapphire, cut with her symbol: an oak tree, with eight sun rays surrounded by an outer circle.

Lothia, the Raven, Goddess of Karakia, was a tall, regal-looking woman with dark tanned skin and long black, straight hair that fell to her waist. She wore a leather top that was embroidered with colored beads, forming the silhouette of a raven against a full moon. Tied with leather strips to her hair above one ear and on her bare ankles were black feathers, which floated as unaffected by gravity as Pualla's cloak. Her hair was pulled around into a ponytail held with a hammered silver clasp, also tied with leather straps. Unlike Dalpha and Pualla, Lothia floated a full hand above the ground.

As Dohma approached, Dalpha's bright emerald-green eyes jumped from Duke to lock onto him. They bored right into his soul. A gentle smile grew on her face, and she continued to stare at him, only glancing down once before continuing her gaze.

Pualla watched Duke with furrowed brows.

Lothia held up a silver medallion, which hung around her neck, for inspection. It looked out of place with the rest of her dress.

Concentrating, Dohma focused his excellent hearing and caught the last part of what Lothia was saying to Duke.

"...Argos has granted me his voice and will also attend."

"That could complicate this more," Duke said.

Dohma stepped up next to Duke and dropped to one knee, bowing his head.

Dalpha's gentle tones washed over him. "Rise, Dohma Uriosal. You shall not kneel to us again."

As Lothia's and Pualla's oversized eyes shifted to him from Duke, he stood.

Pualla spoke first. "So this is the restored child of House Uriosal. I'm pleased to be with you here."

Taking a deep breath, he tried to relax the tightened muscles in his chest. "Lord Pualla, Lady Dalpha, and Lady Lothia, I welcome you, and am your servant always."

Lothia stepped closer to him, her eyes looking into his. Then she saw something behind him and gasped, putting her hand to her mouth and stepping backwards. "It can't be."

When Pualla turned to see what Lothia was talking about, his mouth dropped open. He shook his head and then jumped past Dohma. "It cannot be! By the heavens, how can you be here?"

Dohma turned enough to see what was going on, careful not to put his back to the other Gods.

Pualla picked up Orahda in a hug, patting his back and

shaking him at the same time. Orahda played the part of a limp doll while still grinning ear to ear.

Dalpha did not appear to be surprised.

Although Dohma had not personally seen Dalpha on more than a couple of occasions, he knew she spent a lot of time in Llino.

Of course she knows who Orahda is. She had to have been watching over us all these years. He's the second greatest warrior in all of history and a true hero of the Alliance. He must be well known to the Gods. I'm surprised Dalpha didn't mention to the others that he was in Llino. I thought the Gods were a close group, sharing information freely.

The other rulers and regents came into the room, and an eruption of chaos ensued. Pualla and Orahda exchanged some quick comments in a language Dohma didn't recognize. Afterwards, Pualla acted as if Orahda wasn't even visible. Pualla rejoined Dalpha and Lothia, making some comment to them that Dohma was surprised he couldn't hear.

A reception line formed. Kings, queens, and regents each bent knee, greeting the deities. Dalpha smiled through it all, catching a glimpse of Dohma from time to time like she didn't want to let him out of her sight. Lothia stole several sideways glances at both Dohma and Orahda while receiving each ruler and regent in no particular order.

It was only after the chaos began to subside that Dohma noticed Duke was no longer in the room.

Now, how did he slip out like that?

The participants began to file back to the assembly meeting chamber, where servants were rearranging the tables, adding four silver thrones to a small dais, which had risen out of the floor. One of them was more ornate than the others. The three deities took the lesser thrones.

Dohma glanced back at Orahda. "Who is the fourth one for?"

Cundia stood to one side while Orahda was on the other. Both of them scanned the other attendees as if nothing was different. Without looking at them, Orahda said, "It represents the All Father Lord Argos, who is attending through Lady Lothia."

"So she has his proxy vote?"

"No, m'Lord. Lord Argos is watching and will speak, if he so desires, from his throne in Miniath-Tur at the center of the universe."

Lord Argos is watching this directly? This must be more important than I thought.

Duke had still not arrived, yet everyone was in their places, shuffling and straightening their papers, glancing around nervously for ten full minutes. Only the Gods sat comfortably in their thrones, straight-backed, with the appearance of infinite patience. Lothia and Pualla sat so still they might have been statues. Dalpha, in contrast, was somewhat animated. She would shift her left arm from her lap to the throne arm, and back, while continuing to regard Dohma.

Lord Menthran, the Imperial regent, glanced at the Gods and kept adjusting his seat. Finally, as he rubbed his face and started to stand, Duke walked in. Lord Menthran looked relieved until he saw, following Duke into the room, seventy Daggers who took positions against the walls around the room. Duke walked to his position like nothing unusual was happening.

The Imperial regent took one last glance at the new Daggers and then stood and rapped his gavel. "The Assembly of the Covenant of Duianna is called to order."

Lothia stood, looking at the Imperial regent.

He cleared his throat. "The chair recognizes Lady Lothia, the Raven."

"I speak for the Circle, Lord Argos, and my two companions. We're fully aware of all circumstances leading to this meeting, as well as the debate to date. There's no need to repeat what is already known by all present. I move for an immediate vote on the motion before the assembly."

Duke stood and bowed, but before he could speak, a deep, booming voice came out of the air all around the chamber. "I second the motion for a vote."

With his eyes narrowing, Duke looked at Lothia. The Imperial regent rapped his gavel. "The motion for a vote is made and seconded. The floor will now accept comment upon the motion before a vote. The chair recognizes His Excellency Duke of Greyrhan, Lord of Aelargo, for discussion of the motion now before the assembly."

Duke scanned the room before he bowed his head. "I was going to second the call. I have nothing further to add." Duke said in an even tone. He then sat back down and started mumbling something to his senior staff Dagger, Elades. Elades' hands started moving in the pattern Daggers used as he listened to Duke with a tight-lipped expression.

Duke is pensive and I'd more likely be a jester than that being what he intended to say. He thinks the Gods are making a mistake.

The Imperial regent glanced around the room. No one else indicated a desire to comment. "So be it." He declared rapping his gavel again. "A vote on the motion to declare war on the Nhia-Samri is to be made. Secretary, you will call the vote."

The secretary called, "Lord Argos the All Father of the Universe, what is your vote?"

"NO." Lord Argos's voice boomed throughout the room, causing many to jump.

The secretary recovered from the pronouncement and marked his tablet.

He nervously looked at the physically present deities. "Lady Lothia the Raven of Karakia, what is your vote?"

"I abstain until the end of voting." Lothia's voice was quiet and washed around the room as a summer breeze closely followed by her gaze. Most in the room looked down, unable to meet her eye to eye.

The secretary glanced at the Imperial regent who made

a get-on-with-it gesture. The secretary looked back at the deities.

"Lady Dalpha, Lady of Light and Nae-Rae, what is your vote?"

"I abstain until the end of voting." She said in a soft tone as lovely as the dawn as she fidgeted with her left bracelet, her eyes glued on Dohma. Her brows creased slightly, intensifying her stare at him.

The secretary marked his tablet without looking down. "Lord Pualla, Lord of Air and Yur, Patron Chair of the Circle, what is your vote?"

"I abstain until the end of voting." Pualla declared, his voice the deep baritone of a master of the hunt. Pualla leaned forward in his chair making eye contact with Duke. Dohma saw Duke subtly shake his head 'no' and Duke seemed to plead something that Pualla understood as he sat back straight in his chair with a frown.

The secretary again marked his tablet without looking and shifted his gaze onto the Imperial regent.

"Imperial Regent Lord Aphastes Menthran, what is your vote?"

"Yes!" The Imperial regent exclaimed as his gaze swept the room, defiantly challenging all present.

The vote continued around the room.

Dohma voted 'yes' without hesitation when the vote for Aelargo was called for, receiving an approving nod from the Imperial regent.

After the last member voted, the tally stood six in favor and six opposed. Everyone's eyes turned to the Gods as the secretary again called for their votes.

Lady Lothia, frowning at the room, voted defiantly, "No."

Lord Pualla stared at Duke and voted just as defiantly, "Yes."

All eyes in the room now rested on Lady Dalpha as the

secretary called, "Lady Dalpha, Lady of Light and Nae-Rae, what is your vote?"

Dalpha had stared at Dohma throughout the entire vote. Occasionally, she adjusted her left hand's position, while her right hand remained perfectly still. She did not answer as she continued to stare at Dohma, her left hand shifting slightly. Dohma's instincts screamed at him to act, but what he should do escaped him.

Why is she so interested in me? She's the Goddess of Healing and Life — she won't agree to war. Her own disciple Sayscia told me once that Dalpha never agreed with violence. Yet, she's nervous and trying to tell me something.

The secretary called again, his voice holding steady. "Lady Dalpha, Lady of Light and Nae-Rae, the vote is deadlocked. By the rules of the assembly you are compelled to vote. What is your vote?"

Lothia wore a small smile, while Pualla frowned, as Dalpha took a breath.

Her left hand! She has always had only one bracelet, on her right arm. Why does she now have a second on her left? Dohma's stomach dropped from a cliff into the cold dark sea. *That's the purpose of her actions. I alone have enough memory of her visage. She desired I notice it. Perhaps she's compromised in some manner. I require Orahda's knowledge.* Dohma pointed his nose directly at Dalpha and discretely tapped Orahda's and Cundia's knees.

Dalpha clenched her fists tightly, closing her eyes, and said softly, "Yes." Her voice trembled and pleaded for sympathy. Her voice carried with it a blast of cold air that rushed through the room. Duke's mouth dropped open.

Dohma murmured, "Dalpha has a left bracelet."

Orahda drew his blades and leapt over the desk to the floor, as the Imperial regent rapped his gavel. Orahda's reaction confirmed Dohma's worst fears, and he started to stand reaching for his weapons.

Lothia's jaw dropped as she turned to face Dalpha. Pualla

also turned to face Dalpha, his eyebrows nearly vanishing into his hair.

Before the sound of the gavel finished echoing, the crash of a dozen blades rang out, along with the screams of dying people. Nhia-Samri were pouring through four glowing disks on the walls, cutting down everyone in their path.

Electra's Jewel Case

CHAPTER 2

EVERYONE BLEEDS

Countess Electra Neyon of Waylisia, the youngest Chief Deputy Secretary of the Duianna Alliance to an Alliance state — her new love, the Kingdom of Aelargo — stretched and yawned. She'd been working hard to set up the Alliance secretary office in Aelargo's capitol, Llino.

Looking over her twelve busy staff members, she took a deep breath and exhaled it, enjoying the feelings that washed through her. She couldn't wait for Lord Dohma to return; her whole body shivered at the imagined smile and congratulations she was sure he'd give her when she showed him her tidy new office. It was the model of efficiency. Everything was clean and orderly, with rows of empty filing cabinets, which would soon be filled with all the deeds, disputes, and investigations she and her staff would have to handle. It was a lot of work to run an office for the Duianna Alliance of Realms.

If someone had said to me, even four cycles ago, that I'd be placed in charge of my own office, I'd have called for the physicians and some priests of Dalpha to bless the mad fool. With my Lord's rise to power came my own rise. I know my grandfather had something to do with them considering me for this, but the secretary of the Alliance is no fool. He would never allow someone to take such a position, let alone give them the responsibility of establishing a new office, if he didn't have confidence in them. I've surpassed by thirteen years my goal of becoming a chief deputy secretary by age thirty-five! I'm the youngest to hold this position in the 10,061 year history of the Alliance. How can my Lord not be pleased with these results?

With the thought of Lord Dohma, she recalled the image of his face, her heart rate picking up. She clasped her hands in her lap and swallowed to clear the dryness of her throat. She knew he was in the assembly meeting that would be attacked by the Nhia-Samri just after the vote to ratify the war against the Nhia-Samri took place.

He's one of the best warriors there, captain of the guard. And he has Daggers protecting him, she tried to reassure herself. It helped, marginally.

Again she considered asking Vesta to help keep him safe. She was aware of Vesta's potential powers, but she set those thoughts aside. Both Vesta and Arkady were afraid of being discovered by the assembly.

Shaking her head she stood and looked out the window across the palace grounds. She knew Vesta was watching over her here, but Arkady had fled to the moon. He had been worried Duke would detect he was awake and according to Vesta's monitoring he was right. Duke had been cross checking all the Gracian systems as well as unsealing some emergency corridors for the rulers' expected retreat.

The moon. She looked up and the third moon was visible in the darkening sky. *They can travel to the moon. They have such powers, yet they fear to use them.*

She recalled the night she'd helped Vesta and Arkady attack the Nhia-Samri base. The three of them had used an army of steel-encased crabs the size of horses to attack a Nhia-Samri base. The Nhia-Samri had lost thousands of warriors, yet they'd won that fight. Vesta and Arkady were ancient powers, sentient beings made of pure energy and machines with powers that rivaled the Gods, but they'd still lost.

That same night the main Nhia-Samri stronghold, Hisuru Amajoo, survived an attack by Arkady that should have created a new mountain lake.

I've seen their power. They can do so much that the assembly voted to force them to sleep over 5,000 years ago to prevent the misuse of their knowledge and power. And yet the Nhia-Samri have proven strong enough to face their legendary powers.

I don't wish they'd never woken up, but I do wish we'd been able to be more open about our preemptive strike on the Nhia-Samri. Because of the need for secrecy, Vesta and Arkady could not deploy the full level of forces they had at their command. The attack had not succeeded. She clenched her fists in frustration. *Yes, we cut the Nhia-Samri forces by more than half. But the remaining forces were better, stronger, and I think angrier, which does not bode well for my beautiful Gracia or for my love, who will be at the center of the first attack.*

Shaking her head out of her worrying, she examined her staff as they worked. More than a few quills were moving slower, and some hands were even a little shaky.

"Everyone, that will do for today. Go get some rest. Tomorrow I have meetings in the morning. There's nothing outstanding that requires being here before noon."

Their actions sped up noticeably as they cleaned their desks and put everything away. After they left, she took a quick tour to make sure all was in order before locking the doors. It was nice, having an office provided by the state in the palace. Her rooms were also provided by grant of the regents. As she walked back to her room, she passed patrols of four guards led by two Daggers.

For the uncounted time that day she patted her breast pocket, the soft crinkling of paper making her smile. The letter from Dohma was still there and real. Her steps quickened with the desire to sit in her private chamber and read his juvenile attempt at being romantic once again. *It's so sweet, silly, just like a young boy trying to impress his girl. His sister said no lady has ever turned his head. She's so happy for us.* When Regent Ellua had given Electra the letter, she'd also confided that she'd given up hope that he would find someone to love and be loved by.

Approaching her room, she noted there were six Daggers on guard in the hall leading to her door. *No one else is here, so this must be for me. But we're at the center of one of the ancient cities, the capital of Aelargo, in the very heart of the palace. Surely Dohma doesn't expect the Nhia-Samri to strike here, too.*

She acknowledged the Daggers, reading their body language to identify the senior one. All of the Daggers were women, and they looked like they were each a whole guard squad. The senior Dagger was a full hand shorter than the rest, with a strong, square face. She had a trim but muscular build and sported as many knives as would be expected of an assassin. She also wore small shield bucklers on both arms, with some rather expensive looking custom-armored gloves.

Electra stepped up to her. "Captain, why do I have six guards?"

Right eyebrow rising, the Dagger asked, "How'd you know I was in charge?" Her tone was exactly like that of Electra's matronly tutor: tough, no-nonsense, and used to being listened to seriously. A shame, as it was also a lovely mezzo-soprano, which made Electra think of the very best smoky tavern singers.

Electra waved, indicating the others. "They all glanced at you when I looked them in the eye. Also," she said, leaning in closer and lowering her voice, "I've noticed the shorter women Daggers are usually far more dangerous."

The Dagger captain laughed an interesting, bouncing laugh that Electra liked. "You're classic. Name's Mandy. And yeah, I'm the lead. I received orders making me your personal guard captain. I picked the roughest and toughest I knew. I understand Lord Dohma has a personal interest in keeping you safe, so we're taking this very seriously. The assembly is expected to vote any time now. You'll have at least three of us with you at all times from here on."

Electra's stomach did a flip. *Oh, no! How can I use the equipment Vesta gave me if they're watching me?*

She chewed her lip, trying to decide what to do. As she puzzled over the dilemma, her concentration was broken by the ringing of bells. The sound vibrated through her. They weren't just any bells, but the big palace alarm bells, signaling the city to go on alert.

Before the second ring, three of the Daggers had drawn weapons and closed into a protective circle around Electra.

The others had run in both directions down the hallways, to check around the corners.

Mandy grabbed Electra's wrist and stared into her eyes. "Listen carefully. That can only be one thing. If we're attacked, you're to run away. Don't worry about us. We'll stay with you as best as we can. You *must* escape, even if that means abandoning us or fleeing the city. If we can, we'll be with you or close behind. You're smart and resourceful, according to everything I've been told."

Electra tried to break Mandy's grip, but for such a small woman, she was as strong as steel. "Mandy, you're being ridiculous. I'm not important."

Mandy reached out and poked her in the chest, just over her heart, and the letter there crinkled audibly.

"Lady, listen to me. You're more important to Aelargo than you can imagine. And this is just one part of that. Everyone, and I mean EVERYONE, knows about you and Lord Dohma. Just as everyone believes Lord Dohma will be the calm in the storm that can save Aelargo from the Nhia-Samri. If you're captured, you will be the end of Aelargo. You're also a secretary of the Alliance of Duianna with Imperial authority, which will open many doors the Nhia-Samri are interested in."

For a second, she felt dizzy and wobbly, as if the floor had fallen out from beneath her.

I'm only twenty-two. How can I be so important?

Her diplomatic training reasserted itself, and she slowed her breathing, looking at Mandy. "I understand. Let go. I need to get into my room."

Mandy held her gaze a moment more before releasing her wrist. "Check her room," she barked.

One of the Daggers moved over to her chamber door and slipped through it, closing it behind her.

"Do you expect an attack so soon?"

Mandy had turned so she could watch both ends of the corridor and the Dagger at each end, checking around the corner. Mandy shook her head. "No. We were told Gracia would be the primary target. But it won't take them long to mobilize. The supreme commander believes they'll attack all the old cities first."

That makes sense. The old cities are strongholds and also symbols for the people. If the old cities fell, it would be demoralizing.

The door to her chambers opened and the Dagger slipped back out, holding Electra's weapon belt, some clothes, and a few essentials.

They're going to move me. I need to get to Vesta to see what's really going on.

The Dagger stepped over, handing her the rest of her belongings. Electra shrugged into her light leather armor and strapped on the weapons belt.

This is going to be the dress of the day for some time.

She rolled her things into a tight ball and tucked it under her arm.

"There's a green jewelry case on my night stand. I need that."

Mandy looked at her with wide eyes. "You're worried about your jewelry now?" she said incredulously.

"It holds more than you know. If you're going to move me, I cannot leave that behind," she said in her own commanding voice.

Mandy took in the tone and her serious stance and nodded. The other Dagger slipped back into her room and returned in seconds with the case held in one hand. Electra accepted it and then let the Daggers escort her to a room deep inside the palace, with no windows and a strong door.

"Two questions: There's no back door, so what am I to do if we're attacked? And when can I see the regents?"

"I was told by the regents to put you in this room; they seem to think it'll be safer for you. And they said they'll meet with you in the morning, once they have some reports sorted out."

Electra sat down on the freshly prepared bed. There were empty bookcases along the wall.

This is an office converted recently for me. When did they decide to stuff me in here?

She thought back to the night a few days back, when Regent Ellua had given her the letter from Dohma. The letter had come with 250 reinforcement Daggers for the city.

I bet they picked this room the next day.

Her eyes landed on an old piece of furniture, a chamber-pot chair.

Oh, my Lady! Are we really going to that extreme?

Mandy and two other Daggers stood inside her door, blocking the way out. Mandy was watching her and chuckled, noticing what she was looking at.

"No, you don't have to use that. There's a privy and bath nearby. Still, someone thought ahead," Mandy said lightly.

She felt odd with them standing there watching her. "Are you three going to stand there all night?"

Scanning the room, Mandy said, "Aren't any chairs. Was planning a three-way rotation; meaning yes. The plan is three inside and three outside."

Electra had a sinking feeling and caught herself petting the jewelry case. She glanced up and saw that all three Daggers were watching her closely.

I can't slip on the neural band with them watching, can I? An idea came. *If I don't explain, it could pass for magic. In fact, it really is Imperial magic, just of a different type.*

Placing the jewelry box on her bed, she stood, stepping in front of all three Daggers. She placed her hands on Mandy's shoulders and stared into her eyes.

"Do you swear you are a loyal servant of Duianna?"

Confusion danced in Mandy's expression for an instant. But she put her hand on her Dagger hilt, standing as tall as she could and meeting Electra's glare.

"I am Mandy Gurlan of Gare Town, Dagger in service

to the Duianna Alliance. I swear I'll die before I betray the Alliance."

The rock hard resolve in Mandy's eyes told Electra everything she needed to know. Electra repeated the question with the other two Daggers, making them swear to die before betraying the Alliance.

Satisfied, Electra went back to the bed and touched the box's lock. Keeping her fingers in just the right places she concentrated on her memory of the Neyon valley wheat fields, her home. The memory evoked a longing in her to once again walk through the fields of golden grain, letting the plants tickle her palms. A slight tingle passed through her fingers as the box's systems confirmed her biological signature and brain-wave pattern, which together made an unduplicatable key for the lock. The box clicked open by itself.

Mandy raised her eyebrow, moving closer. "That isn't a jewelry box, is it?" she said conspiratorially, a slight waver in her voice.

Electra gave Mandy a friendly smirk. "This is an Imperial secret of the highest order. If anything happens to me, you're to put everything back into this and close the lock. Once sealed, even the Gods would have difficulties opening this box." She recalled Vesta's undersea worker crabs that labored to keep the merchant channels clear and safe. It took willpower not to smile too much. "Then, if you can, throw it into the deepest part of the Loren Sound you can reach."

The other two Daggers had also come forward. Electra glanced at each in turn, and they all nodded to indicate that they understood the orders.

She lifted the lid, revealing the slim leather journal with gold filigree bindings, and the other compartments containing the technological treasures Vesta had given her to ensure their secrecy. She lifted a device that looked like an ornate silver plate normally used for holding small jewelry parts while the lady applied her makeup or prepared for the evening. She connected the plate to the box by an intricate rod that lifted out. Once the plate was in place, standing above the box on its rod, she activated the box. Although nothing appeared to happen, she knew that Vesta's security systems had been engaged to block and scramble any signals trying to trace the transmissions from the device.

Pointing to the journal, Mandy said, "That's a royal archive. I've seen one in the throne room of Gracia."

Ah, good. That will reinforce the idea this is Imperial magic and not to be spoken of.

"Correct."

She lifted the silver band from its compartment. "Now, I'm going to lie down and put this on my head. I will seem to be sleeping. I am not. If you need me, touch my arm. It might take a minute for me to know where I am. Do not, I repeat, DO NOT take this off my head without giving me a minute to return."

"Return from where?" Mandy asked.

Oh no, I shouldn't have phrased it that way. Electra felt her cheeks and ears heating up as she blushed at her mistake. *What should I say?* She recalled something her grandfather said often to junior courtiers when they made some inappropriate disclosure. 'When you slip you don't have to slide, just take the fall and you won't lose as much ground.'

"That I cannot tell you. Now, I need to find out what's going on."

Mandy was smart — she had to be, in her position — and she jumped to a semi-correct conclusion. "You're going to communicate with the Alliance. I see why that's such a secret."

As Electra lay down on the bed, Mandy and her two Daggers took their guard positions. With a last glance at them, she slipped on the silver band and closed her eyes, letting her head drop onto the pillow.

After cycles of working with Vesta, Electra was no longer scared as she felt her mind connecting to the city's network.

She was able to travel the networks, taking control of many of the devices and systems at will.

Vesta had introduced her to the idea of programming, and Electra had taken up the skills as if born to them. Arkady, the artificial sentient who lived in Gracia, believed her talents were inherited from her family through extra-natural means. Electra's ancestor Muriel Neyon-Banaschel was the architect of the Imperial security overrides that had broken the assembly's and Duke's best coded locks, waking both Vesta and Arkady from their 5,000-year imposed slumber. Even Vesta and Arkady had so far been unable to determine exactly how Muriel's releases worked. Muriel had been a genius systems engineer with a rare talent for complex systems, and Electra was proving to have comparable talents with the ancient systems.

She searched the network connections for Vesta's presence. She was sure Vesta would be using a façade simulation of a city control room because Vesta liked the feel of moving around it to focus her work. It didn't take long to locate it. Electra connected her data streams to the control room simulation and moved from the network into the half-real, half-projected control center of the city.

Vesta was not manifested in the control room, but the status displays showed that she was focused on some specific incoming signals. Dozens of monitors were showing satellite images of cities and the few Nhia-Samri bases they'd managed to locate. Electra ignored most of them, even though there were six cities with images of fires and panicked people fleeing.

She stepped over to the displays Vesta was so busy processing that she had dropped her projection in the control room. A whole wall of displays showed dozens of areas in Gracia. As she looked over the screens, Vesta materialized next to her. Nhia-Samri were fighting guards and Daggers in every display. Blood flowed freely down the floors and streets shown.

"What can we do to help?" she managed to choke out of her tightening throat. She fought tears, managing to hold them in check.

Vesta put a hand on her shoulder. "Nothing. In addition to Duke, there are immortals present who would immediately know what our actions meant. It would mean Arkady and I would be forced back to sleep. Even worse, Duke would take whatever time was needed to dig out Muriel's security overrides to make sure we did not wake again until authorized by the assembly."

"But Gracia could fall! Even with the extra Daggers and the Gods there. What if...?" Her throat tightened so hard she couldn't finish the question.

My emotions affect me here too much. I really need to find a way to keep them tempered.

Arkady appeared, his voice cracking slightly as he spoke. "I have done all I can."

Vesta blinked over to another panel and made some adjustments. "Arkady, can you boost the power? Your signal is still not stable."

Arkady worked for a few seconds before he answered. His hands kept reaching out and typing or twisting things until his voice was slightly clearer. "I don't want to boost the signal too much. If someone scans, we can't let this link be discovered."

Vesta blinked back next to Electra.

I'm glad they trust me so much now. In the last week, both Arkady and Vesta had stopped bothering to act like humans. Electra knew it was because they'd decided she could deal with what they really were. It had taken a little time to understand that they weren't beings like all the others she knew. Electra had decided to classify them as spirits. Beings of energy, yes, made by her ancestors, but still beings with feelings and maybe even souls.

Electra realized she'd let herself drift from needed tasks. Looking at all the destruction occurring not only in Gracia, but also around the realms on all the monitors of the control room, a cold chill formed in her core.

"Arkady, what would it take for me to visit the moon?"

It took several seconds before Arkady turned towards her. The time delay caused by his distance was more than a little disconcerting.

"I told you this is only temporary, until it is safe for me to return to Gracia. If we connected you here, it wouldn't look any different than where you are. You've already seen the external displays," he said.

She shook her head. "No. I meant really go to the moon. You said it was possible."

Her eyes moved from screen to screen; tears were now truly running down the side of her real head back in her room. Try as she might she couldn't move her hand to wipe them dry.

Mandy and the Daggers are probably staring right at me. They'll know it isn't going well.

She forced herself to keep a businesslike attitude as she scanned each monitor. There were many civilian bodies in her view; thankfully, most of the dead were Alliance soldiers or Nhia-Samri. The one man she wanted with all her heart to find, Lord Dohma, was not present.

The God, Lord Pualla, had pushed his defense out into the city. Vesta followed his fighting on the monitors. Pualla was leading a dozen Daggers, who ran directly into a pack of Nhia-Samri. Lord Pualla threw his staff in the air and drew his curved swords. The staff hung just above him as he engaged a pair of Nhia-Samri. The Nhia-Samri combined their attacks, trying to make contact with Lord Pualla, but he parried them.

Lord Pualla swung his blade at one opponent, who managed to parry just in time, but there was an explosive crack of thunder, and the Nhia-Samri was thrown back at least five feet to slam into a wall. The other one sliced at Lord Pualla's exposed arm. He pulled his hand back just far enough to catch the blades on his red bracers. With a motion so fast it didn't show clearly, he swung his arm up and around to thrust his own curved blade through the Nhia-Samri.

With his direct opponents neutralized, Lord Pualla sheathed his blades and reached up, grabbing his staff. Pulling it down, he stepped back, holding the staff before him like a bow. He motioned as if drawing an arrow, and an arrow made of shimmering gold and blazing with red fire appeared in his grasp. He let it fly. It slammed into another Nhia-Samri, who fell dead with the burning arrow skewering him clean through. As the warrior fell, the arrow fell apart into sparkling dust, and was gone by the time the body hit the ground.

Lord Pualla called to his warriors and ran, shooting arrows faster than the Nhia-Samri could react. The Daggers and city guards took care of any of the Nhia-Samri Lord Pualla missed or that came from the side alleys. Lord Pualla made a line of dead bodies all the way to the magical gate the Nhia-Samri continued to emerge from like a wave of locusts. He started shooting the glowing focal points of the gate with his fiery arrows until it flashed and was no more.

Vesta replayed the moment of Pualla breaking the magic gate on a side monitor.

"That would be very dangerous." Arkady's response finally came; he'd obviously been dealing with some other issues as well as considering her question. Electra felt a twinge of pride — one cycle before, Arkady would've dismissed her question without much thought. "We'd have to use a much larger vessel than the one I used for my core and extra communications gear. A ship that size would be hard to hide. Why the sudden interest?"

Still fighting to hold back her tears, Electra said, "Evacuation. If we can't stop them, we need to go where they can't."

Vesta stopped and looked at Arkady. "You were checking on the other worlds. Have you found anything?"

"Other worlds?" Electra asked.

"This isn't the only world in the universe," Vesta said.

"We were able to make seventeen inhabitable planets like Niya-Yur. Not everyone came here. There are also 1,654 other worlds where you could not survive without magic or technology to preserve your form. We're also unsure how many other stars might have habitable worlds. This is a much smaller universe than our original one. I don't think you fully comprehend that thousands of sentient races from two universes worked to save as many worlds, plants, animals, ecosystems, and cultures as they could. Uncounted nonillions died, yet billions were saved. We...."

Arkady started talking, interrupting Vesta, a side effect of the time delay.

"There are no detectable signals, and the Pilum-Gate was shutdown cold a few years after we were put to sleep. They didn't even leave the Tunnelnet active. Only the shielding and minor systems are operating. If anyone's still out there, they haven't been here since we were put to sleep. The only means of communicating between the other planets now is magic. If we start to reactivate the Pilum-Gate, you know that would be noticed."

"Why would they go to the trouble of a complete cold shutdown of the Pilum-Gate. That'd take years of work."

Vesta and Electra watched Arkady, waiting for the answer. He paused longer than just the delay. "Niya-Yur is quarantined. Messenger probes were launched to the other worlds with the Imperial order. No details are in these systems."

"Quarantine." Vesta started chewing her fingernail. "Why not order medical support? The Empire has never abandoned any protectorate. Why would the Emperor order the capital, with the Imperial family, closed off without assistance?"

Arkady stopped tugging on his beard to wave his hands in the air. "Hell if I know. When I get back to Gracia I'll check the imperial archive. Oh and Electra, to answer your question, yes, we can evacuate some to the moon. But again, it would give us away."

Electra stopped making notes of new words to find the definitions for, to stare at both Arkady and Vesta. "If it comes to evacuation, I doubt anyone will care if you're awake or not."

One of the displays flashed a picture of Lord Dohma fighting the Nhia-Samri. Electra's heart jumped to her throat and a tingling feeling bounced around her body with joy. She flung herself at the controls, activating as many monitors as she could control that showed what was going on. "He's still fighting! Curse that man's sense of duty! He was supposed to run!"

DOHMA

Dohma flew over his desk, throwing off his mantle of state. For weeks he'd sweated, wearing the double layer of clothing over armor. At that moment, he was immeasurably glad he had. Cundia drew her weapons as she spun over his desk, landing on the opposite side of him from Orahda.

Lord Pualla practically carried the Imperial Regent, Lord Menthran, personally out of the room down one of the many escape routes to the city. Lord Menthran had a shimmering sword out and Dohma's last glimpse of his face showed tight-lipped anger at being dragged away like a child.

Good, Lord Pualla will make sure the Imperial regent makes it to the elven patrols. Lord Menthran wouldn't dare oppose an order by Lord Pualla.

The extra Daggers around the room were already fighting, trying to block the Nhia-Samri from getting through the gates. They were having some success. The other assembly members all looked relatively calm as they and their staff rushed towards one exit or another, avoiding the Nhia-Samri as planned.

Orahda started to move in the direction of the unblocked escape route they'd planned for themselves.

"Not yet," said Dohma firmly, shaking his head.

"Dohma, you must run," Orahda said. "This is not the time or place for heroics."

Dohma ripped the hanging cloth cover from the front of his desk to get at the small shield held under the desk with some break-away leather straps. "I'm commander of the Aelargian Guard first! I shall not flee before ensuring the safety of my fellow rulers. Aid me in getting those we can to safety, then I too shall retreat."

Cundia smiled. "You owe me another cross."

Orahda exhaled loudly, but Dohma saw the gleam of pride and purpose in his eyes. Orahda's face tightened as he examined the situation. Nhia-Samri were coming through the glowing gates rapidly, but only two could cross at a time. The Daggers and guards were managing to hold a line against them, but the defenders' numbers were dwindling. "If we close these gates, all assembly members will be able to make it to the first checkpoint." Out of the side of his mouth he added to Cundia, "And no, I don't. We didn't shake."

Dohma smiled and slapped Orahda and then Cundia on the shoulder.

"Time to get to work. We must end this gate first," he said as he jumped for the nearest gate. Cundia and Orahda were right next to him. "Cundia, help me. Keep them busy and slow the flood. Orahda, do what you must, but close that gate."

Dohma jumped into the fight. Three Nhia-Samri had managed to get a clear foot inside the room, and a fourth was joining them through the gate. Five Daggers were fighting the three.

Dohma lunged in as Cundia delivered a head blow. The Nhia-Samri blocked both of their attacks. A Dagger thrust in between them, stabbing her all the way through. Dohma didn't pause, riposting the soon-to-be-dead warrior, who was still trying to kill them before she died.

The fourth was emerging, weapons out. Orahda dove between the feet of the semi-circle of Nhia-Samri, protecting the gateway, rolling forward and then kicking up hard, catching the warrior by surprise in the crotch. Orahda's kick sent him backward through the glowing gateway, arms flailing.

The wounded Nhia-Samri struck at Cundia slower, allowing Dohma to block the attack while Cundia brought her blade down, cutting off the Nhia-Samri's hand. The Nhia-Samri fell to her knees and glared at Cundia before finally collapsing.

Dohma didn't have time to consider much else as another Nhia-Samri brought his blades around in a sweeping onslaught with a scream of rage. Cundia dropped flat on the ground to avoid being hit. Dohma stepped over her to engage in a series of rapid strikes, parries, and ripostes.

Cundia rolled onto her back and swung at the legs of the new assailant, who thrust both his blades at Dohma and jumped almost ten hands high, bringing his armored boots down towards Cundia's chest. She slapped the ground with her elbow, rolling out of the way just in time to avoid being crushed by his weight. Something hit Dohma hard in the back, throwing him forward. To avoid stepping on Cundia, he jumped onto the Nhia-Samri warrior, who managed to get one of his odassi positioned to stab Dohma through the left side of his abdomen. Pain burst through him as he and the warrior went down together.

If I'm not dead yet, I will be if he works that cut wider.

Dohma dropped his sword and grabbed the hand that was holding the blade thrust through him. Fear gave him strength to hold it in place. The Nhia-Samri head slammed into the stone floor with a nice thud, and Dohma was sure the wind was knocked out of the man because he'd landed squarely on top. The man glowered at him through slightly glazed eyes. Nose-to-nose, Dohma glowered back just as intensely. A loud bang, accompanied by a brilliant flash of light, shocked both of them. From their position on the floor, they looked up to see the glowing disk of the gate wink out, leaving the ordinary wall in its place.

A Nhia-Samri screamed and fell to the ground, his eyes wide, because the lower half of his body was on the other side of the closed gate. Blood poured across the floor, out of his upper torso, as he twitched violently and died with a long sigh.

Orahda turned and stomped on the throat of the man under Dohma with such force that his neck flattened. Blood burst from under Orahda's boot and out of one of the eyes of the warrior.

Gore sprayed onto Dohma's face as his nostrils filled with its salty odor. The warrior's body convulsed, and his grip on the odassi finally lessened, but not without first vibrating the sword, causing shivers of pain to threaten Dohma's consciousness. He clenched his teeth against the pain and concentrated on holding the odassi with all his strength to keep it as stable as possible.

Cundia got back to her feet and pulled the half-torso away. "Oh, Lady! Lord Dohma!" she cried, dropping to her knees next to him.

"It isn't that bad," he lied.

Orahda knelt on one knee. "I told you we needed to run."

He shook his head. "You're needed, my friend. Go, close the other gates. Worry then about me," he said through gritted teeth.

Cundia and Orahda looked at the chaos of the assembly chamber, and Orahda's face hardened. "No. Cundia, aid me."

They grabbed Dohma by the shoulders and lifted him to his feet. Pain ripped through him, but he bit his tongue to keep from screaming. Giving them a weak smile, he allowed Cundia to take one arm as Orahda supported him from the other side.

"Come," Orahda said grimly.

Orahda kicked a desk, sending it flying into another

Nhia-Samri, knocking him down. Then he dragged Dohma to where Lothia and Dalpha stood together.

Daggers were pushing the Nhia-Samri back, but it looked like no reinforcements had come in, which meant that an even larger battle must be taking place outside and around the palace.

Dalpha wasn't fighting. She stood regally and made gestures, causing a green beam of energy to envelope wounded Daggers as they fell. Anyone touched by her power would miraculously stand up, unwounded yet still covered in their own blood.

Lothia was facing a pair of magic gates, sending radiant bursts of white and gold at any warrior coming through them. Her magic blasts exploded, throwing the warriors back through the gates, knocking down others who were trying to force their way in.

As Dohma approached, carried by Orahda and Cundia, a Nhia-Samri jumped at Lothia from the side. She twisted out of the way in a blur of motion and reached out, grabbing his wrist. In a single motion, she flung the man through one of the gates. It was clear that as long as she stood there no one was coming through either gate.

She's magnificent; I never dreamed to live long enough to see the wife of the All Father Lord Argos in battle.

Orahda pulled Dohma directly to Dalpha, releasing him one step away, letting Cundia balance him. He tried to stand before the mighty deities on his own, but he couldn't find the strength. His pants felt wet, and he looked down, picking at them with his free hand. He sighed with relief when he realized it was only his blood. Cundia caught his eye and shook her head with an annoyed grunt.

I care not what you think. I swear I'll not be known for pissing my own pants in battle, especially in front of these beings!

Orahda was glaring, face to face with Dalpha. His grim expression made Dalpha take a half-step back, and his hand snapped out to grab her. When his fingers were two inches from Dalpha's left arm, lightning cascaded around his hand and around her. It didn't even slow him. He clamped down on her forearm and pulled her towards him.

How much power does Orahda wield?

"Why have you betrayed the world?"

Lightning continued to dance around Orahda's arm and Dalpha. She looked down, her eyes watering. "I had no choice. I tried to draw attention, yet none noticed."

Ripping the bracelet from her wrist, Orahda said, "There is always a choice."

Dalpha screamed, "No! You've killed her!" She fell to her knees, but ended up dangling by the arm Orahda held. Dalpha, Lady of Light, wailed in mourning and defeat.

Orahda held the bracelet up to examine it more closely. His eyes narrowed as he held the Goddess. He squeezed her arm harder, and she whimpered; her other hand shot up, trying to loosen his grip.

Lothia turned to witness the scene, but did nothing to protest the treatment of Dalpha.

Who is Orahda that he can act so?

Orahda's eyes dropped to the sobbing Goddess. In a hard, commanding voice he pronounced, "Shar-Lumen would not. That you believe such speaks much. First, you will heal Lord Dohma." He turned, dragging her to Dohma, and released her arm. Dalpha fell at Dohma's feet, still wailing.

Orahda's brows furrowed; his mouth tightened, showing the tendons in his jaw. He turned to Lothia and then glanced around the room. "I'm tired of hiding, and I'll have the answers."

Dalpha pulled herself up, tears running down her face. "Then I will do what I must," she whimpered.

She concentrated, touching the blade protruding from Dohma's torso. Sparks flew at her from the sword, and she yelped in pain, yanking her hand back.

She looked at Dohma, and he saw, deep in those large eyes, something unexpected behind the anguish and despair:

anger. He felt a surge of energy pass between them. Dalpha's eyes changed from misery to a determination Dohma couldn't understand.

"We shall stop him," she whispered under her breath. Orahda's eyes locked onto her as she wiped the tears from her face and glared at the blade, lips flattening to a tight line.

"Hold him tightly," she snapped at Cundia.

Cundia shifted her grip to hold him with both arms. Dalpha didn't wait or give warning. She remained on her knees, but moved to face Dohma, her back rigidly straight. Dohma felt her presence grow.

She braced one hand on his stomach next to the wound and grabbed the blade by the hilt. Both of her hands flared with a golden light, and lightning from the sword danced over her hand and arm.

Pain flared throughout his body, and it was as if her hand on his stomach was a white-hot brand. He could feel the blade trying to twist in her hand to kill him. The blade's energies spread out into hundreds of barbed needles, ripping his flesh away with them.

As Dalpha ripped the sword free, Dohma's blood cascaded out into the air, raining down onto her and Lothia. She finished the motion by releasing the blade, which flew away, followed by droplets of blood, to bounce across the floor.

Agony seared through his body as his muscles vibrated against the onslaught of the furious energies Dalpha poured into him.

Dalpha twisted on her knees, shifting to his side. Her hands clamped down on the entry and exit wounds.

The world narrowed, and he became only the pain and a blazing fire that spread over him. And then, as suddenly as it came, it left.

Dohma felt detached, with no control over his own body. His muscles relaxed, and he would've fallen if not for Cundia's strong support. He also realized he was still screaming but there was no air in his lungs. He gulped the air back in, trying not to throw up.

Deep in his mind, he heard a soft whisper and knew it was Dalpha. "Your spirit is strong. Use this gift well. Forgive me."

Dalpha slumped to the floor and rolled over. She was completely drained and pale, but she was breathing.

Cundia lowered Dohma to a sitting position on the floor. The remaining pain drained away, and his heart slowed. Stars still floated around him, and Dohma blinked, trying to focus on the situation.

Only one gate remained open. Orahda was leading a pack of twenty Daggers, fighting in a close semi-circle around it. The Nhia-Samri were trying to break through the line. Although Orahda and the Daggers were bleeding from their wounds, they fought on just as hard as the enemy.

The smell of blood was overwhelming. It steamed and flowed around the room from hundreds of bodies. In places, the bodies formed dams, the blood pooled almost two hands deep. In other areas rivers of blood wound their way out the doors.

Dalpha lay next to Dohma on the dais, above the bloodline. Lothia floated nearby, and her eyes squinted as she returned to the fighting with magic and sword. All who attempted to attack her were cut down or thrown away.

Many additional warriors burst into the room to join in the assault on Lothia. More rushed to the gate, pushing the Daggers back. As Dohma watched, three of the Daggers were cut down, allowing more attackers to enter the room through the remaining magical gate.

Dohma shook his head to clear the fog and pushed himself up. Standing still, he let the pain echo through his body from the stab wound, but it felt like it was nearly healed. He picked up a sword, grabbed a dead guard's dagger from her belt, and moved towards the gate.

Cundia leapt in front of him. She held a restraining hand

up, looking him in the eyes, and then she dropped it with a sigh. "You cover me."

Dohma nodded, not trusting his voice yet. As they ran, he felt increasingly better, as his body finished recovering. There was no more time for self-contemplation.

Almost instantly, Cundia's blades cut down a Nhia-Samri. Orahda grunted at their arrival. Dohma sensed himself detaching from the horrific scene. He had to use every ounce of his long years of training to fight.

As his vision widened, his sight filled with not only the warriors in front of him but also the path of bodies leading to this position from the last gate Orahda had closed. Orahda fought as the arrowhead, with Cundia on one side and Dohma on the other. Only eleven out of nearly three hundred Daggers remained with Orahda; two other pockets of fighting held about as many Daggers and guards. Hundreds of fallen warriors covered in gleaming blood made the hallowed hall of the Duianna Alliance Assembly into a macabre painting.

If it wasn't for Orahda, we would've already lost this battle. His blades danced in shimmering waves of death, blocking every attack at him and cutting or stabbing any warrior who stood before him. Their circle of soldiers closed the distance to the gate in steady but difficult steps.

They were almost in position for Orahda to destroy the gate when Dohma's heart sank and a small groan escaped his lips before he clenched his jaw tightly shut. Two squads of Nhia-Samri rushed into the room, through the main door, and headed straight for their position. Behind them, another group of at least three more squads, covered in blood and led by a tall woman in red-enameled battle armor, raced in.

The woman glanced around the room and then pointed to Lothia. "Take her!"

Before they were assailed from the rear, Dohma yelled, "Defensive circle!"

Cundia, Orahda, and the remaining defenders joined Dohma, standing back to back. Surrounded, they fought the desperate battle of fighters who knew they weren't going to survive the day, yet dared to hope they might.

Dohma's wider perception allowed him to witness every barely parried blade and frantic counter-attack. Several cuts burned painfully on Dohma's arms, face, and torso. At his side, Cundia and even Orahda had similar wounds. He cast about for some brilliant strategy that might help. They were overwhelmed, and he knew there was no escape. Two more Daggers fell, either dead or near death.

The light from the gate rippled, attracting Dohma's attention. A lone figure stepped through.

Lords and Ladies help us, Gracia is lost! Dohma realized that his plea was of no avail. The Lords and Ladies were already trying, and failing. There on the dais stood Lady Lothia herself under heavy attack, trying to protect Lady Dalpha. Lord Pualla had already abandoned the hall to give protection to the fleeing rulers.

Dohma's heart rate doubled, tears burning in his eyes, and a painful lump in his throat made him swallow. The tall, muscular warrior wore grey and black armor, which flared dramatically from his heavy shoulders. He stood a full hand taller than Dohma. The new warrior did not have his swords drawn, yet Dohma's heart and soul screamed at him to run instead of challenging him.

This is Shar-Lumen! This last gate must go directly to his fabled impenetrable fortress, Hisuru Amajoo.

Shar-Lumen's violet eyes took in the room. He moved towards the dais, where Lothia was holding off a ring of Nhia-Samri with a shield that surrounded her and the collapsed form of Dalpha.

They pounded on the shield, slowly collapsing it. She gestured time and time again. Each gesture produced a powerful burst of lightning that burned and threw a warrior violently back to land in the pools of blood that filled the chamber. But they continued to come in through side doors to join the onslaught on the Goddess. The woman warrior was also there, pounding on Lothia's shields and dodging every attack Lothia threw at her.

"Lumen!" Orahda's thick orotund voice cut as sharp as his sword through the sounds of battle. The hall's acoustics added resonance, elevating it to the very voice of legend described in dozens of stories Dohma grew up listening to.

All combatants were stunned, and looked around for the source of that call.

Shar-Lumen stopped in the middle of a deep pool of blood, his head spinning back to look at who had called out. As his eyes landed on Orahda, his magnificent face contorted into a mask of rage and hatred.

Without any motion, Lumen's swords were in his hands, fingers clenched so tightly every muscled fiber stood out. In the peculiar silence of the room, the leather grips creaked as loudly as a falcon's shriek. "YOU!"

Lumen dove at Orahda, knocking aside one of his warriors who stood between them. Blinding flashes of light strobed as Lumen's blades clashed with Orahda's weapons. Battles resumed, and the Nhia-Samri fought harder than ever, refreshed and confident in their victory.

A scream pulled Dohma's attention from the two fighting legends. On the platform, Lothia's shield had collapsed, and six Nhia-Samri were beating her with the hilts of their blades as she fought back.

The female warrior had sheathed one blade and was using it, with its polished scabbard, like a club. Strike after strike landed on Lothia's body and head, making her yelp in pain as she tried to protect herself with her bare arms. Lothia's eyes bulged, and she spun around, trying to fend off the blows, but there was no escape.

Surrounded by nearly a dozen Nhia-Samri, Dohma cried out, "Move to aid Lothia!"

He tried to shift the ever-decreasing circle of Daggers towards the dais as additional warriors punched through the Hisuru Amajoo gate and the hall doors.

Dohma's legs screamed in pain from multiple cuts and fatigue, and his arms were no better. Still they fought. Only a couple of Nhia-Samri could engage them at a time, and the remaining Daggers were their equals in combat. The problem was that they had the odassi, which gave them the advantage.

Lothia fell under the onslaught, curling tightly into a fetal position, covering her head with her arms as best she could. They continued to beat her after she had fallen.

Dohma wasn't sure if he could believe his eyes. Lothia was bleeding from many wounds, and her blood emerged the color of dark amber. As it flowed, it turned a clear pink, running over the dais, being smeared and mixed with the blood of others.

A loud howl echoed through the chamber. Hundreds of Daggers rushed into the room from almost every entryway. Duke, supported by at least three teams, forced his way into the room. The Nhia-Samri fought hard, making Duke struggle for every step. He had dozens of wounds, and on his left shoulder, his skin hung open, exposing the muscle beneath. Duke fought on regardless, using every trick he had.

Nhia-Samri warriors continued to rush in, but with the Dagger reinforcements joining the fight, Dohma felt his spirits rise.

We may yet survive this day.

Dohma brought his blades around and slipped past the defenses of one man, cutting his throat. As he fell, Dohma checked on Orahda's fight. Shar-Lumen had cut Orahda across one shoulder, and blood was pouring from a wound in his side. He was favoring his right side, trying to keep Shar-Lumen from getting a clear strike.

Shar-Lumen glanced at Duke, and a frown formed as he breathed out through his nose. He ducked low and spun, kicking Orahda so hard that he was thrown, tumbling over some desks, which collapsed onto him.

Instead of digging Orahda out, Shar-Lumen spun and ran towards the dais, scooping up an abandoned odassi from the floor. He leapt the last several feet to land on the platform. Lumen spun around, facing Duke, holding the odassi high above his head with both hands over Dalpha. "You're too late, Duke! Learn what it means to cowardly attack mine!"

Duke, Cundia, and Dohma screamed in unison as Shar-Lumen brought the blade down with so much force that it sounded like a massive hammer hitting an anvil.

The odassi went through Dalpha's chest and into the stone below her. The shock must have snapped her into consciousness, because she cried out and grasped the blade. Lightning burst from it, down her arms and across her body, making her vibrate. As fast as the lightning started, it stopped. Dalpha's arms dropped, motionless. Her head faced Dohma, eyes open, unmoving, her pupils expanded to fill most of her eyes. Lady Dalpha, Lady of Light and Nae-Rae, was dead.

Rage tore through Dohma's mind. Lady Dalpha, who had given immeasurably to the world, had saved him, using so much power that she'd passed out, helpless to defend herself. Because of that sacrifice she now lay pinned to the stone platform by a Nhia-Samri odassi. She'd had no chance.

His soul screamed out for vengeance, his vision blurring with a red haze. Dohma kicked the warrior before him out of the way. Ignoring that the man flew backwards six feet before collapsing in a pile, Dohma ran, roaring, for the dais. Waves of blood sprayed all around as he cut through the crimson liquid pools as through air.

Shar-Lumen picked up Lothia by one arm as a parent might lift a broken doll. He ripped the silver medallion off her neck, throwing it into the pooled blood on the floor

As Dohma raced nearer, Shar-Lumen produced a golden collar, which he snapped onto Lothia's neck before tossing her aside to the Nhia-Samri warriors led by the woman in red armor.

Dohma leapt the last few feet to the platform, his blades held above his head. As he landed, he brought them down on Shar-Lumen's head, all his strength focused on that single action. The attack should have cut Shar-Lumen in two, except that he had drawn and parried in a single fluid motion.

A brilliant spark of lightning exploded from their blades, illuminating Shar-Lumen's silver skin, making it look like liquid mercury. Nose to nose with Shar-Lumen, Dohma cried out his rage at being denied revenge. Shar-Lumen's violet eyes took him in, measuring him as a collector might evaluate a rare prize. As they stared at each other, Dohma's vision fogged in a red haze, making Shar-Lumen's eyes appear pitch black.

Dohma screamed again, letting the fury take him, giving him speed and strength like nothing he had ever experienced. His blades and body moved as one, faster than he thought. The entire world forgotten, his mind would accept nothing but killing Shar-Lumen.

Daggers and guards continued to flood into the room, their forces beginning to push the Nhia-Samri back. The pitch of the battle started to change to the sparking concussions of Dohma's and Shar-Lumen's blades. The fight began to tip in favor of the assembly's forces. Duke barked and yelled obscenities as he crushed and mangled those who blocked his progress. Ignoring all else, Lumen and Dohma determinedly fought each other as the Nhia-Samri tried to stop Duke. Dozens more on both sides died each moment as the battle raged on. The Nhia-Samri did not falter, even as their numbers dwindled.

Shar-Lumen's face remained tranquil except for the corners of his mouth, which became tighter as they fought. They spun, kicked, struck, parried, and riposted. Anyone, Nhia-Samri or Dagger, that strayed too close to their mortal combat whether by design or accident, they kicked or batted away as if mere insects.

Dohma's attacks continuously pushed forward. Shar-Lumen's eyes never wavered from his as they fought. Dohma's perceptions tunneled until there were only the two of them in the entire universe, which was too small to allow the other to continue to exist.

He drove Shar-Lumen back until he was near the wall. Shar-Lumen nodded ever so slightly. "The day is yours, Lord Dohma Uriosal. I will not underestimate you again."

He performed a rapid series of attacks, forcing Dohma to step backwards for the first time since the beginning of their combat. Instead of following up on his advantage, Shar-Lumen spun and dove sideways through the remaining portal, which vanished, leaving only the blank wall in its place.

A primal shriek escaped Dohma as he pounded the wall where the portal had been, with his blades chipping away large chunks of stone. The fury finally ebbed, and he bent over, breathing deeply. Dohma straightened and turned, lifting his swords to continue the battle only to find the assembly chamber filled four hands deep with blood, bodies, and a hundred Daggers, staring at him with open mouths and wide eyes.

Lady Dalpha's body was sprawled on the dais like a tragic sacrifice, the odassi blade pinning her to the rock. Her clear pink blood ran through the dark red of the dead, as rivers through tilled farm fields under a colorful sunset.

Shivering, Duke stood over her body. With his head bowed, bleeding from dozens of wounds, he mumbled, "How many more, Lothia? How many more?"

Lady Lothia was nowhere to be seen.

Cundia and Orahda approached him, supporting each other, their own blood adding to the deep pools of spent life.

Orahda shook his head, unbelieving. "My Lord, I believe I was incorrect in my estimate of when I needed to start wearing armor for our sparring."

War Reports

CHAPTER 3

FIRES THAT BURN

EMOTIONS FLOODED ELECTRA IN AN uncontrollable tidal wave. She felt nauseated, and her heart beat a painful, staccato pulse. Each broke down a different reinforcement she had built to hold back the guilt from ordering the attack on Hisuru Amajoo.

Although the attack had failed, she still had nightmares of what could have been: hundreds of thousands of innocent men, women, and children burned to ash in the rain of fire from the sky.

She turned away from the console showing her love, Lord Dohma, being cheered by the remaining warriors for forcing Shar-Lumen to retreat. Her emotions didn't let her see the other displays showing the fighting ending in and around Gracia as the remaining Nhia-Samri retreated through their gates. She started to cry, both in the virtual world and in reality.

Vesta appeared next to her, crouching down. "What's wrong, Electra? Dohma lives, and Gracia has been saved."

"I killed her," she sobbed, wrapping her arms around her knees.

Vesta looked over the monitors, her brows furrowing. "Dalpha? No, you didn't. That was Shar-Lumen's madness. Dear child, you are not to blame."

Electra whimpered, "Yes I am," and shook her head in disagreement. Her emotions boiled over, and she lost all control, falling out of her seat to the ground. She cried into her knees, trying to squeeze herself tighter and smaller.

"Let the world swallow me forever," she wailed into her knees. "He should have killed me! Why Dalpha? What had Dalpha done to anyone that caused her to deserve anything but love? Dalpha served everyone equally, healing and caring for the lost and forgotten."

Vesta sat down cross-legged next to Electra and placed a hand on her shoulder. She began to sing. Electra didn't comprehend the words; or maybe her mind was so wrapped in sorrow that she couldn't understand language. But she knew the songs that Vesta sang spoke in tones and music of losses and regrets. Vesta's own tones wavered, and without looking, Electra knew she was crying, too.

Marks later, Electra sobbed and uncurled. Pushing herself up, she saw that Vesta had bloodshot eyes, and her face was as wet as Electra's. It didn't matter that Vesta was a creation of technology. She had regrets, and Electra was sure there were far more than she knew of. Vesta's voice quivered on the last forlorn note of a song, and they sat, looking into each other's eyes.

Something inside of her felt changed. Her mind had cleared slightly, and the edge of the guilt dulled as well.

Electra leaned over and pulled Vesta into a hug. They sat that way for an eternity, the soft hum of the city around them as they cried silently together.

Arkady's soft voice was a shock. "I'm sorry to interrupt, but you're about to be under attack."

Vesta squeezed Electra one time, hard, and then stood up. "What do you mean?"

Electra wiped her face, and yet it still felt wet. It took her a few moments to realize it was from her real face, not the virtual one, that the sensation of wet tears was coming. She had forgotten that only her mind was here. She returned to her body and sat up, wiping away the tears.

I wonder if Vesta did something to me. She said that many problems living beings had could be eased and addressed. Maybe there was magic in those songs she sang.

"That bad?" Mandy asked.

Electra stiffened, recalling that she wasn't alone in her room. The idea of telling anyone the news caused her throat to tighten. She sniffled, and the tears started again. Looking at Mandy and the other two Daggers, she decided they needed to know. She took a deep breath to steady herself. "Gracia stands. The assembly was attacked. I don't know how many leaders still live. Lord Dohma is alive."

Mandy crouched in front of her and put a hand on her knee. "That's not what your face and tears say. Something else has happened. What?"

She took another breath.

I can't tell them everything.

"Shar-Lumen killed Dalpha, Lady of Light, in the assembly hall battle." Tears flowed from her eyes, and her throat tightened, making it impossible to say anything else. The guilt flared less than before, yet it still hurt.

Mandy rolled backwards off her feet to sit on the floor. Her eyes darted back and forth, from one of Electra's to the other. Finally she got out, "Why would he kill Dalpha? Was she fighting him?"

With her head down, Electra sobbed. "He.... He killed her because he believed the Gods attacked him and his people."

"Did they?"

She tried to swallow a few times and looked up at the ceiling for an answer. "No, they wouldn't have failed," she said, just above a whisper.

When she looked down, Mandy had one eyebrow raised and one side of her mouth was curled up.

She knows I know something more.

Just then, they heard a knock. One of the girls by the door turned and listened without opening it. When she turned around, her face was grim. "An army is approaching. The city has been sealed, and the regents request that you join them in the throne room."

Her mind was moving slowly, and there was a pressure in her temples as if her head was packed with cotton.

At least I can function.

Electra stood and put all of the gear away. After strapping on her sword belt, she followed her guards to the throne room. She saw that several nobles were present. However, instead of wearing the normal fine clothing, everyone was dressed in armor of one type or another.

A large table now stood in front of the regents' thrones, covered with maps, papers, and small figures. A palace officer was placing the figures on a map of the city as he spoke.

Electra tapped her fingers together in a quick pattern, activating her recently enhanced hearing device. The audio processors under her covert control easily locked onto and amplified the officer's report for her as she walked across the room. "...burnt and fell. The city's defenses seem to be keeping them at bay. We've added a dozen additional perimeter patrols on the walls. So far, I'm reasonably sure they haven't entered the city."

Regent Bayion, Dohma's brother and co-ruler of the Kingdom of Aelargo, tapped the map near the eastern docks. "What about that fight in the Blue Dolphin that was reported earlier?"

The officer consulted a small paper booklet. "The final report lists twenty-three Daggers killed, eleven Nhia-Samri dead, ten Nhia-Samri thugs, possibly hired locally, dead, and one combatant escaped. Another dozen surviving Daggers, heavily wounded, are at Dalpha's temple now. The most notable point is that the clash included a unique group: Ticca, Duke's Dagger General on special assignment; Lebuin, a Guild mage; and an elite group of eleven including some well-known Daggers. Ticca, Lebuin, and six Daggers raced out of the city on expedition-packed horses heading west before the battle ended. Four other Daggers in the fight left immediately after, also heading westward on expedition-packed horses. We have positive confirmation Ticca is heavily wounded. The others had visible wounds as well. One of the dead at the inn is Tuage, a senior engineering Dagger who was part of Ticca's strike team."

Regent Ellua, Dohma's sister and the third co-ruler of Aelargo, looked concerned. "So Ticca escaped with most of her team. Do we have any knowledge of what they're up to?"

"We only have a vague report about investigating some stronghold for intelligence."

"You said one Nhia-Samri is missing?" Ellua asked.

"Yes, the area is well-lit," he said, head down, staring at the little notebook. Flipping the page, he continued, "We have quite a few eye witnesses, including four senior Daggers. They describe a dark-skinned, middle-aged woman, possibly Rhonian. She's roughly seventeen hands tall, thin build, with medium-length brown hair. More distinguishing is that she didn't have a cloak, and appeared badly burned on the left side of her face. The Daggers suggest she's a mage, due to claims of lightning shooting around behind the Dolphin by the stables, which is where she fled from just after Ticca's team left. That could explain the burned face. The upper rooms across the stable alley from the Dolphin had charring on the windowsill and curtains. Two of the dead Nhia-Samri were in the alley under that window, one decapitated."

Bayion exchanged glances with Ellua. "Have you reported this to the Guild?"

"Yes, m'Lord, and they've provided two strong mages to magically protect the palace. They say they were given some special instructions for facing Nhia-Samri mages by Lebuin the day he returned to Llino. We're advised to not engage directly. They'll let us know if they have any news about this rogue mage."

Electra took out a mirror compact and pulled on her left earlobe. Holding the compact before her, she opened it and covered her mouth as she looked into the mirror, dabbing the edges of her eyes, removing some of the evidence of her recent trauma. She whispered, "Rainbow, there's a rogue mage in Llino. Check the last minute of data for details."

"Okay, checking the records. Stand by." Vesta's voice was as loud as anyone else in the room, and Electra scanned the chamber, confirming she was the only one who heard it. No one else appeared to notice.

Have to remember to thank Arkady for pointing out the imperial spy implants like the middle-ear audio processor Vesta assembled with the nanobots in my ear.

Feeling like she was getting back to working order, she returned the compact to her belt pouch. When she looked up, Bayion was glaring directly at her. She tried to not appear guilty, and nodded to him.

Bayion put a hand on Ellua's arm, stopping her from what she was going to say next. Ellua glanced at Bayion, then at what he was eyeing, which meant Electra was being watched by the two co-rulers of the kingdom.

She bowed formally. "You called for me?"

"You've been crying," Bayion said. "Is everything okay, Countess?"

Oh, he thought I was trying to hide that I was crying. Thank goodness, he didn't hear what I said.

"I'll be fine. I can explain later."

Bayion and Ellua exchanged a glance, and Ellua took over. "Countess, we've received a warning that the Alliance is at war. We were given specific instructions from Duke on what we should do. Have you received any new instructions from the Alliance?"

"We have a means of communication. However, I haven't received any specific instructions yet." Glancing sideways at Mandy, she saw her look of surprise, which she quickly hid. But Electra was sure Bayion saw it, too.

That man is far too observant. Normally I'd be pleased, but this is going to be difficult.

"A large force is approaching," Ellua said to the nobles, officers, and Daggers. "There have already been attempts to breach our defenses. Don't hesitate to bring any news to us, no matter the time. As of this moment, we're declaring martial law. All judicial functions are suspended. Everyone in this room is ordered to be on twenty-four-mark call. Rooms are being prepared here in the palace for you all. The library's conversion into a war room will be finished today. We all live and work here till the end of this conflict is declared."

A chill ran down Electra's spine at the pronouncement. It wasn't out of line, but in saying the words, Ellua cemented the situation and its importance in the minds of all present.

A soft chime in her ear made her jump. Bayion looked over with a raised eyebrow as Vesta's voice came to her. "The rogue mage is close to the palace. Do you need precise coordinates?"

Electra gave him a quick "I'm fine" smile. *How can I do this with Bayion watching me?*

She moved aside, looking around for somewhere private. Everyone's attention was on setting up protocols for work, sleep, and other mundane tasks involved with shifting into a military mode of operation. She spotted a regular guardswoman and walked over and mumbled, "Is there a toilet close by?"

The guard nodded and gave her the location. Moving quickly, with her six Daggers following close behind, she ducked into the restroom. Closing the door, she whispered. "Rainbow, how can you know that so fast?"

"She's wounded, and the nanobots reported in."

Oh, my Lady! The nanobots in the city water.

The nanobots were one of the most interesting things Electra had learned about. It was a long-known fact that visiting the ancient Imperial cities was a curative for many diseases and made wounds heal faster. That knowledge fueled a large health spa trade in those cities. There were even special hostels for pregnant women, staffed with midwives, as elder-city born children usually grew to be healthy and vibrant.

Electra, as many others, had noted years ago that all of the same health benefits were present down river for about a mile from the cities. Many also noted that the first thing done in any healing temple of Dalpha was to clean wounds with temple water and if possible, have the patient drink some temple water. Most believed all this was because the Gods had dwelled in them in ancient times and their blessings continued in the waters.

Now Electra knew the truth. The ancient cities had vast armies of machines called nanobots, so small they could only be seen with powerful microscopes. The cities pumped nanobots into the water for the city's population. These miraculous machines worked constantly to improve health, repair damage, fight diseases, and correct minor genetic defects during pregnancy.

The nanobots were a part of the city systems and part of Vesta, Arkady, and the other sentient machines. In spite of the sentient machines being forced into an eternal slumber, their systems continued to work, just as people continued to breathe while asleep.

Nanobots weren't perfect, and they had limits. Still, they were a testimony to the powers once wielded by the ancestors of Niya-Yur. A major problem the nanobots could not cope with on their own was mages. Magic didn't interact well with some ancient Imperial technologies; it easily interrupted or burned mundane technologies and organisms. Heavy use of magic rapidly wore nanobots down, as magic continuously burned the users. Hence, nanobots in a mage were under constant attack and forced to work harder repairing the damage caused by magic.

If someone was seriously injured, the nanobots called for reinforcements. Since Vesta was awake, she could review the reports from all of the nanobots in the city. In this case, the person they were looking for was a mage who had been burnt, meaning the list of possibilities had to be small.

The problem was how to draw attention to the rogue mage without tipping anyone else off.

I wish we'd started recruiting people sooner. I know Vesta wants only me to know about her; still, we need a way to get our information to the authorities without sounding alarms that could be noticed by the assembly or Duke.

"Give me her location."

"She's staying at the Lion's Gate Inn two blocks north of the palace. She's currently in a second-story room. I have a few of my little friends nearby watching. When you need an update, say, 'The mage was last seen....' If you pause, I'll tell you what to say."

Electra exited the restroom. As she walked back into the war room, she studied everyone with a critical eye.

Who can I trust? And how can we get this news to the guards without revealing that we have a miraculous source of information?

That was when an idea hit her. She glanced back at Mandy and the other five Dagger guards. Mandy caught the motion and stared back as if she could read Electra's mind. She stood taller and nodded with a clear "you can trust me" expression.

Electra stepped into one of the side rooms, which had been turned into a meeting room. It had a second set of doors, but they were closed. She motioned to Mandy to step in with her and to come close.

"Yes, m'Lady?"

"Mandy, who assigned you and the others to me?"

"Not exactly sure. We were in Fox Squad, and our squad commander told us we were assigned as your personal guards until further notice. I didn't think to ask for the source of the order."

"I've trusted you with some Imperial secrets. I'm lost, and I don't know what to do."

Mandy gave a hand sign, and the other five Daggers moved. Three stepped back, out to the throne room, and closed the doors. Two went through the other doors, closing them as well.

Mandy held out her hand. "Tell me what you need."

"I haven't had time to set up lines of communication. I need to get information to the guards or the regents in such a way that they don't know I'm the source. If I'm discovered, I could be killed."

"Surely you're exaggerating m'Lady. Political games aside, intel is intel."

Appearing as earnest as she could, Electra said, "Not this. This you would not believe, and if you did, you would likely be killed, too."

"Okay, I can play cloak and dagger for you." Mandy smiled at her own jest.

Electra put a hand on Mandy's shoulder. "I'm not joking or exaggerating. If discovered, you will be killed as a traitor to the Alliance."

With shock in her eyes, Mandy said, "Traitor? But I thought this was good intel. Why would I be a traitor?"

"I can't tell you that. The less you know, the more insulated you might be from accountability if we're found out. I know everything; I'll be named a traitor if discovered, and the penalty is death by quartering. But I swear, I'm acting for the right side, for the Alliance."

Mandy eyes examined the floor for a few seconds, considering the gravity of the situation, and then she raised her gaze to Electra's. "I'll kill you *myself* if I find out you've lied. But.... I don't know. There's something about you that makes me want to trust you. When can the truth come out?"

Electra felt a twinge of guilt. "Probably not for the rest of our lives, and possibly our children's lives, too."

Mandy took a step back, her face going white. "This isn't about the war?"

"No. The war may be part of this. But this started before the war, and will likely take hundreds of years more to end, if it ever does."

"Can I just promise to do this one thing for you? After I see how that comes out, I'll tell you if I will help more. But this I promise: so long as I never find out this was an evil deed, I'll keep your secret."

A soft chime sounded in Electra's ear, followed by Vesta's

voice. "You can offer her the same two days' memory wipe I offered you."

"Mandy, I can do better than that. I have a magic that can completely erase your memories for a specific period. If after we do this one thing, you decide you don't want to continue, I can remove all memories back to entering this room."

Vesta's voice sounded a little annoyed when she said, "That isn't the same deal I offered you."

Electra ignored her.

"I presume this will mean a long-term contract with your family?"

Electra laughed. "Lifelong, if you stay."

"Okay, let's see how this plays out. What do I need to do?"

"The Nhia-Samri mage we're seeking is in a second-story room at the Lion's Gate Inn two blocks north of the palace."

"You don't mess around." Mandy paced a few steps and then snapped her fingers. "I'll take care of this. If you'll excuse me, I'll be back after it's been passed on."

After Electra nodded her acceptance, Mandy ran to the inner doors, pulling them open and revealing her two Daggers standing guard there. "You two, do NOT leave her side, no matter what. I'll be back." Mandy rushed past them without another word. They walked back into the room to stand with Electra.

Electra turned and opened the doors that led into the throne room, walking past her other three Daggers there.

Once back in the throng of war preparations, Electra tried to pay attention, but between worrying about what Mandy was doing and thinking about Dalpha's death, she was glad she wasn't critical for any task.

Time seemed to slow down and then speed up. The attacking force was going to arrive at the city's perimeter just after dawn, but a sizable force was already blockading the main gates. None of the guards or Daggers were sent out to fight them; everyone considered that a suicidal tactic.

Electra wasn't sure when, but she fell asleep in a side chair.

She heard Vesta say, "Wake up, Electra. Mumble 'what time is it?' so I know you're awake."

"Huh?"

She sat up and rubbed her eyes, trying to focus on the room. A young servant brought a platter over to her with a selection of finger foods. After putting the tray down on the side table next to her, he went and got her a cup of hot arit. Taking a bite of food started her mind moving, and the hot arit was nice and bitter.

"Mmm, what time is it?" she mumbled.

One of the Daggers answered, "Just past three-thirty, m'Lady."

"Mandy is a smart one," Vesta said. "There are fifteen mages surrounding the inn, with thirty-two Daggers and another thirty guards. They're moving in now."

Electra wished she was in the control room, where she could watch everything that was going on. Instead, she munched on the food and drank the arit, getting her body back into motion while Vesta gave her a play-by-play.

"Four mages with six Daggers each are going in, half in the front and the rest in the back. The remaining mages have begun some kind of spell. It's pretty — a giant glowing sphere around the whole inn. That sphere is interfering with my connection to my dragonflies inside. The mage either wasn't asleep, or maybe had some kind of alarm. She's throwing lightning out her window at the mages outside.

"Hang on. I'm boosting my signal to a dragonfly inside. The mages and Daggers inside are sneaking up the stairs. Outside, it looks like the Nhia-Samri mage has managed to break through the barrier in one spot. She's wounded two Guild mages.

"And the door to her room is blown apart by the mages inside. Three of the mages in the hall are shooting her with what appear to be a series of pulse attacks. Explosions are pounding her. Wait, I think…yes, her shielding's failed. She's been blown out the window.

"Oh, I thought she was going to hit the ground. They want to take her alive. The mages have caught her with some kind of magical bands. The Daggers are running back out, surrounding her, and four are slapping and punching her as she hangs in front of the inn.

"A really huge mage, and I mean *huge*, has run up behind her. He's four hands taller than all the rest, with rolling muscles. I can't get his vitals, but I'd swear he's a Zielat. There shouldn't be any of them on Niya-Yur. He's pointing, and a blue light is pulsing from his fingers to the back of her neck.

"Oh, that's interesting. They removed one of those necklaces from her, like the one we pulled off of Hiri-Rula. That seems to be about it. The Nhia-Samri mage is unconscious and being taken off in magical restraints by the Guild mages. It looks like the guards are being left to clean things up with the innkeeper."

Electra wasn't surprised when only five minutes later, Mandy walked up to her and smiled. Ten minutes later, a guard came in with a report that the Nhia-Samri mage had been taken into custody of the Guild. A number of people clapped before they got back to preparations for the coming day.

I'm not doing anything useful. I think I'll get some real sleep.

She started walking for the door that led to the halls where her new room was. As she approached the door, Lord Bayion intercepted her.

Walking close to her, he leaned in. "We've received a report — Gracia has repelled the first attack. My brother lives and is apparently a hero." His voice held a small hint of jealousy, mixed with a lot of pride.

Electra stopped and looked at him. "Why haven't you announced this?"

"It's an early report. There's disturbing news with it we

desire to confirm. I thought you'd rest better hearing it before you retire."

"You're more than kind, m'Lord. Tell me, will Llino's defenses hold?"

Bayion scanned the area. "We've reviewed the city's ancient defenses. Unfortunately, none of the commands in the city archives appear to work. If the Nhia-Samri can breach the protective fields we have, it will fall to our warriors with sword and blood. Our guards are expert soldiers, trained by the best, and we have many Daggers. I must admit, we're slightly outnumbered, and honestly, it isn't a fair one-to-one comparison of skills."

Vesta spoke into her ear. "Tell him your family records speak of things called Imperial enforcer sentinels in Gracia. Ask him if there are any here."

Bayion was about to leave when she touched his elbow. "My Lord, I spent time reading my family journals from the early Empire. They spoke of something called Imperial enforcer sentinels protecting the Empire's cities. Do you know what those were? Are there any here in Llino?"

Bayion looked back at her, his eyes squinting as he thought. "I do recall a mention of such in an ancient text. I must check this. Thank you, Lady Neyon. Please rest well, while you may." He hurried off to the other end of the throne room. Electra watched him as he went to a tapestry hanging to the side of the throne dais and pulled it aside, revealing a vault door. Turning the handles, he pulled the door open and slipped into the room, closing it behind him.

A number of nobles, as well as his sister, Ellua, noticed Bayion's rapid departure and exchanged quizzical glances. Ellua excused herself and followed Bayion. After she had closed the door, the discussions broke into many pieces as everyone grouped up to review their critical areas.

Mandy asked, "What's behind that door?"

"Knowledge. That's the royal archives. Each kingdom has

one. Legend and all attempts to date indicate that only the royal line or their regents may enter the royal archives."

"Oh, I've heard of those. I didn't expect them to be so..." Mandy looked up, trying to find a word. Giving up, she shrugged and continued, "...well, obviously vault-like. Have you seen inside one?"

Electra felt a little rush of joy as Dohma's face flashed through her mind. "No, but if Lord Dohma returns, I might. Come, we need to rest."

Back in her room, she prepared for bed as the Dagger guards also organized themselves to rest and guard the door. Electra climbed into bed, and Mandy turned the lantern down low. Wiggling around, she found a comfortable position, and the blankets warmed. As she stared at the dark ceiling, the day's events spun through her head.

She wrangled her lists of things to do for the next day into enough order that her mind quieted. Closing her eyes, she felt herself falling into the gardens of her dreams when Vesta's soft voice came to her. "Bayion has managed to break the system locks on the Imperial enforcer sentinels. They're already flying a patrol pattern. Llino should be safe for a while."

Try as she might, all she could say was, "Mmm-hmm," before sleep took her.

TICCA

Ticca rubbed her healing shoulder to loosen it up as she rode through the trees. It had been a few days since they'd left Llino, and thanks to Kliasa's boots, she was almost healed, although there was a small ache that wouldn't stop.

They'd decided to stay off the main roads and moved into the forests instead, heading generally southwest. The energy source Lebuin had identified was about 250 miles southwest from Algan. The woods of Aelargo weren't dense like the ones in the far north and south of the continent. On horseback, they could move in a direct line and only lose a few days' travel overall.

As she led the team through the forest, she paid careful attention to their surroundings. The forest made it difficult to stay on course at times, but she felt good about their progress. Her mind started to relax a bit as she enjoyed the woodland sounds and air. They'd been moving carefully, using every trick known in the team to hide their tracks. She felt it would take a miracle for the Nhia-Samri to find them now.

Then the hairs on the back of her neck tingled and stood so straight they almost hurt. Turning, Ticca ignored the pull in her shoulder from the knife wound.

The sun filtered through the trees, forming a configuration of light rays with insects and dust dancing intricate patterns. Everything appeared normal, but Ticca's instincts were screaming a warning. She signaled an alert to the team, who silently drew weapons and started scanning the woods.

Lebuin ducked low on his horse, patting it, but Ticca could see his eyes had that golden tone they took on when he used magic. As he scrutinized the area, his expression was difficult to read. Naturally, he was the first to see the danger. He signaled that there was an enemy party spread out on their right side, approaching.

Ticca couldn't see them yet, but she could feel them getting closer.

So much for being beyond their tracking abilities. This isn't a good place. If we have to fight here it'll be hazardous at best, and there's no fallback.

The decision was easy. She squeezed her horse to turn it slightly so her path would angle away from the encroaching danger. Signaling to run, she waited only long enough to be sure everyone was reacting.

With a tiny change in her stance, her warhorse leapt seven feet, landing at a dead run. Everyone else was right behind her, holding tight to his or her horse and leaning down low to avoid branches.

A guttural scream came from behind, followed by the battle cry of many warriors filling the forest. The screams were echoed by birds startled into flight. They all heard the sounds of their pursuers, Ticca tried to count them, but couldn't be sure — there were more than ten.

"We spoiled their plans. I hear twenty at least! Aieee!" Ditani's voice oscillated like a wolf calling out a challenge. The challenged cry was picked up by Risy and Nigan.

Ignoring the taunting calls of the boys Ticca considered the situation. *Lords, how did they find us?*

Letting her well-trained horse decide on its own path, she scanned for a way to survive. Ditani pushed his mount ahead, expertly guiding it between the trees, and continued his whooping challenge calls. Her horse followed in line and Ticca realized Ditani was leading them down a game trail.

How did he spot that at this speed?

They sped through the dense woods for more than fifteen minutes, with the enemy close behind. They weren't getting away, but the attackers weren't gaining ground, either. *We can't keep this up.*

The light ahead grew brighter. Ditani vanished through a wall of brush. Before she could stop her horse it followed, barreling through the brush, out of the edge of the woods, and into wide grassy plains with rolling hills. In the distance stood the dark cliffs of Cawli. Ticca turned her horse to avoid Ditani, who'd stopped and was looking at the open valley. He turned his horse and launched back into a gallop following her lead; they moved parallel to the tree line as she took in the tactical situation.

The cliffs cut a rough southeasterly slash through the northern quarter of Aelargo from Cawli, where they stood a thousand feet tall, until near Sharri Town, where they petered out entirely. For most of their span they weren't tall, but there were precious few places to easily climb them. The top of the crags were a yellow-green line against the bluish sky. The landscape looked as though it had once been a series of farms, long since abandoned. The plains' shallow hills and banks of brush were cut into sections.

Do we make a break for it in the open, or try to face them?

Ditani was reading her mind. "If we find a path up the cliffs we'll have the superior position," he called. She glanced back to see him standing bent-knee in the stirrups, looking like a romance story description of the lone-wolf Karakian tribesman racing over the plains.

The rest of the team burst out of the tree line ahead or behind, all turning to follow their lead and looking to her for direction. Lebuin's eyes were still golden as he glanced back at the woods.

"They're only a few minutes behind; five at most," he yelled over the thundering hooves.

Ticca slowed her horse to run next to Lebuin. "Is there anything dangerous ahead? We might be able to make a stand if we find a way to climb those cliffs."

Lebuin turned and gazed at them, his reins loose trusting his horse.

"There's a narrow trail from near that clump of trees to the top." He scanned the rest of the area. "I don't see anything else. I think we're about in the middle of the range. They're not as tall here as they are near the Loren Sound at Cawli." His head turned to the south as his brows creased. "I can't see another trail up them in either direction."

Ticca adjusted her horse's path, turning slowly so the whole group was able to follow her change in direction. "Good, make for that trail. Risy, Epton, and Persa, rear guard. DO NOT ENGAGE! Stay with us. Sabri, Coedy, take point. Find us a defensible point on that trail, or at the top of it."

Sabri and Coedy nodded, turning their horses and kicking their lighter mounts to full speed. The two of them raced for the crags, chunks of sod flying into the air behind them.

They're like the wind.

Ticca forced herself to stop chewing her lower lip as she continued to stare at the magnificent animals.

Ignoring a small pang of envy, she brought her eyes back to the rest of the group. "We try for the cliffs. If we get caught, form a defensive circle and we'll make the best of it. With me!"

The group rode together, the fresh air filled with the rich smell of the yur and grass rushing past, whipping her hair and cloak out behind her. Even as fast as the main group was riding, Sabri and Coedy far outpaced them, disappearing at last over a hill.

The sight of long fallow fields brought back Ticca's memories of her father and farming their lands in Raini Wood.

A small tingle of warning at the base of her neck made her turn to look behind. The pursuing enemy was pouring from the forest. She breathed a sigh of relief — they all rode large, strong, but surely slower horses.

We can at least make the cliffs.

There was no doubt they were Nhia-Samri. Each warrior wore bright enameled armor in an array of colors. Ticca cursed as her count topped fifty warriors. *We don't have a chance, unless there's a remarkably defensible position ahead.*

The Nhia-Samri took the time to form up into clean ranks and then charged after them. There were three groups, each with a particular set of colors. Although not matching perfectly, the themes were red, blue, and orange. Each group also had a banner bearer.

They've sent a full platoon after us. I wish Duke had succeeded at making enough noise in the north that they wouldn't think of us.

Lebuin's mouth was tense inside of a scrunched face. He shouted at her, "Ticca, that's not a scouting party!"

"Not her fault! We underestimated their desire for that

journal you carry!" Ditani yelled from the other side of Lebuin.

"Just concentrate on getting to the cliffs! I hope you were right about that path!" Ticca ordered.

"Should I try to attack them now?"

Ticca tried to determine if he had the power to do anything useful. "Won't they just block anything you do?"

From behind Illa's voice drifted up. "My Lord, no! What if they have a mage with them? You still don't have the power!"

Illa's reading his intent through their connection.

Smiling, Lebuin yelled to both of them, "I have a few tricks!"

Ticca glanced at Illa. Her golden hair flowing out behind her did little to distract from the tight look of concern in her face.

"Can you do them riding?" Ticca asked.

"Most of them, yes!"

"Will there be fewer warriors to face, or will they just be slowed down and madder when they catch us?"

"Both!"

Shrugging, she said, "Okay! Sure, do it! But don't pass out!"

Lebuin looked around and pointed. "Let's cut that way and jump that hedge."

Ticca didn't even bother to check; she signaled and turned her horse towards where Lebuin had indicated. He slowed, falling back next to Risy. Ticca didn't have time to watch what was happening, as the hedge was approaching fast. She signaled to go over, and the team jumped it.

Once she was sure of her horse's footing, she twisted around to see what Lebuin was doing. Risy, Epton, and Lebuin cleared the hedge together. Epton and Risy were on each side of Lebuin, and they held out hands, steadying him as if he'd lost his balance. Ticca could see that he'd made the jump without a problem, yet he'd dropped his reins.

What's he doing?

Lebuin recovered his reins, and they all raced after the group. Glancing back, Ticca couldn't see anything specific, but the hedge seemed different.

She slowed the group down, letting Lebuin catch up. As he pulled even with her, he yelled, "Stop looking! We're running, remember?"

Illa rode next to Lebuin. "You used too much power, my Lord! I felt your concern. You lost almost everything in our escape from Llino."

Lebuin didn't answer, but bent low on his horse, urging it to more speed with a scowl on his face.

Ticca turned her attention back to the flight as they angled up a small hill. Near the top, Lebuin let out a triumphant cry. With a grin, he motioned with his head behind them. Looking back, she saw that the entire group of Nhia-Samri had stopped, and a number of them were sprawled on the ground. About half of the warriors were off their horses, and it appeared that quite a few of the animals had broken legs.

Ticca's heart leapt into her throat seeing the poor horses. "Lebuin, what did you do?" she shouted, scolding.

Lebuin looked a little taken back by her tone, but he yelled back, "When I was pretending to have slipped, Risy and Epton kept me in my saddle while I made the ground soft where all our horses landed when they went over that hedge. When they followed us, theirs were bound to stumble and fall after trying to jump over the hedge, which I also thickened and made larger."

"Why make the hedge larger?"

"In case they had a mage. That mage would think enlarging the hedge was the only thing I was trying to do."

"But the horses?" Ditani echoed Ticca's feelings.

Lebuin blushed. "Sorry — it was them or us, right?"

Ticca frowned but had to admit he was right. "That was good thinking! Congratulations! You got us to the cliffs."

As they topped the hill, she could see two of the ranks had formed up and were once again in pursuit. The remaining warriors were on foot, following behind. She pulled up to take a count.

"You took out five warriors and fifteen horses. Not happy about the horses, but you're right. It was necessary."

Lebuin sat taller in his saddle. His prideful demeanor made her smirk. As she turned again, she saw Risy gazing at her with a small frown.

Sweat was pouring off all of them by the time they finally reached the base of the crags. Looking up, she saw that they weren't exactly huge; maybe 300 feet. Still, it would mean they had a good advantage. Sabri and Coedy weren't in sight, but their trails were clear on the narrow wagon path.

They all dismounted and started leading the horses up the trail. Ticca was pleased to see they'd gained at least fifteen minutes on their pursuers. The trail thinned until it was barely wide enough for a narrow two-horse cart. Lebuin was hugging the wall as they climbed.

Behind Lebuin, walking easily in the middle of the trail and leading her horse, Carda carried something in her hand, which she was examining so closely as to practically be ignoring the trail. It was a chunk of the dark stone from the cliff face. Hefting the rock in her hand, she smiled and ran around Lebuin, causing him to stop and stare at her, wide-eyed.

Carda ran to Ticca. "Ticca, this is oil shale."

"I presume that means something important."

Lebuin forgot his fear, letting go of his horse's reins and stepping between the two horses to take the stone and examine it.

Walking only a hand's breadth from the edge, Nigan approached. Both he and his horse unafraid of the 150-foot drop. He stepped over and slapped Carda on the shoulder, laughing. "You're thinking about lighting it, aren't you?"

Carda smiled wickedly and nodded.

Ticca touched the rock. It was dark and cold, with a rough texture, and it flaked easily. She'd never seen anything like it. "You don't mean what I think you mean, do you? Can this rock burn?"

His eyes going gold, Lebuin pulled a chunk of it off.

"Yes," Carda said. "It can burn, and Lebuin should be able to light this whole trail on fire. That might even snap it off the side of the cliffs."

Whistling, Nigan slapped Lebuin's shoulder. "Please don't experiment till we're at the top."

Lebuin's eyes shifted back to green as he stared at the wall of blackish rock. "I'd have to make it very hot, but you have a point. What would it do?"

Pointing down the trail, Carda said, "This whole cliff might go up in flames. It takes a lot of heat to get it started, but once it's ignited it'll burn strongly for some time. At minimum, it would make this trail unusable for a day or two. At best, it might crumble and fall."

Burning rock? That seems unlikely.

Her thoughts must have played across her face.

Carda said, "Look, my village blacksmith would use this when he ran out of coal in winter. He said it took longer to get going, but was almost as hot. I used to help clean out the smithy, and this stuff cracks and crumbles as the oil in it is baked out by the heat. Oh, and it stinks to high heaven."

Looking back at the fertile farming area below, Ticca felt a twinge of guilt in her gut.

If we destroy this road, these rich fields would be far more difficult to cultivate if some family wanted to move here again.

A shout from below made her mind up.

Better we save the world so there can be *farmsteads.*

Her practical farmer side shrugged, but she remained upset at the possible destruction of a safe road that had likely taken a lot of labor to build.

"Okay, it's a plan. Lebuin, do you have the power to do this? You've been using a lot working on the journal."

Lebuin took a moment to stare intently at the small chunk of rock in his hand. It started to smoke, and he dropped it on the ground. "Some threads yield power, others consume it. I can ignite a section of the road. You need to pick which section — maybe ten feet's worth. I can mark it in my mind on the way past and ignite it from the top."

Looking up, Ticca started moving again. "Mid-section on the next switchback will be as good a place as any. We just need to be sure it's ahead of the Nhia-Samri."

As they continued up, she noted that Lebuin stayed near on the inside, staring down more often than not.

They had to pause while he marked the location in his mind, which thankfully only took a few minutes. After that, they pushed to a run the rest of the way up.

Cresting the top revealed a plain with gently rolling hills and some green woods off in the distance. The wind blowing over the plateau pushed Ticca back towards the cliff, and the scent of grasses ready to be cut for hay made her mind jump back to her family's farm.

For a moment she let the childhood memory wash over her, longing for the summer days of working the fields with her father. He'd known she wasn't going to be a farmer, but he tried to convince her, saying, "The weight of the nation rests on the backs of the farmers, Ticca. It's the highest honor to tend to Yur's soils, saving hundreds from starvation." The memory of her father made tears run down her cheeks.

Ditani stepped up next to her, bent down and grabbed a handful of the dirt, smelling it. "These are fertile lands. I'm surprised that homestead below failed."

"There isn't enough rain in these parts for most crops. You need a good aquifer reserve, well, or river for irrigation," she said distantly, looking back at the fields below and trying to stop the tears. "If they could fence off enough territory it'd work as a ranch."

"Something to do when I retire; I like horses and cattle, just not the butchering," Risy said, stepping up. "But before that we need to get the horses away from any smoke."

"I didn't like farming. I did enjoy herding the animals.

Maybe ranching would work for me." Ticca laughed, tears forgotten, and handed her reins over to Risy, who smiled widely at her and patted her shoulder.

Risy and Ditani took the horses a good distance into the fields away from the cliffs and let them loose to graze on the rich and tasty golden and green blades.

A hand rested on Ticca's shoulder. She saw Lebuin's eyes on her under a raised brow. "You okay?"

Trying to covertly wipe her cheeks, she nodded. "Yes, just catching my breath. If everyone is up, you should try to light that section."

Lebuin's expression showed her he wasn't fooled, nor had he missed her tears.

She called out, "Everyone get away from the cliff. We'll wait a while to see if we have to fight."

Ticca, along with everyone else, stood and waited. Near the edge of the crag, Lebuin concentrated, with Illa next to him, daggers out, watching the trail for any possible attack.

Ticca counted the time off in her head.

After four minutes, nothing seemed to be happening.

He better hurry up. If he takes much longer, they'll be past that section.

Just as she finished the thought, Illa jumped back from the cliff as a blaze shot skyward. The fire didn't die down; instead it spread right and left, black smoke billowing, darkening the sky. A scream of rage rose up to their group.

Nigan laughed and whooped. "It'll take them days, or more, to go around."

"Water the horses and yourselves," Ticca said. "We'll rest here to be sure they can't get past that area. Then we'll continue to the energy source."

DOHMA

Dohma held his horse's reins in his hand as he moved to the edge of the elven forest. The giant redwood trees had given way to spruces and pines a day back. A breeze was blowing towards him, bringing with it the pleasant scents of evergreen and sage.

He had led the escort for many of the assembly to Rae-Na-Rey. The rulers were safely housed in the elven city. Hundreds of mages had traveled with them and had exchanged incantations with the elven mages, so they could send messages back and forth efficiently. The incantation links had been sent on to Gracia, and from there to the respective kingdoms. The rulers and regents were able to coordinate the gathering of the Alliance armies from a command center where Shar-Lumen would never attack.

Duke trotted out of the woods ahead. "The way is clear. I've ordered the Daggers to start forming up the troops. We have more coming from the communities to the south."

Shaking his head, Dohma said, "Farmers and tradespeople are not soldiers."

Duke sat down and sighed. "I know. But I've done this before. The Daggers will push the training. We have another week before we get to that first Nhia-Samri base. We'll make sure our best fighters are in the lead on that one. Soon we'll have hardened veterans at our command."

Orahda stepped out of the brush, startling him. "Dang it, I didn't see you coming."

Patting Dohma on the back, he said, "I'll teach you. We'll add that to your morning and evening training routine. Should only be another half mark of work."

Cundia, Dohma's other personal Dagger adviser, silently leapt from a tree at Orahda's back. He stepped aside, letting her land hard.

Cundia stood up, slapping the dirt and needles from her pants. "Urd, I thought I had you."

"You smell of scented soap and you crushed some dry moss. Otherwise, you did well." Orahda said in his standard matter-of-fact training tone.

"I'd smell worse without my soap," she said with a laugh.

"Possibly not," Orahda said conspiratorially, giving her a hard look.

Duke coughed. "I can smell you both just fine. Now if you two are done playing, we have a few thousand new recruits to teach how to strap on their armor."

Climbing up on his horse, Dohma asked, "The shipment has arrived?"

"Yep, it just came in." Duke said. Glancing at Orahda, Duke grinned. "I can smell the oiled leathers from here. We're the proud owners of 50,000 sets of armor. And, Lords willing, the 100,000 swords and camping sets I ordered to have pulled from the Gracian storehouses. They'll need a lot of cleaning and repair, but we should have a reasonably equipped division."

Elades rode up with a huge smile. "Sir, the northern troops were spotted two days away. The report is a 50,000 regular army, fully equipped."

"Excellent. Any word about the other divisions?"

"The mages are transcribing some reports. At a glance, it looks like we'll have another full division forming up in Oslald, starting to sweep west from the Darian Ocean. Yalthum has activated their entire guard. Between them and Laeusia, there'll be three full divisions sweeping south from the Skogen Forest."

"Now we can truly get to work. Come on, we have some recruits to beat into shape," Duke said as he jumped away, landing at a run.

Elracian Recorder

CHAPTER 4

POWER CONSUMES

"**E**VERYTHING OKAY UP THERE?"

Illa stepped over from the direction of the blasted doors to the edge of the pit made by the explosion here. The Nhia-Samri's once-grand throne room was completely destroyed, with only a narrow strip of solid floor left around the edges, near the walls. Illa waved from almost directly above Lebuin.

"Nothing going on up here. I'm sure you'll know if anything changes, m'Lord."

Lebuin returned her wave, then looked back down at the remains of the second room that had been below the throne room.

I'm positive this is the precise location of Finnba's power source.

He crouched and picked up another bit of twisted gold and platinum metal, dusting it off with his mind and examining the shattered gem fragments.

This was a massive magical machine. Was it destroyed when we defeated Finnba? Or did the Nhia-Samri detect that I'd discovered it and destroy it themselves? Maybe this wasn't the source of the power; there's nothing else in the area remotely magical. I can sense a residue of power only here.

He moved around the area, again looking for any clues to the mystery. A small flash of red light caught his eye. As he moved towards the light, something under his foot shifted with a loud pop. He stepped back and cautiously used his telekinetic incantation to blow the dirt from what had moved. The dirt and minor debris flew away, revealing a section of the cracked stone floor. Lebuin paused for a moment, admiring the intricate runes melded into the floor with crystal or crushed-jewel dust. The item that had popped under his foot was a twisted copper necklace with the remains of a heavy chain attached.

His memory jumped back to the necklace Finnba had worn, which had shocked him when he accidentally touched it. Then he remembered the one around the neck of the rogue mage they'd fought and killed in the Llino Guildhouse. This was identical to both of those. Neither of them had remained as more than a lump of melted crystal and copper, useless for ascertaining what they did.

Shifting to mage sight, he dropped to his hands and knees to examine it closely. The rough copper exterior was deceptive; the device was one of the most masterful artifacts Lebuin had ever seen. Tracing the incantations woven into the amulet, he realized these necklaces were similar to the Argos energy collector artifact. One specific pattern caught his eye, and he sat up straight at the implication. Touching his throat, he felt the power of the exact same incantation laid into him by the Argos artifact.

These are keys to power, unlimited by distance or any normal substance.

It was inert, never used — like a spare, or maybe it had been made in advance for someone who hadn't lived to get it attached. He picked it up and turned it around, examining its construction.

If I can figure out how these tap into the power sources, maybe I can locate the other ones and possibly even access them myself. That would put me on an even standing with the Nhia-Samri mages.

He felt a small vibration of guilt at the thought of tapping in himself.

No, I probably shouldn't do that; it would be wrong on many levels. But I could still create an incantation to block or break these devices. That would cut the mage off from their primary magic source.

Remembering the red light that caught his eye, he turned and located it again. Dropping the remains of the necklace into his pouch, he stood and moved over to the light. Again, he brushed the dirt away with his magic, revealing a flat silver box. It looked like a pocket cigar case. Its surface was scratched, but the elegant engraving of vines across it was still beautiful. A series of six small rectangular crystal surfaces were along the narrow top edge. The second crystal rectangle was glowing red. If he hadn't been in that exact spot, he would never have seen the dim light.

It wasn't emitting magic. Lebuin slowly reached for it, ready to pull his hand away instantly. His fingers lightly touched the silver surface; it felt as if it held no surprises.

Picking it up, he was amazed that it was so light. It weighed less than his hairbrush, maybe three ounces. The case fit neatly in the palm of his hand. Turning it over, he tried to fathom what it might be. On what he presumed was the face of the case, a pair of equal rectangles were etched, side-by-side, which encompassed most of the face's engravings. After fiddling with it a few seconds, he found that the long edge sides felt like something softer than metal. As he pressed one side, it yielded slightly. When holding it in his palm, it was a natural feeling to squeeze both edges at the same time.

Pressing the sides simultaneously resulted in the two rectangles on the front popping open. They were doors, which dropped into the case, completely disappearing. Without the door covers, the device presented a new face, divided in halves, upper and lower.

The lower face consisted of a number of circular indentations, with odd engraved symbols on them. Around one depression, a set of three circles inside each other formed something like a bull's eye. The center of the bull's eye was painted bright red. The top half of the face was a large, grey rectangle.

Running his thumb over the indentations, he concentrated, trying to get some kind of reading on it. Although it had a glowing light within, there was no magic flowing through the device at all. Even stranger, the device felt odd to his magical senses. It was unexpectedly magic-proof. The ambient energies flowed around it as if it were a rock and the magic was water.

As he touched the indentions, he felt them move, and realized they could be pressed down further. One was the universal symbol for power.

Curiosity won over caution, and he pressed his thumb down hard on the power symbol. The empty grey rectangle on the upper half of the face turned pitch black, with pictures brightly lit like a lantern shining through small slits in the surface. There were a number of mathematical graphs labeled in a language he recognized. Shivers ran down his spine and he felt a slight chill in his gut as he realized where this thing came from.

That's Elracian. Oh Lords, this is an Elracian device!

Holding it closer, he read the labels. *Available Power, Ambient, Focal, Argos Observed,* and *Recording Time.*

All of the graphs were either percentages or some scale he didn't understand, except for the recording time. That was clearly counting up in the Elracian time notation, and was at 463 years, six cycles, one week, one day, and twenty-three marks.

Just seeing this thing is an instant death sentence to anyone I don't approve of.

Lebuin looked around, glad the team was outside of the main building, patrolling. Only Illa remained close by, but she was guarding the entrance in the main room.

I need another opinion on this.

He moved under the hole in the roof. With a telekinetic incantation, he created a force under his boots and pushed himself off the floor, back up to the main room. Illa saw him coming and walked over.

"Did you figure it out?" Her voice was relaxed and oddly pleasant to listen to, probably due to all her vocal training as a singer.

"Yes and no. What I'm about to tell you is for you alone. I need a second opinion."

Illa kicked a rock into the hole. "Understood."

"The truth is the Circumveni Desert is all that remains of the Elraci nation."

Illa gave him her best *tell-me-something-I-don't-know* look.

He held up a hand. "Let me work through this. I'm trying to organize it."

Illa grabbed two intact chairs, dusted them off, and placed them facing each other and the hole. She sat in one and pointed to the other. "Care to sit and talk it through?"

Lebuin waved one hand in the air. "No, let me pace. I think better that way."

She shrugged and leaned back, placing her wrists on her thighs, both hands still holding her daggers.

"Okay.... I'm the guardian of Elraci, but I don't know how much to say or not say. I'm lost in this. I haven't said anything about Elraci because of this."

"Yes, we noticed. Are you going to tell me now?" She tried to keep her voice even, but her curiosity was sufficiently intense to cause her tone to step up enough for Lebuin to hear it. Illa shifted to lean towards him.

Lebuin tried to ignore her sudden penetrating stare and continued to pace, trying to organize what he knew. "For over 5,000 years, all knowledge of Elraci has been banned. The stated reason is that none of our races are ready for the kind of power Elraci had. It was an amazing nation based on the principles of science. The scientists there studied mundane and magical technologies, trying to combine them. From what I've learned, they'd amassed knowledge from all the races of the universes under a democratic-style system based on logic and reason. They had a blended society that was supposed to be the model for all of our peoples in this new universe. They took a conservative approach to research, favoring patience with oversight, focused on protecting and working with nature."

Illa leaned back again and said, "That's in all the legends about the fabulous shining society of Imridu-Nam, which was destroyed by its own hubris. They thought they knew better than the Gods, and destroyed themselves." Her tone urged him to get to something new.

Lebuin shook his head. "Not exactly. Yes, something went terribly wrong. However, many of the Gods believe a rebellious faction, which had been debating endlessly that the combination of sciences wasn't safe, had purposefully tried to demonstrate how unstable the blended technology was by building a small version of the great power sources, and lost control of it prematurely."

"Really? No one ever says that."

"Of course not. The Gods have hidden the history, turning it into a mythical parable about the dangers of going too far too fast. As far as I know, no one knows what happened. Lord Argos recorded exactly what occurred after the initial accident: without warning, an immeasurable blast of power slammed into Imridu-Nam, the great spiral capital city of Elraci. That blast overloaded the unique power systems there, and Imridu-Nam simply vanished in a release of power beyond anything thought to be possible.

"The energies, magical and mundane, rolled across Elraci, tearing the ground apart and destroying almost everything in its path. City after magnificent city was destroyed as the wave of power washed over the inhabited green lands of Elraci. Each city's energy system exploded and added even more power and chaos to the forces of ruination. All of the Gods and thousands of mages leapt into a defensive fight that all thought impossible to win. They couldn't stop the wave of destruction. Many of the Gods perished trying to block or absorb the energies."

"Well, that last bit is part of every story I've heard about the loss of Imridu-Nam."

"Yeah, I grew up reading the same tales. According to the records, it was Lady Dalpha who took charge and, with the help of many Gods and mages, managed to funnel and redirect the energy flood back into Elraci. The Gods and mages who tried to intervene directly died. Dalpha used forest fire tactics to fight it from a distance. They created massive magical fire lines. They chose to abandon all of Elraci, because they needed to direct the energies into the oceans on the east and west, where it could burn itself out, evaporating and destroying the waters.

"It worked, sort of. It took weeks before all the energy from the explosions of the Elraci systems finally dissipated enough to see past the fire lines, and the containment had cost even more lives from many of the magical races and the Gods themselves. In the end, all that remained of Elraci was a desert, which they named the Circumveni Desert."

He paused, staring at the device in his hand. Illa stood and looked at it, too.

"What is it?"

"I'm not sure. But it's Elracian."

"Okay, so what are you saying? This was a leftover, previously unknown Elracian outpost, with one of those power sources down there?"

Meeting Illa's eyes, Lebuin said, "That wasn't the end of the disaster. A dramatic change to the world came soon after, as the climates shifted, making the central band of the Duianna Continent far hotter than it had been. Even worse, a surprising number of animals that had lived in Elraci survived, but they were horribly mutated by the energy storms that had washed over their lands. Most of the new creatures died, and those that didn't were monstrous, with a thirst for killing. Many more people and animals had to move to survive the deadly climate changes and creatures. For years, the Gods worked to hunt down and kill the mutated animals."

Illa sat back down, shaking her head. "Lords and Ladies be blessed! Never have I heard this."

"It was 5,000 years ago, and most of the effort was by the Gods. The things they were forced to do changed many of them. Never before had such destruction been wrought with magic, and they decided then to keep it safe. Understanding the full extent of the damage, and with the agreement of the Duianna Empire, elves, dwarves, and another race hinted at in the texts but never named, the Gods decreed the ancient knowledge was to be temporarily banned. All the races were to turn their attentions to evolving into a stable society that could exist in harmony and balance. Only when all agreed such a society had been achieved would the ancient knowledge be unlocked. The Mages' Guild of Argos was established to police the world, ensuring early detection of any advancements in either the technological or magical sciences that could lead to the discovery of the banned knowledge."

Talking it out helped; everything fell into place in his mind. Like puzzle pieces, the necklaces, the power, and the fact that something was coming that no one could stop or detect, which would wipe out the world and possibly more, all came together.

Looking down into the hole, Lebuin whispered, "This wasn't an old, lost Elracian power system. This was a *new* Elracian power source. Somehow, the Nhia-Samri have discovered how to build one. Only this was more than what I read about. They have advanced that technology further! They found a way to let their mages tap those energies for magic, to tie their odassi blades to the power, and to construct these power systems hidden from the eyes of Argos and his mages. In many ways, the Nhia-Samri achieved what the Elracian scientists and mages had been working towards!"

Illa stood, her face going pale. "My Lord, if the Nhia-Samri have these power systems, then they have the power to cause the end of everything, exactly as Elraci ended. They could burn the whole world if they had enough of these." Touching Lebuin's arm, she said, "I overheard my father once commenting on the fact that we no longer sent expeditions into the desert. I thought he was talking about some of the deserts west of the mountains in mid-Laeusia, but maybe he was talking about the Circumveni Desert."

"It might have been the capital. It would be a large enough landmark to find, even in the ruins of those lands. Maybe a library or research facility was strong enough to survive the devastation. If so, we have to find it and seal it. I might be able to add some of its knowledge to the Argos Library for future needs." Thinking the plan through, he felt a tingle down his spine. "Then, we have to go to the Nnia-Samri and ensure this knowledge is erased."

His thumb toyed with the other depressions in the device. The glowing graphs shifted, showing an image of himself looking at the necklace.

"This thing was watching me?"

Peering over his shoulder, she said, "Apparently."

He pointed at the bottom left of the image, which had the date in Elracian. "This thing had a display that said it had been recording for 460 years. Could it have been recording what it saw?"

After trying a couple of other controls, he still couldn't get it to go back to the original images it had showed him. Instead, he discovered it had dozens, if not hundreds, of abilities. It displayed images labeled *visual spectrum analysis, shielding control, remote link control, global position, local telemetry sources*, and other things that provided waving patterns of light across the device screen. None of it made much sense, and through all of them, the lower right corner continued to count in marks and seconds.

Pushing the control for power made the device stop working, but the little red light was still glowing.

"I think it's still watching us. It can show me images from its past. If I can figure out how to direct it, I can see what that room looked like before it was destroyed, and exactly what happened to it."

"And then what?"

He paused, considering everything he knew. "This was Elracian technology. It was destroyed by some force or accident. I don't think there's anything else I can find here. I need to try to figure this device out, and then I might have a better idea about what we'll be up against. No matter what, we need to penetrate the Circumveni Desert and find the knowledge cache the Nhia-Samri found. I might be able to learn the same thing they learned from it. This is worse than we thought."

Illa looked around at the destruction. "We're at war, being hunted by a Nhia-Samri death squad, and Nigan is cooking tonight. How can this be worse?"

Despite the gravity of the situation, Lebuin laughed. "He isn't *that* bad a cook."

Illa scrunched up her face. "The next day, I always have to deal with his cooking a second time."

"I really didn't need to know that."

"Well, you asked for it."

He could still feel some turmoil in her. "What? This isn't worse?" he asked, gesturing towards the large hole in the ground.

Illa fiddled with her daggers. "I'm thinking about it."

He laughed as they turned and walked out the corridor. They were halfway down the hall when he felt an odd tingling as magic passed through the area. His senses screamed as the power grew stronger and focused in on the corridor they were about to exit. Adrenaline blew into his system as he spun around.

Illa sensed some of the danger through their shared connection. Turning, she dropped into a defensive stance.

The magic built quickly, and the far end, near the main chamber they'd just left, began to glow in his magical sight. The power continued to increase, and the glowing soon grew into the visible light spectrum.

Illa screamed, "RUN!"

Lebuin, having felt Illa's alarm even before she cried out,

whirled around with her to bolt. Together they ran as fast as they could for the exit. Leaping down the few steps to the ground, they raced across the training courtyard.

Illa yelled the whole way, "GET OUT! GET OUT! WE HAVE TO RUN!"

Ticca and Nigan burst from the kitchen building's doorway when Lebuin and Illa were nearly across the large yard. Ticca's eyes were like saucers as she took in their approach. She didn't even bother to ask.

Leaping over the railing, she ran towards the stables, joining Illa's screaming with her own, repeating, "RABBIT RUN!"

Nigan ran a short distance down the kitchen's patio before vaulting over the railing, landing at a run only a few feet behind Ticca. She and Nigan disappeared behind one of the barracks, well ahead of Lebuin and Illa.

As they rounded the corner, the stables came into view, and they saw more of their team were also running for them. Only a few were carrying their gear. Ticca and Nigan arrived first, pushing the doors open.

The team's horses immediately came out, herded by Epton and Persa. Ticca had ordered that the horses be kept ready. Nigan grabbed his mount and tightened the saddle straps with a few yanks before jumping up into it, while also grabbing some other horses' reins.

Carda and Malla came from behind the stables, quickly tightened their saddles, and mounted. Ticca was on her horse by the time Lebuin and Illa got to theirs.

Nigan yelled, "Aside from away, do we have a specific direction?"

Spinning her horse around to face Lebuin, Ticca asked, "Got a preference?"

Lebuin took longer than most, but not by much, to tighten his saddle and climb up. "South to Elraci."

"You heard him," she told Nigan. "Get the rest of the team, and if we get separated, we'll regroup in the south."

"Don't worry. Sabri and Coedy will be able to find you. GO!" Nigan shouted.

Ticca turned her horse and it leapt into a gallop. "Come on, you two! Move it!"

Towing four horses for Ditani and the three team members with him scouting their back trail, Nigan galloped off towards the east.

Taking the reins, Lebuin turned to follow Ticca. Digging his heels in hard, he held on for his life as his horse launched.

The animals picked up on the mood, moving faster than Lebuin could remember. The wind whipped past, howling in his ears. Looking back, he saw that Epton and Persa were staying behind him and Illa. Ahead, Ticca was concentrating on the ground while Carda and Malla were watching for any kind of threat.

Epton bellowed, "We got company!"

Lebuin wasn't sure if Ticca could hear him, so he repeated it as loudly as he could. As he looked back, he could see that there were at least five people on horses pursuing them at a distance.

Ticca signaled to continue running.

"Should I attack them?" he yelled at Ticca's back.

She glanced over her shoulder at the pursuers and then signaled him to wait.

As they topped a small rise, Lebuin's stomach sank when he saw there were three other riders ahead. Initially, they weren't moving. Within a second, that changed as their horses leapt into a gallop, heading straight for Ticca's party on an intercept course.

She saw them, too, and slowed to fall back near Lebuin. "Can you drop those three?"

He considered his choices. He could soften the ground, but not at a long distance. He didn't know an incantation strong enough to take out a group of men. There were explosive incantations, but he'd pretty much ignored them, thinking he wouldn't need them in the library.

I really wish I could have been warned I would need those incantation formulae.

"All I really know will only work on one at a time, and I might miss, especially riding a horse."

"Well, don't wait! Get busy!" To her team, she yelled, "Lebuin's attacking! If he fails, be ready to circle up when they get to us."

Oh, thanks. No pressure at all.

His heart raced, and his senses were still tingling from the magic energies surging at the base behind them. Taking a deep breath, he forced his emotions away. Concentrating on the lead rider, he recalled the incantation, creating the magical formula's channels in his mind and filling them with enough power to begin to focus the incantation.

The world turned to the gentle colors of magic as his senses shifted to the magical aspects. The area was strangely saturated with mana, as if they were riding through a pool of power. He didn't have time to experiment with drawing mana from the surrounding area, so he forced himself to ignore it. He found the energies of the lead rider, and he concentrated on connecting his incantation's flow to the man's center of power.

Tendrils of magic flung out from his magical construction, latching onto the rider's core. Lebuin felt a surge of pride that he had managed the connection under those conditions. Then he threw all the power he could into the incantation. It rushed into the channels, swelling them, and was filtered to the connection as the construction burned itself out, sending all the refocused power down the connecting strands.

In the rush of things, Lebuin tried to put too much power into the incantation. It warped under the pressure, and some of the excess energies rebounded to him, singeing his own magic channels. Still, the effect was spectacular.

A twisting beam of blue and orange leapt from him, to slam into the lead rider. With a splash of blue light, the man was thrown off the horse backwards, slamming into the horse behind him before falling hard, causing the second one to trip over his body. It cartwheeled, breaking its neck and landing on top of its rider, crushing him. Lebuin's magical sight showed the splash of energies, indicating that the man was killed as well.

The third rider's horse was startled by the flash next to its face, and it dug its feet in, trying to turn away from the unexpected light. That caused it to flip sideways as its rider was thrown off. The man flailed in the air before landing poorly.

Ticca whooped. "Impressive! This way!" She zigged her horse to angle away from the bodies of the three men.

Their group shifted with her as a ball of fire shot past. If they hadn't turned, it would have hit at least one of them. The blazing sphere landed only twenty feet farther on and exploded, throwing bursts of flame two stories into the air.

Looking back, Ticca said, "The one in the middle is the mage. Lebuin, can you do something about him?"

His moment of pride was gone, replaced with cold chills running down his back.

I can't face a Nhia-Samri mage. They have all that power at their command. I can't possibly fight that!

Ticca yelled a warning; the group made another hard turn and another ball of fire exploded even closer than before.

Carda was shouting something at Ticca, but Lebuin couldn't hear it. Ticca glanced back towards their pursuers with a frown.

As best he could, Lebuin looked, too. The base behind them was glowing. He shifted to mage sight, and his thoughts scrambled. It was as if everything he thought he knew about magic was meaningless. Five mana lines were focusing on the center of the base, and a sphere of mana was growing like a soap bubble. It was almost as large as the central building.

My Lords, how can that be possible?

'They have channeled the power through a Loehesh Pattern, stabilizing and transmuting it to a near-physical state.'

Lebuin almost fell off his horse at the answer to what had been a rhetorical question he'd only asked himself in despair. The deep resonance of the presence left no doubt in his mind that it was his grandfather, Lord Argos, the All Father. Lebuin's hopes lifted instantly, knowing that Argos was watching.

Grandfather, please help! The other mage has power I cannot match.

'*You are looking at power.*' Argos's tone was almost reproachful.

Ticca turned them again as the other mage threw two more burning orbs. Instead of turning with her, Lebuin set his jaw and yanked back on the reins. Spinning his horse around, he reached out with his will to the sphere of mana forming back at the abandoned base. Tendrils of control launched from his hands, traveling the distance in an instant.

As the masses of fire flew towards him, he strengthened his shields and pushed them out, feeding them from his reserves. His magic tendrils were unable to gather, hold, or control any of the mana in the growing sphere of magic at the base.

I need that power. It isn't normal; it's been changed. I wonder if that's the same power the Nhia-Samri mages use.

Both fireballs hit his shields, creating a wall of flames and explosions. At the last moment, his shields buckled under the pressure, and he was pushed back by the remaining force of the blasts. His horse neighed nervously, but didn't panic. Shaking his head, Lebuin quickly reconstructed the protective barriers. At the same time, he patted his horse's neck and tightened his grip on the reins.

'*Warning: Energy levels low.*' The Argos energy collector's voice came again. '*Two thousand eight hundred and eighty-one point six rellums remain. Current load is negative fifty-five point nine four one six. Failure in fifty-one point four six seconds.*'

I really need to figure out how to shut that thing's warnings off.

'Its guide is in the library,' came Argos's impatient reply.

It's not written in Imperial! And there are no language books for whatever it is *written in. Also, this is NOT the time. We're under attack.*

Ticca and the others had turned around and galloped back to him. She looked at the fast-approaching circle of riders and the glowing air behind them. She managed to appear heroic. "Um, didn't I say 'run'?" Glancing back, she added, "I don't think we can deal with this."

Ignoring her, he tried again to gain some control over the growing mana.

'It is as water,' Argos prompted, almost apologetically.

The other mage was launching another pair of fireballs at their group.

Desperate for power, Lebuin refocused, using more magic to change his tendrils of control into hardened spears of energy. As his efforts rushed down, hardening them, the ends snapped straight, like a whip, and it worked. His tendrils penetrated the thick wall of the growing mana bubble.

The connection established huge amounts of energy, which rushed towards him, threatening to destroy his control channels. A wave of cold fear washed over him as he saw the power approaching through his own channels. He reacted instinctively, altering them, reinforcing them from his core. He felt them begin to swell and strengthen, and he used more of his own energy to speed up the process.

He split his concentration and began preparing a stronger shield incantation, as well as another pattern for a force attack; they were ready just in time. The power poured into him, and the force was like hitting a brick wall. He swayed under the magical pressure, again altering his channels and core to reinforce them further, allowing them to withstand the level of power filling him. It was amazingly pliable. It had no real nature of its own; it was ready for use as he saw fit. The energy filled him to near bursting. Before it could burn him to ash, he directed it to the shields and the force bolt.

The nature of the power was such that it caused all of his incantations to swell, taking in more energy than they should've been able to hold. His shields grew to surround the whole group, and even dug a deep ditch in a perfect circle around the team.

The Nhia-Samri attacks exploded in fiery bursts, insignificant to the new protections. Lebuin's force bolt snapped out the connection strands, looking more like ropes than the fine, thin threads they would normally be.

The Nhia-Samri mage altered his shields, and power flowed from his necklace into them.

Lebuin's strands speared the mage through his shields and connected to his core. The mage screamed out in surprise, slicing down with his hands, spraying magic from his own channels as he tried to break the connection.

He wasn't fast enough. The power gushed through, and Lebuin's pattern transformed into a force strike that shredded the mage's body, but didn't stop. Instead, it expanded out, pulping the entire group of Nhia-Samri into a red mist.

Lebuin's mouth dropped open in shock at the level of force he'd just delivered.

'You must expend all. It will destroy the area, just as you destroyed your attackers.'

With that thought came some understanding of the destructive power he held. *They're destroying this base. They know it's been compromised.*

The power continued to surge into him. *I have to get rid of this. I can't hold so much power.*

Ticca touched his arm, and he twisted in the saddle to look at her. She jerked back with wide eyes and a white face. The rest of the group froze, staring at him open-mouthed.

Illa spoke for them, and even she appeared ashen. "My Lord, your visage...." She ground to a halt, trying to find the words.

The power continued surging into him, and it was beginning to burn through his reinforced channels. He felt like he was physically expanding under the internal pressures of the magic.

First, I need to deal with this power. How can I expend it safely?

He cast around frantically, trying to think of a way to discharge it.

Light and fire burn the most power. But how can I...? His eyes shot up. *The sky...nothing is up there. Safe distance, just in case I burn up, too.*

He leapt from his horse and dropped his shields, jumping over the nearly five-foot-wide ditch they'd created. His pants held him back as he ran, until, with a ripping sound, he gained complete freedom and surged away from the team.

Running as fast as he could, he began to create a mixture of light and fire incantations. As they formed, he focused them upwards. The magical tendrils all stiffened, pointing straight up like steel blades.

The incantations were ready just in time. He was sure he couldn't continue to contain the power any longer. He looked up and cried out to the sky to take the energy.

He lifted his hands above his head, palms up, focusing all his will on sending the energy into the heavens. Releasing all constraints on the power channels, Lebuin let it flow through him from the bubble.

The world became a blaze of white, and the roar of fire was like a long, deafening thunderclap. Once started, it rushed through him like a hurricane. He had to fight to reinforce his magic channels to prevent the power from consuming him like a river carving away rock.

Above him, he could sense a presence watching him. *I can do this, Grandfather!*

Every fiber of his being burned with the power; every ounce of his will was focused on holding himself together against the colossal pressures of the energies burning through him. With a hard twist at his core, his channels widened even more, and it flowed through him rapidly, smoothly, and without destroying him.

He directed it up, to the fire and light incantations that converted and consumed the energies. Despite the smooth flow, he felt himself tiring, and his concentration started to waver. Pushing himself to hold it together, he managed to finish the job. At last, he felt the flow ebbing. The bubble of power had shrunk to about the size of a rabbit. Exhausted, he sank to his knees.

That won't hurt anyone.

He knew he was losing control and would pass out, but first he redirected some of the remaining power, shifting it to help heal and restore him. His internal channels responded and shrank with a comforting release of energies into his abused body. As he slipped into unconsciousness, he broke the incantations to stop the flow.

"Am I going to pass out after every major confrontation?" He heard himself chuckle as he fell to the surprisingly comforting warm ground.

'*No,*' came the proud response from Argos. He said something else, but Lebuin couldn't make it out.

ELECTRA

Electra jumped back as the three console screens in front of her flared white and then went black.

"What just happened?"

Vesta was frozen, not even breathing for a full minute. Then she started moving again. "He destroyed the satellite."

Electra tried to wrap her mind around the idea that a single mage could reach out so far and destroy one of Vesta's devices, which was supposed to be heavily armored. "Did he attack it? Do the immortals know about us now?"

Vesta was distracted and paused before answering, "I don't have the resources to build another one. I need the crabs to collect more raw materials, but most of them were destroyed in the failed attack on the Nhia-Samri base." Vesta's tone quivered as she held back tears. She plopped down into a chair that hadn't been there a moment before and put her head between her knees and her hands on the back of her head.

Electra walked over and touched Vesta's shoulder comfortingly. "Are we discovered? I swear, I'll defend you to my last breath. They'll have to kill me to put you back to sleep."

Vesta looked up at her with bloodshot eyes. "Thank you. This is more. We failed to stop the Nhia-Samri. We failed to destroy Hisuru Amajoo. We failed utterly to stop the attack on Gracia and the assembly. Lady Dalpha is dead, Lady Lothia is captured, and heaven only knows what else is coming. Now we can't track the empress to ensure her safety, unless we divert the satellite watching Hisuru Amajoo. There aren't enough hawks or dragonflies left. The Nhia-Samri are beating us, and they don't even know they're fighting us."

Vesta grabbed Electra's waist and hugged her tightly.

"What the hell is that?" Arkady barked, making both of them jump.

They looked over and saw that Arkady's ghostly image had appeared on the communication platform.

"Vesta, you could've warned me that was coming!"

Confused, Vesta sniffed and stood up. "Electra, I'm okay now. I just needed to let a little of that pressure off." Turning her attention back to him, she asked, "Arkady, did that energy strike the moon?"

Arkady was frowning at them with one eyebrow raised. The communication lag between Yur and the moon was only three seconds, but it was still annoying.

"Strike? Lady, it's still burning a new crater into the moon!"

"Sorry, Arkady. When I lost the satellite, I didn't consider it would get that far, and without it, I didn't know he was still shooting."

Arkady was looking at a data pad that had appeared in his hand. "Did you know…" He stopped suddenly, listening to what Vesta said before continuing. "…that beam attack is half magic? You're not going to believe this. It registers roughly 700 gigarellums and 600 gigajoules."

After a whistle, Vesta said, "Well, no wonder my satellite doesn't exist anymore. That level of power would've completely vaporized it on contact."

"What do you mean, vaporized your satellite? Was this an attack on us?"

Vesta motioned with her data pad. A few seconds later, Arkady was staring intently at his own.

As she checked one of the creature monitors, Electra found a pair of hawks that weren't mated and set them on course to where the empress was.

Even if we can't find her, we need to see what was going on there.

When she looked up, Vesta made eye contact, smiled, and nodded her approval. "It will take them just over a day and a half to get there. We might be able to pick up their trail, but I'm not exactly hopeful."

Arkady made a coughing sound. They looked over, and after the time delay for him to see he had their attention, he waved the data pad. "Luckiest diurdu shot I've ever witnessed! If you look at the data, there was a massive buildup of magical energies at that base, enough to power that beam. That was what was interfering with our sensor readings. We couldn't get a solid image because of all the radiant light and energies it was giving off. I bet the Nhia-Samri were trying to destroy that base. I'm more than a little concerned about whether or not the empress and her team survived. The sensor data looks bad.

"Vesta, I didn't want to alarm you, so I held some info back. If those gates they use are based on the original Elracian research, they can blow sky-high if they're fed energy and then shorted out or aborted. The first one took out a small section of a hill. That was when the emperor, on Brandon's recommendation, classified all such research and had it moved outside of the city to Kiliun Lol and Niuni Lol. Based on these readings, I bet they activated a gate there and then tried to detonate it. Lebuin somehow detected this and redirected the energies. The last moment of data shows the built-up magical energy dropping rapidly, but I don't know if it was enough."

Nodding, Vesta said, "Ticca has gotten away from the Nhia-Samri before, but this wasn't a direct attack. I hope they were able to move fast enough to get away. We'll know when the hawks Electra sent there have a chance to check it out. I agree that it wasn't an attack on us, just bad luck. If Lebuin was directing the energy up, without any specific direction, while converting it, it would've acted like lightning and jumped to the best conductor around.

"Ticca and the team will likely head for the nearest town. They'll want to report to Duke what they discovered. If they survive, we'll reestablish our tracking of them when they get to Algan."

Electra was filing many new words away to be looked up, but was proud she was able to follow the conversation.

Vesta spotted the confused look on her face. "Have you seen lightning rods?"

"Sure. All the large buildings have them. They attract the lightning and safely channel the energies to yur."

"Correct," Vesta said. "So, in this case, the lightning was Lebuin trying to expend as much power as possible to prevent an explosion, and he just happened to aim up, which was good thinking, really. Unfortunately, our satellite was directly over them, so it acted like a lightning rod."

A couple seconds later, Arkady piped in. "And the next things in the path were likely a few more satellites, followed by the moon. Luckily, he didn't hit anything critical."

Electra felt the joy of learning more about technology wash away as her quick mind also served up another fact. "Lebuin can attack the moon?! How powerful is he?"

"Not precisely," Vesta said. "Like anything else, he needs the power. In this case, the Nhia-Samri provided the power, and he drained it away. Like when a lake with a dam starts to flood, and you have to open the sluice gates to prevent the water from destroying the dam and everything downriver with the flooding."

"Yes, I understand that. But this Journeyman Mage and young immortal stood in front of that dam and controlled the flood. How much power can these immortals control?"

Vesta looked at Arkady for an answer. He finally shrugged back. Turning to Electra, Vesta said, "We were never able to measure their upper limits. Our time in their universe before the Great Migration was limited, and we'd only started to develop the additional technologies to measure and experiment with mana. They measure mana in units of rellums. Argos tested beyond the measurement capabilities of our initial equipment for magic before he was altered, and that was at 2,200 gigarellums. That level of mana is generally no longer available."

Electra typed out the numbers onto her pad. "Vesta, Arkady, I've been studying your records for the Elraci accident, trying to see if there was a legal argument I could bring before the assembly on the grounds of reviewing past orders, to get them to reconsider the order to keep your kind asleep.

"At that time, all of your systems and satellites were fully operational, people knew far more, and the equipment for measuring magic improved. I've been wondering about some of the readings. According to this data, the power system explosions initially registered 1,500 gigarellums.

"I didn't fully understand what that meant to the immortals until just now. The energies peaked as all the cities' energies were combined and reflected back at just under 9,000 gigarellums. Shouldn't five or six immortals be able to contain and redirect that level, working together, kind of like Lebuin just did? Why did so many immortals die when Elraci's power plants failed?"

Vesta turned to Electra, and a moment later, Arkady was also staring at her. Then the two sentients looked at each other with the intense exchanging data stares.

At last, Arkady said, "That question was never brought up. It was always framed as beyond their control. Of course, there was also the atomic element to that energy wave. Still, they'd demonstrated an ability to deal with physical energy using mana."

"You two," Vesta said, shaking her head. "Honestly, I'm not going to fall into conspiracy theories. That much energy sloshing around chaotically is different from a huge surplus contained in a device like a gate."

Raising an eyebrow, Arkady said, "I'm not so sure. I'm going to poke at this when I get a chance."

Electra was looking over the last, fuzzy data from the satellite before it vanished. Something bothered her, so she played with the visual inputs, zooming around.

The empress was left with the few remaining Daggers and horses just inside the edge of the glowing light from the Nhia-Samri base that Electra, Vesta, and Arkady had attacked weeks before, which made a clear picture impossible. Lebuin ran back towards the base. He came out of the radiant light far enough for a clear picture. He had moved at an amazing speed, a great distance away.

Looking at what was visible of Lebuin's path, she wasn't surprised to see he'd left a serious dust cloud; he had been moving faster than a horse.

Probably motivated to try to keep his friends safe. I hope he succeeded. He must have used magic to move faster.

At the end of the recording, Lebuin looked up as he raised his two massive arms towards the sky. Electra's finger jerked on the controls, freezing the image at the exact instant he was releasing the energies that would destroy the satellite and burn a crater in the moon.

Lebuin stared at her from the frozen picture. His body had swollen to almost double its normal size, shredding his shirt and trousers. His large eyes hadn't changed size, but were glowing a bright gold. His face was barely recognizable as the handsome man she'd come to know from observing him for weeks — his face was elongated, covered with golden scales that reflected shimmering rainbows from the other light sources. His nose was flattened, with a small white horn sticking out of the tip. His jaw was pushed out and his mouth was open, showing two rows of polished, pointed silver teeth that appeared to be capable of ripping through heavy armor. His hair and narrow beard had turned silvery. His arms had also become much bigger, with rolling muscles under the same golden scales, ending in a pair of clawed hands, each with three fingers and two opposable thumbs.

White energies emerged from Lebuin's mouth and palms, but it was the power in his eyes that sent a chill down her spine. It was as if he was looking at her right then and there.

"What happened to him?"

"Nothing, dear. Why?" Vesta asked.

Pointing to the monitor, she said, "That's not Lebuin. What is that?"

Vesta's eyes met Electra's, and after a brief pause, she said, "You mean you don't know what an immortal looks like in natural form?"

Turning back to the console, Electra asked, "You mean all the Gods look like this normally? He looks like a fairytale creature called a dragon; something from a romantic fable. But dragons are just fantasy. They don't really exist."

"Of course they do. The immortals are capable of changing their shape with magic. They find the human form extremely pleasing, and have preferred that appearance since the time our races first met. When they change shape, they almost totally become their new form. But Lebuin couldn't possibly control that much magic in his human state. He had to switch to his natural form in order to do that."

The universe seemed to shift beneath her as Electra tried to align her views with this new knowledge. The stature of the immortals shrank and she felt sadness at the passing of her belief. *They are not our Gods.* It was like learning that one's cherished childhood beliefs were just your parents trying to make the world a more wondrous and joyful place. And, like your parents, you perpetuated the belief in the very young, trying to let them keep some of that childhood innocence as long as possible. The immortals did not deserve the reverence of being called Gods, as the creature to its creator. They had powers and abilities near to gods, but that was all. They were beings equal in rights to everyone else on Yur.

Electra sat back, slumping her shoulders. "As far as I know, no one knows this. Everyone I know thinks they look like their gods, but you say it's the gods who are making themselves look like us." Electra heard it herself; her tone would never again hold the reverence for the immortals it had just one minute before.

A few seconds later, Arkady coldly commented, "Now, that's an interesting change we didn't know about. Don't you agree, Vesta?"

DOHMA

Dohma moved cautiously. Cundia and Orahda circled him, searching for an opening. They lunged in together, and he parried Cundia while dodging Orahda's attack. Spinning around, he riposted at her. She managed to bring her blade up in time to parry.

Orahda slipped past, moving faster than Dohma expected. Orahda dropped into a crouch, swiping his leg under Dohma, trying to trip him. Dohma danced over the leg, scoring a hit across Orahda's chest, but Orahda's blade slammed into Dohma's chest at the same time. The force knocked him backwards.

Putting her knee out, Cundia caught Dohma in the back as she dropped one blade to grab his head, bringing her dagger around to his throat.

"You're dead, m'Lord…again. You needed to kill us both."

He straightened up, rubbing his chest. "Thanks. Advice I shall heed fully."

Orahda pounded his shoulder. "Worry not. The surviving officer would've only slaughtered the rest of your battalion," he said in a steady, ominous tone, glancing at the practice field where hundreds of Daggers were trying to drill some weapons skills into the recruited soldiers.

Wiping the sweat from his face, Dohma said, "Be charitable. They're learning. We succeeded in trouncing the last Nhia-Samri base."

"A thousand dead against a few hundred Nhia-Samri is not an acceptable loss," Cundia said.

As Dohma looked at the training going on, he sighed, "I know. They're making progress; some take longer than others."

Orahda's eyebrows furrowed, and he glared at Dohma.

Dohma waved his hand at the training ground. "Very well. Go cull the ones with no chance. Reassign them to safer duties. There's no shortage of jobs needing hands."

"Thank you," Orahda said. He turned and strolled out into the training field, unbuckling his chest armor and tossing it to an aide.

Picking up her sword, Cundia wiped it clean before sheathing it. "If you're not careful, he'll boot all the new soldiers out of combat duty."

"No, he won't. He knows well we need fighters. Also, I agree we shouldn't throw young kids without a chance into the fight. I swear, this will not become a war of attrition."

Elades rode up. "Lord Dohma, you should come see this. Your horse is being prepared. Duke is already en route."

Jogging towards the horse rope-pens, Dohma asked, "What has happened?"

"You must see it to believe it. I don't know what to make of it. Perhaps Duke will be able to sniff out what occurred."

Several officers left with Dohma, Cundia, and Elades.

Elades rode hard towards the Nhia-Samri outpost the division was approaching; it was only a half-day's ride away. It was a large installation near the eastern edge of Duianna, directly east of Gracia. They were sweeping west from the elven lands. Once that area was cleared, they were going to move farther west rapidly, combining with other units before moving to attack the largest outpost in Duianna, located southwest across the Vendis lakes. The plan was to attack this particular base the next morning. "Elades, is it wise we ride at the Nhia-Samri base with so few?"

"There's no danger. Duke is likely already there."

"What do you mean, there's no danger?"

"It's empty."

"What?"

"I swear — our scouts reported the base is empty."

They rode through a thicket of trees, coming out on a small hill to look down on the valley in which stood nearly a thousand small homes and buildings. The entire area was well-tended, and farm fields surrounded the core of the base. It looked like any other Nhia-Samri base, only larger.

All of the structures had solid brick foundations with white plastered walls and red tile roofs. The roof lines were decorated with carvings, and the corners swept up.

The buildings all surrounded a central structure that should have dominated the entire area, but it was evident even at that distance that a burnt shell was all that remained. Blackened support beams stuck up into the air like the skeletal remains of a dead beast. Smoke still plumed into the air from the pile of remains.

Dohma spotted many of his division's Daggers riding around the valley, to the farmhouses.

A Dagger scout rode up to meet them. "Lord, all of the farms have been stripped of almost everything useful. There are no animals, no people. They even took the anvils from the blacksmith's shop."

"Where did they go?"

"Very few clues, sir. There are no major tracks out of the valley. All of the animals were driven into the central building."

"You mean they stuffed all their animals into there and then burnt it down?"

"No, sir. There are no animal remains in the ashes. It was empty when it was burnt down. They likely evacuated through one of their mage-gates."

They spent the rest of the day exploring the valley. Everything was in pristine condition; there were no broken windows, no signs of devastation. There were also no possessions left behind. Every structure had been neatly stripped of everything it contained, including the furniture. They were cleaned, windows closed, shutters locked, and then the doors closed.

The only building that had been damaged was the central command, which the outpost's commander and officers would've lived and worked out of.

Dohma found Duke looking at the practice field.

Duke said, "They evacuated through one of their mage-gates, essentially vanishing into thin air. Do you see what I see?"

As he scanned the area, Dohma saw nothing was there but some empty built-in weapons racks and a large stone-tiled field. "An empty training field?"

"Exactly. They even took the practice dummies. I don't like this. Every man, woman, child, animal, tool, weapon, utensil, and food store has been removed. They even cleaned up the homes. Hell, they dusted all the shelves! It's like they're giving this to us as a gift. We could move a few hundred families here right now and have a happy new town instantly."

"Where did they go?"

Duke turned to the burnt central structure. "They all went into that. I've tracked a thousand different people today, and they all walked calmly in there three days ago. This was at least a week's worth of effort. I thought it might be a trap of some kind, but Orahda says it isn't, and I'm inclined to believe him."

"Why burn the central building?"

Duke growled. "To destroy the mage-gates. They aren't coming back."

"Do you think they moved to another base?"

"I don't know. I can't track through those diurdin gates," Duke said as he stood and started walking away. "And right now, I'm pissed we couldn't tear them out of this place by tooth and blade. I need a drink and some meat. I'll meet you back at camp."

Dohma turned and jumped backwards. Orahda was standing there.

"Diurdu, don't do that!"

"Sorry, m'Lord." His tone was completely unapologetic. "Duke is right. This took considerable work. They treated all the exterior wood and fences with preservative oils for the winter. I found roof repairs that were completed only a few days ago. This is an honor gift. Even one blemish would be considered dishonorable to the family responsible. They meant for us to take possession. This wasn't a small base — there were at least 500 families living here."

Kicking a rock, Dohma said, "Hmmm, well, send a communication to the Duianna regents. There's a free town for the taking. I'm joining Duke in that drink."

"I'll take care of it. At least we have another couple of weeks for training before we get to the next base."

"That's the really big one, right?"

Orahda nodded. "Maybe ten times larger than this one."

Capture of Princess Sheila

CHAPTER 5

WAR DESTROYS

FIRST WARLORD MARU-ASHUA STOPPED HALFWAY down the stairs, calming his mind and controlling his breathing. He shifted the large, heavy tray, balancing it in one hand, freeing his other. He gripped his odassi and directed his blades to shield his mind and wrap him in a cloak of silence. A warm, tingling energy flowed from his blade's hilt, through his hand to the rest of his body.

He held the platter, heavily laden with food, perfectly still, a feat many of the warriors under his command would marvel at for its display of strength. Any lesser man would've had a hard time lifting the tray, let alone holding it out in front of himself singlehandedly, like it was just an empty plate.

Feeling the energies from his blades settle into a smooth, even flow, he knew it was time. He summoned the image of the captain of the troops on guard to mind and laid the image over the energies his blades were providing. To almost anyone he knew, he would be taken for the captain, instead of himself.

He took the last steps down into the corridor, his feet making not even the slightest sound to betray his approach. He was pleased that the thirty guards in the hallway stood ready for a fight, odassi drawn. Ten were facing him, ready to cut him into small pieces. The remaining stood ready but still close to the large iron door, with its heavy chain inlaid with silver and gold.

When they saw who it was, three warriors started to relax, and the warlord let his eyes narrow in contempt. The guard commander called out, "DON'T YOU DARE LET THIS IMPOSTOR PASS WITH HIS BLINDING ILLUSIONS!"

The three warriors realized their mistake, and their eyes hardened as they once again stood ready to cut him to ribbons.

Maru-Ashua nodded and gave the first part of the passcode. "The moons shall guide."

The commander scowled at him. "Tis a cloudy night."

Maru-Ashua drew the one blade he could, holding it so the bands showed to the guards. He let the illusion of the captain drop as he gave both the final pass and the proof of his identity. His maker's mark glowed white as he said, "Clouds cannot block my sight."

Most of the warriors sucked in a short breath of air as he revealed himself, but they were unwavering, their blades remaining ready. The commander stepped forward, and they crossed swords in salute. His blades glowed momentarily after coming into contact with Maru-Ashua's ancient odassi.

The commander and all the guards sheathed their swords, almost in perfect unison, and bowed to him.

"Commander, most excellent. How did you know I was approaching?"

He stood tall, and pointed to a medium-height female warrior. "Numio-Yantha signaled the warning. I have not had time to ask her why."

The warrior appeared to be in her late twenties, but only wore the rank of corporal. However, she wore two ancient odassi blades that predated the ones commonly issued. She was marked with potential greatness by being selected by them to be their bearer. He addressed her. "Corporal Numio-Yantha, explain how you knew someone was approaching."

She bowed deeply and then stood straight. "First Warlord, I heard your footsteps upon the stairs. I correctly identified you. However, when you paused, I realized you wanted to test us."

The commander couldn't stop himself. "You will show respect, Corporal!"

It took some willpower for him to control his reaction and not laugh at her brashness and wit.

"Commander, do you value this corporal?"

Facing him, he came to attention. "Sir, she's a worthy warrior. However, I have had to discipline her too often."

Which explains the rank.

"Very well. I wish to see to her personally. Corporal, at the end of your shift, you will pack your gear and report to Barracks One. Tomorrow, you shall have to deal with *my* trainers."

The corporal was smart enough to realize that this was a unique opportunity, which was also dangerous. She had enough common sense to keep her mouth closed, although he could see her cheeks turn pink, and her eyes first widened and then narrowed.

Maru-Ashua laughed inwardly. *Oh, you will be very interesting. Excellent control. Smart enough to be scared almost to death at first, but resolved to fight your way into my personal ranks.*

"Yes, sir!" She responded with enthusiasm he hadn't seen in a while.

All distractions aside, it's time to do what I really came for.

Stepping through the guards, he touched the chains with his odassi. The gold and silver inlays glowed, and the door groaned under the release of the pressure the chains applied to keep it sealed tight.

Stepping back, he ordered, "Open the door and close it behind me. You will all stand on the far side of this chamber, isolating yourself from all sound, until I open these doors again. If you hear anything at all, you will be executed."

Eight warriors leapt to pull the chains away and then release the catches that had been held in place. For their size, the doors made little sound as they were pushed inward, revealing a room filled with silks and deep fur rugs. On the far side of the room, the beautiful Lady Lothia sat up from her bed. Her pale skin was mottled with amber bruises, and her face was a mask of dark purple scabs with swollen, cut lips. Her jaw was misaligned, enhancing the general look of grotesquery.

Before he stepped into the room, he looked back at Corporal Numio-Yantha. "Except for you, Corporal. You will stand guard and listen for intrusion. If you hear any of what transpires, you will not speak of it." Ignoring the commander's eyes, he turned his back, stepping into the room. The guards pulled the doors closed behind him.

He bowed, keeping the heavy tray level. "Lady Lothia, I am First Warlord Maru-Ashua. I apologize for taking so long to welcome you to Hisuru Amajoo. We have had a busy cycle since you first arrived here. I see that the collar is doing its job a little too well."

Lothia tried to respond, but her misaligned jaw made her unable to speak in more than a grunt.

Stepping over to the dining table, he placed the tray on it and lifted the silver dome off, revealing ten purple teardrop bottles of ancient sharre wine and a small glass with a straw. Also on the platter were four full roasted chickens, two beef roasts, a bowl filled with steaming fish, and two large portions of fresh vegetables and fruit.

After opening the first bottle, he put the glass straw into it and stepped over to Lothia. "Lady, I am truly sorry. Before you drink of this, I must correct your jaw. And I'm sure you understand the result and consequences of both actions."

Lothia was sniffing the air, and she looked at him as her eyebrows raised.

"Yes, this is what you think. Will you allow me to correct your jaw?"

Lothia stared at him before she nodded and sat straight, thrusting her chin up towards him. She closed her eyes and grabbed the bedding with both hands.

"Thank you, Lady." He set the bottle down on the nightstand by the bed. He carefully felt the broken jaw, deciding on the necessary steps. It would take a lot of force to rebreak the bones of an immortal. He knew that if he missed, it could cause more problems. With his ancient odassi, he had the power. It would be a true test of his precision and control.

Positioning himself for the proper leverage, he took her head into his arm and, squeezing tightly, he pulled his other hand back. With the energies from his blades, he struck her three times. Each strike caused her to scream and twist In spite of her amazing strength, he held her head where he needed it. As soon as he finished, he manipulated her jaw into the correct position as Lothia exerted an impressive amount of willpower, holding her head almost still.

He inserted the straw into her mouth and, with a single draw, she emptied the entire bottle.

He leapt back as her body started to glow. She sat stiffly, concentrating. The golden collar did its job — lightning leapt from it, racking her neck and upper torso with fire. She screamed as the collar drained off the magic from the wine. When the final magics had been drawn off, she was still bruised, but her face wasn't as swollen. She looked at him, sweat pouring from her skin.

She tested her jaw. Although she winced, it seemed to be correctly placed and partially healed. "More," she said.

He opened the next bottle and filled the small glass before putting the straw into the bottle. He held both out for her to choose. "The glass will take longer, but the collar shouldn't react to small doses."

She stared at them and sighed, pointing to the glass. He nodded and moved the straw to the glass. She took it and sipped until the glass was empty. She began to glow, and the collar drained away the excess before she could use it for something else.

Pulling up a chair, he sat across from her, filling her glass as she worked her way through two more bottles.

She looked like the perfect image of a Karakian woman. Lithe, with lightly tanned skin, her face was a painter's dream. Maru-Ashua knew she was fully healed, but he let her keep trying to overcome the collar through another bottle.

"Are you satisfied you will not be able to escape that on your own, even with all this power?" He gestured at the remaining six unopened bottles.

She touched the collar. "I'm surprised you found one of these. Honestly, I'm also surprised it still works, considering where you had to have found it."

"We found a remote Elracian station entirely intact. It held numerous treasures."

She gave him a cold glare.

"Yes, Lothia. We know a lot of things your kind tried to hide from the world. I had started learning about these things years ago. Although, I admit I was ignorant until I became First Warlord and gained access to the archives here. The Grand Warlord doesn't know how much I have learned, or how much I already knew."

"I cannot discuss this with you."

"Yes; I know the ruling body of the immortals, which you call the Circle, has forbidden it. In fact, if I'm right, my admitting I have this knowledge to you means a death sentence for me and everyone around me. Doesn't it?"

She had the decency to look away.

He stood and picked up the remaining bottles, leaving the food. "I know your kind needs magic to live. Your internal stores should be as replenished as that prison collar will allow. I'll leave you what remains of that bottle there. If you nurse it correctly, you will be able to live a few years in good health. You know as well as I you will be in better health if you eat mundane foods. I don't know what you like or dislike; eat what you desire, and place the tray on the floor by the door. The guards will take it, and I promise that only what you eat will be provided. You may ask for mundane items that cannot be used for incantations. You have paper, ink, and quills in the desk. Use them to ask for what you want, and I will approve each item personally. If you wish to speak with me again, you have but to ask. I will attend you as my duties permit."

She stood and, probably for the first time in thousands of years, did not float above the ground. "Maru-Ashua...."

"First Warlord Maru-Ashua, or Warlord," he corrected.

Lothia stared at him before nodding. "Apologies. First Warlord Maru-Ashua, you will not be able to hold me. You know the other Gods will come. If they fail to free me, I fear my husband will come." She touched the collar. "And I tell you this because you're obviously a fair man. You will not get one of these onto him."

Without fear, he said, "You are not gods. Lord Argos may or may not be able to penetrate here. But surely you know now that our defenses are equal to your mightiest blows. You have already failed once to destroy this place, and yet here you are, our prisoner. Do you not realize how many people you could have killed if not for Grand Warlord Shar-Lumen's foresight?"

Lothia pulled back from the venom in his tone. She was about to answer when the doors thundered open. They both turned to see who was there. In the open doorway, Grand Warlord Shar-Lumen stood in full armor. Maru-Ashua was taller and far more heavily muscled than him, yet Shar-Lumen's presence filled the room with such force that Maru-Ashua felt like a lion cub watching an adult alpha male in its prime.

Looking at Lothia and the bottles in Maru-Ashua's hands, a small smile creased the Grand Warlord's face. "Lady Lothia, I'm pleased my First Warlord has tended to your needs." He raised an eyebrow. "From my personal reserve, no less."

Maru-Ashua felt his neck heating up; he knew he had overstepped his authority. Still, he stood proudly, not reacting to either the grand entrance or Shar-Lumen's seemingly casual tone.

"Grand Warlord Shar-Lumen, please. I voted against attacking the Nhia-Samri. We can end this if you let me go."

Shar-Lumen laughed curtly. "My dear Lady, what makes you think I want to end this? I forced Lady Dalpha's vote to ensure war was declared. Of course, that was not punishment enough. I then executed her for her countless crimes against my people."

Lothia cried out, falling to her knees. "NO! How could you?" she screamed as she collapsed into a heap.

Shar-Lumen watched as Lothia wept on the floor. "I'm sorry. Didn't First Warlord Maru-Ashua tell you this?"

Maru-Ashua stood still. *He's playing a much larger game than I ever expected. I can't tell if he's truly insane or so cunning he appears insane.*

As sobs racked her body, Lothia held her head and curled into a ball. Tears poured from her tightly closed eyes, across her contorted face, as she screamed and hugged her knees in a futile attempt to comfort herself. Her wailing continued as she shook her head back and forth, trying to deny what she knew was the agonizing reality. She started coughing and gagging on phlegm.

Stone-faced, Shar-Lumen watched briefly, then nodded to Maru-Ashua and turned, leaving the room.

Realizing he needed to follow, Maru-Ashua took a final glance at the devastated Lady Lothia before he walked out of the cell. He wasn't surprised that Shar-Lumen supervised the resealing of the prison door.

Climbing the stairs the hundred meters back to the entry level of the palace had Maru-Ashua panting, but Shar-Lumen appeared to be fresh, like he had just awoken from a light nap. Shar-Lumen didn't say a word until they returned to the throne room. He stepped up and sat in the throne, peering down upon Maru-Ashua.

With a slight wave at a butler, he said, "Take those from the First Warlord and put them back in my personal reserve."

Glancing down, Maru-Ashua realized he was carrying the unopened bottles of sharre. The butler rushed over, taking the bottles, and ran out of the room.

Because his throne was on a dais two meters above the

floor, when Shar-Lumen looked straight out across the vast throne room, he saw over the heads of everyone there.

Maru-Ashua waited, either for a rebuke or instructions. Finally, Shar-Lumen took a deep breath, and Maru-Ashua internally braced for what might be coming.

"First Warlord Maru-Ashua."

"Yes, Grand Warlord. I am your servant."

Shar-Lumen laughed. "Thank you for tending to our guest of honor. In spite of her participation in the attacks on our own, I should have seen to her wounds earlier. It was rude of me to ignore her needs. You have done well. I was about to call for you when I sensed where you were.

"Since that has been addressed, I request and require you to resolve a developing problem. I am dissatisfied with the field commander ordered to take the city of Allornia. He stupidly attacked guards there, slowing his forces down, allowing someone in the palace time to activate the ancient defenses.

"He has since been unable to penetrate the palace and is, therefore, killing everyone there so he can provide me with an ever-increasing death count with little or no casualties to our forces.

"Take what you deem necessary and finish capturing Allornia. I want that city under our control, and every last person in and around it who is not loyal to the Nhia-Samri eliminated within three days. Do you know how to penetrate an ancient city's defenses?"

"Yes, Grand Warlord. I have studied the techniques you developed. I will need to see what is active. I may require additional resources."

"You may have all you need. If you require additional mages, there are more here and at Outpost One. In fact, the second-in-command of Outpost One is a seasoned warrior-mage with experience fighting ancient technologies. Her name is General Hiri-Rula, and she successfully led the defense of the outpost, completely defeating the Gods' ancient creatures with new incantations she personally developed after her original outpost was attacked and destroyed by the same."

Maru-Ashua bowed and turned. Just as he was about to exit, Shar-Lumen added, "Oh, and before you go, please look in on the needs of our other guest. You might want to inform her she is now the Lady of Healing for Niya-Yur. I'll have a less aged bottle of sharre waiting for you with her guards."

"Lady Sula lives? You promised she would die instantly if Lady Dalpha removed your device."

"So I did. Lady Dalpha did not remove the device willingly. The Traitor, Amia-Dharo, now known as Orahda Ima, did. I am a lord of my word."

Shar-Lumen's eyes revealed his emotions as he spoke the Traitor's name. Maru-Ashua was sure he could feel waves of hatred and anger wash over the room from the Grand Warlord.

Cunning and *insane. I'm sure of it now. He's after something. I must discover it before we all pay the price.*

Outside the throne room, he ordered his generals to assemble a special detachment for him. Once the orders were dispatched, he hurried to the other end of the palace complex, where the better prison cells were. There were several guards, and two of the fifty cells were locked and magically sealed.

Stepping over to the first cell, he opened the view port and looked in. A warrior was confined to the back wall with iron chains inlaid with gold and silver.

This must be Magus Cune, the Dagger follower of Dalpha assigned to protect Lady Sula.

The man heard the slot opening and lifted his head. He had the crusted lips to be expected of prisoners not given enough water, and his cheeks hung like someone being starved. He was dirty from head to foot, and his forehead was dark purple from a healing wound. He'd obviously not been allowed to clean himself or shave in the last six weeks, from the time they'd been taken prisoner.

"Magus Cune, I will have proper food brought to you and fresh water, so you may clean yourself. And I'll have your cell cleaned. If you do not make trouble, these privileges shall continue."

The man didn't know exactly who Maru-Ashua was, but he must have recognized the tone of authority. He sat up and held himself straight. "That would be an improvement, but I shall not give up seeking a means of escape. After what you have done to my charge, *I will kill you all* if I get the chance."

What does he mean by that? Maru-Ashua considered for a time his original offer. *We can try to be reasonable.*

"No Dagger with your level of experience would. Still, we can be civil. Now that war has been declared, and the Daggers made officers of the Imperial Army, you're technically an enemy officer. You shall be treated as such, so long as you act as one."

Closing the slot, he glanced at the guard next to the cell. The guard nodded and ran out to execute the new instructions.

He then motioned for the other door to be opened. The vision that greeted him made his heart leap in sympathy. Lady Sula was spread out on the floor with dried purple blood around her. Her hands and head had large gashes, and her clothes were dirty and caked with more blood. He stepped into the cell and said, "What have you done to her?"

Two guards stepped into the room with him. "Nothing, First Warlord. She did this herself. About a cycle ago, she went berserk, screaming and pounding on the doors and walls with her hands, head, and feet. She would do it for marks before knocking herself out. As soon as she wakes, she starts all over. We can't open the door when she's awake. We asked our commander what to do, and he ordered us to ignore her until she regained some composure."

Maru-Ashua was sickened to see that blood spatter decorated the entire cell. He lifted her hands and saw she had been clawing at the stone walls, rending the ends of her fingers into bloody nubs.

"Has she eaten or drunk anything?"

The guards looked at each other. "We're not sure if she

drank. She hasn't eaten." They pointed to a corner, where a pile of rotting food had been thrown.

Gently, he lifted her head and examined the bruising. She had given herself multiple concussions, at the minimum. Her neck had deep scratches where she'd apparently tried numerous times to force off the golden collar.

I don't think I need to tell her that her mother is dead. She's clearly aware of that. I can only hope she's still sane.

"Bring me Magus Cune NOW."

The guards rushed to fetch the Magus. When they brought him in, he let out a cry of anguish upon seeing the condition of Sula and her cell. He fell to Sula's side, touching her neck and checking her wounds.

Maru-Ashua touched the Magus's shoulders. "I will put you in the same cell with her if you swear to me now on your honor as a Dagger that you will not attempt to escape."

Cune looked up, tears running into his thick beard. "Why? What has happened? I heard her screaming; I thought you were torturing her. But..." He paused, looking around. "...this...is self-inflicted. Tell me, please, what is going on?"

"I cannot tell you all, but Lady Dalpha was killed in the assembly chambers after they voted to declare war on the Nhia-Samri. Lady Sula is now the Lady of Healing for Niya-Yur, and she must have somehow felt the truth.

"It appears she started these insane attempts to escape, or to kill herself, at the moment her mother was killed. This should not have been possible with the prisoner collar.

"I need her alive and sane before her father and the other Gods come. Will you serve her in her time of need?"

Magus Cune gazed down on the broken form of Sula, pain evident on his face. "Forgive me, Lady, I must." Looking directly into Maru-Ashua's eyes, he said, "I serve Lady Sula. I swear to you, on my honor, I will not attack or cause the guards any trouble or attempt to escape."

Maru-Ashua nodded. "Quickly, before she awakes. We need to move her to a better cell and clean her up. I want a full set of mage chains to hold her in place. I cannot allow her to continue like this."

When the guards moved to pick her up, Magus Cune held up a hand. "No, she is my responsibility. I will carry her." He gently picked her up and cradled her in his arms, placing her head against his neck.

Although Cune was standing, Maru-Ashua noticed the man was a little wobbly as he stepped out of the cell, so he followed close behind to catch both of them if he fell. But Cune surprised him; he carried Lady Sula the entire distance, and even grew steadier as they progressed.

He put Magus Cune and Lady Sula in a set of store rooms. It was still a prison cell, but those rooms were easily made far more comfortable. They even had narrow windows. The instructions were carried out, converting the chambers into a space fit for a royal visitor.

Sula was attached to the wall by a few mages who sealed the special chains, which Maru-Ashua was sure would hold her. She wouldn't be able to go far, but at least she could move around her room, to the toilet, and to a small reading or dining room. Maids were summoned to strip Sula down and clean her and then to put her into a comfortable set of silk robes.

Once all was taken care of, Maru-Ashua looked at Cune. "You know she needs magic, yes?"

Cune nodded.

Maru-Ashua held out a bottle sent by Shar-Lumen. "This is sharre. If you give it to her in small sips, the collar will not hurt her. If she drinks too much of it, the collar will drain the energy and punish her for attempting to build up the power to do something. Your chains and collar will do the same. This is old enough to heal and to give her the magic she needs to live. When you run out, the guards will provide more."

Cune took the bottle. "Why do you do this for us and offer up such treasure?"

"I am not a monster." Maru-Ashua took one last look at

the sleeping form of Sula in her new bed, then turned and left the room. He heard the guards close and lock the door as he walked away.

- - -

Outside in the training fields, Maru-Ashua found his generals waiting. He followed them to where his warriors were assembled. Looking over them, he nodded in approval. His armor was waiting in a nearby tent. He prepared himself for battle and then stepped over to the wall, where a gate was built.

He wanted to use the gate closest to the palace. With 300 warriors already there, he only needed to place his additional 300 warriors close to the palace to take the city as quickly as possible.

Taking the control from the niche next to the gate, he held the wide, almost flat, silver bowl in one hand. As he touched the large red gem set in the center, the inlaid pattern on the bowl started to glow. He tapped the patterns, indicating west. Six symbols appeared in the air above the bowl, and he selected the one for the city of Allornia.

A semitransparent model of the city rose up out of the control, and with it, five pulsing spheres, each of which was at the relative position in the view of the city where a gate was. He touched the sphere for the one he wanted in a mansion closest to the palace, and it changed to glow blue. He pressed the large one in the center, and the magic gate arch before him shimmered as it established the link.

Placing the control back into the niche, he turned, drawing his swords, and said, "You will kill only combatants. You will inform all warriors you contact that full rules of engagement for formal armies are to be used. There will be no destruction of property. Stop anyone taking advantage of the situation to loot. Do you understand your orders?"

All 300 warriors saluted by tapping their odassi together.

His generals, although surprised by the altered orders, wisely stayed silent.

Yes, I'm interpreting the command differently than most would have.

To his two generals, he pointed and said, "You take half the division to the city districts and police the area." Pointing to the other, he said, "You bring the other half with me. We will take the palace and end this before nightfall."

The portal showed a large empty room with a pair of closed double doors. Maru-Ashua signaled for the scouts to go through. Five warriors ran full tilt, drawing their swords as they leapt through the gateway. Each scout had angled in a bit differently, landing either on their feet or rolling on the ground. The result was a precision team circle, covering a complete 360 degrees, both high and low. The scouts paused to listen, and then they moved as a team off to the right, out of view.

He patiently waited as he considered the possible scenarios that lingered on the other side of the gateway. He wanted to examine the warrior structure there, but at that distance, it would be better to do it when he could enter.

The scout team came back into view of the gate from the opposite side and signaled *all clear*.

Maru-Ashua stepped through into the huge entry foyer and examined the rest of the area he had been unable to see before. The room had a pair of graceful spiral staircases leading up to the second floor. The ceiling was domed with a crystal chandelier. The gateway residences close to the palaces were usually extremely opulent.

Surprisingly tasteful.

Windows looked out over the front courtyard and carriage house. A circular drive led to a tall fence with a pair of ironwork gates to the street that had been left open. Random items were scattered on the floor and stairs, indicating that whoever had lived there had left in a hurry, trying to take as much as possible with them. The scouts had moved to cover all the entries to the room, with two watching the front of the house.

Maru-Ashua picked up a baby pacifier from the floor. Looking at the evidence of children, he sighed before dropping the pacifier back to the floor.

"Scouts, check the nearby houses and streets and report back in ten minutes."

The scouts moved out through the front door as a well-coordinated team, checking for any possible attackers, with a speed Maru-Ashua noted with pleasure.

A breeze brought smoky-flavored air through the open front door. A dozen identifiable burning smells were on that wind, and each one was a vital part of any community. The waste and destruction weighed heavily on his heart as he signaled for the rest of his divisions to cross over.

Standing aside, his generals began staging the divisions into the front courtyard. Warriors streamed past, efficiently grouping into their teams. In less than two minutes, teams were moving out of the gates and into the city on their assigned missions.

Maru-Ashua concentrated on feeling the area. Gripping his odassi, he pushed his mind out along the connecting streams to every warrior in the area. As First Warlord, he could not only see the command connection streams provided by the odassi, he also had direct control over those connections.

Pulling all the connecting streams into a reasonable order took far more time than he liked. He saw that his generals noticed his frown, and they also looked in on the command streams as he worked to correct them.

What angered him wasn't the time it took to correct the organization of the in-theater warriors. It was that he had to do such a complete reorganization in the first place. The hundreds of warriors present were organized poorly. Instead of being grouped into triangular sets of five warrior teams designed to support each other, the entire area was set up in paired teams, based on time in service and rank. Worse, all twelve mages were lumped into one team that was following the local commander around, doing little good for breaking the palace defenses or securing the city.

He was able to accomplish the complete restructuring in only ten minutes, and he acknowledged more than a few senior and junior warriors' feelings of relief at the revised structure. Across the city, hundreds of teams broke away from losing battles and started connecting with their newly assigned teams, which they were able to find through the connection links Maru-Ashua had built between the odassi blades.

The feel of the battle was better. The whole theater was functioning with a proper order.

He communicated openly for all Nhia-Samri warriors in theater to hear, "Commander Herno-Grie, you are relieved! Report to General Yedo-Onu at once." He let some of his annoyance filter into the announcement.

Turning his attention to the mages, he reviewed who was there and their skills. Choosing three with strong wills and imagination, he called them to his personal unit. He assigned the rest of them to various teams around the city. He didn't need to check their feelings about the new assignments; the fact that they moved faster than his scouts to connect with their assigned teams said all he needed to know.

Satisfied that the fundamental organization was in place, he connected the theater regiment to General Yedo-Onu. Again communicating to all warriors in theater, he delegated responsibility and authority. "General Yedo-Onu, all city forces are yours. Begin pacifying the city properly."

The general acknowledged him as well. "Yes, First Warlord!" he said, and started issuing orders to his division.

Maru-Ashua ignored them and concentrated on his own division. Looking at the mage-gate, he saw that all his warriors were in theater, so he called on the gate to close. As he waited, he watched its energies fade, and the staging field of Hisuru Amajoo turned into a marble-tiled wall with no hint of the gateway embedded under its stone surface.

Satisfied that it was secure, he stepped out into the courtyard. The three mages were standing next to General Alamal-Zura.

"General, surround the palace. Do not attack it. Hold a strong line and pacify all surrounding neighborhoods. I require your four strongest strike tri-teams. Have them meet me at the front gates to the palace."

It was a short distance, with many dead bodies belonging to warriors, Daggers, guards, and citizens lining the streets to the palace gates.

The palace wall sported the ancient defenses of all old cities: Impenetrable walls of white towered thirty meters high, topped by another five meters of steel-like plating, with silvery balls on spikes every five meters. Lightning danced on and between those silver balls. Using the magic sight provided by his odassi, Maru-Ashua looked upon the glowing dome that surrounded the air over the entire palace and extended to the base of the metal plates.

Before him was the shiny, perfectly smooth metal surface of the palace gate door. He knew from his studies that this ancient door was slotted into all three sides of the gateway and held in place by something with more power than even all of his mages could overwhelm.

He ran his hand over the mirror-like surface, feeling the cool metal. His fingers didn't even leave a blemish on it. Every attempt to melt or force such a door failed. Even the immortal gods could not breach the doors or walls of the ancient palaces and cities.

Our ancestors made these walls. And it was human engineers who forged this door, built the machinery that moves it, and installed it here with such precision. Now, we might as well be cattle.

His fingers curled into a fist in anger as he considered the implications.

Stepping back, he looked up at the only weakness in the palace defenses. It wasn't visible, but he knew it was there. The silver spheres glowed with their own power, and lightning danced over them. It was suicide to attack the spheres, but if done correctly, a sphere could be damaged. However, it would repair itself eventually if allowed.

He motioned for the mages and General Alamal-Zura to step in close. To the mages, he said, "Two of you, shield the four of us from those things. You must use numerous shields of varying design and change them rapidly. Those things understand magic and will penetrate your shields."

He tapped another mage and pointed at the sphere on the right side of the gate. "You are to lift all four of us up in front of that sphere and keep us there. When the sphere is damaged, a hole will form in the shield. Put me down inside and bring all the teams over the wall as fast as possible. Watch the sphere, and if it starts glowing, blast it again."

Facing General Alamal-Zura, he continued to explain the plan. "All warrior teams are to shield from archers as they're being brought inside the defenses. The mages are to concentrate on moving the teams only. Once inside, this is a capture mission. Kill only whom you must to ensure victory."

Addressing the mages, he said, "With all teams inside, you're to provide standard combat support to any team of your choosing. It will be a hard fight to take the palace."

He looked each individual in the eye to be sure he or she clearly understood the assigned roles. Satisfied, he stepped over to the teams General Alamal-Zura had assigned to him. "We do not stop to engage. We must strike like the arrow through armor. They will put all their defenses between us and whoever is in control here. We must capture the highest authority quickly. You will support me."

Again, he looked each individual in the eye, ensuring their readiness. He then moved between the mages.

As he drew his odassi, so did the 200 other warriors. The sound, no doubt, carried well over the wall to alert the defenders.

You think yourself safe inside this fortress. Oddly enough, I wish you were.

The mages took his cue, and the four of them lifted into the air. Maru-Ashua braced himself and steeled his will.

I cannot waver.

As he pointed with his odassi at the ball, the mage controlling their flight brought the group right up to the edge of the shield. The defenses reacted, and lightning and fire lashed out at their group.

Maru-Ashua called on all the power of his mighty blades and thrust them at the sphere. The first attempt failed; the shielding was back before his strike landed, a small portion of the attack succeeded in getting to him.

He ignored the pain and pulled on his odassi for more speed.

The lightning built up, and he timed his thrust. Lashing out just as lightning, fire, and a blaze of light cascaded around the group, his blades struck metal.

Lightning danced on his swords and arced to his arms. He pressed harder on the device and felt the tips of his blades penetrate the outer lining.

Sweat ran down his face and his arms as his muscles burned with the effort. As the blades made it through the device's armor, supplementary lightning from the internal defenses flashed down the blades and over his arms. He could smell his own flesh burning. Letting out a battle cry, he pulled back and struck forward, putting all his strength and willpower behind the thrust.

His blades broke through the sphere's skin and plunged through the device, only stopping when their tips hit the far side of the sphere.

He twisted and moved his sword around rapidly, trying to damage as much of the internal workings as possible.

With a deafening boom, the sphere exploded into a fireball. Lightning sprayed out in all directions. The mage's shields stopped most of the blast from getting to him.

He was thankful the mages did their job, holding the shielding for the group. Once his eyes cleared, he saw that he was descending towards the interior yard. Guards were standing there slack-jawed, staring at him as if he were an avenging devil. The Daggers present recovered the fastest. The alarm bugles sounded a breached defense. Blades were drawn, and more combatants ran to the gate from every direction.

As his feet touched down on the ground, he pulled healing energies from his odassi to relieve some of the muscle fatigue in his arms and legs. Both of his forearms were severely burned. Ignoring all of the pain, he brought his blades around, batting a guard out of his way with the sides of his odassi. The man fell, and Maru-Ashua started walking towards the palace as ten defenders ran to stop him.

The first real defense group to reach him was four guards. Knowing it was going to be a long, hard fight, he used the energy from his odassi sparingly, only enough to provide restoration for his muscles and healing for the burns. The power flowed smoothly through his body as the magic washed away the fatigue.

A senior guard led the group that faced him. He lunged in with no form. It was a desperate move, and both he and Maru-Ashua knew it. The look in the man's face told Maru-Ashua how truly experienced he was, as well as how desperate he was to protect whoever was in charge.

Out of respect for that loyalty, courage, and expertise, Maru-Ashua spun out of the attack and delivered a precise hit to the base of the man's skull, rendering him unconscious.

After that, he was under attack by too many to be so generous. Four Daggers and three guards surrounded him. The Daggers were the real threat. Two coordinated their attacks, lunging in together. Maru-Ashua calculated the exact distances. One Dagger was support, and the other was the spearhead.

He twisted to avoid a feint and parried the real attack with enough force to knock the Dagger's blade wide. He stepped in closer to the lead Dagger, coming face to face with her. Bringing his other hand up, he punched her in the throat, collapsing her larynx. Spinning away, he kicked the incapacitated Dagger into one of her compatriots. Those two warriors fell together, entangled.

The other Dagger had recovered from his failed feint and, together with yet another Dagger, began a rapid series of attacks. Maru-Ashua parried and kicked, trying to disable them. More defenders were coming.

I need to get past them to whoever's in charge, if I'm to end this quickly.

Behind him, he could sense his three support teams approaching. The Dagger finally overextended, and Maru-Ashua took advantage. Bringing his first blade around, he struck the Dagger's arm hard enough to break the bone. His second blade knocked the Dagger's other knife out of his hand. It flew towards one of the guards, and Maru-Ashua brought his own blade back around fast enough to catch, propel, and direct the knife into a guard's chest. Pulling more power from his blades, he kicked the stunned Dagger away.

His warriors worked in coordinated teams. Guards flew in all directions from kicks and sword strikes. He paid little attention, just enough to be sure the fight remained in their favor. The few Daggers concentrated on him.

They know this is a lost fight, yet they fight with confidence.

Two, three, and four fought him at once. He moved with precision. Each step planned, each strike deadly. The guards and Daggers fell.

With his teams supporting him, he fought in a straight line for the palace entrance. The main courtyard filled with more of his warriors as the mages lifted the teams through the breached shield. The defenders' bodies were strewn around like leaves in fall.

At last they made it to the palace doors. They were sealed against the attack. Maru-Ashua moved up close to them and pulled as much strength from his odassi as he could. Spinning, he delivered a roundhouse kick that would've reduced any normal door to splinters. With an explosion of sound, the doors vibrated but didn't break. Stepping back, he again drew power from the blades and kicked. The doors still did not yield.

Summoning his mages, he pointed. "They're strongest when pushed upon. Use all your powers combined to pull them open. The bolting mechanism probably isn't designed to withstand force in that direction."

The mages nodded, and so much power flowed from their hands that it was visible to all. The doors glowed a brilliant blue that brightened until it was almost as bright as the white-hot sun. A creaking sound was followed by the doors bursting open, revealing several Dagger warriors with bows. Bow strings rang out as arrows flew at Maru-Ashua and the other warriors standing at the front of the line.

He reacted faster than the arrow, willing his odassi to shield him. Two arrows bounced off thin air before him. All but one arrow were also deflected. One of the mages wasn't fast enough, and took an arrow in the arm. His scream was echoed by both the Nhia-Samri and the defenders in the palace foyer. Both sides ran at each other to the sound of dozens of blades striking armor and other blades.

The other mages waited only a second before they released wave upon wave of power that threw the defenders away like small papers in the wind. In a short time, Maru-Ashua was walking boldly through the palace, looking for whoever was in command there. His men were also searching.

The fighting drew him, and he joined a strike team who'd found a gang of guards and Daggers. The defenders were extremely competent, but what he was most interested in was the girl in battle armor who fought with them. She wasn't as good, and they were trying to protect her.

His men had caught her and her guards as they were heading towards a doorway on the third story of the palace. As they fought, they worked their way backwards until they opened the door, revealing a large balcony.

Three of the Daggers broke away and practically dragged

the woman with them. They had ropes and were securing one end of them to the balcony's balusters. Before they'd finished, another team of warriors arrived with one of the mages.

Pointing to the remaining group, Maru-Ashua ordered the mage, "Stop them!"

His necklace glowed with power as he weaved his spell. Maru-Ashua wasn't sure what it was going to do, but he took his original instructions into mind. The six surviving defenders, including the young lady, let out startled squawks as they all fell to the floor with their arms and legs held out as if tied to posts.

His warriors disarmed them. Maru-Ashua walked over to the woman and motioned for the mage to release her. Bending down, he pulled her up to stand before him as he regarded her.

The armor she wore was not her own. Someone had given it to her, but she moved comfortably in it. She had also fought exceptionally well, so she had superb weapons training.

Something about her tugged at his memory. He couldn't place her, but he knew she was important and could be trusted to keep her word. Her head was down, and her hair was matted with sweat and fell forward to hide her face. He grabbed her chin and tilted her head up to study it. Her countenance did not reveal a defeated woman — her eyes burned with rage and defiance. He still couldn't identify her.

"You're obviously the leader here, but you're not of Baron Allornia's line. Who are you?"

She stared at him, and her lips tightened as she steeled herself against him.

He grabbed one of the older men who had not fought well and pulled him up. He was also dressed in borrowed armor. The man tried to fight him, but Maru-Ashua easily held him in check as he removed the man's armor, revealing a set of fine robes underneath. The robes were torn and stained with sweat and blood, but he could see they were high quality.

Holding the man before the woman, he demanded, "Who

are you? You have to be somehow in charge here to activate the defenses. Or is the baron still hiding somewhere?"

The woman stood stiffly and refused to answer.

Maru-Ashua pulled one of his odassi. "I don't have time for this."

He stabbed the man, careful to not strike a vital organ. It was effective. Blood ran, the man screamed, and the woman collapsed to the floor, crying out, "Lord Anduelo, no!"

Maru-Ashua released the man's arm, letting him fall to the floor dramatically. The woman slid over to Lord Anduelo and tore some of her sleeve off, twisting it into a wad, and then applied it to the wound. Lord Anduelo put his hand over hers and shook his head.

Lord Anduelo is the privy councilor for King Laeusia!

Then it struck him. He recalled his visit to Laeusia, a number of years back, when he was inspecting the northern outposts. He had observed the royal family at their famous horse races.

He laughed. "You're one of King Laeusia's daughters! You have your mother's fine features. You're too old to be his youngest, so you must be Princess Sheila, heir apparent to Laeusia. Where is Baron Allornia?"

Princess Sheila didn't answer.

"Your Highness, Lord Anduelo will live *if* I get him treated." He looked back at the other prisoners; at least one of them was another adviser. "I suggest you start cooperating. I don't need all of these people alive."

He bent down and picked up the other man who was not a career warrior. The man whimpered.

Princess Sheila stood and faced him. "Leave them alone! Baron Allornia is taking his family to the capital, and then he's bringing back part of our army."

Dropping the whimpering adviser, First Warlord Maru-Ashua gazed down on the burning city below. He sighed, being careful to not let it show on his face.

Time to end this.

He grabbed the young princess's neckline. With a jerk, he picked her up off the ground and held her before him, so she could see her burning city. She had blood on her face and down her front from the floor. Tears ran over her cheeks, washing the blood into a series of slim red stripes, yet she didn't make a sound. Maru-Ashua admired her strength.

She has been well trained. She must see they have lost. He reconsidered his plan. He had decided to not follow the original spirit of the orders. He wanted to spare as many people as he could, and unfortunately, the intent of Shar-Lumen's orders was to kill every person in the city and surrounding areas.

Urdu, I'm second-in-command. I'm supposed to have nearly equal authority. These people are not at fault, nor related in any way to the deaths we're supposedly avenging. This is a dangerous move. I hope it doesn't get me executed.

"Princess Sheila, you can end this now and spare your people. Surrender the city and province of Allornia to me. I promise that you and anyone who desires to go with you may leave peacefully for your father's remaining lands."

With her feet dangling a full hand off the ground, being held aloft by the scruff of her neck, she still managed to turn her head enough to spit at his feet. She glared at him. "Laeusia will never surrender to mercenary terrorists."

"I did not ask for Laeusia to surrender. I asked for you to surrender Allornia to me."

Princess Sheila's tears and stare continued, yet she said nothing.

You're strong, but you are not without feeling.

Turning, he held her so she could see the dead guards and Daggers that had fought so valiantly to protect her. Pointing to the bodies, he shook her like an errant child. "Cast your eyes on what your father's vote has produced! These noble and honorable warriors have laid down their lives for you."

He then thrust her out over the edge of the balcony, so she was looking down, unhindered, at the full sixty meters to the flagstone courtyard of the city palace. She squeaked at the sudden and dangerous position, whether in fear, surprise, or both, he didn't know.

Another fire flared with pitch black smoke as a warehouse was attacked. Behind him, the whimpering man found his courage and tried to get up to stop him. His honor guard hit the man so hard, he dropped like a sack of flour.

"This is only land, stone, and wood. It is all replaceable. Your kingdom has many thousands of square kilometers of empty and fertile land for these people to build a new home on."

Pulling her back, he set her down in front of him, still facing the burning city. He put his mouth to her ear and pointed at the fires over her shoulder, whispering, "But those lives are your true kingdom, and you alone can save them."

She finally broke. With a forlorn wail, she covered her eyes with her hands and started shaking in violent sobs. Through the anguished bawling, she managed to cry, "Yes, yes! It's...yours! Spare them! Oh.... Lords and Ladies, forgive me! Spare my people!"

He pulled his odassi and held it before the princess. He willed it to broadcast his voice to all the odassi present "All combatants cease hostilities immediately. Princess Sheila has surrendered unconditionally to the Nhia-Samri. All Laeusian defenders, tie your blades. All soldiers and lawful citizens who request to join the princess are guaranteed safe passage " He heard his own voice echoing back across the city as it came from every odassi in the area.

Holding the blade before the sobbing girl, he said, "Princess, please confirm your surrender and my guarantee."

She stood straighter, and through pained cries, she said, "Stop fighting. We've lost the city. I will not allow further loss of the lives of my people. The Nhia-Samri commander has promised that any who wish to come with me will be allowed to leave in peace and with what they need. Allornia belongs to the Nhia-Samri."

Maru-Ashua nodded and announced, "This is First Warlord Maru-Ashua, the new ruler of Allornia. Any lawful citizen who desires to stay in Allornia will be given full rights as a Nhia-Samri provisional citizen. The city guard is now under the command of the Nhia-Samri officers. Any crimes shall be punished according to Nhia-Samri law."

He pulled the princess along with him. "Bring them," he said, indicating the prostrate defenders. "And see to Lord Anduelo's wounds."

He marched the princess back to the throne room. Once there, he stood with her before the throne. "Now, say, 'Allornia, hear me: I, Sheila Laeusia, name Maru-Ashua, here before me, as the ruler of Allornia. I relinquish all authority for both the royal and regent lines of Laeusia to the city and province of Allornia to Maru-Ashua. *Me ut hic coram Sheila Laeusia nomen Maru-Ashua rector Allornia. Remitto etiam potestatem omnis gubernator, et de semine regio, et familias suas, civitates et provincias Laeusia Allornia ut Maru-Ashua, secundum omne tempus.*'"

She did as instructed. She didn't even try to mispronounce the command language words. Maru-Ashua felt a small tingle in his chest at having captured not only the city, but also the entire region.

"Whisper to me the commands to activate and deactivate the palace and city defenses."

She whispered the phrase. Stepping over to the window, he saw that the palace defenses were still active. He said, "*Allornia excitant, omnia praesidia.*"

Nothing happened.

He pulled the princess over to the window. "Why did it not stop?"

She looked out. "Did you expect it to stop?"

"You lied."

She held up her hands. "No, I didn't. Watch. *Allornia excitant, omnia praesidia.*" The lightning stopped, the walls began to settle into the ground, and the palace gateway door slid down, into the ground.

"It should have worked. Why didn't it?"

"Are you going to change our agreement?"

He thought about it and then shook his head. "No; you and those who wish to leave with you may go. This is Nhia-Samri territory now, and at the moment, you are not welcome here."

Rapid Retreat

CHAPTER 6

BATTLES WON OR LOST

TICCA STOOD NEXT TO HER blindfolded horse, holding its head, gently patting and reassuring it. While she tended to it, she also tried to keep her own emotions under control. It was all she could do to not jump up and race after Lebuin to make sure he was okay. Tears kept threatening to break free, and her heart couldn't make up its mind if it wanted to hammer its way out of her chest or strangle off her breath.

Not too far off, most of the team were doing their best to keep their own horses calm and under control. A few of the horses weren't trained and needed a lot of handling being blindfolded. Illa walked over to Ticca, her blindfolded horse docilely following her lead even though it had initially resisted the blindfold.

She's only been riding that horse for a few weeks. I wonder when she had time to train it to trust her so well.

"Illa, what happened to Lebuin?"

Illa looked off in the direction Lebuin had fled, her smile looking a bit more prideful than usual. "I'm not sure. He's finished his task, and I feel he's safe and unharmed. I wanted to ask if you'd agree to go to him now."

Ticca shook her head. "That isn't what I meant. I know you saw what I did. His eyes looked like glowing cat's eyes and his face was more like a reptile than a man. What happened? Are we at risk if we go find him?"

Illa turned her head back to Ticca, her eyes going wide as she stared at her. Her mouth dropped open for a second before she replied. "Lebuin would never harm you or any of us here." Her normally musical tone had shifted up slightly. "When he fled, I felt his fear that he wouldn't be able to contain the Nhia-Samri magical attack. His only thought was to protect us," she said reproachfully.

Ticca took a deep breath and held her hand up to Illa. She looked at where the glowing dome had been. A tower of fire had risen from that half sphere, which she figured Lebuin had been at the center of. The tower blasted a hole in the clouds, leaving a clear view of the stars. The clouds had shifted back now, and the odd glowing from that direction had ceased.

I can't believe you survived that attack. This is the second time you have put yourself in the line of fire of a major magical attack on me by the Nhia-Samri. Glancing at Illa, Ticca reconsidered. *Well, this time, you were protecting more than just me.*

The horses were calm now. The roar and light of the flaming tower had been more than even the combat trained animals were prepared for, forcing the team to blindfold their horses. No one was hurt, and the highly trained horses had remained generally tame.

Ticca pulled the blindfold off her horse and patted it. It blinked, looking around, and then nuzzled her and snorted. Satisfied the horses wouldn't panic at some residual magic they might be able to sense or see, Ticca swung up into her saddle. Her heart began loudly thumping in her ears at the idea of reuniting with Lebuin. Ignoring the odd feeling as just concern she stood tall trying to get a better look at the land in the direction of Lebuin.

"Mount up. Let's go collect Lebuin and get away from here." She ordered as she turned her horse in the direction Illa indicated. The rest of the team followed behind, keeping their alert eyes out for any further trouble.

Lebuin had managed to get a considerable distance away. She had thought he was only a few hundred yards off, but at nearly a mile and a half from where they started, they found a pit with smoke rising from it.

Unsure, Ticca slid off her horse and approached the edge. It was a round, bowl-shaped indention in the ground — a small crater. Waves of heat came from it as all of the dirt inside the circle let off a yury-smelling smoke that wasn't too thick. At the edge, she could make out a whitish form, lying on the ground at the center of it.

She reached down, touching one of the blackened rocks on the edge. A sharp, burning pain made her snap her hand back. Blowing on her fingers, she pulled out her gloves.

"This was that fire dome." Standing, she assessed the area. The burnt-out bowl was at least 200 yards wide, and it looked like the bottom half of a sphere. "I take it back. That was a fireball."

Illa stepped up next to her and pointed to the vague form in the center of the crater. "That's Lebuin. I'm sure of it. He's not conscious, but he's okay."

Epton knelt down at the edge and ran his hand around without touching any rocks. "I think our gloves and boots will protect us, as long as it doesn't get hotter towards the middle."

He stood and pulled out his leather gloves. Illa was also putting hers on.

Ticca put her hands on her hips. "What the heck are you two doing?"

Epton looked at her, asking silently, *'Isn't that obvious?'*

Illa faced her and put her hands on her own hips. "We're getting Lebuin out of this thing, so we can make sure he really is okay. And so we can get out of here, like you said." Illa's eyes sparked in challenge.

Ticca glanced around again. *If that is him, we should get him out. Lady, how did he get this far so fast?*

She sighed, pulling her own gloves on. "Okay, just the three of us." To the rest of the team, she said, "If something happens, pay attention and make sure to rescue us."

Persa smiled and winked. The others had ropes out, and started tying them together to make lines long enough to get them down the steepest part of the crater's edge safely. After that it was hot going, but not too difficult to climb down to the base of the crater.

As they approached the center, Lebuin came into clear view through the haze. All around him, the ground was turned up as if it had been agitated. Most of Lebuin's clothes were gone. What remained were burnt shreds of cloth. His leather belt was almost destroyed, and the knives he had on it were charcoal-black, in heavily damaged sheaths. The buckle was bent and melted, and the belt was almost three times too large for his waist. His shoulder pouch fared better; it was only singed...a lot.

Lebuin appeared to be almost normal. The strangest thing was that his skin was a softly glowing gold. He was lying on his side in a slight indention made by him moving back and forth in the soft soil.

As they approached, Lebuin shifted as a sleeping person would. He stretched and rolled onto his back, leaving nothing about his form to the imagination.

When he fled, he had been 5'11" and 160 pounds. Thin, but handsome in his own way. Ticca would've described him as *svelte*. But as she stared at him, he was another two or three inches taller, and he'd picked up a lot of muscle. His body looked like a statue of a God with distinctly chiseled features, along with strong, solid arms, and the legs to match any athlete or warrior she'd ever seen. His other features were nothing to be ashamed of, either. In fact, she felt a strong longing to curl up into the nook of his arm.

Lords and Ladies, has he filled out!

Illa nudged Ticca hard in the ribs, and Ticca glanced over at her raised eyebrows. Realizing she'd been standing there staring at Lebuin's naked form, her mind started moving again, and she felt her face start to burn.

"Um.... Should we...uh...carry him, or try to wake him?"

Illa smirked as she stepped over to Lebuin and shook his shoulder. "M'Lord, can you wake up?"

Ticca glanced at Epton, who was trying to not look at her. "And you keep your mouth shut."

"Me? No problem, sir."

"I can't wake him." Illa said, slightly worried. "I sense him through our connection. He's not distressed, yet something is happening. It's like he's talking to himself very fast."

Epton stepped up. "And that's why I came along. Unless you want to carry him, General."

Ticca coughed and glanced again at Lebuin.

I can't believe I ran from the market to Dalpha's temple carrying him, once. There's no way I could carry him out of here. He has to weigh about 220 pounds now.

Diverting her eyes, she pointed. "Just give me his...uh, gear."

Epton stepped over, dancing a little as he got close to Lebuin. "Lords! It's hotter here." Moving fast, he cut the belt off with his knife and handed it to Ticca. Grabbing Lebuin's hand, he yanked him up to hold him against his chest while he took the shoulder pouch off for Ticca. "He feels fevered."

Bending down, he pulled Lebuin over his shoulders in a guardsman carry and stepped out of the center area, still dancing.

At the edge of the crater, they realized they couldn't carry Lebuin up and out. A stretcher was made and passed down. Ticca helped Epton get Lebuin onto it. Just touching him sent shivers through her body. His skin was smooth, and she felt a tingle any place her skin touched his.

After getting Lebuin onto the stretcher, Ticca looked at her gloved hands. "Do you feel that?"

Illa and Epton turned to look at her blankly.

"What? You don't feel that tingling?"

They glanced at each other and then shook their heads.

Placing her hand on Lebuin's bare shoulder, Illa said, "He feels hot, like he has a high fever, but I don't think this is an illness. At least, not like one you or I would get."

Ticca pulled her glove off and touched Lebuin's arm. A

tingling ran up from her fingers and into her arm, like sparks from metal. Her heart raced, and she felt herself going flush in anticipation or excitement. She yanked her hand away. After taking a moment to recover, she pulled her gloves on and touched him again. The feeling was still there, but the glove insulated her enough that she wasn't distracted by it.

"I'm getting a magical tingling from him."

Epton looked back up to the top of the crater. "Maybe it's something to do with your heritage. Is this going to be a problem, lifting him out of here?"

Ticca was busy taking in Lebuin's pectorals. Epton repeated the question, and she pulled her mind back to business.

"What? Oh, uh...." She stared at the steep incline. "No, I can do this."

Epton turned to her for a few seconds before asking, "Sir, are you here?" in a serious tone.

Ticca ripped her eyes from Lebuin and turned to Epton, which allowed her mind to work better. She shook her head to clear it. "I'm here. To the job. Illa, go on up and tell them to tie our ropes to the horses." She made a rope harness around herself.

After a grunt, Epton did the same, as Illa climbed out. With the horses pulling, Ticca stayed in step with Epton, and they were able to keep Lebuin's stretcher level as they climbed out.

Ticca helped build a travois from the debris. After getting Lebuin's horse set up, she turned to see what the others had been doing. On the ground was Lebuin's pack, with his clothes picked through. She was relieved to see that Carda and Illa had managed to dress Lebuin, but she noted the clothes weren't his. The shirt was Epton's, and likely the trousers, too. Even Epton's much larger clothes were too small for Lebuin.

She tried to take a clear stock of his condition, but her heart wouldn't stop hammering in her ears.

Urdu! I'm not fifteen. Why am I reacting like this? I have to get control of myself.

A whoop in the distance drew her attention. Nigan was approaching on horseback, with four riders behind him. She started to draw her weapons, before she saw through the dust and smoke that the other riders were Ditani, Risy, Sabri, and Coedy.

Ticca laughed and yelled, "Oh, sure! Show up after the hard work is done!"

Nigan jumped from his horse, landing right next to Illa. He wrapped his arms around her shoulders and squeezed for a second before releasing her and turning to the team. "I'll happily do some work. I'm glad all of you are still here!"

Putting her hands on her hips, Ticca said, "I don't see you giving anyone else a hug."

"If you want one...." He started walking toward her.

Holding a hand up to stop him, she put her other hand on her dagger hilt. "Only if you want to be stabbed."

As he back-pedaled back to Illa he said, "Then don't complain."

Ditani jumped off his horse, and started examining Lebuin.

"Where were you?" Ticca asked.

Swiping his hand over his head, Nigan said, "I decided it was best to ride away as fast as possible from anything glowing. After the firestorm I went hunting for them, and almost rode right over Ditani. Been scouting around to find you and search for signs of other pursuers."

"Find anything?"

Nigan glanced at Coedy, who answered, "We've scouted the eastern side of the base lands. That area is clear...for now. The west was clear yesterday."

As her eyes rested on Risy, Ticca was surprised she didn't have the racing-heart reaction she'd grown used to the last few weeks. Still, she felt a slight longing for him.

Suddenly I'm barely interested in Risy? I know they say hearts can be fickle, but this is too fast and too weird.

She glanced at Lebuin, and her heart leapt as it had just the day before for Risy.

I need to keep this under control and under wraps until I can find out what just happened.

Lebuin's hair was sweat-soaked and caked down, and she had to fight the urge to go finger-comb it straighter.

I need to do something else.

"Ditani, do you know what the golden skin is about?"

He was touching Lebuin's forehead with the tips of his fingers, staring at Lebuin's blank face. He didn't answer. She stepped over behind him and patted his shoulder, careful to keep her eyes off Lebuin. "Hello, Ditani, any hints? Is this unsafe? Do we need to do something?"

Ditani stood and faced Ticca, his face a mask of concern. "It's clear he's hot, but he's not fevered. A God could do this if so desired, but Lebuin hasn't learned to alter his shape yet. To do this would require more magic than I believe he has right now. I've not heard of any condition that would affect our kind this way. Best guess is he's in a spirit trance, or soul quest. If so, Argos will be watching over him, or may even be guiding him. Illa, you have a connection. What say you?"

"I can feel him; he's not distressed. I feel as though he's a short distance away, but just at the edge of my hearing. What I can hear isn't clear — he's talking so fast I can't understand. I wish I could explain it better."

Ticca looked around. "We should move. I don't like being here." She could feel something pulling her. "South. Sabri and Coedy, wolf-trek south. Make sure the trail is feasible for this travois."

They nodded in salute, and Sabri said, "Sir, do you want to head due south, or is there someplace specific we're going to?"

After a brief pause, the name rolled out before she could stop it. "Imridu-Nam."

The entire team stopped what they were doing and stared at her. Illa's expression was unreadable, but definitely not surprised.

Carda broke the silence. "Sir, that place doesn't exist. It's just a myth."

"It's there," Illa said softly.

Ticca shook her head. "Legends say it was the capital of a mighty nation that vanished in a single day 'in fire'. Lebuin's last words on this subject were that we needed to go to Elraci. I'm betting Imridu-Nam was the capital of Elraci. Like Illa says, it will be there somewhere."

"Urdu," Nigan said, looking south. "I thought it was hot now. Do you have any idea how hot the Circumveni Desert gets? I've heard it can kill at midday. Who has the desert training to even attempt this?"

Ticca raised her hand, as did Persa. Ticca nodded. "Good. It's at least a cycle to get to the edge of the desert. We still have to find a path through the Razor Back Mountains. Everyone needs to be fully trained on desert survival by the time we get there. Persa, you and I need to work out a list of minimum essential supplies to gather on the way. We need to make some water packs."

Ditani said, "I've trekked in the southern deserts before with the dwarves. I know of their skills."

Ticca patted Ditani's back. "We'll need every trick if we're to survive the Circumveni Desert. Move out."

It only took a few more minutes to properly distribute all the gear for getting their journey underway.

They all mounted up and followed the trail left for them by the scouts. Illa began to give a complete rundown of the group's investigations for Ditani, including the gating in of the Nhia-Samri, and finally, Lebuin's heroic actions to save them from some kind of magical attack.

The team moved on as fast as possible, pulling Lebuin in the travois. About the time they were to crest the valley edge, which contained the abandoned base, Illa finished the narrative.

Ticca turned around to tell Ditani that Illa's rendition might have exaggerated Lebuin's actions a bit. "Ditani...." was all she got out before her mind finished registering the scene behind them. Everyone noticed her sudden silence and stopped to look back.

Nigan whistled.

The green valley was beautiful. It sloped down towards the center, where a river ran through, cutting it in half. Near the river, above all the flood lines, was where the base had once been. Instead of ornate red and green buildings with sweeping tiled roofs, surrounding the central structures and training grounds, there was only a circular crater. Its far walls shimmered and reflected the sky in the waning light. It was lined with a kind of polished reddish glass.

A mile or so from the large crater, which had been where they slept for the last few days, was the much smaller, smoking pit they'd found Lebuin in. It looked minuscule and primitive next to the larger one.

Ticca swallowed to get her mouth moving again. "Uh. Never mind. We need to get as far from here as possible. Illa, come back with me. I need your help to erase our trails."

- - -

Ticca wiped the sweat from her forehead and grabbed her shirt, whipping it back and forth to move some air over her body. It was hotter than she'd ever experienced.

I can see why Duke went north to the colder climates. We're nowhere near the desert, and it's already hotter than Rhini. The temperature is climbing steadily as we get closer.

After they'd ridden for five days, the Razor Back Mountains were finally in full view in the distance.

As Ticca was coming over the top of a small rise, she spotted Sabri's horse, tied to a tree not far off.

She stopped her horse before it was seen and slid off. Running up low, she stayed in the grass line. As she moved into position, she took her cloak out of the belt pouch. Unfolding it near the ground, she pulled it around her and put the hood, with its sheer front edge, over her entire head.

From near the apex of the rise, she scanned the area. It took only a few seconds to spot Sabri, sitting, leaning back against a tree in the shade. She didn't move.

Might be sleeping. If they needed to check in, where's Coedy?

She pulled a mirror out of her pouch to signal the rest of the team to stay back and go on alert. It wasn't needed; being senior Daggers, they'd already realized something was up, drawing weapons and scanning the surroundings for danger. She made sure they had their position under control, and then continued to look for any sign of trouble.

Sabri moved, but Ticca's gut screamed a warning. Her mind caught almost instantly that *how* she moved was all wrong — too stiff — and that made Ticca's neck muscles tighten. Her hair was standing on end, making the soft warm breeze send chills up her arms and down her back. The wind picked up, faintly rustling the tall grasses in the field, and there was the answer to all the warning signals she was feeling. Six spots in the tall grass did not move right. There were ambushers hiding in the tall grass.

She turned and moved away from the apex as quickly as she could. As soon as she was out of sight from the ambushers, she stood and ran for her horse, pushing the cloak back over her shoulders. She signaled that it was a trap. Again, the team already knew. Twelve mounted warriors had just come over another hill behind them and were galloping towards her group, swords out.

Ticca vaulted onto her horse as the team quickly encircled Lebuin's travois. Only ten Daggers, plus warhorses, stood between the Nhia-Samri charge and Lebuin. Her stomach turned, realizing the odds were heavily against them.

She reached her team a mere moment before the charging

Nhia-Samri. The team looked unsteady. Deep inside, Ticca felt a roar of anger boil up through her. She spun her dagger in the air and shouted, "If I charge, follow me. If I retreat, kill me. If I die, finish our work! OORAH!"

The team swelled, daggers and swords out, and they all shouted as one, "OORAH!"

Ticca screamed, dropping the reins and controlling her horse with her legs, as the Nhia-Samri charge slammed into them. The first warrior's blade sang in the air as his powerful slice came at her. She blocked the attack, and her horse reared, attacking the enemy's mount and ripping open its side, exposing ribs and muscles. It shrieked in pain and reared, putting the warrior off-balance.

Ticca took advantage of the momentary opening. Bringing her blades around, she cut the man's throat, even through the leather armor. The warrior rolled backwards, off the horse, as it tried to move away but fell too.

She had only a second before a Nhia-Samri, in painted green armor with a blue symbol stamped on the front of both shoulder plates, rushed her. That one's horse was just as highly trained as hers. On the backs of the mighty animals, she and Ticca exchanged blow after blow, both of them working to control their horses and their blades.

Beside her, something or someone screamed in death. She didn't have the time to see who it was. Spinning around each other, the horses pawed, bit, and body-slammed each other as their riders exchanged furious attacks.

Ticca knew all four of them were taking serious wounds. She had a series of cuts, as many as her opponent. Still they fought. The horses slammed into each other, and she lost her balance. The Nhia-Samri was in perfect position, and her blade drew near to Ticca. There was no stopping it. It was the strangest feeling — time slowed to a crawl, and still she couldn't move fast enough, forced to watch her own death approach. A primal scream escaped her lips as the Nhia-Samri blade hummed through the hot air, leaving a shimmering trail behind it as it headed straight for her neck.

Another blade came from nowhere and caught the warrior's blade, stopping it cold an inch from her neck. The ringing sound of the weapons connecting vibrated through her body. Ticca kneed her horse, causing it to dance back. Another man, in painted blue armor with the golden symbols of an officer stamped on his shoulders, was holding the blade that had saved her.

"She's mine!" the officer yelled.

The first warrior caused her horse to dance away, and with a sword salute moved to attack someone else.

Ticca couldn't get the sight of the sword coming at her neck out of her mind. *Lords and Lady, I should be dead. Thank you.*

Ticca's attention snapped to the officer. His voice sounded familiar. Her mind was racing, trying to recall where she could have heard it before. She gladly focused on trying to identify the man; anything to stop thinking of that blade coming for her throat.

He kicked his horse and had started to come towards her, sword held in a salute, when there was a flash of light from behind Ticca. He pulled back, looking past her.

He sputtered, "Illa? But how?"

Finally recognizing the voice, Ticca said, "Colonel Runa-Emry?"

The ice blue eyes behind the blue painted face armor flashed at her. "YOU LIED!" His tone was one of deep betrayal.

Ticca felt suddenly sick that she hadn't told the colonel the whole truth. Her instincts told her she owed him far better treatment.

A shriek pierced the air. Turning, Ticca saw that a Nhia-Samri had jumped off her horse to spear Runa-Illa clean through with her odassi. Illa was bending backwards, screaming, as lightning and a golden, shimmering energy poured from the wounds, encasing the odassi and the woman holding them in a bright fire. The Nhia-Samri warrior was also crying out in pain. Their screams mingled, amplifying each other.

Colonel Runa-Emry joined the wailing, adding his own, "NOOOO!" to the cacophony.

Behind Illa, a bright golden radiation erupted. A fourth voice joined the cries, making a strange harmony. Ticca knew instantly that it was Lebuin. He wasn't screaming — he was yelling a savage, raging challenge. The travois he was strapped onto exploded, and he snapped to a standing pose behind Illa, looking every bit the role of avenging God. His skin glowed brighter than a fire, bathing the area in his golden light and casting ominous dark shadows that stretched out across the field.

His hands pointed to the warrior who'd stabbed Illa, and a stream of golden fire flew at the woman, throwing her into the air like a rag doll. The warrior had held onto her odassi, so when she was thrown they were ripped out of Illa's body.

Illa fell to her knees as Lebuin pointed to other Nhia-Samri warriors, hitting each with a similar burst of flames. Illa's wounds oozed a shimmering, golden blood. The air was filled with bodies, all burning like kindling.

Colonel Runa-Emry yelled, "Withdraw!" He turned his horse and dug his heels into its shanks. As he practically flew away, he looked back over his shoulder at Ticca. She clearly heard him say, "Pray my daughter lives. If not, I will find you and kill you."

Only one Nhia-Samri warrior joined Colonel Runa-Emry in his retreat. The field around them was dotted with burning heaps, which only moments before were warriors.

Lebuin had fallen to the ground behind Illa, and she'd lain down so that her head was on his chest. The back of her neck tightened as intense waves of tingles rushed through her head and shoulders. The wave of jealousy hit Ticca harder than an enemy blade. Flexing her fists she slid off her horse and stomped towards the pair, intent on jerking Illa off of Lebuin.

Just as she reached the pair, Ditani called out. "We must put those fires out before the grass goes up in flames."

Ditani's voice touched something in her mind freezing her in place. The memory of a grass-plain fire near her family farm when she was a child washed over her, bringing with it a shiver of terror and a moment of clarity. Looking around, she couldn't concentrate enough to count the team, but the threat of a massive fire kept her focused. "Get out there and put them out — fast!"

She raced back to her own horse, mounted, and rushed towards one of the burning heaps. The farther away from Lebuin she got, the clearer her head became.

I have to control this. Dear Lady, what is going on with me? I have no reason to be jealous of Illa! But as the thought crossed her mind, she felt her heart skip. *Oh, no, you don't,* she said to her own heart. *This is MY LIFE! I choose my own path. And I know I wasn't attracted to Lebuin before whatever happened at that base. This has to be some kind of spell or something. And I won't let it take me over!*

Her conscience disagreed with her.

Okay, okay. Yes, I was a little attracted to him. He was kinda cute, especially after he put on some weight. But that was just cute. I mean, he's an okay guy, but not the kind of man I want to spend my life with.

Her conscience gave her one last nudge, as if to say, *'We'll see.'* But then her feelings finally fell into place.

That's better, Ticca. Stay calm, stay focused, and do the work.

Her arms ached from shoveling as fast as she did to get dirt on the fires, but she did it. She saw no more smoke columns, and there would be no out of control fires. She stood and looked back down the hill to where the team was gathered. She breathed deep and stood still, until she felt she'd achieved a balance. Precarious as it was, she was in control.

Breathing slow and controlled helped keep her feelings in check. She headed back to her team, concentrating on staying in control of herself. As she approached them, she saw that Malla had been dressing wounds. Two bodies were laid out; those of Sabri and Epton. Her throat tightened as she choked back tears.

Nigan stepped over, carefully slipping a different shirt on over his bandages. "We need to get away from here before they attack us again."

"No," Ticca said. "We should build funeral pyres for Sabri and Epton. We must find Coedy; he might be dead, too. Somehow they know exactly where we are. They got ahead of us and set a trap. I wish I knew how they were doing it."

She looked at the mountains and felt an odd pulling towards them. Something about the jagged peaks in the distance touched her, making her feel safe and calm.

"It's what they're famous for. Being where they shouldn't be capable of being, and surgically performing their assignments. Ticca, we got lucky. If Lebuin hadn't awoken and taken out as many as he did, we would all need pyres of our own."

Steeling herself, she looked for Lebuin. He and Illa were laid out on camping blankets. Both of them seemed to be sleeping. Ditani, covered in dirt, was already sitting between them, eyes closed, touching both their arms. His face lifted to the sky and he swayed back and forth singing something soft that had a deep beat, which his baritone voice gave life to.

Lebuin's skin was still glowing gold, but dimmer. Her heart started to jump around in her chest, but she willed it to be still.

"What about Lebuin and Illa?"

Nigan looked over to them. "I think we'll need two travois now. Neither one woke when we moved them. Although Illa was speared through by two odassi, there isn't even a blemish on her skin. Her clothes are soaked in her blood, which was glowing like Lebuin, but it stopped a few minutes before you got back."

"We do this by the numbers. Send Carda and Persa out to find Coedy. We'll camp here tonight and make the funeral pyres. Tomorrow, we skip the travois and tie Lebuin and Illa in their saddles, and make speed for the Razor Back Mountains. If we push we can get to them in twenty or thirty marks. We'll have to forage for the necessary supplies as we cross the mountains. It might take us an extra few weeks to get through."

"Won't they attack us there, too?" Nigan asked.

"I have a strange feeling we'll be safe there."

DOHMA

Dohma awoke to the sounds of camp being broken. After pulling himself up, he slipped on his boots and splashed water on his face, slicking back his hair. He stepped out into the starlit morning air and put his hauberk on over the padded leather coat. The moons were still out, giving the slight morning mist a ghostly quality. He filled his lungs with the fresh air, enjoying the scent of herbs mixed with the grass carried by the mist.

Cundia, his personal Dagger privy councilor, came into view, leading his eight personal Dagger guards. He noted as she approached that all of his Daggers were fully dressed for combat and were glistening.

How you manage to get up and do drills every morning before me, I can't figure out.

A hand closed on his shoulder, causing him to jump.

"Diurdu, Orahda! How do you do that?"

"I've tried to teach you," he said reproachfully.

Cundia was close enough to hear them. "If you two are finished waking up, Duke has ordered a predawn strike." She bowed to Dohma. "And he asks respectfully that you be so kind as to follow his orders this time, and stay with the rear guard."

"I tried to last time. You saw those other warriors in the barracks."

"I'm merely delivering the orders as instructed. That said, this is a primary Nhia-Samri base with at least 30,000 warriors. They will likely have reinforcements coming to support them if they're not already there."

Orahda patted Dohma's shoulder. "They're also likely to use a gate to send a few thousand warriors out of the base to attack us from the rear. We must be doubly cautious this day."

A deep voice came out of the darkness. "Don't worry, my friend. No plan survives the first encounter with the enemy. I'm sure there will be enough chaos to let you slip into the main group."

They all turned in the direction of the voice as the giant, moonlit grey wolf emerged from the thin morning mist like an apparition. Shivers ran down Dohma's spine at the sight. Duke's eyes were reflecting the moonlight like two silver lanterns.

That any dare stand against him is amazing. If he wanted, I think he could have taken the entire world for his own. We're lucky he believes so deeply in the Dagger code.

All of the Daggers, including Cundia, snapped to attention and saluted. Orahda simply nodded.

His eyes on Orahda, Duke said, "This is the first major base we're going to attack. The other outposts were nothing more than guardhouses. If they have any intel at all, they'll know we're coming for this base."

"Yes," Orahda said. "And Shar-Lumen will let it fall to test you, your army, and your tactics. He knows this is the first time he's truly facing you."

"We've gone over it enough. We'll know how accurate your insights are once we engage them."

As Dohma finished putting his weapons belt on, he said, "What I don't understand is why he hasn't sent any of his kill squads after the assembly. He made it clear he wants to kill every regent, king, queen, and all their families."

Duke glanced at Orahda, who shook his head. "Shar-Lumen will never attack in the elven woods," Duke said. "Not even me, unless it's to defend the elves or their lands. He's not insane, as many believe. He's still an elf lord, and will not violate his people's home."

Flashing his grin, Duke said, "Well then, I believe it's time to get started. The attack is just about to start. I've already sent the orders to the other camps. In two marks, 30,000 Dagger officers will lead 90,000 soldiers in three groups into the base from north, west, and south. We'll be leading the last group of the most veteran 50,000, striking from the east, and 300,000 soldiers are already on blockade patrol. I want to be sure our group goes in first."

After he spun around, Duke leapt out of view in a single bound. Dohma jogged after him, with his own team following. Their horses were ready and waiting. Climbing on, they joined the hundreds of other Daggers who made up the rear guard. The army cantered towards the hills, where the base was located. Their path was lit by hundreds of magical lanterns that burned brighter and clearer than oil lamps.

Their division had been sweeping southwest along the Duianna and Nae-Rae border. The outpost was in a valley only a few days' hard ride southwest of Gracia, across the river channels. Once they cleared it, they could move west near Laeusia and join up with another half-division that was sweeping down from northern Duianna. They'd camped only forty miles from the base's center, only five miles from the nearest Nhia-Samri farm.

Orahda had said there would be no way to surprise the base, even if they tried to sneak in from fifty miles away, so Duke had chosen to have the camps far enough away to make either side have to put forth effort to attack. The base knew they were coming; it was only a matter of the precise time.

It was a large base, larger than most towns. Farmland

spread out twenty or thirty miles in all directions from the core facility, with an estimated 5,000 families. It would be cleaner than a regular city, completely dedicated to the military ways of the Nhia-Samri. Still, he knew there would be red-tiled roofs with upswept corners. Hundreds of core buildings and storehouses surrounded a central practice field for the warriors, which was next to the huge command structure at the center of the complex.

Even over the sound of thousands of armored warriors on war horses cantering through the woods, the battle cry of the attack force was clear. Ringing of metal on metal came only a moment later, signaling that the attack had begun.

Dohma smiled as Orahda held up his hand. With his head tilted back, Orahda turned his horse and then pointed. Laughing, Dohma dug his stirrups into the horse's side.

There are advantages to being in the rear guard. This is a major outpost, and Duke really should've listened when Orahda said they would use their gate. I'm not going to lose a target to a closing gate again!

His thousand-Dagger rear guard unit weren't sure what was going on, but they were all smart enough to know something was up. Swords and daggers were drawn by many, and others lowered their spears as they galloped after Orahda and Dohma.

Ahead, Dohma saw the glimmer of light that marked the gate. As he pointed, four Daggers nodded and, with spears down, charged ahead.

As expected, the sounds of their approach had been detected, but too late. It was acknowledged as being directly for the gate. A squad of Nhia-Samri ran towards the base, and another came out of the gate as the lead forty Daggers plowed right into the group, mowing down all who weren't fast enough to get out of the way. Dohma let out a battle cry that was echoed by his guards as they rushed through the gateway.

As Dohma rode through the portal, he had the strangest

feeling he'd ever experienced. The edge of the gateway felt like a creature's soft, furry skin, stretching tighter and tighter as he went through it. The surface didn't want to break, and it pushed back on him. But the horse was moving, and with a snap, the pressure against him was replaced by a dizzying, tingling sensation as he was flung forward and out, into a large training yard. Dozens of Nhia-Samri were rushing towards him, and the cacophony of battle and confused screams of the officers and warriors was too much.

The warriors were taken by surprise by the sudden attack via a path they thought was their exclusive domain.

Orahda came through right behind Dohma, and leapt from his horse, drawing his blades. Through the din and confusion, Dohma clearly heard cries of, "Amia-Dharo!"

Laughing, Dohma took in the area, deciding on the best tactics. Turning his horse, he ordered it to rear up and attack a pair of stunned Nhia-Samri beside him. As the horse trampled over them, he swung his blades on both sides at those who weren't frozen in shock.

By the time the Dagger rear guard began streaming into the center of the base through the captured gate, Orahda had already slain four and was in the process of taking the head off the mage who held the controls for the gate.

The initial surprise was over. Nhia-Samri and Daggers engaged in the dance of death.

Dohma used his horse to trample more warriors. Breaking free, he turned back and charged a group of officers who were fighting Orahda. One of them spun out of the way and grabbed Dohma's belt. He turned, trying to cut down on the officer. In doing that, another one hit his other side hard, as a third sliced his horse's neck. The wind flew from him as he was thrown, falling onto the man who was holding his belt.

The two of them landed in a pile. They shook their heads and then stood, facing each other.

A warrior in bright red armor stepped out onto the field.

Two ranks of Nhia-Samri were following in formal order behind her.

The officer facing Dohma launched at him. Dohma parried the attack, bringing his own blade in, riposting. They exchanged a series of cuts and jabs. Dohma managed to knock his blade wide, and plunged his own sword into the man's neck. Twisting, he pulled his blade out, causing blood to spray as the man fell.

Turning, he saw the warrior in red walking calmly towards the battle, drawing her odassi. Dohma recognized her from the attack on Gracia. She was the one who'd carried off Lady Lothia, while Shar-Lumen had slain Lady Dalpha.

His vision sharpened, and he felt his pulse quicken. The thought of Lady Dalpha being slain as Lady Lothia lay unconscious on the bloody floor still filled him with rage.

She's one of Shar-Lumen's senior officers. Maybe even a warlord. She'll be able to tell exactly what happened to Lady Lothia — if she still lives, and if there's any hope of saving her.

"WHAT HAVE YOU DONE WITH LOTHIA?"

The woman stopped and looked at him. The other warriors started to move around her, when she shouted, "NO! He's mine!"

Even though his heart was pounding, he moved towards the woman. She took off her helmet and handed it to another warrior without looking. She had a sharp, chiseled face with a small cleft in her chin. She stared at Dohma with intensely bright brown eyes. Her face tightened as she saluted him with her odassi.

For an instant, she looked like she was made of marble.

Then she was water.

In the span of a single heartbeat, she closed and attacked Dohma.

His vision clear and heart ripping through his chest, he moved as fast as she did, parrying each blow. He smiled at the realization that killing her would be easy.

His blades spun around in a series of ripostes. She turned and bent, avoiding his blades.

Growling at her fluid movements, he kicked out, catching her leg with his toes. Kicking up, he lifted her leg off the ground and brought his blades down towards her chest.

Off-balance, she fell backwards and twisted to hit the ground with the back of one hand, her blade never touching the ground.

Instead of cutting through her, Dohma's swords slammed into the paving stones in a shower of dirt and rock.

She pushed off with her other leg, twisting around to kick at Dohma's shin, pushing his leg out from under him. At the same time, she swung her blade around, level with the ground.

His front leg already lifted from her shin kick, he pulled it higher, pushing off with his back leg, leaping. Time froze, as he seemed to levitate directly over her, face to face. She wore a small grin, and her eyes were like twin fires. Her blade sang as it passed harmlessly under him.

She thinks she's toying with me!

Pulling his swords in, he pointed them at her to impale her as he fell, but she rolled out from under him. Together they snapped to standing and squared off, staring at each other, each waiting for the other to flinch.

The sounds of battle had changed around them.

A haunting howl came from nearby.

Dohma's vision was tinged with red again. He fought to keep control, knowing that he needed the woman alive to answer questions. The face-off lasted only a fraction of a second before they both stepped in and exchanged a series of attacks.

His rage thrust him forward. Roaring at the woman, he whipped his blades around and beat her back. She parried and tried returning the strikes, but couldn't penetrate Dohma's defenses. One step at a time, her smile fading like a wilting flower, he drove her back.

Duke's frame appeared between the buildings behind her. He was followed by uncounted Daggers. A gong sounded, deep and loud.

The woman nodded at Dohma. "You're a worthy opponent. I'm sorry you must die today."

He didn't bother to reply, as he needed to keep control of his rage. The woman called out something and then leapt backwards. Instead of landing, she flew higher, accelerating away. The other Nhia-Samri did the same.

Duke and Dohma howled outrage as all the remaining Nhia-Samri warriors flew off backwards and vanished over the top of the tree line.

Breathing hard, Dohma knelt down and scanned the area. He could see he'd lost nearly half of his initial attack force.

Growling, Duke looked at him. "I told you to stay with the rear guard!"

Dohma pointed to the magic gate. "I did, but they stormed us through that."

Before Duke could answer, something hit him. Duke's mouth dropped open and his eyes went wide as a shimmering wave rolled over his body. At the same time, the gateway glow brightened almost twofold, causing everyone to shield their eyes from the glare.

Orahda ran over to him with a panicked expression and yanked him to his feet, screaming, "Everyone, quick! Through the gate and RUN!"

Duke and all of the Daggers took only a breath to react. The wounded were hoisted over shoulders or lifted onto horses as the teams evacuated.

As Dohma pushed through, he was literally thrown several feet upon exiting the gate. Like all the others, he stumbled before getting his feet under him and then ran as fast as he could away from the base.

Single mounted Daggers were grabbing others, pulling them up to ride two and three to a horse before galloping away.

Duke appeared next to him. "Dohma, get on!"

He didn't even question the order. He climbed up and gripped Duke's hair with all his strength as the old wolf launched into a loping run, quickly passing those on horses.

He spotted Orahda running faster than Duke in long, leaping bounds, with someone in a guardsman carry. Then the world went white and silent. For a second, Dohma thought he was dead. But then a powerful explosion hit them from behind, throwing Duke into the air.

Dohma tried to hold on, but debris batted him so hard that he lost Duke, even though both his fists were clenched on clumps of long grey hairs. The last thing he felt was something like a castle wall hitting his head.

Caught Red Handed

CHAPTER 7

LOST

Countess Electra Neyon, deputy secretary of the Duianna Alliance, secret agent of the sentient computer intelligence Vesta, and unofficial fiancée of Lord Dohma, tore the neuro-interface band from her head, gasping for breath, crying out in agony as she never had before. The images of the explosion remained clear in her mind. She'd been the unseen witness. For all the power at her disposal, she was still unable to do anything more than scream out her anguish as her love was burnt to ash before her eyes. All of Duke's attack force were consumed in the fires of the Nhia-Samri explosion.

There had been no warning. It looked as if Duke and Dohma had succeeded in taking the base; then a burst of energies had knocked out or destroyed Vesta's observation bugs. Vesta had previously moved her last satellite over the area, and they'd shifted to its sensor input instantly.

Electra couldn't accept what she saw. Vesta and Arkady had also been shocked into silence as they watched the base explosion via the orbital observation platform.

Arkady estimated that everything within a one-mile radius had been reduced to dust. The full destructive radius was five miles. Although some of Duke's elite troops would survive, Duke and Dohma, who were at the base itself, were guaranteed to be nothing more than powder.

Electra's overwhelming emotions swept her out of the virtual world of Vesta and Arkady, back to her chamber. An unknown amount of time passed before she became aware of two people sitting on her bed, holding her and saying something soothing.

She couldn't make it out. She started to retreat into her mind, when her grandfather's voice boiled up from her memory. *'Life has many miseries, but our family has and will continue to perform our duties regardless. You shall be tested, and remember this: You are Countess of Waylisia, and you have it in you to hold the line. You must never forget this.'*

She tried to push some of the grief aside. Mandy, her personal Dagger guard captain, was in front of her, holding her shoulder. Behind her was another of her Dagger guards. Mandy looked worried.

Electra felt tremendous gratitude for Mandy's steady hand on her shoulder. It gave her something to connect to, something to hold on to. She peered through her blurring tears.

"Duke and Dohma are dead." Even as she said it, her heart pounded, and she felt a wave of stubborn refusal to accept the situation.

Mandy dropped to her knees and pulled Electra into a hug. "Oh, Lady, I'm so sorry for your loss. You two had so little time. Fear not, we will still prevail."

Electra shook her head. "No! You don't understand! Duke, Dohma, and most of Duke's Dagger army was incinerated by a massive magical attack!" A devastating pain shot through her chest as she witnessed the horror in her mind as vividly as when she first saw it. Her throat had the sensation of being crushed as she tried to hold back the wails that longed to escape. She tried desperately to regain her composure, but no amount of strength could stop the river of tears from flowing over her cheeks.

One of the other Daggers tried to speak, choking on her own pain. "Lords and Ladies…that's over 25,000 Daggers… and another 120,000 soldiers. What could possibly do that?"

Mandy continued to hold Electra while she took deep breaths as she also cried.

Muffled words came from the other ladies in the room. For a long time, they all did their best to cope with the news. The other guards, leaning against the door, also tried to imagine the losses.

"I wonder how many we knew," one of them said.

Mandy shifted and sniffled loudly, clearing her nose. "We'll make them pay for this. It might take years, but Daggers never forget or fail to act." She pushed Electra back. "Don't worry! It isn't over. We all lost a great deal today. But believe me, this will really piss Duke off!"

One of the women said, "Lords, yes! When he comes back he'll tear them up like paper!"

"If they're lucky," the other guard added.

Electra tried to open her swollen eyes. She felt out of touch, and angry at the helplessness which ate at her confidence.

"Mandy, how can you say that? Don't you get it? They're gone! At the rate things are going, the Nhia-Samri will completely destroy us!"

Mandy looked at the other Daggers, then back at Electra, and put her hand on Electra's shoulder. "Truly, I know your loss. We've all lost good friends maybe even family this day. I'm deeply sorry Lord Dohma is gone. But Dagger history tells us clearly that being burned to ash only slows Duke down for a while! If we can hold on, Duke will be back, and trust me, he'll be *mad*! This happened once before, and Duke leveled the kingdom responsible, sinking its island chain into the oceans. Duke captured the mages involved and applied some of his secret to immortality to them. So long as they're there, it's said that they remain alive, chained in unbreakable steel, forever drowning in the capital of their sunken kingdom. If they ever do break free, they'll die before they reach the surface. Trust us when we say that this war just took a serious turn against the Nhia-Samri."

Electra had heard the tales of Duke's immortality. They seemed so fanciful, and yet he was still there. And considering what he did from time to time, it was likely someone with enough power would try to rid the world of him.

If only Duke could save those around him, too.

Her throat and chest still ached as her tears ran freely.

She forced the hope of Dohma's survival away, as it wasn't logical. Duke might survive, but Dohma had no such proofs against death. Her heart longed for him, and she imagined she could feel his presence beside her.

Electra stood, and her legs wobbled as she forced herself to balance. "I need to tell the regents." A welcome numbness descended over her as she walked towards the throne room from her secured chamber deep in the palace complex of Llino. She didn't remember actually leaving her room. Instead of taking the direct path, she threaded her way to the throne room through the interior corridors, passing through the halls lined with portraits of Dohma's ancestors. She felt connected to the portraits, as if they were there offering her support and urging her to persevere for the good of the kingdom.

Why should I persevere? What good will come from this? she silently asked the images. Her mind mulled over the last few cycles. From the moment war had been declared with the Nhia-Samri, events seemed to be on an increasingly fast downward spiral. Electra's optimism was gone.

Hope had bloomed when Duke found and restored the regents, naming Lord Dohma chief regent. The Kingdom of Aelargo returned to the Alliance. The secretary sent her here to reestablish formal communications with the Empire and its Alliance. Then Lord Dohma had done what no other man could; he stole her heart. And judging by the letter in her breast pocket, she'd stolen his.

None knew that a true descendant of the great Duianna Empire's royal line, Ticca of Rhini Wood, had returned in secret. Ticca accidentally awakened Vesta, a legendary ancient sentient, who, despite her protests to the contrary, Electra was sure was more powerful than the immortals. Electra discovered and allied with Vesta. Together Vesta and Electra had awakened Vesta's counterpart, Arkady, another sentient power who lived in the Alliance capital of Gracia.

After joining Arkady and Vesta, Electra thought they could easily defeat the Nhia-Samri. The three of them launched a secret attack on a major Nhia-Samri outpost, which was their first and last success. The next attack on the Nhia-Samri home, the mountain fortress and city-state Hisuru Amajoo, was a complete failure that only succeeded in angering the Grand Warlord Shar-Lumen. In retaliation Shar-Lumen executed the Goddess, Lady Dalpha, in the assembly chamber for what he thought was a preemptive strike at him by the immortals.

In only three cycles, all hope was gone. In spite of all the heroes, legends, gods, Daggers, and ancient powers used against the Nhia-Samri, they'd captured the southern half of the Kingdom of Nasur, which was on the western border of Aelargo and just east of the mountains that held Hisuru Amajoo. Even more astounding was that at the same time, the Nhia-Samri had also captured a quarter of the Kingdom of Laeusia, which was on the western boarder of the Nhia-Samri mountain home.

Empress Ticca and the demigod Lebuin, escorted by some of the best Daggers known, might have discovered something critical at the remains of the first Nhia-Samri base that Vesta and Electra had attacked. However, the Nhia-Samri noticed their activity and destroyed the empress's party along with their crippled base.

The world was drowning in blood. Tears poured over Electra's cheeks again at the memory of Ticca, Lebuin, and all their Dagger warriors. The blast craters from the onslaught at that first base were immense, and both Arkady and Vesta held little hope for survivors, despite Lebuin's efforts to channel away the energies used to attack them, destroying Vesta's orbital observation satellite in the process. The energies used against Dohma and Duke were a hundred times more powerful than what had killed Ticca and Lebuin, adding hundreds of thousands — including her beloved Lord Dohma — to the list of the dead.

She passed a painting showing the gods watching over the city. Lady Dalpha stood next to Lady Lothia, wife of the

All Father Lord Argos. Lady Lothia had been in Gracia when Lady Dalpha was murdered by Shar-Lumen. Now she was missing. The Nhia-Samri even defeated her in the assembly hall, taking her prisoner after first brutally beating her unconscious. Everyone was worried about her location.

Both Vesta and Arkady were concerned that Lord Argos would abandon his duty of controlling the universe's magical systems to rescue her. As much honor and sense of responsibility as Lord Argos had, he was still a being that loved. Assuming, of course, that like everyone else Lord Argos was unable to communicate with Lothia. No one was really aware of what Lord Argos was and was not doing, thinking, or capable of.

The real problem was that only Lord Argos had the special powers and enhancements to control the mighty machines that maintained the critical balance of magics in the universe. If he left those machines unattended for too long, the magical energies could become unbalanced with the real potential of tearing the universe. According to Vesta, it would take several years or longer before those great machines became unstable enough to threaten the worlds of the universe.

In Llino, as far east of the Nhia-Samri home as it was possible to be, the situation was getting progressively worse, as well. One division had effectively blockaded the city and port for three cycles. Even though Llino's defenses were still keeping them safe, they were little more than prisoners with a large cell. The regents checked with the city systems almost as often as Electra did through her secret connection to Vesta. The Nhia-Samri hadn't killed anyone, or even tested the city's defenses, since engaging in the blockade. They'd attacked anyone who tried to sneak in or out and turned them around, usually heavily wounded, but not dead.

The Nhia-Samri patrols around the city were being shadowed by Daggers, city guards, and the city's artifacts, known as sentinels, which were automated guards. They had a vast array of weapons from the height of the non-magical people's technology, which were built when the initial cities were being constructed. They'd been turned off and sealed under many layers of locks, but those were easily broken by the regents calling for them.

The regents had specifically ordered the sentinels to guard the city from the Nhia-Samri, but not to go on the offensive. The initial Nhia-Samri attack force had backed off from their onslaught on the western gate the moment the sentinels had soared overhead, blasting at the few of their mages who'd been trying to open a hole in the city's defensive shields.

Supplies were becoming scarce, and that had given rise to increased thefts, attempts at graft, and an entirely new black market on food.

The regents were at a loss for what else could be done. Until some Imperial troops came to break the blockade, everyone, inside and outside of the city walls, was stuck sitting around, waiting for something to happen. Aelargo had the greatest navy in the world, but practically no army. The threat of naval destruction of ports and ships was usually enough to guarantee Aelargo would not be attacked by any of its neighbors.

Electra wasn't sure how long it had taken her to get to the throne room. The portrait gallery had given her some confidence back, but she still felt as though she were tightly wrapped in wool padding. The world seemed flat, and her eyes were red, but the tears had stopped. She wiped her face and straightened her stance as she entered the throne room. Her eyes still were blurry and tiny golden sparks swam in her vision. Ignoring her aches, blurred vision, and dry throat, she concentrated on holding herself together.

A heated discussion was going on in the throne room as Electra entered. She paused to assess the situation before making her presence known. A small pack of nobles was led by the recently reinstated Lord Allusia, chief minister of intelligence.

"They have total control of the southern 950 miles of Laeusia. Now we have definitive proof they have taken control of a similar southern portion of Nasur, leaving only a small region around the capital that's barely big enough to call a county, let alone a country. If they decide to continue east, that will mean all of Aelargo will fall under their control! You have to demand Imperial action."

"I will not demand anything. The report also clearly states that they're giving citizens who wish to leave safe passage with all of their belongings. Princess Sheila is safe in Pentegull, along with her advisers."

"My Lord, you must call for help. Our defenses will not hold against them if they decide to stop simply blockading us. They broke the defenses at the palace at Allornia easy enough. Princess Sheila is no fool, and she was fully trained in controlling those ancient fortifications."

"Llino is not a small provincial city like Allornia. Our city was built by Lord Larak, Lady Dalpha, and Duke! We're far more fortified than any other, except perhaps Gracia. Also, it's my understanding that Laeusia does not have any sentinels."

Lord Allusia dropped to his knees, facing Regent Ellua with his hands gripped together. "Lady, please help me with your brother, for all our people's sake. The sentinels are not proof against the Nhia-Samri. We have a clear report from the Algan battle that a single mage defeated three sentinels by himself. If not for Duke and the Daggers, he would've been unstoppable."

Lady Ellua was clearly sympathetic, and that last plea must have struck a blow. She visibly swayed before turning to her brother. She indicated Lord Allusia with an open hand. "Bayion, he's right. I've read that report. I'm not convinced the Nhia-Samri mages were threatened by the sentinels. It's just as likely that they were ordered to stop their attack to give us a false sense of security."

Bayion sighed. "Yes, yes. I've read the same report. Lord

Allusia, stand up. You look silly like that. But I keep asking myself what they could possibly have gained by giving us that false sense of security? I have no answer. If they weren't threatened, they could have seized the city and us along with it."

Electra felt a chill run through her. What had her crushed so hard was that the Nhia-Samri base Dohma and Duke had just attacked had exploded with much more force than the one that had killed Ticca and Lebuin. The events clicked into place. She stepped out. "Time!"

Everyone turned to see who was speaking, and the regents' brows tightened as they took in both Electra and her interruption.

"Time for what?" Lord Bayion asked.

Electra moved to stand next to Lord Allusia as he got to his feet. "Time to set a trap for Dohma and Duke," she said, her voice strained and hoarse from crying, even to her ears.

Ellua stared at Electra's eyes and glanced at her cheeks. "What has happened?" Ellua's voice was soft and comforting, like a mother trying to bolster her child's confidence.

Bayion's mouth was open to argue the point, but his head turned first to Ellua. He looked into Electra's eyes as well, and promptly closed his mouth. He walked down the three steps and grasped her by her shoulders. Looking to his left, he called for a chair and some sharre, which were quickly delivered. Bayion guided her to sit before handing her a small cup of the sweet wine. "Drink it, my dear. Then tell us what's happened."

Electra was so numb, she didn't even argue with being treated like a child. She tilted her head back and drank the entire glass as one would take bitter medicine. The sharre burned as it poured down her throat. Warmth and energy flowed through her like a wave cresting over her body. Her senses cleared, and both Bayion and Ellua were beside her, each with a hand resting on one of her shoulders.

Even with the comfort of the sharre penetrating her body,

she sobbed as grief beat back the artificial boost. She began, "Duke and Dohma's attack on the major base southwest of Gracia was a trap. The base has been destroyed by a powerful magical attack designed to burn everything for miles to ash."

The room exploded with dozens of conversations. Ellua dropped to her knees next to Electra, shaking her head. Bayion had gone quiet, and was staring out the windows.

Ellua's face tightened. "No. My brother is not dead. He would find a way." Her voice was steady and sure. She had no doubts at all.

The sharre continued to work in Electra's system. The world was a shimmering blur through her tears. The court was like a tide of particles, circling into and out of one conversation or another, as the ocean swept them about.

Wiping her eyes didn't make the shimmering diminish. Blinking her vision clear only made the golden specks clearer. Electra scanned the room. She could see that each person glowed with an aura that ranged in color and brightness. Some had strong golden nimbuses around them; others had blue, and there were even a few red. One or two people had broken patterns surrounding them. Electra had never seen anything so beautiful. She looked up, first at Bayion and then his sister. They both had shimmering silver auras, tinged with gold and blues, that flowed out and connected to the floor in a way unlike any other. A fine golden thread ran from the center of Bayion to the center of Ellua.

Her heart leapt and hammered as she noted there were other golden threads present. She saw three more from the center of Bayion, another four more from Ellua, and surprisingly, a third from herself. Two of the threads from Bayion went towards the east and up, which was where his family's chambers were. Three of the threads from Ellua also went off easterly, towards her family's chambers.

Three remaining threads stole all her attention. One from Bayion, one from Ellua, and one from herself that all shot off in the same direction, north. She brought her hand up and tried to grab the thread, but her hand passed through it, as if it was nothing more than a dream. She stood and faced the same direction as Bayion, trying to follow the thread. Hope bloomed, and her heart raced as she reached out with all her might, her hands stretching longingly.

She felt a tug from the thread, like something at the other end was trying to pull her to it, or pull itself to her.

A forlorn voice came to her. *'Electra. Lords and Ladies, I never should have left you.'* She had that odd, wondrous sensation she felt when Dohma looked at her, even though she wasn't able to see him. Before he left, they'd become so close that they seemed to know each other's moods and thoughts.

She hoped and prayed. *'Dohma? Oh, Lady, let this be real! Can it be truly you?'*

She felt a small surge of hope, combined with confusion, come to her through the connection. *'Electra? Is it you? Somehow, it is you. I can hear your heart. You're crying. Ellua is holding your hand. Lords, thank you! I can say I love you one last time.'*

'YES! OH, YES! My Lord, come home to me! Don't you dare give up! I don't want to live without you.'

'My Lady. I don't know where I am. I can't even feel my body. I'm sorry. I feel you, and your love is giving me energy enough to think clearly.'

"Give him my energy, too," Ellua whispered in Electra's ear with a sense of wonder.

Ellua's words snapped understanding into Electra. The regents were connected by some kind of magic, but something else had happened as well. She'd given herself to Lord Dohma before he left, and he'd done the same to her. In the way of the Empire, the ceremonies were just for tradition and a general announcement to the people of what was already in place. As far as the Empire's magic was concerned she was Lord Dohma's wife, so she was joined into the same network of connections shared by the regents. The sharre, her emotions, Ellua's proximity, Bayion's proximity, and maybe her experiences with Vesta's networks had enabled her to not only sense, but also to use the interconnection. She was unconsciously sending energy from herself, and probably from the sharre, to Lord Dohma. Just like any couple or family, they could sense and support each other on a level beyond mere words and actions.

Electra lifted her other hand. "Bayion, take my hand and give me your energies."

Bayion grabbed her hand without thinking, and then he sputtered. "Wait, what?"

"Just do it, brother. Now, be quiet. Our new sister needs to concentrate," Ellua commanded.

Ignoring them, Electra felt for how to push or let the energies flow. It only took a couple experiments before she found the right feeling. With a surge, the connection opened, and energy flowed from Bayion, Ellua, and Electra, down the thread to Lord Dohma. She could sense his body healing.

'Never give up, my Lord!' she commanded him.

Dohma didn't answer, but she could feel his confidence and determination reasserting themselves. She could feel his love for her adding its own unique power to fight through the pain and return.

The last of the energies she could share left her, and she felt her legs wobbling. She could feel Lord Dohma would be strong enough to recover, as the strength of the link began to fade. Afraid she might not be able to reestablish it, she sent waves of love as she said, *'My Lord, we are safe, but trapped. Llino is sealed under an unbreakable Nhia-Samri blockade. They seem to be waiting for something. Ellua and I both fear the city's defenses are not proof against them.'*

None of the initial hopelessness remained in Dohma's feelings as he responded. *'I'll let Shar-Lumen know how displeased I am with this news. Surrender if you must. You and my family must stay alive. I'm coming.'*

She lost the energy to hold onto the connection just as she felt Dohma's rage at the situation filling him. Electra fell to the floor as Bayion tried to catch her, only to discover he did not have the strength himself. Ellua also slipped to the floor.

Electra laughed as a raging fire of joy filled her heart. Bayion and Ellua joined her laughter as the courtiers and guards ran to lift them into their chairs, and pages rushed to bring them more stout drinks.

Brow furrowed, Mandy held another glass of sharre for Electra. After sipping it, she started feeling better. She tried to find the threads, but she couldn't see them. She concentrated and briefly saw them before her vision cleared.

Power or concentration or maybe some kind of state of mind is needed. I'll have to look into mage meditations and abilities. I might be able to use those threads at will.

As they recovered, neither Bayion, Ellua, nor Electra bothered to explain anything. They kept looking at each other, nodding, understanding that only they and Dohma knew what had taken place.

Mandy finally stood between them, putting her hands on her hips. "What on Yur just happened? And what are you three nodding at?"

Electra sat up straighter. "I think Duke has some competition over who'll do the most damage. It seems getting burnt to ash has the same effect on Lord Dohma as on Duke."

TICCA

Ticca leaned on her horse for support as she made her way down the trail. She had no idea how many times she'd pulled her empty canteen from her belt and shook it, hoping some water had condensed to give her even a sip.

I need to find some shade and wait for the rest of the group. I'm starting to get dizzy from dehydration. We'll have to share out some of the remaining water.

She tried to calculate how much water was left, but she kept coming up with different answers. Even though they'd taken a measure of the water only four marks earlier, she couldn't clearly remember how much it had been. Her trainer's voice came through the small headache and fuzziness of her thoughts. *'Don't ration your water in the desert. You'll have a better chance of surviving if your head is clear.'* Until that moment, she hadn't really appreciated what that meant.

They'd managed to cross the Razor Back Mountains using what they hoped was a trade trail. It was not well-maintained, and showed little sign of being used in years. It had taken them over the mountains, and the view south was nothing but blazing, cream-colored sand dunes. A few twisted and brown mahogany trees grew like bushes along the mountain slopes, dotting the terrain to the east and west. At times, they could see a clear line where the hard dirt and rock of the mountains turned into the sands of the deadly Circumveni Desert.

Heat radiated off of the desert floor, blurring the horizon in waves of light. Even though it was still at least four miles and a couple thousand feet down to the desert proper, the temperature was reaching well over a hundred degrees all day long and dropping near the frost point at night.

The team had made large water bladders for the horses to carry on the ascent. Even though they'd crested the mountains confident in their survival training, the descent had taken a few days longer than expected, due to the trail having collapsed at a deep ravine. In getting everything across, they'd lost a lot of water. The bladders were almost empty, and it had been two days since Ticca had a drop of water for herself. She'd ordered the water held for the horses; she knew they would be critical to the group's survival.

Due to the effect of water deprivation on her brain, it took Ticca a few seconds to recognize that her horse had stopped moving. Like pulling a stick through thick old honey, she brought her focus to what was around her. Her horse was sniffing at a crevice. It pawed at the crack in the wall, whining. Ticca let go of the saddle, which she'd been using to hold herself up. After dismounting, she forced herself to step up to see what her horse had found. A breath of moist, cool air brushed her face, causing her skin to dimple with a brief chill in the heat.

Hope fed her energy, and she started shimming sideways, into the narrow fissure. The smells of ancient granite and dirt, mixed with brownish moss, filled her nostrils.

The faint promise of moisture in the air spurred Ticca to move. The gap narrowed, and she wedged herself in, unable to turn her head. She paused to decide if it was worth the risk. The wind blew another sweet, tantalizingly cool, moist breath over her body, and she shivered in excitement at the promise of water. Ticca worked her way backwards and then lay down on her side to slither through like a snake. She had to wiggle slowly; it was so narrow that she was stopped with each breath and had to exhale to pass the final few feet.

Once through, she froze for a moment as her body was wracked with different feelings. Her spine tingled, muscles quivered, and her skin prickled as she took in the hidden green alcove before her. The water she'd prayed for was there. In fact, it cascaded down a twenty-foot shimmering waterfall, from an opening in the side of the mountain into a clear pool, before running out of her field of vision. There was an area that had signs of being used as a campsite in the past. Without another thought, she dropped to the side and dunked her head in with her mouth open.

She drank and splashed the water over her head as she giggled. If she'd been more hydrated, tears would've been running from her eyes. She drank as much as she could. Finally, she rolled over and looked around.

Not sure why anyone would be coming this way as frequently as this place seems to indicate. But the trail is clean here, and this looks like a perfect camp. If it weren't for the horses and men, I would use this tonight.

She grabbed her canteen and filled it, taking more drinks from it and filling it again. Like everyone's in her group, hers was bone dry.

Then her survival training kicked in. She started to worry about whether or not she was drinking poisoned or dangerous water. She rechecked the pool with a critical eye for any signs of being tainted. She saw no signs of danger, and there was even a small bucket left in a niche for the camp. It was as clean as she could hope for. She knew it wasn't safe to drink a lot, even if it was clean. After going for almost two days without any water at all, it was better to hydrate slowly and deal with any other issues later.

She took the container back through the fissure to her waiting horse. He nuzzled her, licking the moisture from her hair as she emerged. She poured some water into her palm for him to first sniff and then drink. Just as it was all gone, Ditani came walking up the path, leading his horse. Of all of them, he was faring the best for the lack of hydration. She waved at him. He saw her excitement and rushed down the steep embankment to her.

"Water. All we can use, through there," she said, pointing.

Ditani grabbed his own canteen and tried to find a way through. "It's too narrow for me."

Ticca took some rope off her saddle. "Give it to me. We'll have to relay all of them. Not sure what else we can do. But we first need to camp here long enough to get ourselves rested. We're almost at the desert. From the looks of it, it's only going to get worse."

Looking out into the desert, Ditani nodded. "Yes. Are you sure this is the path we should take?"

The rolling sand was shaped into frozen waves by the wind. Heat rolled off, pushing them back towards the mountains, seeming as if it wished to be left alone. Deep inside, she could feel the pull of something out there that held a promise of being a key. The problem was that she wasn't certain what that key was for.

The pull and promise Ticca felt were even stronger than when she'd decided on that course, just after they'd pulled Lebuin out of the burnt crater. She'd said their destination was Imridu-Nam. And there she was, on the edge of the very place that would kill most people in less than a day, and still her instincts said it was right.

"Yes, Ditani. The key we seek is there."

Her voice sounded distant and echoed back with a resonance that made her shiver at its power. Everything around her came into sharp focus. She stood on a wide balcony atop a palace made of blue marble, surrounded by a shimmering city with red-tiled roofs and granite-walled buildings. Her balcony overlooked the green valley which encompassed the city, with its deep blue lake. The wind caused the tall cattails to wave gently as flocks of birds flew around the tree line.

She wore a crimson silk gown embroidered with silver. Its high standing collar bent back like a fountain for her hair, which cascaded down to her waist in a series of braids held with diamond bands. She lifted her hands to look at them and saw golden filigree bracelets on each arm. Her hands were soft, with only a hint of weapon calluses.

"Ticca?"

Ditani's voice came from far off to the northeast, over the rolling hills, carried to her by the wind. It startled her, and she stared in the direction it came from, chills running down her spine. "Ditani, where am I?"

She blinked and was back to reality, standing in the mountain's shadow, looking out on the hot cream-colored sands. Her hands, held before her, were harder, with a few scars and calluses. The strong hands of a warrior.

She looked at Ditani. He was stepping towards her with a look of concern in his eyes under his tightened brows.

"Ditani, where am I?" came her scared voice, rolling in from the southwest. They both stopped and stared off into the desert.

They waited for something more. When nothing came, she asked, "I was in a blue stone palace, and you called to me. What just happened?"

"The Gods have forbidden people from coming here,

because they say it's unstable. Maybe Lebuin can answer your question." Ditani's eyes shifted from her, and he looked hard at the ground. "If he wakes."

Ticca pointed in the direction she was sure the palace was located. A small stone outcropping broke through the sands. "Mark that stone rise there. That's the direction we need to go."

After another moment, she grunted, grabbed Ditani's canteen and the end of the rope, and lay down to snake back in to the water.

It took time, but the entire team, all that remained of it, arrived. Another campsite with a large open cave was found not far off, and they set up camp while Ticca and Persa, the only ones small enough to squeeze through, started water-fetching duties. Using ropes, they set up a way to drag canteens back and forth, letting them deliver enough water for the team and horses. Lebuin and Illa were laid out in the back of the cave by the time all the water bladders had been refilled.

As she walked into the camp, she felt her heart tugging at her to go and check on Lebuin, but she forced the feeling down, barring it from overwhelming her. The last week had given her a lot of practice at controlling the emotions Lebuin evoked.

Nigan stood and handed her a skewer with some roasted meat on it. She sniffed at it, and although she had to resist tearing into the meat, she scowled at Nigan. "Snake again?"

"Snake is better than no meat. Eat."

Ticca was too hungry to argue about it. The only non-reptilian meat available was from the odd little native rodents, a type of mouse with skin flaps that allowed them to perform gliding jumps around the rocky terrain. Unfortunately, those animals had so little meat on them they weren't worth the effort to catch them.

Scratching his beard, Nigan looked around. "You know, this is a strange campsite."

Ticca followed his gaze. The cave was a nice hollow with a perfect entryway overhang that deflected the desert's hot breezes. The fire was set into a small depression that had a rock formation, making a reasonable chimney to vent off the smoke.

"It does look well used."

"That isn't what I mean," Nigan said, shaking his head. "This isn't natural. The rock has been formed intentionally. The fire even has a raised ring for holding skewers. And there's something you should see." Grabbing a torch and lighting it in the fire, he motioned for her to follow and walked back into the cave.

They passed through a couple of chambers, each wide and comfortable. The first was perfect as a sleeping area, and the second had vents and seemed to be laid out as a wide stable for several horses. Beyond that, there was only one passage, which went through a series of right-angle turns, with large chambers at each corner.

She could feel the weight of the mountain overhead. Ticca tried to compute how far they'd gone, and she felt sure they were heading for the center of the mountain. The passage ended in a chamber, which Nigan stepped into. Moving around an outcropping, she watched Nigan lift the torch up and place it in a crack in the wall. It looked like it had always been that way, but with the torch in, it was clearly a sconce.

Nigan pointed to the wall next to the sconce. There was an archway of natural stone large enough for a rider on a horse to move through, except that it was completely filled in with a darker stone, or glass. The smooth surface reflected the light, but there was a shimmering depth to it. The archway was carved with a series of strange patterns that reminded her of the mystical writing in Lebuin's magic tomes, but the ones in the cave were more straight lines and sharp right angles.

She stepped up and examined the material that sealed the archway. It was definitely some kind of glass, perfectly smooth, and it looked like it was bound seamlessly to the stone archway. There wasn't even a crack between the stone and glass.

Nigan stood back while she examined it. "Someone didn't want anyone else going in here."

"I wish Lebuin was awake," Ticca said as she rested her hand on the cool surface.

RUNA-ILLA

Runa-Illa was scared and yet bored. She was lost, and not sure if she was anywhere at all. She recalled the attack that had killed her in great detail. She was certain that it happened.

A Nhia-Samri leapt off the horse with both odassi aimed at me. Like a pair of lightning bolts, the blades came. I had time to think, but not act. I knew they were going to kill me. I didn't have time to dodge or parry.

The pain was worse than anything I could imagine. Those blades went right through me. One in my kidney and the other, my heart. I could feel the blades sliding into me. I screamed... except...that scream carried on longer than it should have. And it reverberated.... I felt warmth spreading through me, and now, I'm dead...or maybe I'm just trapped in my mind. Maybe I'm still dying. This isn't what I expected. I thought there would be something. But I'm totally alone here.

Illa had managed to calm herself. That took a long time. *Why am I alone?*

She started worrying that maybe she was alive and insane. Weeks or cycles had passed, yet nothing happened. Around her were a myriad of colors, but nothing particularly defined. There was no pain. In fact, she felt relaxed and comfortable.

Her mood was shifting, fast or slow, she couldn't tell. Her internal clock told her she'd been there for more than a cycle. From panic, she'd moved on to curiosity, then to anticipation, then concern she wasn't doing something right, then panic again, then anger, which manifested in screaming at the colors, a lot. However, she wasn't sure if that did any good. She had to admit she'd gotten a lot of rest, but there was only so much looking at swirling hues one could do. She was well and truly bored.

Should I be bored? I mean, I'm dead. Yet I still feel like me. Or at least, I think I feel like me.

For the hundred thousandth time, she tried to feel her body. Nothing happened. It was as if she didn't have hands or arms. She tried to kick out. Still, no sensations at all.

Staring intently at the colors never yielded anything. Although, there were some she was sure could not exist going by at times. No matter what she did, they flowed and charged at their own will. There were more than she remembered from life.

Time passed, or maybe it didn't. Illa couldn't find anything else to do.

I expected a little more. I've heard lots of ideas about death. They usually involve going someplace interesting, at least Or nothing at all. But this isn't nothing. This is something. There are things happening. I must be able to do something here.

Once again, she concentrated hard, putting all her will behind pushing, pulling, running, swimming, and many other techniques to move herself. Nothing seemed to change the flow of the colors or anything else.

I'm not dead. This is too annoying to be death! Illa tried to spin and scream into the hues.

She was muttering to herself about the unfairness of the universe when she felt a presence approach her. The colors had shifted and flowed around a floating object with no distinct shape. Illa marveled that she could see all sides and the ghostly center of the thing that had come close.

Not dead. That's something.

She thought she heard someone. She concentrated on the blob.

'Did you say something?'

'Yes. Focus on....'

Illa couldn't make out the rest. But encouraged by communications, she reached out for the object, and it moved closer!

She panicked and started to flee. It sped away, seemingly decreasing in size. Realizing she would be alone, her feelings flipped, and a desire to be with the object or creature flooded her being. In the blink of an eye, it became so large that it filled her field of vision, as if she was directly on it.

'Control your emotions. This is difficult. Do you desire help?'

Elation sprang through Illa. The voice she heard was clear, steady, and female.

'Oh, yes, please! Where am I? Am I dead?'

She could feel mirth from the presence. *'No, child. You are not dead. You are between.'*

That registered. Lebuin had taken her *between* before, but that was the place between life and some other place souls went after death. When she'd been there before, it looked like a library. In fact, it was the Mage's Guild library in Llino, where Lebuin felt the safest.

'I'm between on my own? Can I do anything about this?'

'With concentration, you may form your experience however you choose. If you allow it, you can share your reality with others that are close to your essence here. When you do this, they will appear within your world, but their appearance is theirs to control.'

With the words came knowledge that merged into her being, giving her understanding of what needed to be done.

I'm not dead. I'm between! Okay, like a mage, I can form my own existence.

Unable to think of anything appropriate, she imagined the grass plains where she grew up. Holding the image, like she'd been taught the mages did, and as the shared knowledge indicated, she tried to create her own reality.

Illa stood on the top of a knoll. Before her were rolling hills of grass, dotted with trees, and some mountains off in the distance. She saw a tall black woman with bright white eyes, who was dressed in a northern, flowing fur dress with a red shawl that glistened in the sunlight.

The sun was warm on Illa's skin. Looking down, she blushed as she realized she was completely naked.

Why didn't I imagine clothes for me?

The woman smiled and said, "Good. These are the plains of southern Laeusia. I recognize them."

Trying to cover herself up, she realized it was her own thoughts that controlled the image, so she added her favorite hunting outfit to the pictures she held in her head.

Illa was dressed in hunting leathers with her knives on her belt. However, a golden thread connected to her torso floated in the air before her. She tried to grab it, but her hands passed through it.

"What is this?" She pointed to the thread.

"That is the way to your God."

"To Lebuin?"

The lady nodded.

"Who are you?"

"I am not known to you. My name is Lolenda. I am the Goddess of the Rhonian Empire."

"Why are you helping me?"

"We're all watching. I happened on your presence first."

The ambiguity of the answer irked Illa. She snapped, without thinking that she was talking to a God. "Why not help directly?"

"In time. Failing is not an end, unless you let it consume you. You are centered. Return to your realm by the silver thread, or find your God by the golden thread. It's your choice."

"Wait! I didn't mean to snap." But the Goddess had faded.

Illa stamped her foot, enjoying the feeling of having a foot to stamp again.

These Gods could help more if they wanted to.

She turned around and saw the silver thread Lolenda

spoke of. It stretched out into a small grove of trees. She was surprised she could see where each thread went, no matter how far it had to travel. The golden thread was connected to a small building with a single door.

I need to help Lebuin. I suppose I should take advantage of this and see if he has any instructions.

It took some time, or perhaps little time, to trek to where the gold thread led her. It was a humble shack, with a thatched roof and rough wood door. There was no lock, just the latch. She lifted her hand to knock, but instead, she lifted the latch and entered.

Inside, it was a completely different building. She was awestruck by the palatial library, with marble floors and many soft, comfortable chairs. Three levels were interconnected by spiraling, filigreed wrought iron staircases with gold rails. From the entry, she could see more than one cavernous room of bookshelves. There were three wide halls with actual suits of armor, enormous tapestries, and gold-framed paintings covering the walls.

Shaking her head at the size of the place, Illa wondered if that was Lebuin's brain, or his version of it. The golden thread led into the depths of the library. She roamed the halls, following the thread from one room to another. In each area, books were stacked up on the tables, as if someone had been reading them, but not putting them back.

She stopped to examine a few. The first were history books and almanacs from places she'd never heard of. But in the second room, they were what she assumed to be fictional works. They were stacked high, with publications marked as different kinds of novels. She paused to read the first few pages, and found that they were almost all adventure books.

A frown began to appear, and it got deeper as she followed the golden thread into the library, past multiple heaps of adventure novels.

Has he been here this whole time, reading useless stories from other nations? We have been fighting our way to Elraci to stop the coming catastrophe, and he's sitting in here with his nose in this junk?

She started picking books off the pile, reading the titles aloud. With each one, she got louder.

"In Honor's Name! The Wizard of Rhine! The Adventures of Huckleberry Finn! UNDER THE VOLCANO! THE ILIAD!"

Her heart was pounding so hard, she could feel little else. Her vision sharpened, and as she looked around at the vast room filled with books, she couldn't believe they were all fiction. Moving over to the nearest shelf, she scanned the titles. The throbbing in her head continued to get stronger, as she saw they were all on some kind of energy engineering.

Her blood started to boil as she remembered the days of riding, watching over Lebuin's body, worried about why he hadn't awoken or even moved. She stomped so loudly that her footfalls reverberated around the chamber. Looking at them again, she hoped at least one would not be a fantasy.

By the time she got to the end of the stacks, her hands were clenched so tightly, she could feel her nails digging into her skin. She stomped her foot one last time and swung her arm at the offensive heaps of wasted time. Instead of landing in a satisfying mess on the floor, the books all flew off to the shelves, putting themselves away.

Her anger exploded at that last insult. Lebuin sitting there reading fiction was one thing, but the fact that he couldn't be bothered to clean up his own mess, when all he had to do was toss the book in the air, broke the dam holding her emotions under control.

A scream erupted from her as she turned. The sheer primal rage of the sound was like a call to action. Mind burning, fists clenched, and ready to strike, she leapt in the direction of the golden thread. With her feet pounding, all she wanted was to finish the trek, find Lebuin, and hold him accountable for hiding.

In moments, she came upon Lebuin, lying sideways in a

chair, with one book open in his hand and a stack on the floor next to a glass of wine.

She screamed so gutturally that it felt like her throat ripped slightly in the effort. The volume of the sudden shriek caused Lebuin to jump out of the chair, knocking over the wine and scattering the collection of novels. She raced at him with her hands formed into claws, ready to rend him for hiding there.

"ILLA! WHAT ARE...? I CAN EXPLAIN!" was all Lebuin managed to yell before she pounced on him.

"WE ARE FIGHTING FOR OUR LIVES, AND YOU ARE LOUNGING AROUND, DRINKING WINE, AND READING FANTASIES! I SWORE MY LIFE TO YOU!" She grabbed him, jerked him up, and held him in the air before her, shaking him like a rag doll. He had no weight in the odd place, which added to her anger.

Lebuin was flopping around, wide eyed, as she raged at him. Finally, she tossed him aside, into a pile of books. As they took to the air, Illa remembered the other affront. "AND YOU COULDN'T EVEN CLEAN UP AFTER YOURSELF!" She kicked the ones he had by his chair, and they all flew off, heading for their shelves.

Lebuin had regained his feet and was staring at the scene with his mouth hanging open. He grabbed one from another stack and tossed it into the air, jaws still agape, as it also flew off to find its shelf. "I didn't know they did that."

Illa's blood hadn't stopped boiling, and Lebuin wasn't helping matters, just standing there.

"Of all the men I have ever known, you are the absolute worst! Stay here, for all I care! I'm done!"

She whirled around, and her mind latched onto the silver thread. With a snap, she was in her body. It was incredibly hot, and she started sweating instantly. After ripping off all the ropes that loosely bound her to a cot, she stood up. She was in a cave, and sounds were coming from nearby, through a passage. She followed it out, stomping. Ticca, Nigan, and the other Daggers were around a cooking fire, eating some kind of meat on skewers. She stamped up to them and noticed that Nigan had a pile of bones on the ground in front of him.

"MEN!" she screamed. She then glared at all the stunned men there and stalked out of the only exit she could see.

The Arch

CHAPTER 8
HARD CHOICES

LEBUIN STARED AT THE EMPTY spot where Illa had just been standing. His heart was still pounding, and he felt his face and ears burning red.

She didn't even give me a chance to explain.

He looked at the stacks of books. For the first time, he noticed how many there were in his "already read" pile. He wondered how many she'd encountered.

Dog-earing the page, he closed the book he'd been reading and started walking back along his path.

How long have I been here?

He recalled all the books he'd read and tried to figure out the time there versus the time in the real world. He didn't have enough experience to know. He was ashamed that he hadn't really thought about it before.

I figured I had been here maybe one day, but Illa was pretty angry. I must have been here a lot longer than that. I should've returned when the pain pulled me back.

He recalled the hurt that had hit him so hard he'd almost snapped over into the physical realm. But that hadn't been real. He'd barely had time to consider, and he was really mad at having his book interrupted. In a blur, he'd directed his power roughly at the offending people and then fled to the library again, away from the pain. He wasn't sure what had happened, because he'd fought so hard to stay here that his senses hadn't completely aligned with the physical.

He sat down in the next chamber and gazed at the hundreds of books stacked around the chair.

Why should I go back? Everything I could ever want is right here in my family's library. I can't be hurt here between. *I don't need to eat, sleep, or anything else.*

He eyed his nice silver doublet. His fingers traced

the patterns on his blue trousers. As he stood up, a mirror appeared before him, showing his elegant attire. He looked himself over from top to bottom. There he was, as muscled as his younger brother. He knew he was almost six feet tall, but he seemed taller in the mirror. His green eyes no longer had that tired, sunken appearance. In fact, his whole face was relaxed and perfect. He loved the way his light brown hair was trimmed short, Dagger-style.

With his filled-out frame, he looked regal in the silver patterned doublet, and royal blue slacks with a perfect crease down the front and a red stripe down each side. Soft, shiny black riding boots complemented the entire ensemble.

In the physical world, there's grime, pain, killing, and suffering.

As he glanced around, he felt his stomach tighten.

I'm hiding here. This is what I wanted before I met Ticca.

The thought of Ticca brought her image to his mind. He recalled how attractive she was, no matter what she did. *She never seems to put any thought into her outfits. Though always dressed for a fight, in that style of hers, she's also unrealistically beautiful. Even when she brandishes knives, sweating and covered in dust, she manages to look like....* He stopped on that thought.

She's the empress. She's a royal woman, yet she didn't want anyone to know. She didn't seem at all interested in going to Gracia to take the throne.

He picked up a book and turned it over, glancing at the hand-drawn picture of a spaceship on the cover.

I've been wasting my time here. Ticca would never have sat here reading even one book, let alone.... He tried to count how many he'd read and lost track. *Well, more than a few thousand.*

Standing, he picked up an armful of books and threw them in the air. They raced off towards their shelves.

I should put things away.

Lebuin ran as fast as he could through all the chambers he'd been in, lifting the stacks of books and throwing them into the air to be sent back to their places. It took longer than he thought it would, and with each chamber, the guilt inside built up.

As he stood in the main entrance, he considered his next steps.

I'll have to apologize.

He started pacing back and forth, trying to think of a reasonable explanation. But regardless of what he came up with, they all sounded hollow, especially when he tried them out loud.

He looked back into the library. He could feel an almost tangible pull towards it.

Maybe they can figure it out without me. I can just stay here forever.

The word *forever* stopped him. He glanced again at the books. Being there was not the right thing to do, and he knew it. It was the easy thing to do. There was nothing preventing him from simply letting his body go. He could hold himself there indefinitely, but he'd be alone.

Illa had pulled him out of the novels, making him realize how much time he'd spent there alone. Alone…. He'd been alone most of his life. That was what had really been bothering him about his family and those around him. They all lived with their families, they had friends, and his brother was even engaged. As much as he'd tried to make everyone believe he was okay with being alone, it wasn't what he wanted. That was the draw of those books. They told fantastic tales, but in them all, the characters had at least one close friend who shared in the adventures, pain, and joys of life. Those friends were there, no matter what. He knew exactly who he wanted to be there for him. But first, he needed to be there to cover their backs. There were people he didn't even know who were dying in a war which they had no part in making, but he might have a major role in stopping.

And, of course, there was Ticca. She wouldn't have stayed there at all.

Recalling the Dagger mottos Ticca lived by, he said them aloud. "Never give up! Never fail to do what is right! Never willingly accept second place!"

If I want Ticca to be by my side, I must also be at her side. I have to earn respect.

He turned his back on the library. Placing his hand on the door handle, he pulled it open, looking at the swirling colors of *between.*

"I will not hide in here alone forever!"

Holding Ticca's image in his mind, he stepped out. He made sure the library doors sealed, and watched as they faded into the colors, blending in with the rest of the space around them.

Willing himself back to the physical realm, he felt his body start to move. As he opened his eyes, he saw that he was in a cave of some sort. He realized that he was tied to a cot, although the bindings were more to keep him from falling out than to restrain him.

He reached to untie them and stopped. His hands were glowing. He held them up before his face and turned them over. His skin was uniformly illuminated. As he pulled his sleeve up, he saw his arm was also glowing. He looked inside and found that he had hundreds of additional energy channels in a web under his skin, throughout his whole body. An astounding amount of mana pumped and circulated through this web-work. The radiance was caused by a small amount of residual burn that came from that energy circulating though his system.

I've never even heard of anything like this. How did this happen?

The energies didn't burn, and he could see that he could tap them at any time. *It's like the Argos collector's network of channels. I must have somehow created these channels when I was filtering off the power from the Nhia-Samri base.*

Feeling even guiltier about hiding in the library, he started working on the knots that held him down. It only took a moment to loosen the ropes and stand up, but in that time, he started sweating profusely. The temperature felt high enough to boil water.

He stood, holding his hands before him, still looking at the golden glow emanating from his skin. He heard some muffled voices from nearby and saw a flickering light on the far wall past a bend in the cave or passage he was in.

Ticca, dagger out, came bounding around the wall, where the light and voices told him the rest of the team had to be. She must have heard some of the noises he made and came to investigate.

When she saw him, she screeched, and her eyes lit up like twin suns. Her dagger miraculously shifted to its sheath as she rushed to him, arms out, not bothering to stop. She jumped up, slamming into him and wrapped her arms around him tightly to hold herself head-high on him.

She was wearing a loose shirt over riding pants, and her clothes were dripping wet with sweat. Her outfit was stained with dirt, and where it wasn't wet, it was caked in dust. She'd been eating something a little greasy, as her face had smear marks from the food. Her hair was slicked to her head. As he breathed in, he had to fight not to grunt at the stench that hung in the air from her body. But to Lebuin, none of that mattered. In his eyes, she was incredibly beautiful He grabbed her back and hugged her hard.

He tried to say something but found his throat was too tight to speak. So instead, he just enjoyed being with her. He'd been gone a long time and hadn't realized how much he missed her until that moment. Her feet were dangling in the air as she clung to his chest, and she felt as light as a feather.

His heart rate soared at her touch. The hug was so tight that her dagger and two throwing knives were digging into his belly, but he didn't mind. He could feel her heart pounding, too, and it soothed and excited him like nothing he'd ever known.

Ticca looked into his soul. "I've missed you." Her lips

connected with his, and electric shocks ran through his body at the taste. Her feet lifted up behind her.

The sound of running feet approached, and Ticca pulled her head back, breaking the kiss. She closed her eyes, and her brow tightened. She released him, and he let her drop back to the ground. She stepped away with pain evident on her face.

Confused, he started to move towards her, but she sensed it, and her hand shot up to hold him back. "No, this isn't right. Sorry. I lost control when I saw you."

Before he could comment, Ditani came around the wall. He was also caked in dirt and sweat. His face lit up with a huge smile, and he tossed his head back and screamed an oscillating Karakian ritual cry. Accelerating his approach, he slammed into Lebuin, gripping him in a bear hug and picking him up off the ground.

"Lebuin, thank the Lords and Ladies you've come out of it!"

Behind Ditani, the rest of the team was filtering in. The area became noisy and crowded. Everyone wanted to hug him or slap his shoulder. They all talked at the same time, and the pandemonium showed no signs of letting up.

In the chaotic mix, a smiling Nigan waded in and pushed his way through the team. Holding up one hand, he pointed to Lebuin with his other. "Not to ruin the mood, but are you entirely safe?"

Laughing, Lebuin said, "Yes, I think so. This is just stored energy from that base. Now that I'm back, I'll try to figure out how to stop looking like a lantern."

The team cheered, and the joyful greetings and chatter started again. As Lebuin watched them, he could feel tension behind the ebullience.

It's like they needed something positive. Things must have been depressing as of late. Lebuin tried to ignore the feeling in the pit of his stomach. *And when they hear what I have to tell them, even this moment might be dulled for them.*

Ditani grabbed Lebuin's shirt and managed to pull him,

and the rest of the team, out of the sleeping area of the cave into a large, open cooking and eating area. Nigan handed Lebuin some roasted meat on a stick, and they all settled onto rock seats or sat on the ground, leaning against the wall. Lebuin noticed almost all of them were getting as much contact with the stone as possible, to combat the heat.

As he looked around, he saw that Sabri, Coedy, Epion, Illa, and, surprisingly, Ticca, weren't around.

Where did Ticca go? She was just here.

Assuming the other Daggers were out scouting, he ate slowly as Nigan began filling him in on everything that had happened so far. He practically choked when he learned that the missing Daggers had been killed in a Nhia-Samri trap, which he'd saved the team from after Illa had taken what should have been a fatal strike. His feeling of guilt continued to grow throughout the whole narrative.

"Then Illa surprised everyone, walking out here, maybe ten minutes before you came around. I don't know what happened to her, but she screamed at us and then went outside. I tried to follow her, but she threw one of her knives at me." Nigan held up a knife as evidence.

Carda laughed and patted Nigan's shoulder. "If she was mad at you specifically, that would've hit more than the ground between your feet. Don't worry. When she calms down, we'll find out what got her so spun up."

Lebuin swallowed and glanced at the cave entrance. *Me. That's what she's mad about. She didn't tell them, which means I still have to say something.*

"You might," Nigan said with a smirk. "But ladies don't usually explain things like this to men." Ditani, Risy, and Lebuin chuckled, which elicited scowls from Carda, Fersa, and Malla.

Nigan diverted attention away from himself. Looking at Lebuin, he asked, "So what happened to you? We only saw the pillar of fire, and when we found you, you were in a wide, burned pit. Let's just say it left a lot for speculation on our part." He gestured at Lebuin's glowing body.

Lebuin's throat tightened, and his stomach tensed, doing a few flips to be sure it was felt. *Oh, Lords! What do I say? Illa is furious with me, and if I tell the truth, the rest of the team will be just as mad. They've been carrying my hide across hundreds of miles and mountains, assuming I was injured.*

Swallowing, he tried again to find a way to spin the story so it wouldn't sound so bad. The team had settled into comfortable positions, awaiting his response.

"Uh...." He felt his face flushing, not that it would be noticeable with the glowing energies. Still, he glanced around.

Ditani's brows narrowed.

Oh, urd. He knows I did something stupid. Lords, what should I say?

He felt like he was spinning, and the world was waiting for him to fall off. Many possible excuses about delving into the other realm came to him. He even considered claiming the vast power knocked him out; he could say he was healing and had no real memory of the past few weeks.

A memory of Ticca sitting across a cheery camp fire came to him. It had been in those wonderful weeks when they'd first fled Llino, and Ticca had started training them as Dagger recruits. She'd looked so radiant as she retold the Dagger legends. Her voice was clear in his mind. *'The hardest thing about being a Dagger is doing what's right. There are times it will burn so bad that you falter. But this is the core. If you ever choose to ignore it, it will be you who suffers the most. You must never fail to do what you know is right.'*

Looking Ditani in the eye, he sighed. "I'm really very sorry to you all."

Ditani's eyes softened, although his brow still tensed in expectation of something he wouldn't like.

Lebuin met every person's eyes solidly, trying to keep his back straight and desperately hoping they would forgive him and understand. Everyone had a different expression, but he knew that in a moment, they would all show disapproval.

"I made a terrible choice. I thought I was going to die when I diverted the power at the Nhia-Samri base through myself. It burned so badly that at the end, as soon as I knew Ticca was safe, I fled. I didn't want to deal with the pain, or to find out that I had been wrong, and hadn't saved anyone except myself."

He poked at the fire with the stick his roasted meat had been on. It flared, and no one said a word. They were all perfectly quiet, and he imagined their judging eyes upon him.

Now that he'd started, Lebuin knew he had to finish. He glanced around and realized that none of them had a judgmental look. They had neutral faces, except for Nigan, who still wore his perpetual smile. He waved the knife he was holding, saying without words, *'Don't stop now. Finish what you must.'*

"I left my physical body behind, and went to a place Argos had given me access to. Imagine the grandest building in the world. It's unbelievably beautiful, and it's a library. It has volumes of books from thousands of races, including lost knowledge from before this universe was created. Can you imagine all that knowledge? It's all there. The knowledge, histories, and stories of a thousand lands. And there was no pain, no hunger. Only solitude, and books beyond measure. I roamed the halls, and I saw works of art from species I cannot even begin to describe. There is this fountain that...."

Nigan tossed another log on the fire, jarring Lebuin from his rambling. When Lebuin looked at him, Nigan widened his eyes and jerked his head, as if to say, *'Get on with it.'*

Stalling for time, Lebuin cleared his throat. "But that doesn't matter. I left you here to deal with this mess, while I hid in that complex, reading."

They glanced at each other, keeping their thoughts to themselves, until Ditani finally broke the silence, asking, "Did you discover anything useful in all this reading?"

Lebuin winced. "Well, I started reading some engineering and science books, but...." He searched their faces for any sign of support. Many were frowning.

Ditani poked him in the shoulder. "But?"

Shoulders slumping, Lebuin said, "But then I discovered the library had these adventure novels."

A few of them gasped. Lebuin wasn't sure who, but it didn't matter; all of them looked shocked. Nigan was slowly turning over the dagger Illa had thrown at him, his eyebrows riding high, near his short military bangs.

Silence, broken only by popping from the fire, stretched on. Lebuin swallowed, knowing he had to tell the final bit.

"I could've come back whenever I wanted. Time flows differently there. I thought I was stretching it, so I wouldn't be there long, compared to here. I really thought I would only be there for a day or two. When Illa found me, I realized I'd been there longer than I thought."

Ditani stood. The look on his face was unreadable. "Lebuin, how long did you stay there?"

Lebuin forced out in a squeaky voice, "I lost track, but I'm sure it wasn't more than fifteen years."

They all reacted. His eyes were so full of tears that he couldn't tell who did what. Some made choking sounds, and others went to the back of the cave. He knew Ditani had silently turned and walked out.

"I'm sorry," he said, with his head hung low.

"You ran and left us," Ticca said. "Do you expect us to forgive that so easily?"

Lebuin jumped up, turning around. Next to Ticca stood Illa.

How long have they been there?

Wiping his eyes, he took in the two ladies. Both Ticca and Illa were covered in dirt and sweat. They'd lost weight, and their clothes, once wonderfully fitted, hung loosely on their bodies. Ticca had the hollow, sunken eyes of someone who was starving, while Illa appeared to be in a little better shape.

Lords and Ladies, they look horrible. This hasn't been an easy trek, made even harder by having to carry me. While I read, they worked, and friends died. Even worse, I slowed the team down so much that maybe we won't be able to help end the war.

He started to turn away, but realized that wasn't the right thing. Instead, he tried to face them, but couldn't get his eyes to lift from the ground for more than a second. He wiped his tears on the back of his hand and attempted to look at them.

His one encouragement was that neither turned from him, although both their faces were streaked from crying.

Ticca shook her head after a minute of staring at him. With a glance at Illa, which seemed to indicate that she should speak first, Ticca walked past him, towards the rear of the cave.

As he scanned the area, he realized that only he and Illa remained in that section of the cave. Illa was slowly breathing through her nose. Ice blue eyes locked on him. Her face was a mask, revealing none of the thoughts and emotions that were boiling in her mind.

He could feel that she tried to find something to explain his behavior. But in failing to find any forgiveness she was pushing him out of her mind and building walls against him. She needed to find her balance again. He knew she'd taken her role as his high priestess seriously. All of her training as a Nhia-Samri had taught her the importance of following through on every commitment. In exchange, she was guaranteed that her superiors would do the same. Failure to perform was unacceptable, and even if it meant your death, you did what you were ordered to do. As Lebuin was seen as a new kind of God, a Dagger God, Runa-Illa had applied all that commitment to learning to follow the Dagger ideals, which Lebuin had utterly failed to follow himself.

Unsure about what to do, he glanced towards the back of the cave.

"She said you changed her, just as you changed me. But now, I think you've broken her." Illa's voice was so soft, he barely heard it. The words cut, but he forced himself to keep looking at her.

"I didn't mean...."

"This, I already know. Tell me, *my Lord*. Why come back now? Surely, being discovered by an insignificant, foolish follower couldn't change the will of a *God*."

He couldn't meet her eyes; the guilt was too strong. He dropped his head, looking at the ground, and shrugged. "You're not insignificant or foolish. I am, because it took you to tell me what I should have already known. I came back because it was the right thing to do." It came out barely a whisper.

She stepped closer to him, putting her legs into his field of view.

"Not good enough. The right thing was to never stay there. The right thing would have been to find me lost in the colored realm *between*. Instead, you stayed in your library. Lolenda is the one who found me and guided me to safety. If I hadn't come to you, would you be here now?"

Lebuin knew the answer as she asked the question, and he could feel she knew the answer, too. Shame washed over him, and he started to turn away. Illa stepped even closer and grabbed his arm, preventing him from turning. Her grip was light, and any amount of pressure would have broken it, yet he felt as if he'd been chained into place with iron bands.

"I would've come back eventually." Even as he said it, he knew there was no forgiveness or value in the rationalization.

"Did you even check on me in all the time you were there?"

Lebuin nodded, but not hard. "A few times, just to see if you were still alive, when I first got there."

"Lolenda said something that didn't make sense at the time. But now I know it was meant for you."

Lebuin looked up at Illa, waiting for the final rebuke.

Illa's eyes locked onto his; her lips remained tight, and he could see that her face and shoulders were tensed.

After a quick pause, she said, "Failing is not an end, unless you let it consume you."

Yes, that was for me.

He placed his free hand on her shoulder. "I failed you. I will not let it happen again."

She pushed his hand off her shoulder and her face remained hard, like cold granite. "Lebuin, these Daggers are your followers. Your duty is to serve the world and Argos. All they ask is that what they do for you is not in vain. I'm not sure I can serve you now."

Releasing his arm, she walked past him, not turning to look at him again. Lebuin fell to his knees and ran his hands through his hair. Forcing the tears back, he pushed his feelings down.

I can fix this. I have to regain their trust. Never again.

He sat up straighter, and stared out into the blazing sunlight outside of the cave.

"Never again. I will never fail to do the right thing again. I will prove myself to them."

"If you're finished with the self-loathing, there's work to be done." Ticca's voice was surprisingly close, and he jumped back to his feet, spinning around to face her.

Ticca had changed into a semi-clean cotton shirt, and was near the back of the cave, trying to look casual as she leaned against the wall. Illa stood next to her. Lebuin could sense the tension there — Ticca eyes were as intense as when she was in a serious fight. Illa was frowning and leaned away from him glancing at Ticca impatiently.

He started to walk towards Ticca, but she held up her hand to stop him. "Do not get close to me right now I'm just as pissed off at you as Illa is, although she has even more right than I have. I'm only your hired Dagger. She's the closest thing to a real friend you have, and you left her to hang out there."

Lebuin stepped back and stood straight. "I won't fail either of you again."

Ticca's grunt was non-committal. Illa's silence was even worse.

After looking him up and down, Ticca said, "You've put on a lot of muscle mass for someone who's been lying around in a cot for almost three weeks. One thing, before I take you anywhere near what I want to show you."

He waited for her to continue. His mind kept replaying that electric kiss. Less than half a mark ago, she'd been willing to wrap herself around him with so much joy at being reunited. But at this point, he'd be lucky if she'd continue to work for him even one second past this mission. He resolved to remain hopeful that he could win her back again. He knew she hadn't been there for his confession to the team, but he was also sure Illa had told her everything.

When he just stood there, her face contorted, and she gestured to his whole body. "Are you going to do something about that?"

He glanced down at his glowing hands, remembering he looked a bit like a lantern on low burn. "I seem to have created some new magic channels in my skin. They're acting kind of like a canteen for water. I didn't do this on purpose. In fact, I thought I'd channeled away all the energies from that attack."

Illa straightened a little. Her face was still neutral, but her eyes shone with hope. "You don't feel different. How much of the magic were you able to store in the collector? Do you think you have enough power to defend against a Nhia-Samri mage now?"

His jaw dropped open. *Oh, Lords! Urdu, why didn't I think of that? I could have channeled a lot of energy to the collector!*

Even though he didn't answer, Illa's eyes went wide. "You didn't keep the magic?"

With a little snort, Ticca said, "Well, he was kind of in a hurry."

Illa stomped her foot. "Power! Power has been our primary focus for cycles. And you could have collected a lot." Her hand twitched, and her lips tightened into a line. She shook her head. "I need to get my knife back." Her whole body quivering, she turned, stepping past Ticca and heading into the back of the cave.

Ticca hadn't moved, but she snickered, trying to not laugh.

"What's so funny?"

She shook her head as her eyes teared up. "Nothing.' For a brief flash, she looked like she had in those weeks when they trained in the woods and thought that only some hired Knives were after him. But then weariness and anger fell back over her features. She pointed to his skin.

"Do you have that under control? There's something I need to show you."

He shrugged. "As far as I know, I do. But I only discovered this change in me less than a mark ago. I believe it's under control. I do understand what it is. I just can't explain how I did it. Do you want me to figure this out before showing me?"

Ticca stared at him a bit longer, her face hardening and softening like waves in the ocean. He knew she was trying to decide something, but for the first time since he met her, she was uncertain. It was almost terrifying to see her struggling with a choice.

She jerked her head towards the back of the cave, opposite of where the bedding had been, and started walking that way, grabbing a spare torch and lighting it as she went.

"We need your opinion on what Nigan found. I ask that you be careful. If it's dangerous, I want to get everyone away safely."

That got his attention. The heat and sweat forgotten, he stepped lightly after her. *I wonder what they've found already. We might not have to go into the desert if this is what the Nhia-Samri discovered.*

He had to suppress the urge to hurry to Ticca as they

went past the lantern-lit sleeping area. The sleeping area was far enough inside the mountain that the temperature had dropped to merely 'hot', and the team was all there, broken up in pairs of three, talking. When Ticca walked by, they didn't look at her; all eyes turned to him as conversations stopped. His chest tightened, and he recalled their shocked faces when he'd told the truth.

If I could go back and do it again, I'd ignore the library. But I can't do that. This is my mess, I made it, I have to clean it up…if I can.

Nigan and Illa were well away from everyone else and almost in complete darkness, until Ticca's torch illuminated the pair. Illa was holding a knife between them in the palm of her open hands. Nigan's brows were drawn tightly together, but he smiled at Lebuin and Ticca as they drew near.

Illa huffed, and with a menacing glance at Lebuin, she grabbed Nigan's hand and pulled him away, towards the front of the cave.

I hope she doesn't take out her anger towards me on Nigan.

At back of the sleeping area, the cave narrowed into a passage. Although not wide, it was tall. Lebuin could almost touch both walls with his arms out to the sides, yet the ceiling never came closer to his hands than ten feet, sometimes rising to roughly twenty feet.

In the flickering firelight, the stone walls and floor looked natural. However, the passage sloped downward at a fixed angle, which didn't seem to vary. There was a series of 90-degree right turns; at each turn, they saw a side passage to the left that went straight for a short distance, then performed two snake-like bends, opening up into a fair-sized cavern. The distance from one corner to the next decreased with each progressive length.

Ticca gave him time to poke his nose into each cavern-like room before jerking her head back towards the main passage. Lebuin ran his hand over the semi-rough stone, not finding a single mortar joint. In spite of the rough rock appearance, the

90-degree turns and identical snake bends clearly spoke of a purposeful design.

The tunnel ended at an arched entry that opened into a cavern. The final arch was the first thing that didn't look natural. A faint odor of plants hung in the air. Lebuin stopped and sniffed. Ticca turned and waited.

"Did you bring the horses down here?" he asked.

Ticca shook her head and stepped next to Lebuin. "No. Why?"

"I could swear I smell hay."

Sniffing the air, Ticca walked into the cavern. Lebuin followed her in.

The scent of many horses came to him, along with those of the barn. He smiled and glanced at the princess walking beside him. She was lovely, with her brown curly hair pulled up in a bun, letting a few strands fall down the side of her face. She was wearing a riding outfit in red silks, with a layered petticoat. Her shiny, tall riding boots were soft and well-worn.

"Your Highness, thank you for inviting me on your daily ride."

Ticca's laugh was like the singing bells of the temple. "Lord Lebuin, you would've been terribly put out if I hadn't."

He laughed, too. "Have you told your father yet?"

Ticca glanced around to make sure none of the grooms were close. "Lebuin, please. We need to pick the right time to approach the emperor." Her eyes sparkled, and he was sure several devious plots spun through her head. "What about you? Have you told *your* father yet?"

He stole a kiss before answering. "Yes, but my grandfather might need some convincing."

She danced away from his embrace, giving him a look that said, *try to do that again if you dare.* "I'm sure we can overcome those obstacles."

He started to move after her, but she called for a groom's assistance. Three tall grooms came in answer to her call.

Lebuin laughed and gave her a *just wait till we're riding* look. Her smile said all he needed to know, and he contented himself with preparing their horses. The light greenish-brown skinned elven grooms laughed as they spoke to the horses and helped tighten the saddle buckles. One knelt, offering the princess his knee and hand to mount by.

Ticca performed a rather acrobatic jump into her saddle. The groom lifted his leg as Ticca launched from it, giving her a practiced boost. Ticca landed with that spread-leg jolt she used to make the male riders wince involuntarily. She giggled and pointed to Lebuin. He bowed and executed his own acrobatic mount. The grooms began to lead the horses out of the barn doors, into the wide-open grassy plain behind the palace.

Wait. This isn't right. Memories of where they'd been came back to him in a flash. Turning, he saw Ticca was sitting on her horse, staring at him in shock.

The torch lay on the ground at Ticca's feet, and was starting to go out. Confused, he picked it up. Ticca had stepped back and was leaning against the stone wall.

"Did you...? I mean, were we just someplace else?"

With saucer eyes, Ticca nodded.

"Horses?" he asked.

Again, she nodded.

Lebuin examined himself. He seemed fine, except for the glowing. He noted that his clothes were soaked with sweat and sticking to his thick, muscular form.

I'm more fit than my brother. Ticca wasn't kidding about that.

When he looked back at her, she was staring at him, but with a far-off look in her eyes. She held one hand to her face as her fingers lightly touched her lips, then refocused on him.

"That's the second time I've been somewhere else since getting near the desert."

He stood, and waited for more details.

"The first, I knew instantly I was having a vision or

something odd. I was dressed in something unbelievably fine on the tall balcony of a blue marble palace. Ditani's voice came to me on the wind, and I was back here. Except that I know precisely where that palace is. I can take us there."

Lebuin didn't know what to make of it. "Did we just get ready to go horseback riding?"

"Yes. And we were talking about telling our fathers something. You kissed me."

Lebuin stood taller. "You kissed me a little while ago. I.... Well, I...." He couldn't get it out.

"Something happened to you and me. After the Nhia-Samri base, I thought I'd lost you. But more than that, it hurt. Then we found you. And you...."

Lebuin waited for her to finish the sentence. After a second, her face hardened and she started to straighten up.

"I what?" he pressed her.

Ticca pushed herself off the wall and stepped up to him, standing toe to toe. She looked up into his eyes. "You've put a spell on me or something. These feelings I have are too intense to be natural. I've been fighting them ever since we found you. You put me in a spin. I can't think straight. I can't act right when you're close. I don't know which way is up. Urdu, I'm not even able to stay mad at you, even though you deserve it!"

As the distance between them melted away, he felt an intense desire to kiss her again. Her head was tilted up to him, and her eyes locked on his. Like an inescapable gravity, his head started to bend down. They stared into each other's eyes as sparks seemed to fly between them.

Just before their lips touched, she pushed away from him violently.

"NO! I decide my own destiny!"

"Then what was that?" He waved, indicating the vision. He knew that she knew exactly what he was thinking.

"I don't know. But that wasn't me! It was someone else.

I'm not a princess. Maybe it was some spell you did to trick me."

He stepped back. "I'd never! I don't even know if that's possible. I had nothing to do with that!"

"You said you smelled horses! You took us there."

He sniffed the air, and the musky animal scent was still there. "I do smell horses."

Ticca turned around. "I do, too."

A tall man wearing a formal uniform rode out of the back of the cavern. He carried a strange torch that didn't use fire, but created a bright, non-glaring light. As he approached them, he frowned.

Ticca took a sharp intake of breath and her hand flew to her mouth. She stood straighter, but her face was pale.

"Your Highness, what are you doing here? This is a dangerous...." The rider's eyes landed on Lebuin, going wide as his face went white. "Lord Lebuin! You can't be...." The man and the horse faded, vanishing completely.

Ticca ran to the spot where the rider had been. Kneeling, she examined the clear horse prints in the dirt. Lebuin stepped up next to her.

She looked up. "Look! These aren't just visions. I think they're real. But what do they mean?"

A chill ran through him. "Elraci is unstable. This has to do with Elraci. The Gods are afraid of it. They've locked it down, because none dare to try to fix it. Both Argos and Lothia were sad that I'd have to learn about it. They felt it might be too much."

Ticca stood. "*Unstable* doesn't really describe this. Besides, I knew that man."

Lebuin raised his brow.

"Well, it's no secret. I didn't meet him in person in Llino, but I have seen him a few times. That was Orahda, the weapons master of Aelargo's guards." Her lips tightened and he saw her jaw move slightly. *She's not telling me everything.*

236

"He came from what I wanted to show you. They might be connected" she finished.

She led him to the back of the cavern, where there was a most unusual arch, clearly not natural. It had a black glass-like substance blocking its opening. He felt the truth — the glass was a plug added to prevent passage through it.

There were no other exits from the room. The arch was the focal point and end of the passage. Lebuin examined it, noting its large size and the carving on the stones. Something about it spoke to him on a level above language. He felt a smug attitude emanating from it. It stood proudly here alone, saying, *'Yes, they tried to block me, yet I still stand. This place is for me alone.'*

He stepped up to it and felt power. Shifting to mage sight, he saw that the entire archway was an artifact beyond anything he'd studied. It also contained thousands of glass strands, gold wires, and strange silver plates under its surface.

This is mundane science mixed with magic. Why is this buried in the depths, under this mountain?

An answer he didn't like came almost immediately, as he re-envisioned the path there, the twisting tunnel with open caverns. If an explosion happened there, the power would flow out. But at each bend, the power would flow directly into the chamber before traversing through the sharp corners. It was a containment construction. Looking back at the walls, he saw that they also had magical channels.

The entire tunnel was a blended artifact, strengthened against something this arch could do.

His fingers itched like never before. He wanted to pull the covers off and get a better look at the technology behind this thing. He leaned in to examine it more closely. A faint tart scent with hints of smoke filled his nose from the construction.

That's burnt metal; I know that scent well.

He looked for burn marks, but there were none. Interconnecting magic formulae created a strange array of hundreds, if not thousands, of independent incantations. An unusual grouping of channels on the right side of the archway ended in a series of circular bands on the surface, like an archery target. In addition to its magical properties, there was a significant amount more mundane crystal circuitry in those bands.

His fingers brushed one of the circles. Power surged, drawing his hand to the device. His palm struck the artifact and made an unexpected sound of thunder, which echoed into the cavern and passageway. The surface of the artifact did not feel like stone. It was more like a stiff cake. A strong pull on his hand caused it to press into the suddenly fluid stony surface.

He cried out in shock and terror as magic was ripped from him by the artifact. It had dozens of small tendril channels that pierced his skin and connected to those in his hand. Even more alarming was the feeling of his life being sucked into the archway. Magic flowed from him at a tremendous rate, and he couldn't stop or slow it.

'ARGOS, NUAS ZI MIL,' a voice boomed in his mind. It was chilling and deep, yet it felt familiar. It reminded him of the Argos Artifact's voice, somehow not natural.

He tried to pull away, but the power holding him was stronger than he was. He could feel the level of force holding his hand growing as his power fed into it. He couldn't escape.

Ticca saw his efforts, and realized some of what was happening. She jumped around him to stand between him and the artifact, with her back to him. She grabbed his free arm, wrapping it around her waist, and then placed her back into his chest.

"Hold me and pull!" she yelled.

Fear gave him even more strength. He clamped down on her waist as she lifted her feet, putting them on the face of the artifact. She then slammed into him with all her strength as he yanked backwards.

Pain erupted from every inch of his arm at the pressure.

A sharp stab from his wrist and shoulder added to the torture, making him cry out involuntarily. But their combined force worked — his hand tore free, and they fell.

Ignoring the agony, he untangled himself from Ticca and got his feet under him. Ticca was faster, weapons out she stood defensively facing the device. Lebuin saw that the archway's intricate designs were glowing. Light, like waves of water, flowed over the entire device. On the left side was something that had to be a control panel, with a set of displays. He knew what it was instantly. Although it was technically the first one he'd seen, he'd read enough descriptions of such technology in the library to no longer be confused by them.

He stepped over to that side. Ticca practically knocked him back down.

"Are you insane? Look at your hand!"

Getting his arm to respond, to lift his hand, was more painful than he thought possible. But it did obey. He held his hand up to examine it. Some kind of clear pink liquid was oozing from a dozen holes in his palm, but it didn't look like it would be a serious problem. He wondered what it could be, as he watched it slowly stop. His hand didn't feel bad. Still, he needed to clean it and bandage it soon. Through the drying liquid, he noticed a layer of skin had been peeled off of his palm, revealing tender flesh.

"I'll be okay. That was the feeder port. Now that I can see this thing turned on, I know what some of it is. It recognized me...I think."

Ticca looked back and forth. He tried to gently push her out of the way. "I need to look at the controls before that energy it took runs out. I don't think it got enough to work for long."

Ticca stood aside, but kept her blades out.

He stepped to the controls and looked over the displays. All of them, as well as the labels, were in an ancient version of Imperial.

"This is an Imperial artifact, but it's a blended technology. It has to be Elracian."

Carefully, he touched one of the things he thought was a control for the displays. It changed to show a graph of something. One word caught his attention: *Rellums.* The graph was an energy level readout. Growing more confident, he touched more of the controls, watching what happened, trying to understand what the device showed him.

He noted with his magic sight that his original feelings about the black glass plug were right. It wasn't an original part of the artifact. In fact, it was another magical artifact, now working. It was pulling power from the arch, and sending it somewhere down a conduit that stretched into the distance. Lebuin tried to grab that power and was surprised he could connect to it. With a quick change, he set it up to feed back to him, restoring some of what had been stolen.

As he examined the archway, he saw that it was collecting magic on its own. It had been designed for continuous operation, but the glass plug was pulling that power away faster than the artifact could collect it. The plug would win the race in a short time, but Lebuin would be fed more than had been taken from him by then.

Smiling, he turned his attention back to the control panel. After cycling through the readouts, he found one that was a map, which showed no sign of the Circumveni Desert. Instead, the area that represented the location of the desert was labeled *Elraci,* with dozens of lakes and forests that spanned the entire continent, from east to west. The map showed two highlighted points connected by a line. He guessed the one furthest east was where the team was, assuming they'd headed mostly south from the Nhia-Samri base. It was marked *Origin.*

The line that connected the two dots had a label that read '503.22 km'.

That must mean kilometers. Lebuin tried to remember the ancient measuring system taught in the Guild school. *If it is, then that's about 300 miles.*

The line tilted down at a regular angle, making the other highlighted point west-southwest. More interestingly, that point was due north from the star marker for a large city named Imridu-Nam.

Stepping back, he looked at Ticca. "I think we just found what the Nhia-Samri found. I bet this is a magic gate prototype. According to these controls, it's connected to something here." He slid his finger along the line on the map from what he thought was their location, to the other indicated. "I bet another one of these things is there." He tapped the black glass. "This is a plug designed to keep this thing from working. It might be permanent, or maybe it's like a cork, meant to be pulled out for testing, only put in to keep everything safely turned off when it's not being worked on."

Looking at the map, Ticca said, "I've been taught this language but I don't recall the distance conversion. Do you know it?"

"I was taught it in the Guild. If I remember correctly, 500 kilometers would be about 300 miles. Plus or minus a few."

Ticca looked at him, and her eyebrows lifted slightly. "Good memory; I think you're right. So Imridu-Nam is real. Is this the Elracian language?"

Obviously her family hasn't forgotten its roots.

"Not exactly. This is Imperial. It's the ancient form of it. Languages change over time."

Ticca touched the other dot. "So is this our new destination? I was going to try to find Imridu-Nam. I can't explain why, but I know exactly where it is, and I'm positive the blue marble palace I saw was in the capital."

"If this is to scale, Imridu-Nam is about ninety miles south from whatever this is connected to."

Shaking her head, Ticca said, "That's a very, very long way in the kind of conditions we'll have to travel through in the desert. I'm not thrilled about the 300 miles this seems to suggest we have to go."

Checking his levels, he saw he'd gotten a considerable amount of magic from the Nhia-Samri base and from the plug. His expression reflected his satisfaction.

He touched Ticca's shoulder and, with the brush of a thought, created a layer of cooling and filtering around her. The amount of power it took to hold that incantation was almost nothing, and he activated a second layer for himself. He had more than enough power to do that for the whole team. It would be a slight draw that wouldn't matter much if he had to fight, but it might go a long way to redeeming his recent mistakes.

Ticca's eyes went wide as she registered the suddenly comfortable climate she was in. She looked down and watched the dirt fall from her like rain. Her shirt became clean and stopped sticking to her, slipping off her skin to hang loosely. She shook her head, and dirt slid from her hair, leaving it bright and fresh. She brushed off the dirt, playing with the falling dust and marveling for a full minute at how it didn't stick to her hands, before looking up at Lebuin.

And they thought I was wasting my time with these comfort incantations.

"How about now?"

She tried to frown, but couldn't manage a convincing one. "Are you sure you have the power for this?"

He nodded, and Ticca's frown turned into a smirk as she waved a hand at the map.

"If you can keep this up, then you're right. We could travel between both in about two days, which isn't too far, to maybe find what we need. We still have to get there. Which one first?"

Hiri-Rula's Mirror

CHAPTER 9

TURNING OF THE TIDE

DOHMA OPENED HIS EYES, WHICH was a mistake. Dirt fell into his left one. Further, the effort yielded no useful information. He was still disoriented and unsure of where he was. He closed his eyes again and tried to move his hand to rub the dirt-filled left eye, but his arm didn't move. It was pinned in the general direction of his body, and there was an almost crushing weight on him, making it hard to breathe.

Slowing down his panic, he took a careful inventory of his body. Toes could wiggle, legs could shift slightly, arms and fingers all felt present. If it wasn't for the fact that all his limbs were competing for which could scream most about being twisted, bruised, or otherwise injured, he would consider himself in surprisingly good shape.

He felt like he was upside down, but one arm had been raised to shield his face, and that seemed to be preventing something solid from falling on him, forming an air pocket which smelled of smoke, dirt, and blood. But it could be that the arm was holding him up from falling on his face.

The smell of blood worried him the most, because it was likely that the strong salty smell, mixing with the dust and dirt, was his own life slowly draining away. He had to get free and take a better look.

The existence of the air pocket gave him a lot of hope that he would survive. Also, he knew he was far better off than he should be. *Electra....* He stopped on her name to bask in the love he felt. Electra had sent him vital healing energies, with the help of his brother and sister. How they'd managed that trick, he didn't know. Not being prepared to stop living yet, he was thankful for their amazing feat and intensely curious as to how they'd done it.

Worry about how later, he told himself firmly. *I promised I was on my way. Time to get started.*

Concentrating on the feeling that he was head-down in the dirt, he worked his tongue around enough to make a little spittle. Letting it out of his mouth he concentrated to feel where it went. His upper lip felt wetter and then his nose felt a dot of moisture chill. *I'm head down. I hope.* He tried to move his legs and wiggle backwards praying that was the right direction to get free. It took a few starts and stops, but something fell away from his legs, and they became unhindered.

That small success brought him renewed energy, and after a lot of hard work, he pulled himself out of the hole he was in. In spite of being out of the dirt, it hurt to breathe. He forced himself to take slow, shallow breaths, which helped, but each breath made him gag. It took more willpower not to cough. He recalled the explosion, being thrown like a toy, and losing contact with Duke.

Still blinded by the dirt in his left eye, he realized his right eye had never opened, and was held shut by debris. He shifted his position to get his hands up to his face and wipe the dirt from his eyes. Leaning forward, he slowly probed his eyelids, letting them tear from the pain, which helped remove some of the grit. As his tears flowed, he kept trying to open his left eye, which blinked rapidly, refusing to remain open. He managed to remove the dry, caked-on substance from his right eye as his left slowly cleaned itself till he could glance around.

A shiver of pride at making his eyes work ran through his body — a minor but crucial victory he was pleased to accept. Although his sight wasn't great, he sat up and looked around. The world was white. A heavy fog blocked everything farther than maybe twenty feet around him. Sniffing the pungent, smoky air, he ran his hand through his hair, combing some of the debris out.

There was no hint of fresh forest and green lands there.

Each breath threatened to choke him, and he realized the air was filled with smoke and ash. The ground was random jumble, and strange lumps in the thick layers of ash hinted at the debris beneath the white landscape. He lifted up some of the pale ash and felt it between his fingers as he took in the small circle of reality he existed in. The ash was as fine as the best ground powder; it made his fingers nearly frictionless.

That isn't fog. My Lords and Ladies, what power would turn the world into this?

Tearing a section of his shirt he tied it around his head covering his mouth and nose to filter some of the air. With the cloth filter breathing was easier so long as he didn't take fast breaths. Trying to ignore the devastation, he examined himself. The blood he'd smelled had been his own. Rips and cuts were everywhere in his clothing and armor, yet the skin underneath the blood-soaked spots was the light pink of half-healed wounds.

My wondrous Lady Electra, I must do something truly outstanding for you in thanks.

He dragged himself up to his feet. Muscles and joints recently abused complained, but he knew he would be well enough in a short time.

His sword was gone, and one boot was missing, but he still had his pouch. He opened it and pulled out the compass. It was a tool that he'd gotten many years prior, when he was a lieutenant in the guard. It was bent, smashed, and beyond repair. Sighing, he started to throw it away, but instead he put it back into his pouch and patted the pouch gently.

The sun was up, but it was hidden by the falling ash. As he turned, he realized that there was no hint to tell him where he was in relation to any landmark he might find.

The main camp was east of the base. We attacked from that side. When we fled, I'm pretty sure it was in a straight line easterly. I could walk in circles and die of thirst if I don't get a direction. The camp was five miles from the base. I pray this devastation doesn't extend that far. If I can figure out which way is east, I shouldn't be far from any survivors, and I should be able to get some gear.

He chose a direction and started walking, testing each step before committing any weight to the foot, especially his bare foot. If not for his footprints in the white field behind him, he might have thought he wasn't moving. After an unmeasurable amount of time, he came upon a broken tree. As he approached it, he saw there were more broken branches and stumps. Giant trees had been pushed over, tearing huge root-balls out of the ground.

Stepping up to one such giant, he put his hands on it. It was covered in ash, but it was as real as he was. He pondered the power that could smash such a giant tree down.

We cannot allow this to be used again. I will not allow the Nhia-Samri to continue unchecked.

Leaning on the tree, he looked over it at the other broken or uprooted ones. They all lay in a series beyond the first. It took a few moments to realize two important facts. First, the fog had cleared enough to let him see a few hundred yards. Second, and more importantly, the trees were all laid out parallel.

The force of the explosion pushed them down. The destroyed base would be towards their roots, and... He turned to face the other way. *...our camp should be generally in this direction.*

With renewed energy, he started picking his way through the debris. A sound, the first he'd heard in a while, came from nearby. He stopped and listened for more. It came again: a low, soft neigh. He made his way towards it. On the far side of a tree, two men and a horse were pinned under a limb. He moved over and brushed the ash from the horse's face. It looked at him with its large eyes. Jerking its head, as if saying, *'I'm okay, check them.'*

One of the men wore a grotesque red mask of ash. He'd suffered a head wound that had poured his blood out to mix with the falling residue. Dohma couldn't find a pulse, but that didn't mean much. He wasn't going to give up. The other was breathing. Dohma patted him down, looking for injuries, but couldn't identify anything life-threatening. He didn't recognize the man, but his gear showed he was one of the Daggers from the army.

Dohma started patting the man's face. "Wake up. Time to get to work. C'mon back now." His breathing changed, so Dohma knew he was making progress. His face contorted. Dohma remembered the Dagger motto. "Never give up."

After a few more seconds, the man's eyes opened, and his brows tightened as he tried to focus. Dohma sat back on his haunches as the warrior moved a bit more, lifting his head and looking around.

"What happened?"

Dohma shrugged. "Not exactly sure, but it was a trap to take us out."

The man shifted, and his horse neighed. He put one hand on the animal and checked the neck of the bloody man with the other. "Faint, but he'll live. Shame, now I'm going to listen to his griping for a while."

"I couldn't find a pulse, but I'm glad to hear that."

The man almost smiled. "You might change your mind when you hear his khabing. My leg is pinned under Olly here, and I think the tree has my waist."

Dohma shook his head. "We can talk about this after we get back to camp. Now that I know you're not crushed let's see if I can get you out from under there."

Dohma started looking for a strong enough lever.

The man started working something out from under the unconscious fellow. "I have something that might help.'

With Dohma's assistance, he eventually got a leather satchel out. Smiling, he opened it and produced a camping hatchet. He also took out a small flare and a hunting horn.

Dohma laughed. "That will probably be far more useful than the hatchet."

The Dagger squinted at Dohma. "I agree. Since we

survived, there will be others. You're Lord Dohma, aren't you?"

Dohma started cutting a large branch into a good pole. "Yes. Sorry, I don't know your name."

Waving his hand in a general salute, he said, "Nullo Sidurson, m'Lord. And this," he said, indicating the other man, "is my brother, Essen."

"Sidurson — are you Sidur of Ashkash's sons?"

"Yes, m'Lord. You know of our father?"

"I know your father saved many lives and was instrumental in ending the last war with the Nhia-Samri. I read about him when I was growing up. I spent many days dreaming I was a Dagger under Faltla and Sidur's command."

"Thanks for saying so."

Dohma waved his hand dismissively and finished making a pole.

Putting the horn to his lips, Nullo began to blow a sequence of notes: three long, three short, three long, the age-old cry for help.

When the lever was ready, Dohma worked to cut away the branch that was holding them down. Although small, the hatchet was sharp. He'd already cut through about half of the limb when they heard other horns in the distance.

Warriors gathered, many of them being carried by others who were less wounded. Riders came to the call, as well. Finally the limb was cut enough to allow them to break it. With the aid of some of the others, they used the pole to lift the branch off Nullo and his horse. The horse neighed loudly and then stood, moving around, testing its legs. Nullo stood and stretched, brushing the ash off.

"M'Lord, if I might suggest, why don't you take Olly here back to camp and organize things there? I'll stay here with those who are not heavily injured and start searching for survivors."

Nullo's horse blew its nose, and then nuzzled Dohma.

"I'm not seriously injured. I can stay and help," Dohma said.

"I'm sure. But to be honest, m'Lord, it would do everyone some good if you looked less, um, gutter-dragged. Also, you need another boot."

Dohma had forgotten about the missing boot and looked down at his bare foot. He had to admit that he was far from being inspiring officer material at the moment.

Nullo held out his hand, and Olly stepped over to him. With a loving gentleness, Nullo lifted his brother onto the back of the horse. "Please, m'Lord. Essen needs better care."

As he glanced around, Dohma saw that many of the Daggers were giving looks of approval to Nullo. He gave Nullo his best *I know what you're doing* look. He then took the reins of the horse and climbed up, careful to not jostle Essen.

"All right, but I'll be back shortly. See if you can find Duke. I was with him, but we were separated at the last moment." Dohma pointed, saying, "I came from that direction. You should be able to backtrack a one-shoed man."

"Yes, m'Lord."

He rode slowly as dozens of others followed him. More joined in, and soon they found where the devastation ended. Although the ash still fell, it felt better to ride through the normal grass and trees. The sounds of riders came to him, and he tensed, wondering if the Nhia-Samri were going to ensure that no one survived.

Out of the forest rode teams of warriors, followed by even more people jogging along. He sighed as he noted they were from the encampment. After a few quick exchanges, people were moving the wounded back to camp, and others were being called in to help with the search.

Dohma went to his tent, where he cleaned up. When he finished, he dressed and found a new pair of boots at the front of his pavilion.

The camp was busy with groups of people and horses heading out towards the west. Other groups were returning, their horses laden with bodies. The few living wounded were being brought back in carts.

That had been the largest Nhia-Samri base in Duianna lands. They'd expected at least 30,000 Nhia-Samri warriors to be there, as well as another 50,000 support staff. Duke had committed a large portion of the division to the mission. Their 30,000 Dagger officers had led nearly 100,000 soldiers into the base, attacking from all sides. Another 300,000 warriors were stationed in three rings around and patrolling the fifty-mile-wide area that consisted of the base's lands. The offensive had taken out most of the direct attack forces and many of the patrol and blockade forces.

Dohma spent a full mark touring the hospital tents. Hundreds of stretchers were occupied as more wounded were being brought in. Everyone was trying to clean wounds or provide solace. He found more than a few groups of warriors with their heads down, crying over lost friends or loved ones.

The side of a hill to the north of the hospital tents had been cleared, and more bodies than he could count were laid out in neat rows. Each one was wrapped in a bed roll, and most had a dagger lying on top of the chest. Dozens of Daggers roamed the field, stopping at times to reverently touch the dagger on a body, while fighting to hold back sobs of grief.

There was a continuous procession of honor guard teams for the dead. Daggers had their own rituals for death, as well. Dohma watched the teams. No honor was overlooked for Daggers or guards. Each deceased Dagger was added to the field by a team of nine other Daggers. The teams marched out, one Dagger in front, carrying the dead warrior's bare dagger resting flat on open palms. The lead Dagger stepped with a measured pace, which the others followed precisely.

Behind the lead, six carried the remains. A pair of Daggers, with their own daggers out in a guard position, brought up the rear of the procession, staying two steps behind. They laid the body carefully in one of the rows, at which point the nine would stand around it while the bare dagger was handed around, hilt first, to each person in the procession. The last person to hold the dagger would place it on the chest. The team then returned to camp in the same measured step. For guards, the Daggers gave the same honor guard, except that instead of a dagger, the lead carried a sword or other weapon from the fallen warrior.

Sometimes the honor guard was followed by other warriors. After the honor guard left, the remaining warriors would perform additional honors. Depending on the origin of the deceased, the death honors included placing coins around the head or sheathing the sword.

The Yalthum warriors were the only ones treated differently. They were carried out naked by one of their warrior priests, who was the only one allowed to touch the corpse after being declared dead. The Dagger honor guard escorted the priests, each holding a different part of the ceremony. The priest would lay the remains out and cover the face with a cloth, placing stones around the body. Once completed, it was covered with a special cloth, which Dohma was surprised to learn had been made by a wife, mother, or sister when the warrior had taken up the sword. Yalthum warriors carried their own death shrouds throughout their career.

Dohma looked at row upon row of corpses and the unending procession of others being added. Gracia had thousands of deaths at the assembly battle. But more dead bodies than live warriors were being brought back from the ash fields. His back stiffened, and he clenched his fists.

They will pay for this. All of this could have been avoided. Why did they start this? Why are they pushing it this way? There's more going on here than a dead mage and an old murder.

He was just about to turn away when he noticed a lone figure kneeling by one of the bodies. It looked like Orahda. He ran as fast as he could. As he got closer, he was sure it was Orahda.

Orahda placed something on the forehead, stood, and turned back towards him as he approached. A smile came to Orahda's face as he saw Dohma approaching. The body Orahda had been kneeling by wasn't Cundia, as he'd feared. It was a grey-haired man. On the forehead was a gold coin.

"M'Lord, I heard you survived. I was just about to come look for you."

"Who is that?" Dohma asked.

"He was Brini of Thilis. An old student from before the time I came to Aelargo. He was almost as much trouble as you. But he was a good Dagger."

"I thought I saw you running, carrying someone. I hoped it was Cundia."

"It was. She lives. She wasn't as lucky as you and me. She needs some time to recover. She's in the officers' hospital area."

A victorious cry came from the west. The call was picked up, and dozens of people started running.

Orahda said, "If you don't mind, I'd like to stay with Cundia a bit longer."

Dohma nodded. "Of course. Come see me later."

Waving, Dohma turned from the hill of death and started to run towards the commotion as a distant cheering started. Running between the tents, he came out as thousands of Daggers were gathering and applauding a group of men and women who were leading a series of carts loaded with wounded.

Most of the gathered soldiers were focused on one cart. It took Dohma a moment to recognize Elades as the driver. He was covered in blood and ash, looking like a wild man. His head was wrapped in a field bandage, and he had his left leg in a splint. Despite the wounds, he was waving and smiling. Clearly visible behind Elades was the huge body of Duke.

Dohma's heart raced, and he felt a surge of hope. Smiling, he pushed through the warriors to intercept the cart. As he approached, he noticed Duke's body didn't move of its own accord. In fact, Duke's head was lying on the side, mouth slightly open and tongue hanging out. He showed no signs of life. Dohma's hope fell.

Duke didn't make it. How can that be? I thought of all of us, he was sure to survive this. After all these centuries, to die now?

When he got even with the cart, he climbed up to sit next to Elades and looked back at Duke. The wolf's body was crushed. Upon inspecting him closer, he saw that one side of Duke's head was caved in, looking like a gory bowl. Tears rolled as Dohma remembered that Duke had stopped and probably slowed himself down to carry him to safety.

What happened when we were thrown apart?

He looked at Elades, raising his eyebrows in question.

Elades stopped waving and noticed Dohma's questioning face. His eyes traced the tracks of Dohma's tears.

"M'Lord, he's not dead."

Dohma glanced back, still seeing no signs of life, not even the movement of breath.

"Elades, he isn't even breathing."

Elades waved his hand dismissively. "He'll be awake and yelling orders in a few days. Although," Elades said, glancing back, "without that healer here, I think it will take him a couple of cycles to get back on his feet."

"Elades, how can you jest like this?"

"M'Lord, you know the stories, yes?"

"Stories, yes. Legends, myths only. This is reality." He turned back to the wolf carcass, taking up the wagon bed.

"M'Lord, you shall see. As Duke says, 'Those aren't worth believing, because they're usually *understated*.' If you believe in nothing else, believe in this. Duke will be back. Duke is the only true immortal of this world."

"What about the Gods?"

Shaking his head, Elades said, "You already know the answer to that from what you witnessed in Gracia. Lady Dalpha is gone, and she shall not return. Duke is truly immortal; death cannot take him. He can be laid low for some time. But he always recovers. Once he's freed, of course."

"What happened to him? I was with him until the last few moments."

"From what I have heard, Duke saved those Daggers in that cart over there. He shielded them from some of the falling debris. However, a large tree fell, and Duke threw them to safety, but was unable to get out of the way himself. A second tree broke and crushed him before he could break free from the first."

Dohma looked at the twelve Daggers riding in the other cart. *Yes, he would sacrifice himself to save others.*

As they came into camp, the applause abated, and people returned to the necessary tasks of regrouping. Dohma watched as, in spite of the events, everyone not involved with support tasks or caring for the wounded was busy mending their gear and weapons. A distinct air of battle preparation was underway.

"M'Lord, Duke's last words were, 'Follow Dohma.'" Elades' comment broke him out of his reverie.

One of the Daggers in the other cart laughed and called out, "Not exactly! There were a couple of choice curses leading up to that."

Everyone chuckled, knowing that was Duke's character, as Elades waved away the intrusion.

Dohma let the words drop into his mind. He couldn't help looking at the hill of corpses. The numbers appeared to have doubled and continued to grow. Bodies were laid out so closely that there were hundreds of squares with only narrow walking paths between them.

The other carts stopped next to the hospital tents, and were overrun with people helping to unload the wounded. Elades drove Duke's cart up close to the command pavilions. It took twenty strong men to carry Duke into his pavilion. Ladro, Duke's personal secretary, had the center of the pavilion cleared and dozens of piles of pillows and blankets formed into a bed for Duke's body. As he was leaving Duke's tent, Dohma noticed Ladro was arranging maps and a working table near Duke's head, as if he expected the wolf to sit up and demand the latest information.

Elades waited for Dohma outside by the large fire at the center of the commanding officer's tent area. Elades looked at him and held out a glass vial.

Dohma took the vial and looked at it. It held a silvery fluid that swirled with traces of pink. He was pretty sure it was a healing potion of some type. "What is this?"

"Dalpha's last gift to you."

"What?"

"It's from Boadua. She said that Sula, Dalpha's daughter, was in Llino and had had the temple making healing brews for cycles. Boadua just brought one for me and one for you."

Dohma shook his head and held it out. "I don't need it. Please send this back to her with my thanks. It's too precious to waste. There are many who could use it."

Elades, appearing to be much better, turned and locked Dohma over with a critical eye. "You came through amazingly well, but you're holding your side and limping, and I note there are small spasms in your left arm. I know you were in the center of it. How can you be sure you don't have internal injuries? We need you to be healthy and alive. Duke is the only one who doesn't need one of these."

"No, I was almost killed," Dohma said, shaking the vial. "However, my...family saved me. I don't know how, but they healed me, all the way from Llino. It was very strange."

Elades grunted. "And you don't believe in Duke's possible recovery. It seems there are many mysteries here, and...' he said, glancing at his right hand, "...just as many miracles." Elades reached out and closed Dohma's fingers around the vial. "Still, m'Lord, keep it safe and near. You may yet need it." He looked down. "I'd like to clean up a bit. Or do you have orders for the armies that need attending to now?"

Dohma felt a slight jump in his stomach. "Orders for the armies?"

"Yes. Duke has left you in charge of the Imperial Armies."

Llino is under siege. I could order the armies south to break that force and insure Electra, Bayion, and Ellua are safe.

He turned and stared into the fire. *No, that would be wrong. I must do what is right for the Empire and the Alliance.*

He looked at the hill of bodies. "Continue search and rescue. Secure this location. And yes, you may get cleaned up. I need what officers we have gathered in the morning. Let's give everyone this evening to clean up, get treated, and get some rest. I want to inspect what's left of that base before we decide what to do next. Tomorrow, start the funeral pyres. We will give all honors to our dead before we move on."

Elades raised his hand to his chest in salute and limped off.

Dohma grabbed a chair and sat down to stare at the fire.

We must have lost over half the attack force, if not the majority of them. This weapon was not detected by our mages, and it killed not only the people, but the forests, too. He leaned back, looking at the clear sky. *We cannot allow such weapons to be used again. Imagine the fear if people learned whole towns could be wiped from existence in a white flash. This burden is heavy. I have to stand tall and command. The armies cannot see me bending under the weight.*

HIRI-RULA

Hiri-Rula chewed her lip as she watched Elades walk away from Lord Dohma. He looked like a man with a lot to consider. Since there was nothing else to do, and she didn't want to lose sight of Dohma, she tuned the power flows to enhance her hearing. After a few seconds, she decided it was too distracting. There weren't any interesting conversations in the nearby area, so she reduced the power levels to normal. She continued to watch Lord Dohma as he glowered, transfixed by the fire. After many minutes, Dohma looked up, frowned, turned, and began walking with a purpose. She floated after him.

As she followed, she reveled in the power the small oval mirror in her hand gave her. It was an amazing find. It had been tucked inside of a special book that not only had a padded silk storage area built into it, but held an equally valuable treasure in research into divination incantations. The looking glass the result of a lifetime of work, which was meticulously recorded in the book. The fact that the volume had sat on the shelf untouched for hundreds of years was a wonder. When she'd asked, she found that all the mages under her command had ignored it because of the unadorned binding and title, 'Practical Thoughts on Divination'.

Hiri-Rula had to admit that she'd only picked it up by accident. But the sealed compartment had intrigued her, and opening it had revealed the beautiful mirror. Her curiosity was lit on fire, and she'd spent an entire cycle studying the book, incantations, and mirror before experimenting with the unusual formulae embedded in it. It took another cycle before she'd gained enough understanding to use its most basic abilities.

There were still many incantations she couldn't understand, which were yet to be explored in the compact artifact. But that night, she was pushing her limits. She'd traveled farther than ever before to gather intelligence. The further she pushed her sight, the more power the mirror demanded. She was using an excessive amount of mana, and it was taxing her strength.

She felt like she was in a dream when she scried on people with the device. It allowed her to watch and listen to almost any place she could find with her mind. Getting there was even more dreamlike. Moving out and flying around the world felt like being one of the Gods. She could be present almost anywhere, but she was invisible. She could flow through walls and doors, sail high into the air, or simply float in the middle of a room. In short, she was able to do something she'd often dreamed of doing her whole life.

It was difficult to maintain concentration, and it took a surprising amount of magic to use the device. But she'd always been a superior mage because of her willpower and ability to maintain focus, even when dealing with many things at once.

Through study and experimentation, she'd discovered she could cast certain incantations through the mirror. She could use telekinesis to move things and even use magic to start fires. She wasn't sure what the limitation was, or if it might break the artifact, which was a risk she dared not take, so she kept any such manipulations small.

The fact that she had the mirror, or the abilities, she kept to herself. They were far beyond anything the Nhia-Samri were aware of, and she was concerned with what might be demanded of her, or worse, that they would take it for study if they found out about it. She'd decided to avoid scrying on anything near Hisuru Amajoo. The urge to look in on her father was strong, but her fear of discovery by Shar-Lumen was even greater.

Dohma returned to the medical enclosures and was busy talking to the staff about casualty numbers. Hiri-Rula knew she needed to gather some more intel, but before she left, she cast an incantation to leave a marker on Dohma's new right boot. Her mind could activate that marker and trace it anywhere in the world through the mirror. That would let her find Lord Dohma again easily.

She felt her strength weakening. She couldn't continue to channel that level of power for much longer. She decided to check on Duke. Butterflies fluttered in her stomach as she floated up through the top of the tent. It was easy to identify Duke's tent, so she drifted there, listening for any information as she passed.

Duke was a complete mystery. He had so many unusual abilities that he never mentioned, and yet he would use them without a worry about discovery as needed. It was possible that Duke would be able to detect her presence. What had her most worried was that in her research of past Nhia-Samri encounters with him, Duke had demonstrated the ability to 'smell' magic, as he described it, and identify it.

Inside Duke's tent, his staff had set up a table with food and drink, and there was a work table with maps. Duke wasn't breathing. She floated down and examined him. Blood didn't run from his open wounds; there was no heartbeat to pump it. There was little chance anything could live, given the amount of damage. Yet everyone, including Shar-Lumen, had called that a delaying tactic, and fully expected Duke to come around with a vengeance.

Even Duke's Dagger, Elades, said he would recover. I wonder how it is that Duke can be so resilient.

She resolved to check on the wolf regularly. Looking around the room, she decided one of Ladro's ink bowls would likely stay near Duke. She cast an incantation, placing as small a channel as she could into the bowl's metal to let her find it when she wanted to. She didn't dare put such a hook onto Duke, no matter how tempting that was. He probably had the ability to trace such a thing straight back to her.

How often does Duke inspect his secretary's tools?

She was just about to release the incantation when an officer brought in some papers and gave them to Duke's secretary, Ladro. He put them on the table near Duke's head. Curious, she drifted over and read. Checking to be sure that no one was around, she used her telekinetic power to move the pages enough to read them completely.

They were early Alliance battle reports. Her stomach lurched when one paper revealed the Alliance's estimated casualty report for the battle. She knew they would be bad, but she had no idea until that moment how many lives were being affected. Her own base had been attacked prior to formal war being declared, killing her commander, friends, and teachers.

Many Nhia-Samri bases had been attacked, killing almost

30,000 Imperial warriors and over 10,000 Nhia-Samri. Tears welled in her eyes, and she gasped, losing all control of the incantations. The connection to the mirror lost, concentration broken, she fell onto the carpeted floor, her mind racing. The casualty report numbers bounced around her thoughts ripping her apart. The broken magic channels, so violently lost, burned her as magic spilled uncontrolled into her body causing even more pain. Excess power flowed from her, scorching the carpet and stone floor.

That wasn't a strategic trap or a delaying maneuver; it was a massacre. They had no chance.

She recalled seeing the dismembered head of Colonel Mishia-Ollan staring at her. His last thoughts had been how proud he was of her and that she should avenge him *with honor.* Those last two words burnt as painfully as the wild magic and casualty numbers.

In a single trap, I killed almost 200,000 people. Twice that number are wounded for life. That's more than died in all of the past wars combined!

Her stomach lurched with nausea as painful spasms forced her last meal and bile out her mouth and nose running over her head to pool under her. She tried to move, but all her strength had fled. She could only muster enough willpower to push her head out of the pool of vomit. Lying there, she cried until she had no more tears to shed. Still, she wept for the proud person she once was. She'd become a monster, the very monster most citizens of the Alliance thought all Nhia-Samri were.

The plan was Shar-Lumen's, she told herself, to no avail. She wanted to disappear and cease to exist.

'*No, little sister. You could not know,*' said a deep and caring voice that reminded her of her grandfather.

'*Now, you do know. You must find a way to stop the next,*' added a light and airy female voice.

Hiri-Rula opened her eyes and looked around. The pungent smell of vomit hung in the air, but her private office was empty. The door was still bolted shut, as were the two windows. She weakly uncurled and pushed herself up to sit.

"Who said that?"

She climbed into her chair. The voices had been near; she was sure of that. She summoned her power and made sure her shields were ready. Slowly rotating, she examined every niche and corner of the room. She was alone.

"I left the mage-gate open for them to flee and pushed its terminus farther away from the base before it failed."

The room remained silent. Wiping the dried vomit from her face, she knew the voices had been true. Maybe they were just her imagination. She considered the past weeks. Something had been going on, and Warlord Eshra-Zunia knew. Hiri-Rula had only been brought in a few days before to organize the mages to pull their warriors out of the base before the trap sprung. The base, their warriors, and even Warlord Eshra-Zunia were to be the bait to bring Duke and his best into position.

Hiri-Rula had no idea they were going to detonate the magical generator. That had been intentionally left out of the details shared with everyone she was aware of.

Thanks to the mirror and book on the scrying sciences, she'd learned not only what powered the Nhia-Samri bases, but also the devastating potential it held.

I must make sure it's never used that way again.

Because of the advanced scrying incantations, she'd been able to observe clearly what the warlord had done. She saw how the Nhia-Samri warriors had engaged in combat with Lord Dohma, drawing Duke to the location.

She was aware of how potent Lord Dohma might be, as there were whispered rumors that he'd fought Shar-Lumen to a stand-off in Gracia. Naturally, the warlord wanted to test herself against him. Hiri-Rula had been shocked as she watched Lord Dohma prove superior to the warlord. If it hadn't been for her magical escape, being pulled back to a secondary gate kilometers away, Lord Dohma would likely have killed or captured her.

Hiri-Rula smiled. It was information she might be able to use, if needed, to prevent the warlord from using another Nhia-Samri base in the same way.

Her reputation as the best of the warriors, second only to the First Warlord, would be ruined if that information became known.

Her guilt had ebbed slightly, especially after she considered all the facts. Even more important was that she'd seen how the warlord had sabotaged the magical generator, and that it was something she was sure the warlord and Shar-Lumen wished to keep secret.

Hiri-Rula was also amazed that the new scrying incantations had allowed her to seize control of the mage-gate next to Lord Dohma, keeping it open and moving its terminus farther away from the base, giving the escaping warriors more of a chance. If she'd known the destructive capabilities of the magic generator, she would've pushed the gate even farther away. However, at the time, she'd been worried about the movement of the terminus being discovered by Lord Dohma or anyone else. That was a secret she was worried her superiors might discover, as it would mean her death.

Tapping her own base's magic, she brushed away all signs of vomit from herself and the room. She placed the mirror back into the book, sealing the compartment with even more protections than it had originally. She was just about to put the volume back on her shelf when she paused.

I cannot leave this. My report will not go well.

She opened the book and found an incantation she'd only recently mastered. Refreshing her mind on it, she weaved the channels. She pulled from an air line nearby, instead of from her base's power, to avoid any possible detection by other Nhia-Samri mages. Using the fresh power, she wrapped the book in the sensory-deception incantation. Anyone who found the book would find their attention slipping from it, making it almost invisible. The book then went into her shoulder pouch, instead of back to the shelf.

She stepped out of her study and headed for the throne room. Her pace was the measured step of someone in authority with important business. As she moved, one of her aids noticed her bearing and wordlessly fell into step with her. He did not ask, or even expect to be told, what she was about. He was doing his sworn duty to support her and be ready for whatever was called for.

She considered what she was going to report. Long-range intelligence was always problematic, which was why the Nhia-Samri had their bases and outposts. Spying was still the most reliable means to know what was happening. Her enhanced ability to see clearly at such a distance was entirely unique. Mages had many devices and abilities to see some things or to sense others. Most such incantations involved placing hooks into people, or things that allowed them to become the focus of the divination. She would need to not lie, but then also not reveal too much.

Hiri-Rula considered everything that had happened. Her base being attacked, the attack on Gracia, and her strange feelings. She'd witnessed many things. In the past, she'd often worried about some actions, but it had never bothered her so much. Recently, it was as if her mind had been freed from some kind of binding, and she was able to assemble the facts and reach sound conclusions easier now. Both her perceptions and interpretations were clearer than ever.

She attributed some of it to the advancement in rank and the need to take more note of everyday actions. But she knew that ever since she'd taken up Colonel Mishia-Ollan's ancient odassi, she had a higher sense of purpose. Just holding the blades made her more confident in her decisions, especially when she opted for compassion and the older definitions of honorable action.

The throne room doors were closed, and four honor guards stood blocking them. On her approach, they rapidly came to attention and stepped out of the way. She used magic, instead of her hands, to push open the large doors with their broken-shield handles. They made a banging sound just as she stepped over the threshold.

Warlord Eshra-Zunia remained seated in the carved throne. The other generals and officers present stood and formed a path for Hiri-Rula. They bowed in unison as she moved past them to stand directly before the throne. The warlord frowned at her, anticipating the news.

"General Hiri-Rula, what news of our attack on Duke?"

After a slight bow, she reported, "Warlord, the attack was devastating. We have been able to determine that Lord Dohma survived. Many of Duke's senior officers have also survived. We've reduced the division under Duke's direct command by at least thirty percent, perhaps as much as fifty."

There were more than a few sharp intakes of breath at the news.

I'm not the only one who finds this news disturbing.

Walking backwards in her mind, she identified who had been standing where as she went past. She took note of the direction of the sharp intakes of breath, indicating horror or surprise, and added all five of those people to her list of possible allies against such mass killings in the future. She knew she would have to sound them out, but she was pleased to note that one of those people was her own general.

The warlord did look unhappy, but not horrified by the casualty numbers. "What of Duke?"

"We could not detect Duke's life force."

The throne room doors swung open again, banging even louder than she ever dared to do. The warlord's eyes widened, and everyone around Hiri-Rula prostrated themselves on the floor. She turned to see a magnificently chiseled warrior standing in the doorway. His black armor was beautiful, with a pattern of grey highlights and piping. The armor had wide shoulder plates that turned up from his muscled shoulders.

He stood taller than everyone in the room. The large doorway framed him perfectly, a fact Hiri-Rula knew was no accident.

Shar-Lumen walked straight towards her. She dropped to one knee. "Lord."

She did not look down. Her entire attention was riveted on his violet eyes. He stopped before her.

He looked up at the warlord. "Warlord Eshra-Zunia, you have served well. Not even my most sensitive mage can detect Duke. He's well detained. Hopefully, he's also buried or trapped."

She didn't move a muscle, at least nothing she was aware of. Yet Shar-Lumen's eyes came back to her. "You don't believe we're so lucky?"

How did he know? What did I do?

His eyes remained on her.

Think. How do I explain my prediction? No mage can see clearly at that distance.

"Grand Warlord, Duke was with Lord Dohma. We have detected Lord Dohma. Through whatever means, it's likely Duke saved Lord Dohma, and therefore, will be found rapidly."

Shar-Lumen blinked as he continued to stare at her.

No one dared speak. After what seemed like an eternity, Shar-Lumen nodded almost imperceptibly. "Very sound reasoning, General Hiri-Rula."

Shar-Lumen looked back at the warlord, and it took every ounce of her mage training in control to not let out a sigh of relief.

"Warlord, congratulations on the excellent execution of our plan. Now, you're to take what aid you desire and go to the city of Llino. You are to assume command of all forces there and to take the city. I do not care if the city is destroyed, but you will deliver to me in Hisuru Amajoo Lord Dohma's family, alive and uninjured."

The warlord stood and slapped her chest in salute. "It shall be done."

"Warlord, when I say *family* I mean *all* of his family. His sister, his brother, their spouses, their children, and most especially, Countess Electra Neyon of Waylisia. None of them are to be threatened, mistreated, or in any way harmed beyond the necessary force to hold them and guarantee their passage."

"Understood, sir!"

Shar-Lumen turned and started to walk out, but paused. He turned back, looking at Hiri-Rula, his eyebrows creasing. He then waved for her to approach. She stood and stepped up to him. He placed a hand on her shoulder and drew her odassi of prayer with his free hand. He examined the blade before sliding it back into its sheath.

"Warlord, may I borrow your second-in-command for a special assignment? It may take some considerable time."

The warlord clearly didn't want to agree, but she snapped instantly, "Sir, your will and pleasure. I trust she will serve you admirably."

Shar-Lumen's smile sent chills down Hiri-Rula's spine. He gestured to her aide, who, she was surprised to see, had followed her and still stood ready to assist. "You shall remain here."

He turned and stepped back through the doors and started walking down the long, empty corridor.

Where did the honor guard go?

Without any other orders, Hiri-Rula fell into step with him, the throne room doors closing behind them.

At the end of the hallway, another pair of large doors with shields for handles waited. They opened, either by themselves or with Shar-Lumen's magic. Hiri-Rula wasn't sure, because she sensed no magical usage by him.

The doors opened on an impossibly grandiose room with a tall throne on a raised platform. Shar-Lumen swept through the well-dressed officers and warriors in the room, cutting a path like a ship running through the ocean. Stepping up, he turned and sat on the throne.

We're in Hisuru Amajoo! I didn't feel anything: no gate, no power, nothing. How did we get here?

Mages on the Wall

CHAPTER 10
ANCIENT MISTAKES

Hiri-Rula roamed the great halls of Hisuru Amajoo, unsure of what to do. Shar-Lumen had swept her there in his wake, like the great ships that collected debris as they moved through the sea. She was sure he would demand more intelligence from her, or perhaps accuse her of hiding secrets. The Grand Warlord was a top-level mage, a warrior beyond measure, and mysterious. He never explained his plans, but everyone knew he protected his people. Of those that served him, he demanded perfection of service, and strict adherence to the Nhia-Samri code of honor.

After introducing her to his command staff, he'd dismissed her with instructions to relax and visit her family. Expecting to be sent off on some dangerous mission, Hiri-Rula had found her father, Hiri-Ming. He was Shar-Lumen's chief avenarius, in charge of all the stables for the entire fortress. Her brother, Hiri-Yonu, was following the family's traditional profession, and had just been named avenarius for Hisuru Amajoo's farming stables.

Her brother and father were both busy men, but took what time they could to visit with her and discuss everything that had happened. She felt better, being able to talk through some of her feelings. Her father was truly proud that the ancient blades had chosen her, and he even took her to see the town's leaders, known as the elders' council. The elders had shared wine with her and congratulated her, as each elder respectfully touched the blades' hilts.

In all, she had a wonderful couple of weeks. Every day, she came prepared to leave. Every day, she was told Shar-Lumen was not ready for her.

She'd been tempted to use the mirror, but fear of discovery kept her from even opening the compartment.

She still studied the book, trying to decipher the complex formulae and unusual terminology, which was either made up, or from a language unknown to her.

She'd found the seemingly infinite library complex on her third day. It was filled with texts and books on every subject. Whole sections were locked off, or sealed under the Nhia-Samri preservation shields similar to those she'd used to seal the empty barracks.

The chief librarian was a nimble, smart, and chatty old lady named Olmanna-Yillion. Hiri-Rula had tripped over her when she was carrying too many books to see where she was going. She'd swept up all the books and gotten Hiri-Rula to join her for tea.

Through that entire first meeting, Olmanna-Yillion had chatted almost nonstop, but the tea and pastries were amazing. Since then, Hiri-Rula had tried to avoid her. Every time she encountered her, it seemed she lost three marks of her day. But the chief librarian had different ideas, treating Hiri-Rula like a new prized pupil, giving her access to hidden and locked-away treasures, and often leaving little notes with many references to help her studies.

The main hall of the library was over a hundred feet tall, with a golden dome. The western half of the dome had a masterpiece series of panel paintings, depicting a terraced city that filled half of the ceiling. Opposite the city were panels of men and women dressed in various robes and outfits from many ages. The people were of all ages, and through a clever ploy, they held hands in an unbroken chain. She'd spent a whole afternoon staring up at that ceiling, tracing the hands, only to end up back at the main figure in the front. The figure was a muscular man wearing leather pants and a loose white linen shirt with the billowed sleeves that came and went in popularity. She liked the man. He had a strong face, and she felt he was someone who could be trusted. She'd asked librarians who he was, and they shrugged, suggesting it was just a heroic caricature.

A magnificent chandelier held what she thought was a representation of all the constellations. Each light was artistically shaped like a star, and golden ropes moved back and forth between the lights, which she assumed were some kind of oil distribution system. The lights never flickered, making her think it had been changed out for a more reliable magical light source at some point.

She'd started using the vast resources of the library to improve her understanding of what was in the book she carried. Although there were hundreds of books available on the subject of divination, none of them held a candle to the enchanted text. Divination was considered a shoddy and unreliable science that was best left to lesser-talented mages who needed to impress villagers.

Her stomach grumbled about her light breakfast that morning, but Hiri-Rula had been reading an interesting book on a secondary existence theory about parallel realities. That book wasn't generally available to anyone, but she'd been given access to it. It wasn't allowed outside of the library, so she'd eaten quickly and was rushing back to continue studying it.

I almost hope I meet Olmanna-Yillion today. I would love to get some of her pastries. I really should ask where she gets them. She laughed internally. *That is, if I can get a word in edgewise.*

A junior warrior ran past her, heading for the library. But when she saw Hiri-Rula, she skidded to a stop and jogged back, coming to attention just to the side of her path. The warrior kept turning her head slightly to glance at her. She had a message, but was reluctant to interrupt Hiri-Rula's thoughts. Never mind the fact that her noisy appearance and nervous glances had already done just that.

Still, Hiri-Rula waited a full minute before stopping near the warrior, looking at her as if she'd just noticed her. Unsure about what to do, she saluted, and glanced at Hiri-Rula again.

Trying not to smirk, Hiri-Rula nodded at her. "You have a message for me?"

The junior officer let out her breath. From the sound of it, she'd been holding it the whole time. "General Hiri-Rula, I bring you greetings from my master, First Warlord Maru-Ashua. He requests an audience with you at your convenience."

"Why would he wait for my convenience?" The fact that First Warlord Maru-Ashua would wait for her was so shocking that she asked the question without thinking.

The warrior didn't seem to notice the inappropriate response. "General, First Warlord Maru-Ashua directed me most specifically to not interrupt any research or work you were engaged in."

That explains the odd behavior. She expected me to be in the library, and didn't know how to deal with finding me roaming the hall she was running through. She was probably planning on a more dignified approach.

"Take me to First Warlord Maru-Ashua, now."

The warrior saluted and turned back in the direction from which she'd come. She marched, leading the way. She didn't seem to be paying attention to Hiri-Rula, yet she maintained an excellent distance two steps in front. But Hiri-Rula became curious, and slowed to examine an artifact in the hall. The warrior slowed, and even stopped when Hiri-Rula did. A slight tingle caught her attention, and she shifted to mage sight. The warrior was pulling power from her odassi to enhance her hearing.

Very astute usage.

The girl didn't have the internal magic potential to be a full mage, but she was highly attuned to her odassi, which caught Hiri-Rula's attention. They weren't the new style. In fact, they were ancient odassi, just like Hiri-Rula's.

There are not that many blades of such age left. This junior officer having a set is surprising.

Hiri-Rula pondered the coincidence as she was led through the complex to a set of iron-bound oaken doors.

There were two guards on the door. The guards were both majors, and they saluted as Hiri-Rula approached.

One of them knocked once on the door, and opened it without waiting for a response. As she entered, she noticed that both of the majors also had ancient odassi blades.

Four sets of ancient blades. This cannot be coincidence. But what does it mean?

Stepping inside, she was surprised by the large room. It had a fireplace, with a set of plush sofas around a coffee table. Two of the walls were bookshelves, stuffed with ancient-looking tomes. Her fingers twitched to run along their spines, reading the titles.

At the far end of the room was a beautiful wooden desk, inlaid with gold in a series of sweeping lines that curled in interlocking vines around it. Behind the desk was an almost throne-like, high-backed leather office chair, in which sat a hulking man whose chest and upper arms stretched the wool shirt he wore, revealing rolling pectorals and bulging biceps. This was the man, whom she knew to be First Warlord Maru-Ashua. He looked as athletic as any young warrior, despite being over fifty years old. Only the grey streaks in his hair gave away his age. He was the largest man she'd ever seen.

Before the desk, arrayed in a semi-circle, were six wing-back chairs covered in a blue patterned, tapestry-like cloth. Three colonels and one general revealed themselves by standing up out of those chairs. They turned in a leisurely manner to look at her, all with welcoming faces. None of them revealed much in the way of emotion. Somehow, she knew she could trust them, and that they in turn would welcome her into their midst.

The warlord also stood. His face remained a mask of neutrality. Seeing him standing, she re-evaluated her original estimation of his mass. Saying he was *immense* didn't sum up his presence. He wasn't wearing his armor, but his odassi were in a holder behind him within easy reach. She was sure his clothes had been made for him, yet they were snug, leaving little to the imagination about his muscled torso. He stood well over everyone in the room at two meters tall, and if there was an ounce of fat on his frame, it wasn't visible. His arms were rolling muscles, the size of most men's legs.

The warlord pointed to an empty chair. His hand was large enough to grab her entire head and crush it like a grape.

"General Hiri-Rula, join us." His voice matched his size, but was soft and gentle.

She walked across the vast room, all of the men watching her every move. She felt like some kind of special specimen being brought in for study. None of the men made even the slightest sign to indicate their thoughts.

As she moved before the chair, she realized that every person in the room, including the warlord, had ancient odassi matching her own.

This is beyond coincidence. The warlord has intentionally gathered officers selected to bear the ancient blades. But what can it mean?

She took her seat, and the men followed suit. A porter approached her with a tray of drinks. Glancing at the others, she saw that they all had drinks and small plates of food on the tables in front of them. As she took some of the hot arit offered, she noted that even the porter was an officer wearing ancient odassi blades.

No one said a word until she'd taken a drink. As soon as she placed the cup before her, the warlord continued a conversation that had been going on before she came in.

"Eshra-Zunia will have a hard fight to take Llino. Once the city is breached, the palace will be strong enough to resist for some time."

The general leaned forward. "I could go there as an adviser. I'm aware of the tactics used for penetrating those defenses. Plus, we all witnessed your capture of Allornia."

The others nodded. If the warlord had a feeling about the idea, nothing about his appearance gave it away. He did not respond immediately; he sat and thought without comment or motion. The officers sipped their drinks quietly, accustomed to waiting on him. After two full minutes, he said, "No. There is added danger to Llino."

One of the colonels motioned for attention. When the warlord looked at him, he said, "I do not understand. Allornia was just as old as Llino."

"Llino was Duke's home, and he built it as a fortress for the Duianna Empire. The attack may cause an unexpected response from the city. Should the city's mechanisms become fully engaged by the assault, there's potential that we cannot defeat these defenses. There are records indicating that some ancient cities hold powerful entities the likes of which we are unprepared to face."

The colonel sat back, crossing his legs and placing his head on his hand. He stared at one of the desk legs in thought.

An older colonel said, "If we leave her to her own means, she will eventually lose her patience and use less-than-acceptable hostage and execution tactics to force a surrender."

Hiri-Rula was shocked at the conversation and the blatant opinions being stated. The men spoke of a senior officer with a total disregard for protocol. She was unsure how to react. The warlord didn't respond as many officers she knew through her career would have. If these had been lesser men before a junior officer, they would've been punished, or even killed, for speaking so plainly.

"You're correct. I taught her some patience, but she was not yet ready for command. I had no choice. She's still the most competent officer I could leave behind. She's ambitious. That Shar-Lumen has given her the assignment personally means she will not be willing to use slower tactics."

The general shifted to face one of the colonels. "Now that Hiri-Rula has joined, we should discuss the unique team heading south. Runa-Emry, your report of this team is almost unbelievable. A Journeyman Mage defeated an entire strike force. Your own daughter, who we thought was dead, as her odassi died with Ossa-Ulla and his odassi, was willingly traveling with them. The Gods, or at least one, interfered on your daughter's behalf to save her from your warrior's strike."

The warlord's gaze fell on Hiri-Rula, spearing her like a specimen for study.

The general turned from Colonel Runa-Emry to face her directly. "General Hiri-Rula, you should know Shar-Lumen has sent four separate teams after this junior mage's and young Dagger's team to capture or kill them without success."

Colonel Runa-Emry frowned. "I failed, as well."

For the first time, the warlord responded instantly. "No, you succeeded in bringing back vital intelligence that we had been lacking."

Hiri-Rula filed the face and name away, thankful to finally learn the identity of one of the officers.

The warlord again sat quietly for a few minutes. His eyes were directed at Colonel Runa-Emry, yet Hiri-Rula had the distinct impression all of the men were staring at her.

"General Hiri-Rula, do you know why you're here?"

It took her a moment before she realized he'd addressed her. She sat up straight. "No. Does it...?" Her tongue betrayed her, but she managed to stop before blurting out her idea that it had something to do with her blades.

The warlord turned his head towards her, his eyes like twin suns boring into her. "Finish your question. You may ask or say anything in this room without fear."

She swallowed, feeling even more like a specimen under his direct gaze. "Does it have to do with my blades?" In spite of her tight emotional control, she felt her cheeks reddening.

"She is as observant as reported," the last colonel said.

"Yes. How did you know Duke's body had been recovered before we did?"

Her throat tightened. She fought for the rock-solid control she'd been trained to have, but fear of being stripped of everything locked her mouth and lungs. She didn't think she could even squeak if she needed to.

He waited. No one said a word. The others seemed

prepared to wait an eternity, while calmly sipping their drinks and nibbling their snacks.

She finally managed to regain control of herself. "Warlord...."

"Do not lie to me. We live for honor. That you hold those blades means you know this."

The lie she was about to tell wilted into nothing. She was caught, cornered, and there was no way out. She sighed, "I have learned a rather unusual line of magical science on divination from a unique book I found in the library at Outpost One."

"Let me see this book," he said, holding out his hand.

He knew I had it on me? How?

With nowhere to go, she pulled the book out of her pouch and handed it over. He examined it, and with a brush of power, he broke her incantations hiding it. The other officers sat up and leaned in the moment the perception filter was broken.

"She actually has it," the general said.

Holding the book out to Hiri-Rula, he said, "Can you show me what it contains?"

She didn't know why he asked her to open it, especially when he'd broken her incantations so easily. Still, she took the book back, and opened the compartment that was part of the back cover. As she held up the mirror for all to see, the warlord nodded and smiled.

"We have a diviner."

Her nervousness forgotten, she asked, "What do you mean?"

His face had returned to his normal stony demeanor. "The odassi chose you, indicating you had the potential for greatness. You found this book, of the two that were there. Therefore, you are a natural diviner. You never would've found the book without the combination of the blades and this talent. I tried for many years to open that compartment and failed. I also found the other two caches of secrets when I was still a major. Only one would open for me. It held these." He patted his odassi behind him without looking. "Only later did I discover that I hadn't done anything. They wanted to be found by me. Just as this book and mirror were waiting for the right person."

The general said, "She didn't tell Eshra-Zunia or Shar-Lumen of her discovery. That she managed to produce a believable conclusion via logic kept Shar-Lumen from discovering this book and its treasure, proving her quick thinking."

"Yes," said the warlord. "She was guided by her blades a bit, I'm sure. But that does not negate her accomplishments." Turning his gaze back to her, he continued. "General Hiri-Rula, Shar-Lumen has directed me to send you to do that which no one else has been able to do. He feels your resourcefulness with the attack on Outpost One; your intelligence, your prowess with both magic and sword, and your self-control will allow you to succeed."

She looked at the men. "What exactly am I supposed to do?"

"Intercept Lebuin, and find out what he's doing for Duke. It's clear that Ticca and Lebuin are far more than they seem, and Duke is trying to keep our attention in the north, on him. But Ticca and Lebuin, with an exceptional team of Daggers, have gone south, into the Circumveni Desert, a fact that has Shar-Lumen concerned."

Hiri-Rula's mouth dropped open. "That's a suicide mission."

Shaking his head, the warlord said, "No, we have sent many expeditions into the desert. You shall be escorted by an expert team assembled by Colonel Runa-Emry. You will be in total command. You're to intercept them, find a way to neutralize Lebuin and Ticca, and bring them to me in my city of Allornia. After I question them, we will present them together to Shar-Lumen. Returning her to Hisuru Amajoo is the primary mission goal. We must know what Duke is doing, and Shar-Lumen wants to learn precisely why Duke sent this strike team into the desert. Shar-Lumen gave explicit instructions that you're not to hurt any of them beyond the minimal force necessary to secure them. Ticca, most especially, is to be kept from harm."

Hiri-Rula looked at Colonel Runa-Emry. "Why you?"

"I volunteered."

The warlord said, "He wants to discover the truth about his daughter. He's highly motivated towards your success. I trust him with my secrets, and my life."

"So you expect me to find them with the mirror?"

"That would be inadvisable, without much experimentation from a safe distance. The Circumveni Desert is dangerous and uniquely unstable for magic use and mages. You must be very careful, and keep tight control on your magics while in the desert."

"So how are we to track this Ticca and Lebuin?"

He held up the most beautiful silver cloak clasp she'd ever seen; it glistened in the light, sparkles running down gems inlaid in a flowing pattern across its surface. "With this."

ELECTRA

The regents were reviewing supply reports with all of the office heads when Electra, with her Dagger guards, entered the ballroom, which had been recently converted into a command center. Tables were arranged around the room, each with a scale map of a section of the city. Guard officers were busy placing markers around the maps, indicating levels of crime, types of crimes, persons of interest, and guard and Dagger deployments. She waited to the side, listening to the conversations.

Nothing new was in any of the data being shared. The food and water supplies were sustaining the normal population, along with the evacuated villages from the surrounding areas. The city held just over 460,000 souls.

It's a shame I can't show them that the palace can provide these maps and indicators via voice updates and live monitoring. Still, the regents might discover the instructions for doing this someday. I don't think even Gracia's regents know such things.

The walls held maps of the other countries in various scales. They were being marked with pins, indicating last known troop locations and cities. Similar maps were set up in Gracia as well. Electra was helping to coordinate some of those updates via communications through the Mages' Guild with the Alliance offices around the realms.

The maps were being updated with the most recent data, received a few marks prior. Many cities of the northern realms weren't faring nearly as well as Llino. Of course, Electra had Vesta and Arkady, with all their observation species and the one remaining orbital platform. The generals of the Alliance, under Duke's orders, had assembled six divisions of the Imperial Armies. Each division consisted of nearly 700,000 warriors under the command of 10,000 Daggers. The divisions were marching on all of the known Nhia-Samri outposts and bases. Twenty bases had been overrun, with heavy losses on both sides.

Still, the Nhia-Samri advanced, taking more land across the middle section of the continent. In the southern areas near Aelargo, they had no fear of attack from the south, thanks to the impossible-to-cross Circumveni Desert. So far, what land they'd taken, they claimed as their own.

Farther north, Nhia-Samri attack forces had used their magical gates, striking at individual cities. Six of the smaller, more isolated ancient cities in the north had been bested by the Nhia-Samri, killing only those who stood to fight. Reports stated that ever since the Allusia incident, they'd stopped slaughtering non-combatants. People were being given a choice to leave, or become part of their nation.

At first, there was a sense of urgency to push them back. The Imperial Armies had retaken two of those cities, but the Nhia-Samri had destroyed almost everything in them as they evacuated back through their gates, leaving ruins that were useless to anyone in place of the ancient landmarks. The reports also said that they evacuated their new citizens ahead of the attack by the Imperial forces. No one knew exactly where the people who'd stayed in the cities, choosing to become Nhia-Samri citizens, had been taken. But they, along with all their valuables, had been evacuated.

The new Nhia-Samri tactics had turned some of the general populace's opinions in their favor. Where once they'd been universally viewed as bloodthirsty assassins, out for money and chaos, they were being seen as more lawful, even earning back some of their original reputation for honor. In the latest city to be taken, few of the population chose to evacuate. Many had locked themselves in their houses until the fighting was over, and then volunteered to stay under Nhia-Samri rule.

That tactic had caused a lot of debate. In the end, troops had been dispatched to blockade them inside the cities. No further attempts were being made to push them out. The stalemate left the ancient cities intact. The Nhia-Samri had yet to demonstrate any ability to seize control of the ancient systems in those cities, and many believed it was unlikely they would succeed, especially after Warlord Maru-Ashua had tried to gain control of Allusia's artifacts. Even with a proper royal command, the city hadn't answered to him.

The best estimates placed the death toll at over 200,000 Alliance warriors and another 100,000 non-combatant deaths, to the 40,000 Nhia-Samri confirmed deaths.

At this rate, we'll win the war by attrition. But that price will be too high. We need to find a way to end this without so much loss. But how can this be done? The war seems to have a life of its own, and it's hungry.

Arkady had returned from the moon, and was back in Gracia. He and Vesta were trying to speed up the harvesting of the resources needed to replace the lost orbital platforms. They were also trying to deal with issues affecting other systems by the extreme loss of worker crabs in the failed attack on the Nhia-Samri base. The ocean wave energy harvesters were already starting to get packed with sand and debris. Vesta had to lock many of them to keep them from being damaged. Silt was building up in the Loren Channel. It wasn't bad yet, but without the crabs to help clear it, some shipping lanes would become unusable in a year. Arkady was having similar issues near Gracia in the fresh water channels there.

Ellua motioned for Electra to join her. Stepping around the busy officers, she threaded her way through the room to where Bayion and Ellua were bent over a table of reports and smaller maps with hand-drawn markings and updates.

"I assume you heard that additional forces joined the blockading divisions yesterday." Ellua's statement was not a question.

"Yes, I was just looking at the figures."

Bayion handed her some loose papers. "We have a better count this morning. What has us worried is that many of these new warriors appeared to be officers. There's been a lot of movement outside the city since their arrival. They are shifting troops."

Electra took a moment to glance at the papers. They showed that an estimated 10,000 warriors had been swelling the troops already outside the city walls. If they were accurate, over 40,000 Nhia-Samri were just beyond the city limits.

She looked back at a map of the realms. They hadn't taken a single city in Aelargo. In fact, they'd bypassed Algan and Breorchy, which were both ancient cities, to come all the way to the eastern coast, directly to Llino. There was no doubt in her mind they meant to take Llino.

She handed the papers back to Bayion. "We have double their number in guards, and almost 10,000 Daggers. We can defend the city walls for some time."

A series of explosions shook the palace, causing tables to shake. She felt the vibrations echoing through the floor. Ellua had to catch herself on a table. Cups of arit, tea, and wine spilled, as pens rolled, knocking over inkwells.

After a few seconds, it stopped. Everyone looked around, wide-eyed, without a word. Then through the walls, they could hear the battle calls of thousands of warriors, shattering the silence.

A palace guard ran into the room. "THE SOUTH AND WEST WALLS HAVE BEEN BREACHED! THEY ARE ATTACKING!"

At the same time, Vesta's voice came to Electra through the micro-implant. "Electra, the Nhia-Samri mages blew out seven shield emitters and are destroying the sentinels. Their warriors are running over the top of the walls on some kind of magical bridge made of pressurized air."

Bayion was already issuing attack orders, and ran out of the room with a group of Daggers.

Ellua had grabbed Electra's arm, pulling her in a different direction. "We must get to where we can see. I can't direct the defenses from here. We have to give Bayion and our guards support."

Vesta's voice sounded worried as she said, "I don't know how, but suddenly over sixty mages are out there! They're flinging magic like I've never heard of before. Some of them are attacking the wall's infrastructure. I won't be able to restore the shields if the repair systems are taken out. We're in serious trouble."

Electra's heart raced as much as her mind as she digested their predicament. Her realization that there was no time to hold back made up her mind on what to do. She grabbed Ellua's hand, pulling her to a stop. "No! This way!"

Ellua paused, but then turned, motioning for the other officers and guards to follow. Electra ran, pulling Ellua with her. It wasn't easy, as she was wearing a dress instead of loose pants, but she managed to keep up. A group of guards and palace staff were clustered in the halls. Electra ignored protocol, shoving people out of her way as she rushed to the throne room. Letting go of Ellua, she thrust the double doors open, stepping into the nearly abandoned room.

Ellua slid to a stop as Electra screamed, "*Defensionem et imperium eu monitores!*" She marched towards the thrones, dramatically turning and sweeping her arm, indicating the glowing columns that shot out from the floors and spread, looking like a set of fountains, except that instead of water they were millions of microbots. Rather than falling to the floor, the top of the fountains filled out into radiant command consoles.

I had no idea they would look exactly like they do when I'm working inside the network with Vesta. They're so beautiful. Electra recalled the name *Light-Unit-Microbot-Emitter-Displays*, or LUMEDs, from the technical manuals she'd read.

"We can use the city's LUMEDs."

They finished forming, and the displayed images were perfect, as if they had a window open to the scenes shown. The controls all glowed, but the switches, dials, and keyboards looked solid.

Ellua glanced around at the floating consoles, which showed the city from dozens of positions. Electra reached out and pulled the air that held one of the screens. Her hand gripped the edge of it, and she was surprised that it had a tactile feedback. She'd assumed they would be light images, but there was some form of power that also gave the interfaces a partial, ghostly presence she could touch. Although her hand could press into the surface, deforming it.

She pulled two displays to her, and started adjusting their settings to show the two breaches in the city's walls.

Ellua came up next to her. Her eyes were so wide, she looked like she didn't have eyelids. She stood and gazed around the room at the multiple screens showing graphs of power, defensive system statuses, and highlighted maps with colored dots representing people.

"How?" was the only word Ellua could utter.

Electra heard Vesta's worried voice in her ear. *'Yes, what are you doing?'*

Electra whispered, "Fight them. Rainbow, you can act now, and I'll claim it was me."

Still mesmerized by what she was seeing, Ellua murmured, "What did you say?"

Electra was too busy typing commands into the console she'd taken for her own. She was activating all of the city's defenses she could.

Seeing that the city was waking, she realized she needed Vesta to act as well. She racked her brain to try to find a way to direct her. She almost hit herself when she realized she could use the command language she'd been studying since she met Vesta. It would sound exactly like all of the other ancient artifact commands, and more importantly, Ellua would assume it was something Electra had learned in Gracia.

The command language was an ancient dead language that the Empire had adopted to use for controlling all of its machines. That eliminated the need for massive processing power in the devices to try and separate natural language and commands meant for the machines. Even though she didn't have the permissions needed for most defensive commands, she crossed her fingers, hoping, Vesta would react as if she did have that authority.

"Socium hostemque pugnae signum," she called out.

'Good thinking,' Vesta said as she complied with the request for colored identification of the combatants. The displays started to alter, and the ones tracking people started color-coding into red, blue, yellow, and green dots. All of the forces outside the wall were red, so that was easy to figure out. There were far more green dots than anything else, so they must be the general population. That left blue for guards and yellow for Daggers. One of the dots moving with a large group of Daggers turned into a silver crown.

Electra pointed. "Bayion."

That snapped Ellua back. She looked over the screen, and

began figuring out what it all meant. "Urdu! He's leading the charge. He isn't Dohma!"

One of the red dots, in a large group moving through the streets from the southern wall towards the palace, started blinking and changed to a set of red crossed swords.

Electra noticed and pointed, touching the new symbol. "*Quis est, qui?*"

Some text appeared next to the symbol in old Imperial. 'Warlord Eshra-Zunia.'

Electra's heart skipped three full beats at seeing the name. Her stomach tightened. "What is she doing here? Is Hiri-Rula here, too?" She blurted out, immediately realizing and regretting she hadn't used the command language. She sent a silent prayer up that Ellua was too distracted to hear.

Ellua started touching another display, rapidly figuring it out. She'd been issuing orders, which Electra knew Vesta was complying with, if perhaps altering them slightly to help defend the city better.

"Who is Hiri-Rula?" asked Ellua.

Electra knew her face was stone white as Ellua turned around and stepped over, she still felt light headed from the shock. Electra willed her body to loosen up, heart to slow, and took a deep breath as quietly as she could to regain her composure. Following Electra's gaze, Ellua puzzled out the translation. "Warlord Eshra-Zunia. It's amazing that it can figure out titles and names. I don't see a Hiri-Rula listed here."

Electra swallowed.

Urd, I screwed up! She's smart. I must be more careful to protect Vesta while we save the city.

"I provided a report on Nhia-Samri officers for the assembly, and Hiri-Rula is this warlord's second and a powerful mage. I presume she and her mage came in those additional troops. She must be here to capture the city."

Ellua's lips flattened as she gazed at Electra's face. Then she turned back to the monitor.

Thank you, Lords. I know she didn't buy all of that, she

knows I'm holding something back. At least she accepted most of it.

The warlord had been on the western side, heading southeast towards the palace. But she changed course and was heading north, deciding to go around. She came to an intersection and moved through it rapidly, choosing the more northerly path, which put her on a different street, bypassing the palace complex completely.

They heard more explosions. On the monitor showing the city's shield status, the entire thing vanished. The throne room turned red, and alarm bells sounded.

The warlord was coming to the palace. Why would she change her path?

Looking over the displays, she realized the warlord was on an intercept course for Bayion.

"Lords and Ladies, she's going after Bayion personally!"

Ellua looked around at the screens, and when she spotted the same one Electra had used to come to that conclusion, she choked up. "No! We have to warn him!"

Vesta's voice came to Electra's ear, *'Call for the announcement voice.* Da mihi nuntius vocem.*'*

Electra spoke the command as Vesta had instructed.

Vesta said, *'The whole city can hear you now.'*

Electra smiled. *Good time to turn the tables.*

In a clear voice, Electra said, "*Ostende mihi*, Warlord Eshra-Zunia." Her voice floated in from many directions, like an echo. Ellua stopped to listen, looking back with an odd expression.

A side display shifted, per her request to see the warlord, showing a tall woman warrior in red armor, marching down a merchant street with hundreds of Nhia-Samri behind her. She stopped, her mouth falling open, as she heard her own name booming from around her.

Ellua whispered, "Can they hear me, too?"

In answer to that, they heard her voice coming from the city.

Electra nodded. Ellua smiled and silently mouthed, 'Thank you!' She turned to the screens, calling out, "Bayion, Warlord Eshra-Zunia is proceeding northeast, down Porter, with 300 Nhia-Samri. They have breached the city shields entirely. There are 10,000 coming over the west wall, two blocks south of the west gate. There are another 10,000 coming over the south wall...."

The warlord's face contorted in rage, and she began shouting orders.

"*Tsk-tsk*, Warlord. You didn't think it would be that easy, did you?" Electra couldn't help taunting. In addition to her own voice, she heard thousands of voices cheering. In the displays, she saw that some guard and Dagger divisions were cheering as the Daggers began redirecting their actions based on Ellua's reports.

She's giving them an advantage, knowing where the Nhia-Samri are and what they're doing.

Ellua's voice became steady as she manipulated one of the monitors, dragging her fingers around the screen, scrolling from one place to another on the map of the city. She kept up a continuous monologue, describing Nhia-Samri movements and strength. It didn't matter where they went or what they did; she reported everything. She especially reported on where the warlord was and what she was doing.

Unfortunately, it became less of a morale boost as the Nhia-Samri overwhelmed guard divisions, leaving the streets filled with dead and dying bodies. Electra noticed a new set of light green dots moving around the city. As she touched one, the image shifted to show a priest from Dalpha's temple, carrying a blood-covered pouch, constantly pulling out medical supplies as he tried to tend to the wounded guards and Daggers. Moving the screen out wide, she saw that there were over 300 green dots, indicating healers moving around the city. But as she watched, a number of them went out.

Electra shifted to a visual display and saw that a Nhia-Samri warrior had decapitated the healer, and was pulling his odassi out of the chest of the Dagger the healer had been tending to. It was more than she could take. She turned as her stomach clenched. Dropping to her hands and knees, she threw up on the floor. It took several minutes to pull herself together. When she started to stand, a hand came down and helped pull her up.

She saw all the sympathy and understanding she needed in the eyes of Mandy, her personal Dagger guard captain. Mandy nodded and handed her a cloth, while another Dagger held out a cup of water. Electra cleaned herself up, and turned back to the tasks at hand.

Bayion was trying to outmaneuver the warlord. He'd split his forces and was moving away, trying to take a circular route away from her and back to the palace. Electra managed to get the names of the Dagger commanders added to the displays she and Ellua were using. As soon as Ellua saw those, she bent close to the displays, providing specific intelligence by calling out names before specific unit reports.

"Three hundred Nhia-Samri just turned south onto Silver from Jules. Remdian, take the second right, then left. Daggers out. Oshman, go back one block and connect with the Daggers there. Nhia-Samri have established a barricade facing east on Merchant Way near Olman."

Electra, more determined than ever, searched for what she truly wanted.

Weapons have to be here. I should have figured these out weeks ago, but I didn't think I would be the one trying to use them.

The problem was that many of the weapons would not respond or activate. She tried verbal and typed commands, but nothing worked.

'I've lost the empress's command override. It went inactive when we discovered she'd been killed with her team in the blast zone of the gate explosion Lebuin tried to stop. I can't bring any of the primary weapons online for you,' said Vesta after the third combat system she'd found didn't activate.

Electra recalled the bloody pile of human and horse flesh being picked over by the carrion birds the hawks had found when they got to the power source location where Ticca and her team had been. Vesta and Arkady estimated there was enough to account for the whole team. Lebuin's last location was a burnt-out crater. Given the destructive force, it was clear that Lebuin hadn't been able to stop the attack.

She glared at the defensive and offensive systems that would not respond. Then she noticed one system had a low level of power available.

At last! One palace defense system is online.

"Aperi aestus imperium radio," she said as she touched the system's icon.

Her display shifted to show her a targeting system like the one used during her earlier clandestine attack on the Nhia-Samri base.

Now, let's stop some of those mages.

Using the controls, she scanned for anyone who looked like a mage. Spotting one, she made sure the targeting locked onto him, and pressed the activation button. The air around him burst into flames as he stumbled backwards.

Holding up their odassi, two Nhia-Samri warriors leapt between the mage and the weapon she was using. For a second, she thought they were going to be able to defend against the cannon. Then one of the odassi blades shattered. The warrior holding the broken blade tried to jump out of the way, but he wasn't fast enough, and was also set aflame.

The mage turned back towards her view. He appeared to be calm, and seemed to have already recovered from the initial attack. He stepped out between the weapon and the remaining warrior, as the weapon's power slammed into his strengthened shield. His defenses absorbed the energy, as he looked directly at her. Actually, he was glaring at the weapon, but it was an eerie feeling. He raised both hands, and a few moments later, the display went blank.

'The mage destroyed the photon cannon,' Vesta confirmed.

'*A repair unit is in route. If we can get it back online we can use it against the normal warriors.*'

Electra slapped the console in frustration.

I thought we could get some of them before they took out the weapon. I think all I did was get him upset.

Electra glanced at the screens. In spite of Ellua's reports coordinating the city's troops and preventing any surprise attacks, the Nhia-Samri had taken control of the western and southern portions of the city and were making progress. They weren't suffering many casualties, and it was obvious their numbers were sufficient to the task of subduing the city. Llino just did not have enough seasoned soldiers to face them.

Further, the city's defenses were proving useless. The ancient weapons were easily blocked by their mages, and the flying enforcer sentinels were being blown out of the sky without stopping their advance. It was only a matter of time.

"BAYION RUN! TAKE THE ALLEY! RUN, URDU!" Ellua's screams, laced with fear, caught Electra by surprise, and she looked over to see what was happening. The warlord and her warriors were rushing in on Bayion's position. The entire city heard her cry as it echoed around through the streets.

Bayion was fighting with his personal Dagger guards. As Electra and Ellua watched, a Nhia-Samri cut down two of the Daggers. The warlord ran, slicing into the fight and, in a rapid series of strikes, killed all of Bayion's Daggers and disarmed him. Electra's stomach tightened, and her heart leapt into her throat as the warlord clubbed Bayion down and turned back towards the palace, issuing orders. The warlord's eyes seemed to look right into the display, directly at Electra.

Her whole body shivered with the revelation of that action. The warlord's orders were to capture the regents.

Her mind raced, and her heartbeat rang in her ears. With shivers running down her back, she looked at her guards, imagining Mandy and her team cut to ribbons.

She's coming for all of us! Lords and Ladies, can they know about me? We're going to lose this battle!

Vesta had the same thoughts. *'You need to evacuate.'*

VESTA

The areas around the Nhia-Samri forces were finally clearing of non-combatants. Vesta had been focusing all of the flying Imperial enforcer sentinels on pushing them in specific directions, while she'd taken advantage of Ellua's using the announcement system to issue orders via the same systems, claiming to be by order of the regents for evacuation.

Bayion had taken the lead, combining several Dagger teams into full squads. He'd been directing a platoon of Daggers overseeing the guards, getting people out of the city using the eastern gates. But his position had been overrun, and he was a prisoner of the warlord.

"If we don't get Ellua and Electra out of the palace, they're going to be cut off." Arkady's urgent tone caught Vesta's attention.

She reviewed the data, and saw that Arkady had correctly predicted the Nhia-Samri's goals to take the palace. They weren't fighting as they had in reports from the north. There, they'd focused on capturing the ancient cities, and had pushed out or killed all resistance.

In Llino, they'd attacked from only the western and southern gates in a coordinated assault. Their mages had blown out six shield emitters at both locations, and then created magical bridges over the walls. The use of magic negated the need for any kind of war machinery or siege towers. The Nhia-Samri warriors simply ran over the walls without any hindrance.

Once the attack began, their remaining forces had abandoned the blockade lines to rush to the nearest breach. Since they held two sections of the city, they were pushing in, ignoring the houses and populace and taking only the needed sections to create a path deeper into the city. The two paths they were creating pointed straight towards the palace, except that the warlord had specifically gone after Bayion.

Agreeing with Arkady, she told Electra to begin evacuations. Electra and Ellua were collecting the regents' family and guards. The other nobles had been told to return to their families and, if possible, to escape the city.

With the sixty-one confirmed mages in the city, Vesta almost missed the three mages doing something unexpected. While the other mages were battling with their warriors or attacking the Guildhouse, three mages had split off, and were standing on a section of the southern wall. Away from all the other activities, they bore into it with powerful magical blasts that broke down the molecular bonds of the nearly indestructible materials.

They were a few degrees off from breaching the paths inside the walls. She knew they were looking for those. If they got inside the city's sealed maintenance tunnels, they would be able to find critical systems which, if knocked out, would cut off power to many of the palace defenses, as well as much of her control infrastructure — not that those defenses were useful at the moment.

Given that she was supposed to be asleep, Duke wouldn't care if those systems were fixed. He would probably just fix the wall, leaving those systems to be repaired when she was awakened. But she needed those systems to maintain full control. There would be no explaining how they got repaired when Duke came looking.

"Arkady, can you do something about those mages on the south wall? They'll soon discover they're not in the right place and adjust for their error. I don't know how they know what to expect, but I'm sure they know exactly what they're searching for."

"Got them. Sending sixty enforcer sentinels to keep them busy, but they can defeat them. Any chance we can stop shooting pillows and get serious?" His tone was far more acerbic than usual. He was as worried as Vesta about the outcome.

As he spoke, she saw sixty of the large silver sentinels spin out of the massed group, flying a patrol pattern high above the city, providing most of the visual data they were using to track all the movements. The group of sixty formed into a fighting formation, turning south. Their armored bodies glistened in the sun as rainbows danced off their gossamer wings. Lightning began to arc between them as they dove on the three mages.

"Stand by. I'm working on that. I need at least twelve more minutes. The security override from Ticca's original call for help stopped working the moment we discovered she was dead. We should have considered this contingency, and either cut off the Imperial registry from the main systems, or unlocked everything ahead of time. If I get a second chance, there's no lock I'm leaving in place. I should have released all the locks before she was killed, but I was afraid Duke might check."

Sixty sentinels swarmed the three mages. Vesta sighed, noticing that the lower-yield crowd control weapons the enforcer sentinels had didn't do much against the combined shield of the three mages. Arkady growled, slamming one of the sentinels directly on top of their shield, forcing its internal systems to overload.

Arkady's gleeful cackle caused Vesta to review the results herself. The explosion was massive, catching the mages by surprise. Their combined shield crumpled, blowing them off the wall. All three of them managed to maintain their own personal shields.

"They're certainly well-protected. I wonder how many layers of shields they're maintaining."

Something else registered with her for the first time.

"Arkady, can you take some readings? These mages are expending far more energy than should be possible. There's not this much energy available via the mana lines in this area. I'm sure of it."

Arkady grunted acknowledgement of the request.

Vesta also activated a tracking system like the one in Algan that had triangulated the power source of that mage. Unfortunately, with the Nhia-Samri and Guild mages all using power, it would be really lucky, with the limited magical sensors remaining, to identify where they were getting the power.

"That isn't going to work. We didn't have a chance to get Brandon's latest sensors exported from Elraci before the accident."

"You're too pessimistic at times."

"I'm a realist." He huffed.

The mages twisted in the air, each casting a different spell to soften their landing. Arkady split the sentinels into two groups and had them attack, full force, two of the mages individually. Nine sentinels, combined and coordinated, could effectively cause issues. Although their shields weren't penetrated, the two mages were slammed and thrown around at the coordinated attacks. Vesta enjoyed watching them getting kicked around.

This is more than just an old city. This is my home, and I'll be diurdin if I let you keep pulling it apart.

Just as Vesta managed to release the locks on another hangar of enforcer sentinels, she noticed the city's maintenance system had dispatched a repair unit to the wall. A repair walker moved over the hole, spraying the tungsten carbide and carbon filament repair goo, which was packed with nanobots designed and programmed to combine the elements at the atomic level, creating a nearly indestructible nanotwinned material in a variety of final styles.

In that case, the bots would form the goo into a perfect nanotwinned patch that would be indistinguishable from the rest of the wall, which looked like an ordinary alabaster granite.

The one mage who wasn't dealing with sentinels flew back on top of the wall and rushed to stop the repairs, hitting the repair walker with a magical blast that caused it to explode. Repair materials went everywhere, encasing the mage.

"Oh, ouch! He'd better work fast to get out of that, or he'll be in a lot of trouble." Arkady laughed.

"I liked that repair walker. It came from Duianna Prime," she grumbled.

She let a small amount of her attention stay on the mage, who'd inadvertently attacked himself. The materials were hardening as the nanobots did their jobs. Without the preprogrammed directives, the nanobots were hardening the mass of repair materials in an uneven and chaotic pattern. Small spurs were growing in some places, while other areas went glossy as they hardened into polished stone. It was a rather interesting sculpture.

In two seconds, enough of the material had hardened that Vesta was pretty sure the mage wasn't going to get out of it.

"You know, that might be a way to take care of the other mages."

Arkady's attention came back from fighting the other two mages. "What? He didn't make it? That's interesting! We'll have to put that on display someplace later."

Vesta checked on Electra's progress. She and Ellua had the regents' families together, and were herding them to the throne room. There, Daggers were already gathering the remaining key officials. The plan was to get them out of the eastern palace gates, and to the eastern docks, before the Nhia-Samri realized they had left.

Reviewing the other data, Vesta saw that Warlord Eshra-Zunia had a group of 100 warriors carrying the unconscious and bound Bayion out of the city. The warlord had consolidated the rest of her forces, and they were moving to cut off the palace's eastern routes.

"Urd!" Vesta yelled. "Bayion is almost out of the city."

"She's moving fast. She'll be able to block the routes from the palace to the eastern docks."

As if they could read the situation, the Nhia-Samri all turned as one, and began pushing towards the palace from all sides. Many of their teams began running around the guards and Dagger squads in their dash to form a blockade line around the palace.

Vesta felt herself warming as she realized that they'd probably guessed that the palace was about to be evacuated. Ellua's updates had stopped. In hindsight she realized they should have kept Ellua coordinating the battles. If Electra tried to get out, they would encounter enough Nhia-Samri to slow them down. Outside the palace she and her group would be easy targets.

She materialized all the control room monitors, and herself in the center of them, just so she could slam her fist into the consoles and stamp her feet. She started pacing. Arkady appeared to the side.

"Odd how good that feels, isn't it?"

"Electra is surrounded, completely cut off! Bayion is captured! And you want to talk about physical sensations?" she screamed, stomping her foot.

Arkady took a step backwards. "What else can we do? Unless you want to expose our status. So far, we haven't been able to release any of the combat locks. We could use everything we have in perfect coordination, but that would pretty much shout, 'Vesta is awake,' to Duke. Even then, I'm not sure we could win with just the crowd-control stuff."

She turned and stomped towards Arkady, hands raised in fists. "WE CANNOT FAIL!"

Arkady nodded. "I agree. What we need is Ticca here to call for help. That'd give us an excuse for releasing the locks on the military defenses."

"SHE'S DEAD! THE EMPRESS IS DEAD! NO ONE IS LEFT!"

"Then we have to protect the regents. They're the rulers now."

Vesta had started to walk away when Arkady's words penetrated a part of her systems.

Turning around, she stared at Arkady, open-mouthed. "The regents are the rulers."

Arkady nodded. "Yes, that's what I said. They...oh." His eyes widened as he, too, understood what he'd said. "Do you think it'll work?"

"Like you and Duke, I don't know how Muriel's security override works. If it doesn't work, we would be no worse off. But if it does, we'll have time to doctor up the records like I did at Algan to satisfy Duke that you and I are still locked down. It would give us all we need to regain total control of all our systems."

Vesta spun, finding Electra and connecting to her audio implant. "Electra, you're cut off. There is one hope. You have to get Ellua to cuss and call for the city to stop the Nhia-Samri."

"What? You're already helping," Electra replied, her voice pitching up nervously.

"I'll explain later. This is a long shot," Vesta said.

Electra didn't respond as quietly as she had been, and Ellua heard. "Who are you talking to? Of course everyone is helping." Ellua's voice came through the connection.

Vesta engaged the throne room monitors, and started chewing industriously on her nails as she waited. Electra moved before three of the LUMED consoles, reviewing the situation and pointing. Ellua was standing next to her, looking at the displays as well. Electra made sighing noises, and Ellua's eyes followed her gesture and moved, focusing on the indicated data or image.

Finally, Electra gave an emotional sigh. "We've been outmaneuvered. The palace is surrounded. The Nhia-Samri almost have Bayion out of the city. If they get him out, we won't be able to track him."

Ellua's face tightened, and her eyes teared up. She turned to Electra, shaking her head. "Lords and Ladies, help us."

Ellua turned away from Electra, looking across the

screens floating around the throne room. Electra made a small motion that caused Ellua's eyes to go past the displays, to the children at the far end of the room. Tears ran freely as Ellua stared at the families grouped in the throne room who had no way out.

Vesta calculated that Ellua's eyes were on her own son and daughters. Seven nannies and as many Dagger guards kept the kids in line and quiet.

Arkady stood next to Vesta in the virtual control space, watching. "She's clever."

"Shh. Wait for it."

Vesta pulled up a display that showed Ellua's heart rate had picked up, and her system was flooding with adrenaline as the feelings washed through her. Ellua's emotions were edging in the right direction.

"Even if this does work, it was a poor thing to do," Vesta said.

"We can find a way to apologize afterwards, if this works," Arkady responded.

Ellua flopped onto one of the regent's thrones. She cried softly, her eyes on Electra.

"I don't know how you know so much! Is there nothing more you can do?" she begged. She looked back at the displays, and slammed her fists into the throne's arms. "Urdu, make this city protect us! It's supposed to have amazing powers to guard the citizens and palace!" She broke down completely and cried out in anguish, dropping her face into her hands.

Arkady and Vesta didn't see Electra rushing over to Ellua's side, embracing her in a hug. Their attention was fixed on a large display in the control room wall that had appeared. Tall orange words scrolled across the screen:

IMPERIAL SECURITY OVERRIDE
ACKNOWLEDGED: *SYSTEM LOCKS RELEASED*.
IMPERIAL ATTACK ORDERS *CONFIRMED.*
OBJECTIVES - *PROTECT PALACE FROM AGGRESSORS,*
DEFEND CITIZENS FROM AGGRESSORS.

Arkady looked at Vesta with a wide smile on his face. "Thank you, Muriel Neyon-Banaschel! We have our orders."

Vesta didn't bother to answer, as she was already releasing the locks on *all* of the city's combat systems. Vesta's systems, burning with anger at the attackers, tingled with the power of the reactivated systems.

Combat sensor data started pouring in from the hundreds of preprocessing stations embedded in sensor clusters around the city. Her view of the city grew exponentially clearer, as the processing systems began creating profiles of aggressors and guards.

In the palace, deep reverberating klaxons began to sound. Ellua and Electra stood staring at the multitude of new monitors that had bloomed into existence, each one showing weapon systems' reports and overhead a holographic combat map of the city formed. The natural light of the room vanished as hidden steel panels slammed close over the windows sealing the palace.

Deep in the city, the reinforced combat generators fired off, and power levels spiked across all of Vesta's systems. The structural reinforcement fields in the city and palace walls burnt with the extra energy, engaging the millions of high-energy military shield emitters embedded in the walls. The entire city began to glow a soft white.

Dust and dirt was flung into the air around the palace, blurring it in a haze of brown, as ancient doors surrounding the walls dropped open, and thousands of combat drones took to the air. Nhia-Samri warriors fell back, covering their faces from the rush of debris.

Vesta connected herself to the public announcement system via the automated voice interface systems, so it wouldn't be her voice the city heard.

"Attention! This is an Imperial military action. Hostile forces in violation of Imperial Law have breached the city and have been identified. All citizens are to proceed in a calm and orderly fashion to the closest designated emergency evacuation site or emergency bunker. Imperial guards, all hostiles are to be detained or destroyed." She set the message to auto-repeat every thirty seconds.

In her monitors, Vesta saw that Warlord Eshra-Zunia, the hundreds of Nhia-Samri with her, the tens of thousands of Nhia-Samri throughout the city, and all of the guards and Daggers had stopped fighting. Enemies and allies turned towards the palace, most with their mouths wide open. They all stared at the shimmering wall of Duianna Empire military combat drones from before their worlds existed, descending on them from the air around the palace.

Above the city, hundreds of enforcer sentinels dove as a swarm, each one opening its previously locked military weapons ports. At the eastern and northern docks, the water boiled as hundreds of additional enforcer sentinels leapt from the underwater hangars. The silvery insects burst into the air, spreading their wings as they swarmed towards the palace.

Arkady was dancing as his arms moved in blinding speed over the controls. "Duke's locks on the sentinels' combat weapons have been released. We're weapons free across the board."

Vesta stood in the middle of her control room, using the thousands of new sensors to coordinate the hundreds of thousands of activated combat systems. Her mind spun as the level of calculations and interactions pushed even her to the limits. Still, she laughed. "You thought you could just put me to sleep for thousands of years, kill my empress, attack my city, and threaten my Aelargo without fear? At last, I don't have to hold back, and *I* will show you how wrong you were!"

Royal Gift

CHAPTER 11
MISFORTUNE PLAYS NO FAVORITE

RUNA-ILLA KEPT HER BACK TO Lebuin as they climbed up the sandstone escarpment. Everyone in the group was still simmering mad at Lebuin for taking his extended reading trip, while the team fought Nhia-Samri and hauled his body over the mountains. Her temper flared every time she looked at him. For the last few days she'd made a point to keep her back to him.

She couldn't avoid her connection to him, and although he tried to block some of his feelings, Illa knew it hurt him. Reaching the top, she stepped out of the way of the rest of the team. As she stepped away from the precipice, she got a surge of regret and guilt that was not her own, and she knew Lebuin was watching her.

The only time she didn't feel that guilt from him was when he was working on opening the journal. The needed focus required to unlock the threads took all his attention. Now that she thought about it, she realized that was why he pulled the journal out at every break or rest period. In a way it was letting him escape those feelings, and yet work towards a possible solution to save them all.

Sure, you feel guilty now. But you chose to sit in that library, reading fairytales. What kind of God would do that?

She adjusted her head wrap and cloak again to fully cover her. Through the cloth slits, she looked out over the burning sands of Elraci. The place was so depressing that she hadn't even thought of working on that new song since waking next to it. For her whole life, that place had been the deadly Circumveni Desert, but now she knew it had been so much more.

I wonder who decided to rename this place the Circumveni

Desert. Elraci was wiped from existence, but surely people would want to remember what it was. They had to have had a history.

She no longer wanted to think of the place as the Circumveni Desert. She felt a need to honor the memory of what had once been there. Elraci was once a green and fertile kingdom filled with scholars, scientists, philosophers, and millions of other souls. Her heart ached, taking in the wasteland before her.

Nigan climbed up the opposite side of the small plateau from exploring a little ahead. He stepped up next to her. She stopped herself from grabbing him just to breathe in his intense scent. She'd flirted with him for weeks before they finally embraced. She'd caught whiffs of his scent before, but in that first embrace, she was able to breathe him in, and it shocked her how much she'd swooned over it.

"Looks like another full hot day," he said with his perpetual friendliness. She couldn't see his face through his head wrap, but she could hear his expression.

She grinned as his joy infected her mood.

I do love that man. His ability to remain obstinately cheerful is a miracle.

"Every day is a hot day here," she groaned back, trying to not let him know she was smiling. She had to keep him on his toes.

"Ha! Wrong again. You know, you really should be careful with your pronouncements." He held out something to her in his gloved hand.

Like her, he was covered from head to toe against the intense, burning sun. They'd learned their lesson painfully the first day in the desert. Even with Lebuin's miraculous incantations providing constant cleaning and cooling shields, the sun still caused harm. They'd all ended the first day with every bit of exposed skin badly sunburnt.

Lebuin had been able to apply a little healing magic, but not specifically for burns, and it was only moderately effective. There was a wonderful salve in Magus Vestul's pack that Lebuin carried. It was based on a plant called *aloe,* which they knew grew in Karakia. Lebuin had spent a mark digging through the pack, saying, "Aloe. It has to be in here," repeatedly. When he found it, he practically danced as he rushed to give large amounts of it to everyone. There were a number of bottles of the salve in the pack.

Actually, now that I think about it, why would Magus Vestul have nearly a dozen large bottles of a burn cream in his pack? I doubt he suffered any kind of burn that often.

No one used the salve until Ditani identified it as a medicinal treatment, effective for many skin ailments. The Karakians didn't call it *aloe.* It was called *dilotha,* after the flower dilothalai, or commonly called Lothia's Light. Ditani said that many Karakians, mostly women, also used the cream regularly to keep their skin soft and youthful. Illa had taken a bottle of it and put it in her pack. She knew Lebuin saw it, and his hidden smirk made her even angrier.

Sharing a skin cream won't win me back, Lord. You'll have to do a lot more than that.

Nigan, the only Dagger treating Lebuin like he wasn't a snake, asked how he'd known about the aloe. When he answered that he'd read about it in so many of the books that he was sure it was a real treatment, Illa almost laughed aloud.

He didn't intentionally try to imply that all that reading was useful.

The other Daggers recognized it, too, and that small fact had helped with some of them.

After applying the cooling cream and having the burns rapidly become tolerable, many thanked him. The top priority that evening was shredding blankets and shirts to stitch together desert robes for everyone.

Even though desert travel was normally done in the twilight marks of morning and evening, the team had decided time was more important. With Lebuin's incantations being able to keep everyone safe from the heat, they decided to travel as much as possible through the day. On the second day, a few team members complained they were having a hard time seeing clearly, which was all the warning they needed to avoid sun blindness. The sands of Elraci included a substantial amount of finely ground crystals that reflected the light as much as snow did. That had almost changed their plan. A simple solution was discovered, when Ditani suggested narrowing the gap in their head wraps.

After that, they'd been marching for five days, mostly in a straight line, for the installation Lebuin thought was important to visit. They got up in the twilight marks of morning, ate a light meal, and then walked steadily all day. They all sweated, but not nearly as much as they should have. The environment protection incantations Lebuin provided allowed them to almost act normally.

The only limiting things were food and drink. There was practically no game, and there seemed to be no water at all. They were all carrying their own water, and they had just enough to make it to the other location. Both Ticca and Lebuin were assuming there would be more water there.

I can see why he liked having these incantations running all the time. I'm not sticky, dirty, or uncomfortably hot.

Glancing at what Nigan was holding out for her, she decided it wouldn't be dangerous, or else he wouldn't be offering it to her. Besides, she had gloves on. It wasn't safe to touch anything there with bare hands. If it didn't sear your skin right off, it was likely to be poisonous. She took the object and brought it in front of her eye slits.

Amazingly enough, it was a dried leaf. It was oddly elongated on one side, and had silvery edges along the other. Turning it around, she noted that the silvery edge looked suspiciously like a knife edge, and the opposite edge was prickly.

"Lovely specimen. I wouldn't push through a bush with these leaves. If the silver edges don't cut like sharp knives, I'd be surprised."

Nigan chuckled and held up a glove that had a number

of slicing cuts. "I really should consult you before I reach for something interesting. You're right, of course."

"Thank you, but I fail to see how this makes me wrong about my *pronouncement*, as you called it."

"Water. The plant was nearly dead and dried out, but it was just down there." He pointed over the edge of the escarpment. She stepped over, and saw what he was suggesting. The area below held a number of twisted plants that grew along and through what was obviously a flood water wash bed. There was something wrong. She could sense it.

Turning back around, she noticed Nigan was examining something else that must have been in his pouch. Moving closer, she saw it and didn't like what it was. It was half of a skull.

Ticca pulled herself up and, seeing what Nigan was holding, stepped over. "Where did you get that?"

Nigan pointed ahead at the gully.

Illa sensed power washing over them, making her feel like she was caught in a large wave. Her head spun, and she felt dizzy, grabbing Ticca's arm for support.

Ticca held her hand for a moment, as Illa finished bowing to her.

"I'm pleased you were able to come down from Lebuin's temple in Pentegull."

"I would not miss this for all the treasures in the world, Your Royal Highness."

A smile blossomed on the princess's face. Ticca motioned, and a young girl appeared, wearing a silk dress decorated in the Imperial red and silver pattern of a household servant. She held a small, beautifully carved, wooden box. Ticca took the box from the girl, who curtsied, and then backed away.

"A small gift for you, Your Excellency. From me to our high priestess."

Illa took the time to examine the box, which was likely to be every bit a treasure as that which it contained. Any gift from the heir to the throne of the Duianna Empire should also be accepted with the greatest of attention. It was hand-carved, with a seamless set of scenes that wrapped around the entire box, depicting the local Elracian elves in various endeavors like hunting, craft working, and research. The top of the box was carved with the Imperial seal. The box had no seams she could detect, although it felt far lighter than a solid piece of wood.

"Lady, this is an amazing treasure," she said, genuinely appreciative.

"Thank you. Your reputation of having an expert eye for art is well-deserved. That was made by Amia-Hon as a favor."

Illa almost dropped the precious box.

A hand carving from the patriarch of the Amia family. Lords, this is priceless.

She puzzled over it for a time, and Ticca seemed content to wait. She couldn't find a means to open it, though she was sure the top released or came off somehow. She looked up, and Ticca motioned as a mischievous smirk replaced her smile. "I'll let you figure out how to open it at your leisure. It's a surprise I am willing to wait for."

"Your Highness, I...."

Illa's memory of who she was, and where she and Ticca were, flooded back in. She glanced around at the royal greeting room. Aside from Ticca and Illa, there was the serving girl, and two Imperial elite guards. She turned back, and Ticca was regarding her with glazed eyes, that looked around at the room uncertainly.

"Illa, do you remember a...different place?" Ticca asked pensively.

Am I losing my mind? What is happening?

Her eyes fell to the box she was holding. It was solid.

Ticca is here. But where is here?

She recalled she was in Imridu-Nam, and she'd arrived a few marks before by shuttle.

She shook her head, and remembered she was trekking through the Elracian desert with Ticca, Lebuin, and a group of Daggers. There was no craft like the flying shuttle she remembered riding on. Elraci was a devastated land. Still, she recalled the lakes, flowing grasslands, and forests she'd flown over, coming to visit her God, Lord Lebuin, to help him with some matter involving the emperor and his daughter Ticca, who was a long-time friend and confidant.

I need to be careful. This might just be me. I need to find Lebuin.

She felt Lebuin's presence. *'Illa! I'm coming, so try to hold onto this moment. We must know what is happening.'*

'I don't serve you right now. I'm still mad,' she thought at Lebuin irritably. Illa staggered backwards. *Why did I say that? How can I not do as Lebuin commands?*

Her mind was split. She recalled he'd abandoned her to go read adventure stories. She laughed out loud at the ridiculousness of that idea. Ticca focused on her and raised an eyebrow.

Lebuin has never abandoned anyone ever!

Something inside her told her he had, just not there.

The royal guards sensed something was wrong, and moved with a speed she admired. One stepped between Ticca and her, drawing his odassi blades. The other caught her, giving her a steadying hand, but also holding her with the obvious intent of detaining her if she became a threat to the princess. She noticed they'd tapped their odassi blades, enhancing all of their senses, speed, and strength.

She considered knocking them away, as she had far more power through Lebuin than they could cope with alone. But they were just doing their duty to protect the princess.

Ticca also seemed to be confused.

"Perhaps you were recalling the desert?" Illa hoped that was cautious enough to avoid trouble if it turned out she was wrong.

Ticca's eyes had shifted to look at her guards' swords. She reached up, and held her head a second before replying. "It was a bit hotter than it is now."

She does remember it, too. I'm not under attack. So what is this?

The doors slammed open, and Ticca stumbled backwards, her mouth dropping open.

Illa recognized the intruder instantly, and her legs wobbled under her, going numb. *Amia-Dharo! How can he be here?*

Her mind split again as she wondered at her silly questions.

Something must truly be wrong with me. Of course Amia-Dharo is here. He's been the captain of the emperor's Elracian Imperial Royal Guards for thousands of years. She felt dizzy trying to reconcile her dual memories. She was sure he was a hunted traitor who had betrayed the Nhia-Samri. She also knew that Ticca and her father, the emperor, considered him an Imperial cousin, due to his unusual connection to the royal family via his prototype odassi blades and imperial nanobots. He'd protected the Imperial family from all dangers for over five thousand years. His blades and special nanobots were the first of their kind, the genesis of the five thousand year Elracian research project about to be completed.

Amia-Dharo's lips were drawn in a flat line, and his brows were so far down, his eyes looked like slits. He held his longer odassi blades in his hands. The silver surfaces of his blades reflected and bent the light around them, making them shimmer. His eyes first went to Ticca. "Your Highness, are you okay? I felt a strange shift in...." His eyes landed on Illa. "Runa-Illa? Your Excellency, you...."

Illa felt that strange wave coming again. Her mind felt the weight, and she grasped the guard who was holding her for more support. Power flowed through her from an unknown source. The guard looked around, as if he could sense some of what she was feeling and was seeking the cause. He pulled power from his odassi, and used it to ground himself harder. Illa knew exactly what he was doing, even though she'd never held an odassi. She shook her head, trying to clear the sensations racing through her.

I got my odassi when I turned seventeen, two years early. Father was so proud that his eyes teared.

Still shaking her head, she twisted her arm up and out with all her might, breaking the guard's hold on her. In a swift move she put the box into her pouch as her other hand came down. With her free hands she drew both his odassi blades while simultaneously kicking him so hard that he flew backwards two feet before falling back, smacking his head on the smooth marble floor, and sliding three more feet, coming to a complete stop. Using the raw power flooding her, which she assumed was from Lebuin, she bent the odassi to her will. Their bands shone as they became hers to command. She pulled their power and used them to anchor her against the coming wave. With a crack of thunder, she shifted her stance, rooting her feet to the marble floor, bracing against the force that was washing past her.

Ticca grabbed her for stability; Illa wasn't sure how she managed to hang on, but her grip was like a steel band pulling on Illa.

"Use your legs. Root!"

Why would I say that to the princess? She hasn't been trained in those kind of martial arts.

Ticca understood, and shifted her feet to match Illa's stance. She also opened herself to allow Illa to feed power from both Lebuin and the odassi blades to her. Ticca's feet made the same thunderclap as the powers reacted, and she stood, bracing against the force.

Light shimmered around Amia-Dharo, and his eyebrows shot up as if they were launched by a pair of ballistae. A kind of terror swept across his face. Sheathing one sword, he used both hands and his weight to thrust the other blade into the stone floor. Sparks flew, and the marble floor trembled as the sword sank almost two feet into the stone as he dropped to his knees. He shifted into a tight one-handed grip, pulling out leather strapping from his pouch with his free hand. He wrapped the leather around his hand, binding it tightly to the sword's hilt. He fought the same powerful force, which wasn't affecting the guards or the serving girl.

All the while, he was yelling at them, "I wasn't here! I don't know what happened! I suspected treason, but I can't find the proof! Elraci is too unstable. Every time I've tried to enter it, I'm practically ripped apart by the instabilities."

The invisible force hit them all harder. Amia-Dharo was lifted off the floor, only held in place by the sword he was bound to. One hand shot towards them as tears came to his eyes.

"I ordered searches, but they just found some of the lost technology. Ticca, please, I beg you to leave! Don't stay! There's more that can kill you than you can see! I can't protect you here! You need help from the Gods, but they won't give it...."

The wave hit with so much power, it whipped Illa around. She tried to hold herself in place. Ticca screamed as she was thrown into the air and out through a wall, taking a portion of Illa's sleeves with her. She tried to hold onto the place, but the force was too great. The odassi blades disintegrated into dust, which flew away as if taken in gale-force winds. She lost contact with the floor as the world spun around her. She wrapped herself in protective shielding, pulling on Lebuin's powers freely. Then she slammed into something, and blackness enveloped her.

Ticca, Nigan, Ditani, and Lebuin were all calling her name when she opened her eyes. Nigan was holding her; she smiled and nuzzled closer to him. His strong arms felt good around her, and she liked the feel of his muscled chest against her cheek.

She wanted to ignore everything else and stay there in his embrace. It was so comfortable. She knew she could trust him, and that she was in a safe place. Her mind slowly started moving again, and she recalled who and where she was.

Opening her eyes, she saw that Lebuin was kneeling next to her. Ticca was standing a bit wobbly, bracing herself with Ditani and Risy's help. She looked up and found Nigan's warm brown eyes and smiling face. He'd thrown off his head wrap, and was staring at her critically.

Illa made a shooing motion at Lebuin. "Still mad at you."

"Fair enough," he said. "Were you there? Did you see the blue palace? I felt you were there this time, inside somewhere. But something more happened. I didn't get to you in time."

She smiled and snuggled tighter into Nigan's grasp. "Yes, I was there with the princess. She gave me this." She reached into her pouch and pulled out the wooden box.

As she held it up for everyone to inspect, her mind snapped into place fully. She stared at the amazing carved wooden box. *How can I have this? That was a dream, wasn't it?*

❦ HIRI-RULA ❦

The sky was blue, and the green field spread out, rolling down to a vast lake. The songs of hundreds of birds played in her ears. Hiri-Rula turned around, looking at the beautiful city that blended with the forest. She stood on a wide stone path that meandered down to the water's edge, where it continued across the lake over a stone bridge, straight and level, with rising stone arches and black hanging lanterns that would light it at night.

She breathed in the fresh, clean air; it was moist, cool, and smelled of the late summer flowers she loved so much. They only grew there, and they defied her every attempt to take the seedlings to her northern home in Yalthum. The climates were almost the same, yet something about Elraci was special.

She saw some elven workers moving across the path below and laughed as a thought occurred. *Perhaps the flowers need something more than good soil, water, and sun to grow.*

She shifted to mage sight, and the golden mana lines in

the streets emanated soft magic like a warm candle shed its light. Elraci's uniquely filtered magic bathed everything here; the void system collector generators provided a lot of energy.

Maybe when these lines are installed in Yalthum, the flowers will grow there, too.

A bright beacon of power ran around the palace corner and headed towards the main gateway. She shifted back to normal sight, weaving her magic into a vision-enhancement incantation. Her sight focused in on a running man, whom she recognized instantly.

Lord Lebuin is visiting here. I didn't know he was interested in the emperor's plans.

A wave of energy passed over her, and she felt dizzy. Her stomach turned as her legs collapsed. Someone caught her.

She lifted her hand to her head, but it didn't move. Or maybe it did, it was impossible to tell. Her eyes either wouldn't open, or weren't working. Her mind was under siege by a massive headache that was causing convulsions in her muscles.

"General, are you okay?"

"Sir, we're assembling a shelter. We've all lost the elemental protections."

"Yes, I know! Help me. Grab her pack."

"Sir, do you see that? Some of their team are down, too."

"Later — we have to get out of sight. All of the general's spells have collapsed. We're not being hidden from them. Set...."

Strong arms lifted her as she slipped into unconsciousness.

- - -

Water trickled into her mouth. She coughed and tried to wipe her face, but her arm was so heavy, it flopped across her chest instead.

"Careful, sir. Here, drink more. You need water."

More was dripped in, and she moved her mouth, recalling

how to swallow. She drank, and the warm liquid brought more life to her. Opening her eyes, Hiri-Rula saw a fuzzy blur hovering over her, wearing a striking halo of light. Blinking, she tried to clear her eyes.

"Ath affin o ee." Even to her own ears, what she said was unintelligible.

"General, I don't know. You said something none of us heard clearly. Then all of your environmental protection spells stopped, and you collapsed. We've erected an emergency shelter in a rock gully. Two have already collapsed from heat sickness."

Hiri-Rula considered this answer to her correctly-interpreted question.

Whoever that is, I'm impressed with his ability to translate gibberish.

She flexed her fingers, trying to feel them. There was a light tingling, and then sharp needles started piercing her skin. It rushed from her hand, up her arm, and across her whole body. The pain wracked her as muscle spasms shook her violently. She couldn't focus, and panic consumed her.

Screaming, she arched her back and rolled off the bedding. Her head hit a rock, and the impact added stars to her vision. Something gripped her tightly. It felt like cycles spun by as her form quivered in agony. After an eternity, the stars still floated, but the pain ebbed, and she felt completely exhausted. She didn't want to move, but something was crushing her. She found she could control her arms, and tried to push at whatever was on top of her.

"Colonel, the seizure has stopped. Can we get up?"

"No. Hold her. Don't let her hurt herself. It's the mage sickness this place causes. The seizures can happen multiple times over days before abating. We have to wait until her mind returns to us," Colonel Runa-Emry commanded.

"G'off ee!" she managed to grunt.

"Sir?" asked the warrior holding her down, unsure.

"It's over. Get off me!" she commanded again, finally finding her voice clear in her ear.

"Sir?" A second voice, female, came from somewhere near her legs.

The weights lifted from her. Her vision cleared, and the three warriors who'd been pinning her with their whole bodies came into focus. They were in a rocky shelter under an open-ended tarp roof. The tarp barely stopped the sun, heat and light radiated down through it.

She took a moment to breathe and center herself. It occurred to her that she wasn't maintaining the environmental shielding Lebuin's artifact let her extend to herself and the whole squad, yet she wasn't uncomfortably hot. All the other members of the expedition were stripped down to light cotton garments, which were soaked in sweat. Colonel Runa-Emry knelt, facing her, and although the three warriors had sat back more casually, she could read that they were prepared to jump on her if the spasms returned.

Sitting up was difficult until the colonel helped her. She noted that most of the group were leaning against the rock wall of the gully. Three warriors lay unconscious, as others dunked some cloths in a water basin, dabbing their comrades' faces and necks first before doing the same to themselves.

"Report."

"Lebuin, Ticca, and Illa fell at the same time you did. Lebuin was only down for a moment. We lost your camouflage spells, so we have only been confirming their location periodically. No one can stay out in the direct sun for too long." He indicated the unconscious warriors. "Even with ample water, the heat is too much."

She nodded, taking a long drink from the water bladder Una-Omda handed her.

Runa-Emry continued, "Their team has set up a camp, as we have, a short distance away. We're well outside of their normal patrol distance. We weren't spotted. You've been unconscious for three marks. You passed out after...."

Hiri-Rula held up her hand, saying, "I heard your earlier description."

She realized why she wasn't feeling the heat, as she looked down to see Lebuin's cloak clasp fastened to her clothing. Its magics provided her with continuous cleaning, and more importantly, temperature-controlling shielding.

He left this on me, knowing it would protect me from the worst of this place.

She lifted her hand to touch the silver clasp and acknowledged Colonel Runa-Emry. "I was drawn into a vision in which I was someplace I don't know called Elraci. But I saw Lebuin there, and knew him as a God. Lebuin made this." She tapped the cloak clasp. "He doesn't need it, so it must've been for Ticca. He's been planning on coming here for a long time." She slapped the clasp. "No mage would waste this much effort for spells he could maintain for himself, unless for the purpose of coming here, and needing someone to operate independently."

"Do you trust this vision? If Lebuin is a God, we must be more cautious."

"We will confirm this information. But for now, I'm feeling better; you've done well."

Hiri-Rula reached for her reserve powers, and extended the clasp's incantations out to the whole team. Many warriors sighed with relief, feeling the change in climate. Those who could, turned and bowed to her in thanks.

"This clasp makes more sense now. Ticca and Lebuin weren't working for Magus Vestul and Duke. Magus Vestul was working for Lebuin. Duke is, too. That explains why Vestul and Duke went to Llino to meet with Lebuin. The Gods must have discovered something and sent Lebuin to investigate. Lebuin used the Guildhouse to hide his activities while he researched and made this. Llino is the only city shielded from our mage-gates. Lebuin did not want us to discover his activities." She tapped the clasp again. "But what can be here that's so important? And why is the Grand

Warlord so concerned about this group's activities here? What would need so much effort and time from a hidden God?"

Hiri-Rula sat there, thinking, as her unit readied themselves, putting their armor back on. Finally, she stood and motioned for her armor. After she was dressed, she stepped out, looking at the setting sun.

"Colonel, come with me." She put on her wide-brimmed sun hat, and slipped on dull black sunglasses with leather side shields that cut off almost all the extra light, except what came through the smoky glass.

She looked at Runa-Emry until he realized she was asking him to show her the way to Lebuin's camp. He indicated the direction, and they slipped through the gully so stealthily, there was no trace of their passing. They came upon the observer on duty, and she extended the clasp's incantations to that warrior, too.

Using hand signals, Hiri-Rula ordered the warrior back to camp. Then she joined Runa-Emry as he peered over the edge of a small rise.

A good distance away, a tarp shade was erected against the sun, using the side of another wash gully for additional shade. She shifted to mage sight. Magic was rolling around the area. It moved fast in some places, and slow in others, and it changed shape, temperature, and color as it moved. She marveled again that so much power could be there. It was also one of the reasons it was so hot — the magic generated additional heat as it rolled and moved.

She concentrated on peering through the swirling magic, but due to the distance, she couldn't see the shelter. She considered the many scrying incantations she'd studied, settling on one she felt was small enough to work as needed in that environment. Pulling the power, she formed the pattern with her mind and fed energy to it. That created a small invisible third eye for her perceptions. Pushing with her will, she moved it closer to the shelter. She had to move it just past the halfway point before the lean-to came into clear view.

In spite of her self-control, she sucked in her breath. Lebuin glowed like a sun. He had an unbelievable amount of magic flowing around him. She had no way to even quantify what she saw; it was beyond anything she'd witnessed in all her years of study.

Runa-Emry motioned, asking if she was okay.

"It's confirmed. Lebuin is a God. Hold on, there's something under that hill," she whispered to him.

A pair of energy sources were beneath Lebuin's shelter. She moved her perception down and closer. As her magic eye circled the area, she found a narrow, elongated cave-like entrance into the hillside nearby. She added sight perceptions to the incantation and slipped it into the cave.

Two magical beasts were resting inside, the larger one half-propped up on the other. They had translucent armored shells that showed some of their internal organs. They pulsed with magical power. Each of them had three enormous pincers and two long, curling tails, which ended in one-meter stingers that looked like serrated tri-blade swords. Every inch of their enormous bodies was heavily armored. They appeared to weigh at least 5,000 kilograms. As she watched, she noticed they also had six smaller pincers around their mouths that continuously grabbed floating particles of magic and shoved them into their mouths.

They live on magic. Probably magic plus something else; those large pincers must have a purpose.

The creatures reminded her of the huge crabs that had attacked Outpost Two, killing everyone but her. They only had two pincers and no tails, and they'd been magical constructs.

Maybe these are escaped magical constructs.

As she started to move her perception spell out of the cave, one of the creatures sprang at it. Its large pincers closed on the incantation. The backlash of the break slammed into her, and she felt her channels burning with residual magic.

She leaned on the rock to shake off the adrenaline surge

from the surprise attack. Runa-Emry placed a steadying hand on her shoulder.

"What happened?" he whispered, since she had her eyes closed and he couldn't use hand signals.

She shook her head and held a hand up for him to give her a moment. Gaining control of her powers, she opened her eyes and looked at him. A distant chittering roar came from the direction of Lebuin's shelter.

Carefully poking their heads up over the rise, they saw both creatures scrambling over the top of the small hill. Their tails were curled for an attack. Her body involuntarily shuddered as she placed the creatures' origins. Their movements were purely scorpion. Except for the extra pincer, second tail, and six pincers around the maw, they would look like man-sized scorpions. The two beasts stopped at the crest of the hill, swinging all their pincers in the air.

The hairs on the back of her neck went up when she realized both creatures were staring directly at her.

As if purposefully waiting for the perfect dramatic moment, they clipped the air together and raced down the side of the hill, faster than she thought possible for their size. They made a direct line for Hiri-Rula's position.

The monsters didn't realize Lebuin's shelter wasn't part of the hillside, and they stepped out onto the flimsy tarp, both dropping on top of Lebuin's unfortunate group. Screams came from the shelter as they reacted to the apparent attack.

Lebuin and Ticca appeared from under the collapsed tarp. Together, they grabbed the edges of the tarp and ran towards the beasts, trying to entrap or entangle them in the canvas. It worked momentarily, and uncovered more of their group. Ditani and Runa-Illa joined Ticca and Lebuin in trying to distract or lure them away from the destroyed shelter. Ticca leapt in, landing on the back shell of one of them. Her knives moved as fast as Nhia-Samri, cutting off a few of the smaller pincers and stabbing the beast in a tender spot.

The creature's stingers thrust at her, but she dodged both

of them by turning and leaning back gracefully. It screamed, and its large pincers swung in to grab Ticca. She ducked under one. Before the stingers had finished pulling back for a second shot, she vaulted off, using the second pincer like a gymnastic brace. Lebuin hit it with a series of magical blasts, which did nothing at all. The beast was immune to magics, and its attention was locked on Ticca.

Illa had found a bow and was shooting arrow after arrow at the one going after Ticca. None of her arrows found a soft target. In the meantime, Ditani was pulling the other Daggers out of the collapsed shelter.

Hiri-Rula didn't have time to see what else happened. The second animal hadn't been distracted by Lebuin's group, and once it recovered from the surprise drop, it raced directly towards her.

Hiri-Rula turned, pulling Runa-Emry with her. "RUN!"

LEBUIN

Where the beasts came from, Lebuin had no idea, but it was apparent that they were immune to his attack incantations.

Strange visions, pissed-off teammates, and now oversized... whatever these are. Why did they attack us now?

Illa was standing next to Malla, their medic, who held three quivers and was handing Illa arrows as fast as the priestess could shoot them. Illa created a steady rhythm of *schhwaff-whack, schhwaff-whack*. The iron hunting heads bounced off the armor plates without much effect. The rest of the team was at least out from under the canvas, and miraculously, it looked like no one had been seriously injured when the monsters had jumped on their shelter. Persa was pulling their gear out, trying to get at more weapons.

Ticca kicked him in the hip, throwing him to the side. A pincer slammed into the ground where he'd been standing. Sand and rock pelted him, accompanied by a loud thump from the narrow miss.

"Wake up!" she shouted as she grabbed the back of the pincer. Persa threw a short sword to Ticca, who caught it. A stinger shot forward, narrowly missing Carda, who rolled out of the way.

The creature lifted Ticca into the air, and she slid down its arm to land on its back. It paused as it tried to understand where she'd gone.

While it was confused, Carda stepped inside its mandible zone, and sliced off a couple of the smaller pincers around the gaping mouth. She leapt backwards, doing a spin into a sideways roll as it reacted to her attack.

Illa was aiming at different locations, and with the satisfying sound of *schhwaff-THUNK*, an arrow lodged in the front area near its mouth, between two plates. The beast chittered, and one of its smaller pincers near the mouth ripped the arrow out, crushing it in the process.

Yes, wake up. Right. It's sensitive in the mouth area.

Rolling to the side, Lebuin got to his feet. Reinforcing his shield, he recalled a lightning strike incantation and quickly formed it, feeding it a lot of power. He targeted the same place where Illa's arrow had hit it. Lightning arced from him, and slammed into the creature. It reared up with a grating scream as it recoiled from the attack.

"Ha! Got you!"

Ticca was thrown off, but she landed with an acrobatic twist just behind it.

The second beast had been running off. At the scream, it turned, sliding to a stop. Its feet were digging troughs as its eight legs were already running back in their direction. Its open large pincers stretched out directly at Lebuin, and it screeched as it came.

The first beast landed with a thump and turned towards Lebuin. Two of the large pincers were coming for him so fast that he didn't have time to register the attack before they gripped his shields, crushing them. He strained to keep them up under the gigantic pressure. He couldn't move, and his heart pounded in the certain knowledge that the pressure would break his protection, and him, any second.

"Lebuin is pinned!" Persa called out.

Nigan and Risy came running in with swords held high. Together they brought their weapons down with massive, meaty thuds, at a joint. It worked, and the creature let go of him, yanking the pincher arm-high.

That didn't stop its third pincer from swiping at the attackers. Risy dropped to the ground under the claw. Nigan was a fraction of a second too slow, and was clipped by the claw, which threw him at least ten feet. Risy jabbed up at its underside, causing it to jump.

Illa screamed and ran towards Nigan. Malla ran towards Persa, who already knew what she was after. Persa picked up and threw the medical pack to Malla, then jumped out of the way of one of the stingers as it struck the ground where she'd just been. Catching the supplies, Malla turned and started running for Nigan.

Illa didn't pay attention as she ran for Nigan, bringing her into the path of the second creature. The intersection surprised both of them. It bowled Illa over, smashing her to the ground, as it tried to bring its pincers into play. As fast as the things were, it still missed Illa by a few inches.

Ditani, Persa, and Ticca were keeping the other beast busy. For a moment, Lebuin thought Ditani was going to get skewered, but he was able to parry the stinger with his blade. However, the power behind the attack still knocked him down, and as he fell, his sword went flying away. As Lebuin dodged, he spotted Risy's body on the ground, blood covering his head.

Anger flared, and Lebuin pushed to finish constructing the twisted channels of the lightning-bolt incantation, targeting the creature's open mouth. The attack sizzled, and the thing shook violently. Its pincer opened as it stepped back, shaking from left to right.

"HA! You're not so tough on the inside." Lebuin ran

around it, heading for Illa. She was unconscious on the ground. He picked her up and ran with her to where Nigan was pushing himself up to a sitting position. Malla was sitting next to him, looking him over.

He laid Illa down, so Nigan could hold her. "Take care of her."

Lebuin grabbed Malla's arm, and squeezed to get her attention. He pointed to Risy. Malla tapped Nigan's shoulder, grabbing her medical supplies, and launched towards Risy.

Motioning towards the fight, Nigan said, "I've got her. Go help."

As he turned and ran back towards the fighting, Lebuin saw that the rest of the group was trading off, pestering the second creature. As the first one stood there, vibrating, the second one was fighting the team effectively with its three large pincers. Its dual stingers were only missing the Daggers as they dodged by an inch.

Lebuin threw more lightning at its back, but the attacks dispersed across its armor plating. It snapped at Ticca, but she managed to leap over the pincer. The beast seemed to be learning, because it appeared to be anticipating her moves. Its stinger was already shooting down the length of its arm, right at Ticca.

Lebuin's mind blazed, and in an instant, he'd reached out with his telekinetic incantation and shoved Ticca out of the way. The stinger slammed into the ground, but a part of Ticca's ripped shirt and a little of her skin were on its serrated edges.

Ticca, caught off-guard, slipped and fell. But she turned that into a roll, coming up directly in front of another pincer. The creature snapped out, and Ticca bent back as the pincer closed over the top of her.

Ditani raced in with Ticca's black sword, and when he struck, the sword bit through its armor. The thing stepped backwards, away from Ditani, as he swung the sword in a swirling pattern. Carda and Persa were trying to kill off the first one, stabbing it with their swords. Still, it stood there, shivering.

The second monster noticed their attacks on its partner and turned, rushing towards them. Lebuin's heart pounded, and he felt a tingle of elation when a clear view of the mouth area on the second one came. He threw his power at it. The lightning didn't hit precisely where he wanted. His attack didn't stop the creature, which literally ran over the top of the first one. Carda and Persa saw it coming and dodged. Carda almost made it, but the claw slammed into her, and she flew backwards on impact.

Still, she fared better than Persa, whose dodge was a fraction of a second too slow. It grabbed her in its claw.

A guttural scream came from Ticca as Persa was sliced in half.

Lebuin ran, trying to find another clear shot. As he moved, the thing sensed him and turned, covering its mouth area with one claw as it swung its pincers at him. He saw that one of the stingers was lining up on Ditani. With a brush of his telekinetic incantation, he pushed Ditani clear of any attack. The creature paused, and swung its huge pincers sideways, both half-open. The lower edges scraped the sand, and the upper edges were beyond his ability to jump over. He could only backpedal, but he couldn't move fast enough.

The impact sent stars shooting through his head. The world spun, and he felt the air rushing past him. He didn't know which way was up, and none of that mattered. He knew that all their lives depended on his being able to stay in the fight, but all the willpower in the world couldn't clear his mind or vision fast enough to land in anything other than a jumbled heap. The last thing he heard was Ticca shouting something that sounded like what he imagined a Karakian war cry would be.

Llino Defenses

CHAPTER 12
ANCIENT ARTIFACTS

ESHRA-ZUNIA

WARLORD ESHRA-ZUNIA GLARED AT THE glistening wave of things between her and her goal in the Llino palace. Things she'd never imagined in her whole life — she didn't even have a name for.

These are not in any report we have! They must be part of the original city's construction.

She kept her face neutral as her mind raced over possible actions. Nothing she'd studied had prepared her for facing thousands of ancient war artifacts.

"The palace has sealed itself. Electra, what is happening?" Regent Ellua's voice came from dozens of locations around her.

The regents don't know what's happening either.

She tried to guess at what the things were. They flew in tight formations; it appeared their flight was provided by three smooth rounded holes mounted inside of fixed fin-like wings, two towards the front, and one on the fixed upright tail. She could see dust swirling down from the disks. She assumed the buzzing had to do with whatever mechanics were used in those circular holes. The things also had a series of at least seven holes that expelled fire in small bursts.

The artifacts were narrow-bodied like sharks, and their fins were swept back, contributing to that shark-like impression. They had a rounded section mounted across the front. She recalled the drawings of sharks found in the Rhonian island chain called *hammerhead* sharks. The artifacts looked like that; they were even about the same size as those sharks. But the shape and smooth body were where the similarities ended. These were painted with red and black stripes, and bristled with tubes mounted on the bottom and on each side.

For a second, she let herself laugh as she recalled her fear at facing Duke, remembering Llino had been Duke's original home on Niya-Yur.

I knew it was going to be difficult, with many surprises. But this? Why here? Why now? No other ancient city had anything like these.

She used the power of her odassi to enhance her vision. There were far more of the flying things than was possible to count. The front portion of the wave cleared the dusty air, and she began to get a good look at them as they rushed outward from the palace and across the city, in all directions at once. The volume of dirt that accompanied them as they flew, or were thrown out into the air, blurred the palace behind them.

Through the dust filled air, she could make out the glowing palace. Its walls had brightened behind the silver wall of flying combat artifacts. It glowed a gentle white, adding more contrast to the scene. The shields that already encased it brightened, as well. Behind the shields new steel plates had appeared sealing the windows and doors.

None of it could be good in any way.

The flying artifacts were coming out of the ground, surrounding the palace in what she hoped was not an infinite flow. A strange buzzing sound, along with the regular rattle of metal on metal, emanated from them.

Sharks. They buzz like bees, but they move together like a school of sharks, and there are so many. Might as well call them airsharks. I need a name for them.

Powerful exploding arrow-like weapons shot from the airsharks, filling the air with the bodies of her warriors. Shouts near her drew her attention. Eleven of her warriors had just exploded.

Urdu! We were so distracted by those airsharks that we didn't pay attention to what else could be happening.

The six mages with her were putting up additional shielding. She had over 300 of the best warriors with her. They all knew how to use their odassi. Two loud explosions happened above a few of the remaining warriors, who, like the mages, had adjusted their shields from their blades to cover them overhead, as well as around.

Looking up, she saw hundreds of the Imperial enforcer sentinels flying in.

We have defeated these easily in all of the other cities. Does Llino have special ones?

The man-sized chrome steel enforcers, with their long thoraxes, and flexible segmented bodies, looked like a child's oversimplified drawing of a hornet. She examined them more closely, using the enhanced vision from her odassi. All of the sentinels had opened a series of six panels along their heads, each panel revealing three circular tubes that varied in size and color. What the tubes did was still a mystery to her. They'd all grown spikes or stinger tails, and their thoraxes were pulled under to direct the stingers forward.

As she watched, dozens of sentinels bulged, and through their skin, like something emerging from water, appeared a long tube with an arrowhead and things that looked like fletching. Fire erupted from the tail of each of the tubes, and they flew with a speed and bending flight path that shocked her, to slam into the shields of her warriors. They looked similar to what the airsharks were shooting at her other squads around the city. On impact, the things exploded with so much force that many warriors were knocked down or killed, even through the shields.

Grabbing her odassi, she opened communications. *'All mages, concentrate on shielding the warriors. Be sure you can hold against these new threats before attempting anything else. Pull together into full regiments! No one fights alone. The things coming from the palace are designated airsharks. Find a way to deal with them. All majors to coordinate their brigade communications.'*

The warriors around the city moved with odassi and, she suspected, a healthy dose of real fear, fueling their speed to comply with her orders. They fought hard, and they fought with honor. She maneuvered her group through the streets, every step getting closer to the palace.

That woman's voice came again. "Attention! This is an Imperial military action. Hostile forces in violation of Imperial Law have breached the city and have been identified. All citizens are to proceed in a calm and orderly fashion to the closest designated emergency evacuation site or emergency bunker. Imperial guards, all hostiles are to be detained or destroyed."

The voice never deviated from the same tonal quality. The precise nature of that voice sent more chills down to her gut than anything else.

This was supposed to be easy! We had the mages and more than enough warriors to take this city. Throwing out the silly worries about non-combatants made the initial strikes highly effective. This should be just about over.

"Warlord Eshra-Zunia, you may surrender now if you wish. Order your warriors to lay down their weapons. You cannot win this." That was a young woman's voice, and the accent screamed Gracian. Eshra-Zunia was sure it was Countess Electra.

If she wasn't a primary target, I'd love to take her head back. She brought knowledge from Gracia about the defenses. She's responsible for this sudden change.

She kept her warriors moving and dodging as they rushed towards the palace. Around her, the sounds of battles raging kept the adrenaline flowing.

Two women's voices had been tracking her movements everywhere she went. The other was constantly reporting on all the Nhia-Samri activities. Eshra-Zunia had enjoyed the other woman's voice. It kept her updated better than her own officers on all her warriors' activities. She was sure that woman was Regent Ellua, especially considering how much she'd screamed when they captured Regent Bayion.

Ignoring the voices seemed prudent. She was sure they could hear her perfectly and probably see her just as well.

The regents hadn't wasted time in learning to use the power of their ancient city.

The wave of airsharks was almost to her position.

We need to stand and figure out their weakness. I doubt we'll get any closer until we know how.

She ordered her own regiment to form up around her. The warriors and mages lined up almost instantly. Blades out, they braced for the coming wave of artifacts.

More explosions vibrated the ground. She looked up just in time to see at least fifty sentinels twist together, spitting a strange ray of light from those front panels. The fifty individual rays combined in the air and slammed down on the ground, melting the dirt into lava instantly. The ray moved with a speed no one could match and mowed down a line of her warriors, the mage and odassi shields having no effect on the attack. As the ray brushed over her warriors, they blew up like a pot left sealed on the stove too long. The remains touched by the ray vanished into a black smoke.

The deadly ray of light swept down a line of warriors, killing twenty in less than a second before it stopped.

Her heart rate leapt to an uncontrollable level, and her blood boiled.

To face us and fight is one thing. But to sit safe in your palace while we're defeated by a bright light! I will make you pay, even if it violates my orders.

Without another thought, Eshra-Zunia leapt with all her speed, knowing full well she was a primary target. A white ray of energy brushed past where she'd just stood, burning and exploding the mage that had been next to her.

She rolled back through the gore to grab the mage's odassi. Whirling, she pushed herself into a forward roll, coming with as much force as she could muster. She threw the odassi at the group of sentinels firing the ray at her warriors. The blades flew hard and true. They went clean through one sentinel and embedded in another.

The first sentinel exploded a fraction of a second

later. The force of that explosion threw her to the ground. But better, it took out at least half of the other group. The remaining sentinels in that group, their wings broken, spun out of control, crashing into buildings and the street with great force.

"The artifacts' armor is not proof against our odassi!" she yelled to her troops.

The remaining mages had combined shields, and were holding off the ray attack of another group of enforcers and their exploding arrows. She rolled to her feet. She felt her face going red, burning with anger.

The mages all looked strained, their power channel amulets burning brighter than Eshra-Zunia had ever seen before.

The airsharks had already engaged five of her regiments. She could hear the commanders calling out, trying to coordinate. Two regiments had lost too many mages, and were being wiped out. She ordered them to break and reform with the remaining units.

A large wave of the airsharks was heading her way. Drawing her own blades, she pulled power like she'd never tried before.

If the enforcer armor isn't proof against an odassi, maybe those airsharks are susceptible, too.

"We must take the palace!"

She ran at a low building and, screaming a warrior's raging battle cry, leapt to its roof. Using that as a springboard, she pushed off in a different direction at a thick-walled building made from the same strong white stone as the city's walls. From that wall, she launched herself into the air like an arrow, aimed straight at a new group of sentinels that had started to form together the same way as the first group.

She turned in the air, catching the wing of one sentinel, and twisted herself over to land on top of it. She swung her swords so fast that even she could barely tell where they were in time to adjust them to come back in for another attack. The power flowed through her, and she loved it.

Her sword bit and cut the sentinels so fast, they didn't even have time to change their course. As the one she stood on began to fall, she pushed off from it and swung at another. Her warriors, witnessing her display, all broke and ran to jump into the air, cutting at sentinels and airsharks.

The airsharks had weapons similar to the enforcers, plus something new. Four of them would hover together into a diamond formation. Once in position, their skins would sparkle, and a ball of lightning formed around them. Once that weapon was fully lit, fire erupted from their tails just like the exploding fire arrows the enforcers used. As a unit, they ducked and swerved, racing at a speed unmatchable. If the ball of lightning brushed the edge of a sword, armor, hand, leg, or head, lightning would instantly blaze around the warrior. Even though the touch was only for a fraction of a second, the warrior would be covered in lightning, burning them to a blackened husk.

Landing, she dodged such a ball. It missed her by a hair's width, and at that moment, she knew she was lucky to still be alive. Rolling, she dodged more of the exploding fire arrows. The lightning-ball attack was only good for a few seconds. The group that missed her broke apart, and went back to shooting other missiles. She brought her odassi up, creating a firm shield around and above her, as a dozen of the airsharks swerved gracefully towards her.

As soon as they were pointing right at her, she heard dozens of pops, and minute smoke puffs blew away from some of the narrow barrels mounted on the side of the airsharks. Hundreds, maybe thousands, of sling bullets slammed into her shields with far more force than a sling could produce.

She rolled to get out of the line of fire. She could hear all her warriors reporting in on types of weapons, effect ranges, and deadliness. The casualty reports were coming in so fast, there was little else.

She muted all the other communications and broadcast

to all the warriors, *'Stop all casualty reports, unless requested. Report weapon strengths and enemy activities. All units, continue to palace. Capture the throne room, and remember your orders!'*

A group of airsharks was heading for her remaining mages. She ran and leapt, intercepting them as they swung into alignment, aiming their weapons at the group. She allowed herself to smile as her odassi sliced them into halves. One exploded as her blade cut through it, throwing her to the side.

She landed on her side. Wounded and bleeding she pushed to get up. Her wounds were not serious enough to stop her. Her blades were already healing her. As she finished getting her feet under her a battle cry came from behind. Spinning in time to parry the swords of a group of city guards, rushing her position. She quickly dispatched the seven guards.

I don't have time for this. She thought as she wiped blood from her face, some of it her own.

She ordered her regiment to regroup in a small open courtyard. The remaining 134 warriors formed up with her. She gasped at their number.

I've lost over a hundred warriors in five minutes! We're taking too many casualties.

Less than a second later, she made the hardest decision of her career. It would be a bad mark, but it would be worse if she died for pride. Using her odassi, she created a communications channel to her commander, First Warlord Maru-Ashua.

'Sir, Llino is attacking us with artifacts and weapons I've never heard of before. We're taking heavy casualties. The palace is sealed behind a new kind of shielding. We will persist. However, primary targets Regent Ellua, Countess Electra, and their families are likely to escape.'

TICCA

Rolling as fast as she could, Ticca got out of the way of one of the large claws that snapped at her. The second and third claws were already moving, and opening to grab her. She managed to get her feet under her, and sprang up, grabbing the creature's arm just at the base of a claw. Hanging onto this, she swung herself up to straddle its arm, temporarily safe from the claw as the creature stared at her back.

The beast made a clicking sound that reminded her of what the old ladies used to do when she was a little girl and did something unladylike. She wasn't sure if it was her imagination, but she had the distinct impression it was moving from mad to frustrated.

Maybe we're more difficult meals than it thought.

Taking advantage of the second she had, she glanced around to assess the situation and look for inspiration. She was still wondering what set the two things off; they'd attacked without any provocation or warning. This was the first time she'd even seen these kinds of creatures in the desert. She wondered if they were common. Their team had been trekking across the desert for five days, and the worst they'd encountered before were some spiders that were so brightly colored, no one wanted to go anywhere near them.

The first beast was still standing, still vibrating, and didn't seem a real threat, even though all the damage that had been done to it had not yet killed it.

Ditani was down again. Nigan was down, but he was nursing Illa, who appeared to be unconscious. Persa's body halves lay apart, still oozing blood, creating a bright red river in the glistening sand. Risy had a grievous head wound, and Malla was trying to drag him away from the fight with a grim expression. He was bleeding heavily. A red trail followed Malla's efforts to get him off the battlefield.

Lebuin had been tossed twenty feet. He was upside down, his head either in the sand or almost so, arms under him, and his butt stuck up in the air. She'd seen a number of men land in that position after getting so drunk that they passed out. It would've been humorous, except that she was worried. He wasn't moving, and couldn't be breathing well in that position. Worse, she was sure he was knocked out. The moment he hit, the temperature-controlling spells he had been maintaining for all of them stopped working.

Only Malla, Carda, and I are still in this fight. And with the heat protection gone, we'll be in trouble. With Lebuin down, someone has to be able to put the sun shelter back up and get the team under it. Otherwise, everyone will die from the heat.

She made up her mind. Lebuin was the one who needed to get the information and figure out how to use it. It was up to her to give him every chance she could.

This one was after something, but came back when the other one was wounded. They're probably mates, and I know they're at least minimally intelligent.

The second creature started moving again. As it swung its other giant pincer towards her, it came open and twisted to pluck her off its arm. She knew she'd been in one spot far too long.

Ticca put her foot on the arm. With all her strength, she shoved herself off, trying to leap clear of its base attack range. Something slammed behind her, and the beast let out a burr of frustration.

Is it bad that I'm starting to understand these things?

Rolling to a stand, Ticca saw the first one pick up Persa's lower body and turn it over, as if it was wondering what it was and why it was there. She braced herself for what came next. It brought the body close to its mouth, and the three remaining smaller pincers began to rip chunks out before shoving them into the open maw.

I need to get these things away from here.

Before she knew what she was doing, she was in motion. She ran and leapt on the back of the first animal. The second one paused before deciding to follow. Ticca drew one of the razor-sharp blades she'd gotten from the Knife, so long ago it was a different life. She slid down the front of the other creature, past the mouth and three smaller pincers, still busy tearing away pieces of her dead friend.

Ticca put all she had into the slicing cut that removed all three of those pincers. Landing on the ground, she rolled, popping up to a run to get clear. The first one let out a surprised chirp of pain, and the second one gave one of those chittering roars. Any reluctance to chase Ticca vanished. It launched at her like it wanted to rip her apart just for the joy of it.

Ticca turned, spotting her black sword on the ground nearby where Ditani had dropped. Sheathing the knife, she ran, scooping up the sword, and sheathing it as well. Then she moved as fast as she could, with the sound of the pursuit in her ears. Although they were fast, they weren't as fast as she was. She knew she was the one in trouble, as she had to deal with the heat and dehydration. Without Lebain's temperature-controlling spells working, she wasn't sure how long she could withstand the heat. She was already sweating liberally.

All I need to do is get them to follow me for a mark, and then I can lose them and circle back. That should let the team find a more secure spot and get under some shade. I hope Kliasa's healing boots can help keep me going in this heat. If the heat gets me, I'm dead for sure, either from exhaustion or those beasts.

Ticca had two canteens on her, and she didn't bother trying to save the water. She jogged and walked up sand dunes and then used gravity to run down the far sides in seconds. After several marks, she'd gained a good lead, but the heat was stripping her of energy, and the beasts were better at tracking her than she'd anticipated.

As the sun was starting to set, she ran out of water. They continued to follow her, but were still some distance behind. She took advantage of the low sun to hide in shady spots, resting. Once the sun was down, the temperature plummeted. The creatures slowed, yet every time she stopped at a peak and looked back at her tracks, eventually she would see them crest a couple of dunes behind, still following her trail.

She jogged, walked, and ran all night. The next day, she

was forced to walk. Fatigue dragged at her. She couldn't see the things anymore, but her instincts told her they were still there and to keep moving. A lone, scraggly tree on the top of a hill gave some shade and a view behind. She dug down into the sand underneath it and lay down in the cool trough. She only meant to stay there for a mark to cool down, but she woke with a start. She wasn't sure how long she'd slept, but the sun had made some progress. She needed water, but had none. Kliasa's boots could only help heal her. They weren't proof against starving or dehydration.

Pulling her head up, she saw the creatures coming up the hill she was on. One was leading the other, and they marched in unison.

Skeed! I lost all of my lead on them!

Scrambling out from under the tree she ran down the steep side of the hill, starting the jog-walk-jog pattern again. Night came. The moons passed slowly overhead. She was so tired, she fell face-first into a flash flood gully.

Might be water if I follow this.

She moved up it, desperately, looking for any sign of water. Near morning, with the horizon beginning to blaze orange, she found an area lined with ragged plants that still had some green leaves. She dropped next to the rock wall by the plants and dug. Four feet down, between one scoop of sand and the next, water filled in the bottom. She tore off her head dress and soaked the cloth. Lifting it up, she squeezed the first precious drops of water in over twenty-four marks into her mouth.

Sighing with the pleasure of moisture, she dug deeper and drank as much as she could. A precious mark passed as she filled her canteens with the priceless treasure, every minute checking for the sound of the beasts approaching up the gully.

Her instincts sent chills through her body. She stood, listening to the desert silence.

I can feel those things. They're not far now, time to go.

Moving was living. Day came and passed. No food, no rest, and by the end of the day, again no water. Then it was night's turn. The pattern repeated she wasn't sure how many times. The only break was when she found a sign of water. Sometimes she was lucky, most of the time she wasn't.

She stood on the crest of a high sand dune. Looking at the rising sun with her canteens empty again but her belly busy with protein from a handful of crickets she'd caught in the blade-trees, Ticca tried to count the days. She wasn't sure if it had been three or seven mornings. She was trying to decide how many days she'd survived, where none should have, or had before.

She looked back for the creatures, squatting to rest. There was no sign of pursuit. As she started to move, she spotted some berry-bearing brush in the gully ahead. She ran down and ate as much as she could find. The fruit-filled hedge meant there was a lot of water below, so she dug down, finding it rapidly. Maybe half a mark later she sat in the shade from the side of the gully, feeling better than she had for some time. Before moving on, she spent a couple of marks harvesting berries into her belt pouch, and filling the canteens again.

Somewhat refreshed, she climbed back up the tall dune. The bright, burning sands were all she could see. Soon the temperature would be beyond anything she could take, and she prayed for some better shelter. She was exhausted beyond description.

The land was barren, rolling up and down in a series of gullies and sand dunes. The only distinguishing feature was the mountain range to the north. That was almost 200 miles away, and still, she could just make it out. Otherwise, the desert had little else. Sparse, scrubby plants dotted the landscape, and there were lots of flash-flood wash basins. She couldn't see anything that looked like a tree line or an indication of water.

I need water and rest. I can't keep this up. At least I don't see those things. This is as good a place as any to fully rehydrate and restock my energy supply.

She stood up, preparing to build a small shelter, when a roar came from the distance. She saw the two creatures walking over the top of a hill a few dunes away. They were still on her trail.

Patting the magic healing boots, she sighed. "Okay, not done yet. I'm not certain if having these is good or bad. They've kept me alive, but they have also kept me alive."

Gotta find something. I have to sleep for real, and I need to find another good water source and more food. Sleep first. Maybe I won't wake up.

She'd only gone a short distance farther when the scenery changed. As she started down one dune, she noticed there was a gully, and the far side of it was perfectly straight. She could see a flat surface on the far side, and it looked like a road. But there was one section her eyes locked onto, where the flat surface split and warped up, creating a jagged outcropping with a small cave. It was the only one she had seen since entering the desert.

She was already squeezing into the small cavern backwards before she realized she'd made the decision to hide in it. Her hips got stuck. She wiggled to try and get in, but it hurt. She started to get back out, when the creatures appeared at the top of the sand dune just across the gully. She shoved herself backwards into the hole, freeing her hips by leaving behind fabric and skin.

Ticca's senses screamed at her to run. Despite the knot in her stomach, she held her breath and pressed harder, squeezing farther under the warm rocks, scraping her exposed back and burnt hands.

I might kill myself if I get wedged in here.

The rocks above her simmered in the midday heat, and she prayed it was enough to hide her body heat from the beasts.

A shadow passed over the narrow entry fissure,

momentarily blotting out the sun's glare. The beast snuffed about, trying to find where Ticca, in the form of the tasty but annoying morsel it had been chasing, had gone. The rock above her vibrated as they tried to dig through the thick stone to get to her. Their claws made sounds like a work team chiseling stones to fit a building.

Panic rose as she heard the rock cracking under the extreme pressure and strength applied by those monsters. She could hear pebbles flung by the digging, shooting away as if from a sling, ricocheting off other nearby protrusions or exploding on contact.

A series of metallic rings came next. The beast stopped its digging, letting out a chirping sound, like it had been stung by something. It moved back to the entry fissure, snuffing and poking some of its long, sharp claws into the fissure, trying to hook her out. The translucent claws refracted the killing sun in beautiful rainbows on the cave's surfaces as they swiped at her.

Ticca held her breath and didn't move, the claws passing only inches from her.

The scraping and sniffing stopped, and time crawled on as the shadow at the entry gap grew longer. Ticca was about to start trying to wiggle out when the beast's angry cry curdled her blood, making her shiver. Another call came in the distance. The beast roared directly over her. A minute later, a sad warble of failure came to her, followed by scraping and pounding as it moved away huffily, like a child purposefully stomping to display its anger.

Long after the sounds of the beasts had vanished, she kept still, except to breathe slowly through her nose. The entry shadow grew longer, and heat radiated down through the rock to her back. Precious water was dripping into the dirt below her. As the fear-fueled adrenaline waned, her willpower lost the fight to exhaustion, and she fell asleep, wedged under the rock that had saved her life.

- - -

Ticca sat beside the cool lake, next to which Rea-Na-Rey was built. Elven dwellings, evident to her experienced eye, lined the irregular western shore of the lake. The silver elf, Kliasa, strolled up and sat next to her, holding out a silver goblet filled with fresh water from the lake. Ticca took it and drank.

"It can't sustain you much longer. To be honest I'm surprised it has worked this long."

"It doesn't have to. I think I finally lost the diurdu things."

"Do you have any idea where you are? Or more importantly, where your comrades are?"

Her throat tightened, and she looked away from Kliasa, to the lake.

Kliasa frowned and shook her head. "I haven't sensed Lebuin for two days. I can't guide you. Without him or even any supplies, you will not survive in the desert much longer."

Feeling tears coming, Ticca fought to keep them back. "I pulled those beasts off of him and the group. Lebuin is the key. If I saved him, I have served well."

Kliasa wasn't fooled by her bravado, and scooped Ticca up in a strong hug. That was the final straw. Tears burst from her as she sobbed into Kliasa's shoulder. Words flowed between gasps. "I don't want to die here! I knew being a Dagger was dangerous, but I never thought I'd die of thirst to the elements! Lords and Ladies, help me!"

Kliasa held her, petting her hair and back until the emotions broke, and her sobbing stopped.

"Ticca, you know all we have on desert survival. I admit, the Circumveni Desert is many times deadlier than any other desert. Still, creatures live there. You know how to find water and food. The real choice is, do you backtrack to Aelargo or try to find your team?"

"I can't return to Aelargo until I find Lebuin."

Kliasa squeezed her hard before letting go. "Now, there's the Dagger I know. It helps to share our burdens, doesn't it? Never forget to share your problems with your trusted friends. If you don't, they can fester and consume you."

"I'm so thankful for you and your boots. If it wasn't for you holding to life here *between*, I would've died already." She looked deeply into Kliasa's eyes. It was impossible to lie in the *between* realm that bridged life with whatever came next. But Ticca wanted to show Kliasa how sincere she was.

Kliasa held herself there, refusing to move on without her love Shar-Lumen, the person Ticca, Lebuin, and half the world was trying to stop or kill. The same person who was trying to destroy the entire Duianna Empire and all of its allies in a rain of fire. Kliasa had somehow clung to the living realm at her death by holding to her magical creations. In the 700 years since that time, she'd mastered existing in that space. She even used it to teach Ticca, after she'd accidentally gotten the amazing magical boots Kliasa made, which not only healed, but blended to match what was needed.

Kliasa's connection to Ticca through the boots allowed her to pull Ticca into that realm when she slept. In that place, Ticca could rest and spend almost three full years, if needed, in one night. Over the last few days, Ticca had needed a lot of time there to overcome her fears.

"Are you ready?"

"As ready as I can be."

"Good girl. Now, go find more water and stay alive," Kliasa said, waving her hand as if showing her the world. Ticca's senses spun as her consciousness returned to the living realms.

- - -

Opening her eyes, she found herself in near-darkness. The entry was nothing but shadows. Carefully, Ticca worked her body free and inched towards it. She still had her sword and dagger, and Magus Vestul's magically expanded pouch. Everything else she'd either left at camp, or lost in the cat-and-mouse chase.

The sun had just set, and the temperature was already plummeting. It was going to be another freezing night. She contemplated staying in the small cave. It would be warm, and she desperately needed to rest.

I should travel at night. Without Lebuin's protection spells, I could die in the day's heat here. It's a miracle I haven't died from the heat yet.

The nights were bright, the crystal sands reflecting the light of the moons and stars. Ticca pulled herself up and out of the lifesaving hole. Going from the near-black cave to the twilight felt like stepping out into full daylight. Ticca climbed on top of the rock that had protected her from the creature. She saw that it had managed to dig a depression five feet across and a foot deep. Something in the exposed rock caught the light, reflecting it back. Knowing that every beast in the desert was a deadly predator, she kept an eye out for any as she crawled down the face of the rock to examine the gleaming substance. The stone reminded her of Llino's walls and older buildings. It also had a square corner sticking up.

This is man-made! It really is a road.

The sparkling was from a series of six steel rods, as smooth as glass, with mirror-like surfaces. Not even the diamond-hard claws of the beast had scratched the steel tubes. Ticca bent to touch one of the embedded cylinders, but as she reached for it, every hair on her head stood up. She felt a strange tingling sensation, like small insects dancing over her skin.

This is active Elracian technology! What is it for?

She stood and looked out at the wasteland of sand and rock. The steel rods ran in what appeared to be perfectly parallel lines, east-west. She could see that the surface extended like a ribbon past the horizon in both directions. It was ripped up at points, but it was obvious that at one time it had to have been a perfectly flat, straight line with a uniform width. Pacing out the distance across what had to be an Elracian street, she concluded that it was just over seventy feet.

Roads are built between places of habitation. This is so wide, it has to be a major passage, which means it's likely a commerce route between key cities. She knew they'd been heading generally for the capitol city Imridu-Nam, which was southwest of their camp. She'd kept the sun and major moon in the right positions to travel southeast, as she lured the creatures away from the team.

Looking at the bright stars and the first moon rising, she knew she needed to get moving. She could feel that the blue palace lay ahead down this route.

I can follow this to Imridu-Nam. And if Lebuin lives, he'll continue on his course. Maybe he can detect me. Either way, west will put me closer to the party. When I get to the city, I can turn north and find the team, or get out of this place.

Turning west, she started jogging as she scanned the area for plants or animals that might sustain her one more day.

MARU-ASHUA

Warlord Maru-Ashua sat lotus-style on his office floor, relaxing his muscles and letting his mind flow out through his odassi. The spider web of connections spun out from him to his commanders, and through them to other commanders, and finally to individual warriors. Since the war had started, he made it a point to look in on as many units as possible for a few marks every day.

Some days, his ancient odassi had gently urged him down specific paths to learn of troubled units or problem warriors. He'd spent almost the entire day observing. There had been many issues to deal with. He moved through the web, pulling the patterns out.

It's here somewhere. The pattern must be here. Shar-Lumen forced the war, yet he ordered all the families to Hisuru Amajoo before doing that. Some bases he commands to stand to the last. Others, threatened or not, are dismantled and evacuated.

He concentrated, trying to hold the entire war in his head, every warrior, every base. Still Shar-Lumen's goals eluded him.

He'd spent the last six cycles observing Shar-Lumen's activities and orders directly. He didn't have to rely on reports from others, because as the First Warlord, almost all of that activity went through him. He also had the ability to look in on any warrior within their nation via the odassi web. Only Shar-Lumen's elite regiment of personal advisers and guards did not report directly to him.

It was hard to tell if the war was going well for the Nhia-Samri, or not.

In the south, the two largest single forces of Nhia-Samri warriors ever assembled had been created, and marched east and west, taking land like a regular army. They'd never before engaged in land disputes for themselves. For the first time in their history, they were acting as a nation, intent on carving out a place in the world for themselves.

Shar-Lumen had been pleased with his capture of the southern portion of Laeusia. The surrender document signed by the princess heir had made him smile, a rare display of emotion. He did not even comment that the document named Maru-Ashua as the new lord of those lands.

Maru-Ashua drifted around the world, looking in on all the outposts. The far southern ones beyond the Circumveni Desert, hadn't been affected, other than through the recall of so many of their warriors to the north. The northern outposts were being destroyed or abandoned.

Lord Dohma had brought what remained of his division together and pulled in another one. With the combined power, he'd been marching the nearly two million soldiers as four regiments, all within a day's fast ride of each other, in a line south out of Duianna and into Laeusia. By all reports, he intended to turn that line, sweeping east to cleanse Oslald.

Under his command, the last three outposts in Duianna had fallen to the Alliance forces.

You're predictable. You're heading back to Aelargo first, and then you'll turn west to retake Nasur. Eventually, you plan on bringing your army against Hisuru Amajoo from the east, while the other half of the Alliance forces mirror your movements. They will try to retake Allusia, and then turn to attack Hisuru Amajoo from the west. Even so, it's a good strategy, and may yet prove effective.

One of his generals, Alamal-Zura, was preparing a combined casualty report. The numbers caught Maru-Ashua's attention. A part of the pattern he'd been looking for formed before him.

Opening direct communication, he ordered, *'Zura, add a percentage loss column to that report, and drop the attack at Outpost 12 from the total averages. Bring it to me immediately.'*

He quickly brushed his connection to General Hiri-Rula. He was well aware of the dangers of having that open channel if a magical flare, which was common in the desert, took place. More than one officer had been lost in the past due to disregard for the power and instability of magic in the Circumveni Desert.

Hiri-Rula was up with her forces, following Lebuin's team. He didn't want to spend too much time looking in, but he was surprised to see that Lebuin's team was moving as if heavily wounded, and he could see they were missing three members.

'General Hiri-Rula, did Lebuin's team suffer casualties?'

'Sir!' Hiri-Rula's surprise that he'd made contact was evident. She hid it quickly. *'Yes, Persa and Risy are dead. Ticca is missing and presumed dead. They were attacked by strange magical creatures. It was my fault, sir. The things detected me and were coming for me, when they went through Lebuin's camp and got entangled in a fight with them. We weren't discovered.'*

He felt his heart rate go up a notch. He suppressed the anger in his thoughts. *'I wanted them all alive. Shar-Lumen specifically ordered that Ticca not be harmed. You should have given immediate support. Should they fall into trouble again, you will assist!'*

Hiri-Rula was perceptive, and Maru-Ashua was sure she'd read his anger in spite of his efforts to contain it. *'Understood, SIR!'*

He broke the connection. All of his relaxation was lost as he tensed up over the news. He stood and started pacing. His mind raced through all the things he would do if he was in Ticca's place. Attacked by a monster, due to no action of their own. If the attack was in any way suspicious, he would assume external agents were at work.

Ticca is missing. No. More likely, she recognized Hiri-Rula's mistake and slipped away to check their back trail. Ticca might even discover the Nhia-Samri unit following Lebuin.

He heard a knock, and his guards opened the office doors, allowing General Alamal-Zura to walk in. Zura stepped up to him and held out the report with a raised eyebrow.

"How did you know?" Alamal-Zura asked as Maru-Ashua took the report and pored over it.

The pattern, when laid out, was clear. Except for the one extraordinary attack against Duke, Shar-Lumen had been ensuring the losses on both sides remained relatively equal on a percentage level. Both sides had suffered thirty percent total force casualties. For the Nhia-Samri, ninety-five percent of the casualties were deaths, and for the Alliance, sixty percent of the casualties were deaths. Most of those were Daggers.

Maru-Ashua sensed a surprise rush of adrenaline from the two majors guarding his door. He flicked the report onto a pile of papers on his desk and stepped away just as his office doors opened. Shar-Lumen walked in, his silver face a study in marble. He was dressed in full combat armor, which gave him sharp lines, and immeasurably added to his presence.

Both he and General Alamal-Zura came to attention and saluted the Grand Warlord.

Shar-Lumen ignored General Alamal-Zura and

approached Maru-Ashua. "Warlord, order General Cositel to dismantle all his outposts, A-22 through A-26. Relocate them as you see fit in Hopu Rinyaru."

"Sir?" Maru-Ashua had never heard of Hopu Rinyaru. Out of the corner of his eye, he could see a similar glint of confusion in General Alamal-Zura's eyes.

Shar-Lumen smiled and stepped over to lean on his desk. "That's the name I chose for our new province. I don't think it's wise to leave it named Allornia. That might cause some unnecessary feelings of hope for Laeusia to reclaim it. Have you not heard that the first thing you do when you get a new pet is to rename it? In this way, it does not become confused by past behaviors associated with its old name."

Pet. He thinks of the province as a pet?

Shar-Lumen casually leaned against his desk, waiting. Maru-Ashua tried to decide if he was for or against the concept. After he considered it, renaming the province did seem a good idea. And why not Hopu Rinyaru? It had a nice sound to it.

"Hopu Rinyaru," he said aloud, testing the flavor. He liked it. "I had not considered such an action. The name is both promising and pleasing."

Shar-Lumen nodded, his hand dropping down to rest on Maru-Ashua's desk. Maru-Ashua didn't let his face register that Shar-Lumen's hand was on top of the casualty report.

"I'll let you think of a name for the main city, although I always thought Lumendaria would make a good city name. I have reviewed your report on the new citizens, and signed all the land and title grants you have made or suggested."

Shar-Lumen's hand stuck to the report page, which lifted and fluttered back to the desk as he dug into his belt pouch. He pulled out two silver boxes that looked like small cigar cases with soft, rounded corners and some kind of scrollwork engraving that appeared to wrap around them.

"Warlord, I want you to look in on our guests. Make sure they're doing well, and give them each one of these."

Shar-Lumen placed the boxes neatly on his desk, squarely on top of the casualty report. "They will know what they are." As he moved his other hand, a key lifted in his fingers, which he held up for inspection. "And then, I want you to have a long look at what is in Building 9."

Building 9! That's the huge building with the blue-tiled roof. That thing has been sealed, and all the windows blocked, for centuries.

Shar-Lumen tapped the casualty report, or perhaps just the desk underneath it. "We're missing so many pieces. Llino lit the fire before we were ready to contain it. I'm sure you're beginning to see this. I didn't want things to go this way. But we must do what is needed to protect our own."

He was about to answer, when a communication link was established from Warlord Eshra-Zunia. He shared the communication channel with General Alamal-Zura and Grand Warlord Shar-Lumen. Eshra-Zunia sent a report on the battle at Llino. The memories of the new weapons and the losses taken sent a shiver down his spine. Her conclusion was clearly a request for aid.

She woke the city's full defenses. Those must be the legendary war artifacts Duke's tales warned that people attacking Aelargo would have to face. Once again, Duke's tall tales have proved to not be exaggerations or lies.

He turned to General Alamal-Zura. "Assemble your divisions, and General Enon-Maus's too. Llino is shielded from our gates, but portable termini have been established in the encampments. We will gate there and then move in to assist."

Shar-Lumen held up a hand, standing straight. "No. You have your orders, Warlord. I shall attend to this personally."

He turned, shocked that Shar-Lumen would expose himself to such danger. "Sir, allow us to deal with this. You're too important to risk, especially now."

Shar-Lumen stepped close, and his hand dropped on Maru-Ashua's shoulder. Even though he was a couple inches taller than Shar-Lumen, he felt small. Shar-Lumen's violet eyes looked straight into his own. Their intensity was dramatic, even more so close up.

"No. I cannot allow anyone but myself to be responsible for the conclusion. If it does not resolve quickly and as I directed, I must be the principal. My elite guard and I shall drop onto them faster than you could. You have your orders."

Shar-Lumen let go and walked calmly from the office. The doors opened before him, even though no one touched them.

After the doors closed, General Alamal-Zura waited a moment longer before asking softly, "Do you think he knows we found the ratios?"

"Of course he knows." He picked up the key from his desk. "I think that's why he gave me this. We have discovered something important."

"What of Llino?"

Warlord Maru-Ashua picked up the two silver cases. They were light, and he noted each had a small glowing red gem on one end. They looked identical. He put them in one pocket and the key in another.

"We have our orders."

He needed to look in on Lady Sula and Magus Cune first. Then Lady Lothia. And then explore what was in the sealed building. His thoughts were mostly on what would happen if Llino was destroyed. Lord Dohma was a formidable opponent, and Llino was his home. Even though Duke had abandoned it five centuries before, he was sure it continued to be unusually special to Duke.

Lords and Ladies, preserve Llino for us all.

Shar-Lumen's Fall

CHAPTER 13

STOLEN VICTORY

Vesta's systems were taxed beyond her abilities. She'd been forced to turn over repair and energy production operations to automated computers designed specifically for those tasks. But she kept checking in on them, since they wouldn't deal well with combat interruptions.

She was also forced to shut down the command center. As much as she enjoyed and was comforted by the physicality of projecting herself there, she needed the extra processing power to deal with the 730,422 combat drones and 12,102 enforcer sentinels in the air under her control. Arkady was flying the remaining 19,311 enforcers she didn't have the processing power to deal with.

Still, her systems were overloading with the level of details she was pulling, and her direct control of the combat units. She considered turning all the enforcers over to Arkady, but she resisted, as she wanted to have highly coordinated attacks by both the combat drones and the enforcers.

"You lied." Arkady was using the virtual control room with her. For some reason even the AIs didn't understand, it made coordinating and working together easier. There were less conflicts, and the two massive systems were able to stay in sync as they shared the processing requirements.

Vesta didn't answer for some time. She measured it, being sure she made him wait at least a full 200 microseconds before answering, so he would understand she was busy. In the meantime, she sent orders to 20,000 combat drones to assemble into a tight formation to break through the shields of one particularly lucky or extremely skilled mage, who had an uncanny knack for dodging her onslaught.

With the last attack completed unsuccessfully, she

responded to Arkady's accusation. "I did not," she answered automatically in a tone that indicated she intended that to be the end of it, for the moment. But then her curiosity got the better of her. "When do you think I did?"

"When you implied you needed my military experience."

That caught her by surprise. Her attention fluctuated, and a few Nhia-Samri warriors were able to move out of the way. Frowning, she ignored him in favor of staying focused on the job at hand.

She concentrated on attacking the mage, even as she considered Arkady's accusation. His luck or skill held one more time. He anticipated the threat and added many layers to his shields just in time. Vesta peeled them off as she brought an enforcer wing down, preparing to fire the photon-directed plasma cannons.

The mage performed a spinning dodge. Launching into the air, he was able to cut several combat drones in half. As he landed, he changed his shields a fraction of a second ahead of the cannon firing. Its attack fell on the new shields and was held off.

Blast it, this guy is getting annoying. He's protecting an entire regiment and himself alone. All the other mages have been dealt with. This regiment is getting dangerously close to the palace.

"See, that's what I mean." Arkady gestured at a display, showing the last attempt to get that pesky mage. "That was brilliant. I know it missed, but still, it was an amazing combination. Vesta, I...." He was cut off by an alarm.

They both regarded the display, taking in the data stream. One of the city-defense monitor systems had activated the alarm. What she saw sent a shiver of concern through her.

"ILLEGAL POWER SOURCE DETECTED."

The display screen showed a map, and the triangulation calculations were already running as the defense system used various directional sensors to pinpoint the disturbance. The sweeping sensor's triangles of coverage narrowed rapidly, until they were unmoving lines, which intersected directly on Llino.

"What?" Arkady manipulated the virtual displays, creating a new data stream onto which he overlaid maps and satellite information.

"Well?"

"I'm trying to locate it. Hang on, got it. Huh? That's something new. Vesta, you need to see this."

Vesta gave coordinates to 100,000 combat drones, and let them navigate automatically to give herself the free processing power needed to pay attention to whatever Arkady had found.

Turning her attention to the display feed, she saw Arkady had already added sixty live video streams to it via enforcers that he broke off and had on the way to the disturbance.

"What are those?" she asked as she looked on the twelve glowing, two-dimensional, parabolic arches that had appeared precisely 10,000 feet above the city. They were a slightly different color from the sky, and invisible from one side. Arkady had calculated their size: each was precisely eighteen feet high at the center and eight feet wide at the base.

"I don't know. But I don't like them there. They're emanating 5,322.6 rellums per second each." Arkady began shooting projectile bullets from his approaching enforcers at both the visible and invisible side.

The data stream showed every single bullet's trajectory from sixty different angles. Vesta released another 100,000 combat drones to deal with the additional data, while she continued to harass that annoying mage and Warlord Eshra-Zunia. She hoped she'd get lucky, and they'd make a marginal mistake. So far, both were avoiding her attacks and continuing to make some progress towards the palace.

The bullets reached the U-shaped arches, and the impossible happened. Those that struck the visible side went into the arch as if it was a tunnel or doorway. The bullets that struck the invisible side continued on, as if nothing was there at all. As she was trying to reason out what the things were, she realized there was only one possible conclusion.

"Those are mage-gates!"

Arkady shook his head. "No terminus. Nothing on this end. Could they really have figured them out to this level?"

To confirm her conclusion, a man stepped into view on the central archway. He was a handsome man by any measure. She was struck by his features. He was a silver elf, and tall for his race, standing 6'1", a full 3.5 inches taller than average. She knew it would be obvious to anyone, even without the incredible armor and beautifully carved ivory-handled swords on his belt, that he was a warrior. He had heavily muscled shoulders and arms. She estimated his weight at about 224 pounds, and that he could probably lift 600 pounds, at least.

The armor was in the same style as all the Nhia-Samri, or perhaps it was the other way around. Maybe all the Nhia-Samri imitated his. The glossy black-enameled armor was piped with grey and inlaid with a beautiful vine pattern. His shoulder plates flared out and up into sharp points. His helmet matched, but left his whole face open with a clear field of vision. He had long, silky black hair, pulled back into a ponytail that went all the way to his waist.

Arkady made the same connection she did. "That's Shar-Lumen."

Arkady hadn't stopped shooting the bullets into the mage-gates, and the one Shar-Lumen stood in was no exception. A full 6,489 bullets had already been shot at Shar-Lumen, but they had zero effect. Their momentum was stolen, causing them to stop a few inches from him and drop to the ground. He casually reached out and caught a bullet as it fell. He held it up before him and turned it over, examining it from all angles.

He stepped to the boundary of the gate, his toes hanging out in open air. His boots were so dramatically different from his armor and dress that Vesta spent some processing cycles to examine them more closely. The armor was well cared for and perfect, not a single stitch out of place. But describing the boots as shoddy was an understatement. They were soft, thick leather knee-high boots with soft soles. From the threading, Vesta could see the boots had been repaired many times.

Shar-Lumen's eyes swept over the approaching enforcers, and he examined the open combat weapons port. Arkady took advantage and launched sixty missiles at him. The combined explosion was impressive. Once the smoke cleared, Vesta was surprised to see Shar-Lumen standing exactly where he'd been, still studying the coming enforcers.

He pointed at something to his left, and she saw his mouth moving, but she couldn't read what he was saying. She replayed it a few times, running through all the languages she knew of. There was no match in any of her archives.

Dressed in armor colored similarly to Shar-Lumen's, Nhia-Samri warriors stepped into view in the remaining gateways. They all stood there, waiting for something.

Arkady shifted the sixty enforcers into two groups patterned to fire the combined photon plasma cannon attack at maximum power. As soon as they had alignment, he fired. Both beams were targeted at Shar-Lumen.

His reaction was unexpected. He dodged left, like a bending reed, causing him to fall out of the gateway. As he fell, he drew his odassi blades. Arkady growled and tried to track him, sweeping the beams in a bright arc after him.

Shar-Lumen had a lot more control over his fall than should have been possible without an anti-gravity jet pack. He twisted in a sharp arc and dodged at right angles as the beams swept after him, trying to score a hit.

Vesta predicted the pattern and cried out, "STOP!" But it was already too late. The beams of each enforcer group swept the opposite ones as Shar-Lumen slid between them.

The auto-stop systems of the two groups detected the mistake and cut the attack off, but that still left enough time for the weapons on each side to do significant damage to the opposing ones. A dozen enforcers in both groups exploded, throwing the remaining enforcers in random directions. Some of them were lightly damaged by shrapnel, and others had broken wings or destroyed circuits that couldn't be repaired before they hit the ground.

Shar-Lumen spun in the air, landing with bent knees on nothing, yet he straightened to stand tall, as if he were on the top of a wall. He took in the falling enforcers, his brows narrowing critically with one raised.

"He's surprised that worked. Frankly, so am I."

"Skeed! Sorry about that," Arkady spat as he slammed his fist into the virtual console.

Vesta was redirecting 300,000 combat drones. "We aren't perfect. It might be useful that it happened. It might make him overconfident, leading to a mistake."

"What now?"

"We attack, of course. I'm transferring control of half the remaining enforcers to you, as well as 100,000 combat drones. See if you can slow down this lucky mage. I'll deal with Shar-Lumen."

Arkady turned around, creating three new system displays, and smoothly took over the units she gave to him. "Why do you get all the best targets?" he groused.

"'Cause I'm the leader. And it's my city."

Vesta took direct control of 5,000 enforcers, splitting her concentration. She maneuvered them into a series of attack formations. She could feel the air rushing over their bodies, their wings beating the pattern needed for fine flight control.

Time to step up the game.

She pumped hard once with their wings, and then snapped the wings close to the body in a swept-back position. Firing the jet systems, she felt the sudden rush of speed and G-forces in 5,000 slightly different ways, and the sensations were wonderful.

This is as close to being a flight-capable creature as anyone can come.

She noted the smoke trails she was leaving. The Daggers

and guards needed some moral support. The cost in lives, defending the city, was far too high.

Even one life is too much. I hate wars.

She maneuvered, rocketing groups of enforcers in a series of turns, banks, and spins, keeping the combat formations. She heard cheers from guards and Daggers who were witnessing the first such action in 13,002.61 years.

They think the display of power is a good sign. I hope they're right.

In perfect unison, she lifted all of their noses up, towards the mage-gates. At the same moment, she fired the jet boosters of 200,000 combat drones. She divided them into support groups, each for a set of enforcers.

She smiled, noting that the roar of 205,000 jet boosts caused the Nhia-Samri combatants to duck, looking up defensively. The city fighters took advantage of the distraction and added to the Nhia-Samri losses.

Shar-Lumen pointed down, towards the coming wave of combat units, and spoke clearly in Imperial. "With me!"

Vesta opened fire on him and all twelve gateways.

Shar-Lumen jumped up in a long arc, and Vesta adjusted, keeping him in the dead center of her targeting. Bullets, missiles, and beams of light from the photon cannons flew around him as he twisted and shifted in the air. None of the missiles managed to hit him, but the bullets and cannon fire pounded his magical shields.

He shifted as he started to fall, as if landing on something, with his feet spread apart and his knees bent. He began to spin faster as he fell towards the combat units coming for him His hands pumped and danced, throwing blasts of magical energy almost as rapidly as the missiles fired back at him. He used his magic bolts to destroy 67.4 percent of her missiles, dodging the others.

Vesta compensated the missile trajectories, managing to drop his ratio down to 23.8 percent missile loss. The added explosions around him were now throwing him around. His eyes narrowed as he changed tactics. He shifted to hitting the drones firing the missiles in between, dodging all of the missiles. The drones couldn't maneuver as fast as the missiles, but their armor held up better. It took him several hits before a drone would explode or fail, falling back towards the city.

She managed to begin predicting his next target. That reduced his effectiveness by 29.33 percent, but there were too many variables, and one out of every ten of Shar-Lumen's attacks successfully hit his target. He learned quickly that her enforcers had strong enough armor to withstand his strikes, but the combat drones weren't so lucky. They also had so much ordinance onboard that when his attacks broke through they exploded, knocking some of the other ones out of alignment.

Vesta compensated, bringing her enforcers in tight to protect the combat drones. Still, she had to leave gaps for the combat drones to fire at Shar-Lumen. Those gaps worked both ways; he used them to get at the drones.

Vesta expected what happened next, but she still gasped. Nhia-Samri warriors, all wearing black and grey armor, came running out of the mage-gates, dodging and jumping around the heavy suppression fire she was putting on all twelve gates. She managed to take out twenty-four of the 350.

They jumped far out into the air and began falling. Half of them drew their swords immediately. The others threw magical blasts exactly like Shar-Lumen. He'd been probing and learning how to fight her, and now his group used this knowledge effectively. All of them had shields strong enough to deal with the peppering of combat fire Vesta was able to target them with as they dodged and flew down.

Sixty of them bent forward and rushed downward to form a large circle pattern around Shar-Lumen. When they came even with him, they spread-eagled, lying down like parachute jumpers in a ring, drawing their swords and spreading their arms wide. Three flat rings of warriors formed around him, their feet towards him, looking like the rays of the sun. As soon as they were in position, their swords glowed brightly, and all of the weapons fire Vesta was directing at Shar-Lumen began to strike a wide shield that surrounded the entire group.

Looks like a nice target to me, with Shar-Lumen the bull's-eye!

Arkady said, "That looks practiced."

"Ya think?" Vesta growled back.

Shar-Lumen and his warrior rings came into contact with the combat drones and enforcers. Any unit that came directly into their path bounced off the shield and burst into flames. Bullets, rockets, photon cannons, and every other combat weapon she used had limited impact. Vesta's main group was shattered, with all the other groups of drones and enforcers dodging wide around Shar-Lumen.

Ignoring the fact that if Duke heard of this it would be a dead giveaway she was awake, she activated the aerial defense systems. Hatches on the walls of the palace and city snapped open, exposing the 64,344 missiles loaded in the launcher grids. She overrode the launch protocols that fired the missiles individually and launched every missile at once.

The force blew apart the launcher platforms, causing secondary explosions inside the walls. It worked. 64,344 missiles flew at Shar-Lumen from every side. He had nowhere to dodge — there was no escape. She saw fear bloom on the faces of his ring of protectors. Instead of panicking, their faces tightened into determined glares at the approaching attack. The central circular etching on their breastplates flared, illuminating the city below, and Shar-Lumen wove his hands together so fast they blurred slightly in her high-speed cameras.

The energy shield around them darkened. The explosion blinded her sensors, and black smoke flew across the sky. The concussion threw combatants in the streets down and blew in 163 doors, destroying all the windows and collapsing three wooden buildings in that part of the city.

"That was a bit extreme," Arkady jovially said.

"He made the target," she smirked back.

Eighteen slowly rotating burnt bodies fell out of the smoke cloud, leaving a black trail. Behind them, Shar-Lumen, surrounded by the remaining forty-two warriors, emerged in a tight group. Sixteen were unconscious, carried by their comrades.

"Urdu! What does it take to kill this elf?!" Vesta screamed.

"He does have significant support," Arkady pointed out.

Shar-Lumen drew his blades, and his warriors broke out of their group, moving around as if they were jumping from one platform to another. They continued to fall, but their rate of descent had nothing to do with gravity's expected speeds. They spun, twisted, and dodged the drone attacks, while using their blades against any unit they got close to. The unhindered warriors supported the ones carrying the wounded.

Vesta stopped using most of the weapons. The only attacks that had any impact were the photon-directed plasma cannons, and the hell's-fire electrical attacks of the combat drones. Six enforcers overloading their power packs had a chance of taking out a warrior through his shields and disrupting others to good effect. However, those could ignite other units. Still, she liked the explosions. They had a chance to overwhelm one of Shar-Lumen's warrior's shields.

Shar-Lumen was unbelievable. He'd taken to walking on her drones and enforcers, as if they were stepping stones put there for him. His progress through the drone cloud left not a scratch on him, and yet thousands of her drones were being destroyed or disabled by his actions. He turned, jumped, and cut through without pause. It was like watching a masterful and inspiring dancer perform a unique show exclusively for her — one she hated with every fiber of her being. She sent group after group at him, and she overloaded hundreds of combat drones near him, but his shields remained impenetrable.

When Shar-Lumen was 1,345.3 feet above the city, a dozen bursts of energy rushed towards him, slamming him backwards. He twirled in the air, looking for the source.

Vesta traced the energy bursts' flight paths in the sensor data, and located six groups of six mages on the roof of the Mages' Guild, all waving their hands in the air in various patterns. At their core was the massive Magus Nillo, head of the Guild.

There were 129 mages throughout the city, fighting with the Dagger teams, but this group didn't include any of those she'd already registered. All of these men and women were old enough to look in need of walkers and canes, even though none of those items were present. Only Councilor Nillo had been out in the fighting. In fact, Nillo had a bandage over his shoulder that was oozing blood, dripping down his shirt.

These must be the senior instructors and retired mages. Nillo must have gone to get them when he saw the mage-gates open.

Vesta brought her drones around and swept in from various angles, firing everything they had at Shar-Lumen. Six amazing magical attacks joined in. One group had created a white-hot ball of energy that weaved and zoomed past her drones to slam into his shields, throwing crimson sparks out and inward. He lifted his arm, protecting his face from the sparks breaking through. She adjusted the aim of some of the drones to target the same location.

Another group of mages pointed and closed their eyes. She wasn't sure what that was about. Ignoring them, she adjusted another group of drones to avoid a barrel-width beam of energy generated by another group, directed at Shar-Lumen.

Lightning arced between yet another group of six mages, coalescing in the center of their semicircle, and jumped to Councilor Nillo. He caught it with one hand and focused it, creating a steady bolt of lightning, which he directed at Shar-Lumen. Shar-Lumen brought his feet together and dropped like a rock towards the ground, causing the bolt to miss.

The mages and Vesta redirected their attacks, trying to keep him targeted. The lightning bolt thrown by Nillo didn't continue onward; instead it bent back towards Shar-Lumen, tracking him like a homing missile. He spun his swords in a pattern. The blades flashed a bright white, reflecting the lightning bolt back at Nillo. The bolt hit the roof next to Nillo, and the explosion threw a few mages off the rooftop. All of their attacks were disrupted.

Shar-Lumen spread his arms wide, reversing his fall, and like a bullet shot from a gun, he flew up at the cluster of drones she'd directed down to follow him. He slammed into them with his swords, which were moving so fast that they looked like silver rings around him. By the time he'd passed through that group, another 649 drones were damaged beyond repair. Moreover, 193 of them exploded behind Shar-Lumen, taking out another 10,026 drones in a chain reaction.

Shar-Lumen's Nhia-Samri were doing similar, if not as spectacular, maneuvers. She'd managed to take out another thirty-six of them, but as Shar-Lumen and his warriors struck the ground, her drone force was down to 1,679 enforcers and 115,306 combat drones. Shar-Lumen had only lost ninety-four warriors, leaving him with 256 warriors at his back.

Twenty-three of Shar-Lumen's warriors had landed on the rooftop of the Mages' Guild, exchanging blows and magical blasts with the mages. The Guild mages barely managed to hold their own against the attackers.

"We have 49.3 percent drone losses in twenty-three minutes and eleven seconds, to his twenty-seven percent losses."

Arkady continued to concentrate on attacking the rest of the Nhia-Samri units.

"Well, with the loss of our combined concentration on the already present attack forces, and pulling the drones up to deal with Shar-Lumen, the Nhia-Samri already here have turned the attack around. They have the palace nearly surrounded."

"Did you get the mage, at least?" As Vesta asked, the same mage flashed across a display. "Never mind, I saw him."

Shar-Lumen had started moving through the city with

his personal unit. Vesta fumed at the monitors. He looked completely serene as he sliced through Daggers, mages, guards, drones, and enforcers. Watching their progress, she realized what was different. She reviewed all the sensor logs showing Shar-Lumen's unit as they essentially parachuted into the city.

"All in Shar-Lumen's personal unit are mages!"

Arkady turned around. "That's going to be a problem. We need bigger guns, and lots of them."

"STOP!" Electra's scream caught everyone by surprise. Even Shar-Lumen paused, his blade an inch from slicing into a Dagger. The strike would've probably cut him in half. How Shar-Lumen had frozen like that was remarkable in itself.

Vesta cried out at Electra as she realized what was about to happen. "NO! YOU CAN'T!"

Around the city, everyone was frozen. It was an odd tableau of scenes. Electra had stopped everyone and everything with that scream. Arkady held the combat drones and enforcers where they were, hovering, ready to continue the fight.

"Do we hold?" Arkady asked.

"She's going to surrender," Vesta squeaked out past her fear for Electra.

Arkady looked over all the data. "With Shar-Lumen here, we're going to lose unless we launch the war ships. And even if we do that, they'll take some time to get to Llino. I'm not even sure they could fly at the moment. We haven't activated any of their systems or done even a simple diagnostic on them. In addition, it would take one of us to fly one without a crew on board, and that would reveal our presence to the assembly."

While Arkady was talking, Electra typed a message to Vesta on her console in the throne room. *'Rainbow, I have to.'*

Electra's voice, strong and unwavering, came through the city's announcement system. Ellua had stopped giving updates on the Nhia-Samri movements as well. "Grand Warlord, I know you have come for us. I can't abide any more bloodshed.

If I surrender myself to you, will you order the Nhia-Samri to leave Aelargo, and return Regent Bayion unharmed?"

A great outcry came from around the city as guards, Daggers, and citizens shouted protests.

The Dagger facing Shar-Lumen knocked his blade aside and thrust his sword at Shar-Lumen, but the Grand Warlord shifted out of the way, sheathing his own blades. His hands snapped up to grasp the Dagger's blade and arm. With a painful twist, Shar-Lumen took the sword away and kicked the Dagger backwards, onto his backside.

Shar-Lumen tossed the Dagger's sword aside and looked up in the air. "The Nhia-Samri will abandon Aelargo until invited back by its rulers...on two conditions. One, you shall open the palace, and allow me to escort you out. And two, you and Lord Bayion will cheerfully remain our guests at Hisuru Amajoo until we allow you to leave."

"No, Electra. You can't do this. We will defeat them. I won't allow this," Ellua said.

"Lord Bayion has not agreed to this. I cannot speak for him. I can only speak for myself. I offer only myself as your hostage." Electra said resolutely, ignoring Ellua's plea.

Shar-Lumen stared at the drones and enforcers hovering around him. He grasped the hilt of his odassi, and when he spoke, his voice came clearly from every odassi in the city.

"I agree to your terms, Countess Electra Neyon. I shall speak with Lord Bayion individually. It shall be up to him how he spends his time as a guest of the Nhia-Samri. We shall abandon Aelargo entirely, until we're invited back by the rulers of Aelargo, given that you are cheerfully inviting me to the legendary palace of Llino, and accompanying me as my royal guest to Hisuru Amajoo until such time as we allow your departure."

"I agree. Ellua, please order the city to stop. We cannot win this day. But this will save Aelargo."

Across the city, the Nhia-Samri saluted those warriors and drones they were facing, and sheathed their swords.

"NO! I won't do it!"

Shar-Lumen put his hands on his blade hilts, focusing on the drones hovering around him. Around the city the Nhia-Samri also placed hands on hilts.

Electra said, "Ellua, please listen to reason. Look at how many have died. I do this freely. Besides, Shar-Lumen wouldn't dare harm me. Lord Dohma is already marching for Hisuru Amajoo. We know that's where the final battle must take place. Ellua, please, for me, do this."

Electra's voice was carried throughout the city for all to hear. Shar-Lumen frowned at something for only a second, but then his face went back to a neutral look as he stood, waiting.

Ellua looked at the displays and finally nodded. "All hostilities between the forces of Aelargo and the Nhia-Samri are hereby suspended. Guards and Daggers, attend to the wounded and assist the Nhia-Samri as needed, with courtesy, out of our city. Grand Warlord, you...are invited to the palace."

Electra told Ellua the commands to turn off all the defenses, and to cut off the announcement system, which she repeated. The palace shield winked out as Shar-Lumen walked at a rapid but dignified pace towards the palace. His personal unit formed up into ranks behind him as he moved. Citizens came out of hiding to help the wounded and glower at Shar-Lumen's procession.

Vesta was trying to decide how to react. She and Arkady watched the throne-room monitors, trying to determine what to do. The drones had been set on *auto return*. Maintenance systems were covertly grabbing damaged drones before anyone thought to take the parts. She had repair units moving to get the missile hatches repaired and closed.

Electra hugged Ellua. "Don't worry about me. He'll take good care of me. Please, Ellua. You must do as that new song everyone is humming says, 'Teach the children how to be strong and conquer fear.' Protect our family's future, your children, Bayion's children, and all the children of Aelargo. Keep Aelargo safe and give us all hope. Lord Dohma *will come* for me, I know this. In the meantime...." Electra said, turning to her Dagger guard captain with a grin, "Mandy, you'd best hurry and change clothes."

Mandy looked at Electra and raised an eyebrow. "Into what?"

"I'm not going anywhere without my handmaid. Now, go quickly. You also have to pack some of my things, especially my jewelry box."

Mandy took only a second to process the orders. "Handmaid. Right." She grinned right back, even with a reasonable curtsy. "Oh, yes, m'Lady. Jewelry box. I know just the one." She turned and slapped one of the larger of Electra's Daggers. "You're captain now." She ran full speed from the room.

Vesta watched, feeling helpless, as Shar-Lumen strolled into the palace and up to the throne room. As he walked in, he looked over everything with a keen eye. Of course, by that point, all of the displays and other armaments had been turned off and vanished. Shar-Lumen entered the throne room and walked straight up to Ellua and Electra. The women stood in front of the regents' thrones.

He executed a formal bow. "I am pleased to meet the restored regent."

Ellua's back was as stiff as a sword. "I am not pleased to meet you. I warn you, if any ha — "

Shar-Lumen waved his hand at her. "Lady, you have nothing to worry about. I never intended any harm to you or your family." His eyes moved to Electra. "So this is the woman who shall be the new co-chief regent. I am extremely pleased to meet you, Lady Neyon." He bowed again.

Electra nodded. "A formal announcement has not been made."

"No, but Lord Dohma has already made his choice, hasn't he?"

Electra's cheeks blushed, and she looked away. She stepped up to Shar-Lumen. "I am your hostage, sir."

Holding out his arm, he said, "No, my Lady. You are my guest, with some circumstantial requirements."

Vesta could see Electra's pulse had shot up, and she hesitated. Although her skin indicated she was terribly afraid, she still put her hand on his extended arm and followed him.

Shar-Lumen bowed to Ellua. "Lady, I shall send you news of your brother's decision as soon as possible. I presume it will be allowed for a pair of junior warriors to carry messages between our nations?"

"I'd prefer not."

Shar-Lumen paused and looked at Ellua. "Communications will be difficult without a trusted courier."

Ellua indicated two of Electra's Daggers, dressed in the Aelargo guard uniforms. "Would you guarantee the safety of these Daggers?"

Shar-Lumen looked at the Daggers. "They can stay close to Lady Electra."

Ellua looked shocked that Shar-Lumen accepted the idea.

"We shall leave a single gate terminus outside of your city. No one will come through without first getting your permission."

Ellua's lips tightened, but she nodded once.

He turned and began escorting Electra out. As they moved, Mandy stepped in behind, leading four large trunks carried by some palace servants.

Shar-Lumen again paused with his eyes landing on Mandy, who was dressed in a servant's blue slacks and a white linen shirt and leather vest. His eyes went from her to the trunks, and his eyebrow shot up. "I didn't expect you to pack nearly so much. And who is this?"

"My handmaid, of course. If I am your guest, then I shall require some suitable clothing. I have no idea what Hisuru Amajoo is like, so I had her prepare a limited selection."

"Hmmm...." he intoned as he looked at the baggage, but

he didn't protest. Without a further sign, he escorted Electra, Mandy and their baggage collection out of the palace. The Nhia-Samri took the trunks from the palace servants and fell into line. Together, they walked through the city, towards the western gate. Many of the streets they walked were littered with dead warriors, and all had bloodstains, both Nhia-Samri and Aelargian. Still, people came running to line the streets, many with their hands on their hearts. Guards and Daggers stood at attention and saluted as Electra went by. Shar-Lumen walked, without comment, out of the city.

Vesta paced back and forth as she monitored them walking out to the Nhia-Samri camps. Electra didn't even look back once. She held her head high and stepped with grace through the mage-gate.

Vesta stomped her foot and then kicked a console. "SKEED! HOW CAN WE BEAT HIM?" she screamed as she started pacing twice as fast as before.

Arkady leaned against a wall, silently pulling on his beard. His snappy comment didn't come, which surprised her. Vesta stopped and glared at him. He didn't say a word.

"Nothing?" she finally prompted.

He shook his head and kept pulling on his beard, his mind focused elsewhere.

Vesta huffed, and went back to pacing.

DOHMA

The two weeks of hard travel were finally over. They'd made the rendezvous site ahead of the other divisions. Dohma dismounted and stretched. Patting his horse, he took it to where the officers' horses were going to be corralled. The handlers were all busy, so he grabbed a pair of combs and brushes from one of the supply wagons and set about brushing the animal down. It wasn't hard work, but it took time. Dohma found it pleasurably relaxing as much as the horse appreciated it.

It had taken almost three weeks to finish all the funeral rites, and as much as that put them behind schedule, Dohma refused any suggestion to speed up the ceremonies. The division then force-marched for fourteen marks a day, every day, for two weeks solid to make up the lost time. No one complained about the journey.

As he worked on the horse, the strong musky animal odor was momentarily masked by wood smoke wafting past. The ashy smell brought the remains of the valley he'd inspected back to his mind. There had been nothing left of the base or surrounding farms. In total, an area almost ten miles wide had vanished into ash instantly, leaving a deep crater. The explosion wiped out the forest for thirty miles in every direction.

I wish I could figure out what happened. I'm sure my group was only a mile from the center of that base when we used their magic gate into the complex. There's no way even Duke could have run twenty miles in the few minutes we had before being hit by the explosion, and yet Duke and I were right at the blast edge. I just can't find a reason for this. I hate not knowing what happened. My Daggers and I were diurdin lucky.

Duke still hadn't awoken, and Dohma was slowly losing hope he ever would. Elades kept insisting he would be fine. Carrying his body with them was having a polarizing effect on the troops. The Daggers weren't bothered by it, but the regular soldiers murmured about the apparently disrespectful treatment of Duke. Many were suggesting a bit of a mutiny to build him a proper funeral pyre.

The rapid march had kept that from happening. They were going to settle in and rest for a week while the other troops came in, reinforcing the division to full strength. Dohma was worried the mutiny would be forthcoming in a few days.

When he was finished brushing, he handed the horse over to a stable boy. His saddle and gear had already been taken away while he'd been preoccupied. The boy's hands glistened with the oils used to clean and protect the leather gear.

He headed for the officers' tents. Finding the location was more difficult than he expected. After roaming about for a full mark, finding no clue where he should go in the sea of thousands of tents put up while he'd been working, he asked directions to his own tent from a Dagger. Another long walk through the pungent oil cloth maze brought him to the core officers' area. As he walked past Duke's tent he spotted Elades inside and stepped in to check.

"Lord Dohma," Elades greeted him cheerfully, his voice clean and clear. "I'm told dinner will be ready shortly. I'm just looking over the fresh reports from the Alliance."

His feet hurt and the smells of various meals being prepared filled the air, making his stomach rumble for samples. There were some comfortable seats, so he sat down and put his feet up.

"Hand me some of those, please."

Elades handed him a stack of papers. The reports showed that all six divisions were nearing full strength, which meant that the Alliance had succeeded in mustering almost five million soldiers. Each of the divisions was making progress. So far, no Nhia-Samri base had stood to their attacks. Some of the bases were abandoned, like the one he'd found a couple of cycles back. Others fought to the last warrior to defend themselves. But considering the size of the divisions, the Nhia-Samri bases had no chance.

Their only real chance of fighting us would be to pull together into a single army and face us on the field. I pray that isn't where soldiers from the empty bases are going. We'd outnumber them at least 15:1, and yet with their skills and odassi swords, that might not be enough.

A steward came in with some wine. "Sir, would you care for the game birds or deer meat?"

"BOTH! And get me all the bacon I'm smelling too!" came the deep-voiced reply from behind him.

Elades and Dohma leapt at the unexpected voice.

"Duke?" Dohma yelled as he moved around the body.

Duke's sides were rising and falling with his breathing.

"I sure as hell ain't a dancing girl! Where is that meat? I'm hungry!"

Duke's head, which he'd avoided looking at since initially seeing it crushed was surprisingly normal and was resting on a pile of pillows. As Dohma reached it, Duke's eyes opened, and Duke looked at him, his brows narrowed. "You look half-dead. What on Yur have you been up to?"

Dohma sat down on the floor in front of Duke. "You're alive! Really and truly alive."

Duke lifted his head and winced. "Yeah, mostly. Elades, I know you're back there. I can smell you and hear you breathing. Didn't you tell him I'd be okay?"

Elades walked around. "Yes, but he, and a growing majority of soldiers, didn't really believe it. We've had a hard time keeping them from putting you on a funeral pyre."

Duke put his head back down. "Thanks. I hate getting burnt up almost as much as being crushed. I'll have to make a speech or something to rally them back to sanity." Duke looked at Dohma sitting on the floor. "Dohma, get up off the floor. We can't have anyone seeing you sitting there like that. If you're going to join me for dinner order up some chairs and a table. Elades, get the officers together. But first, get me that bacon! The smell is making my mouth twitch. And wine, lots of wine."

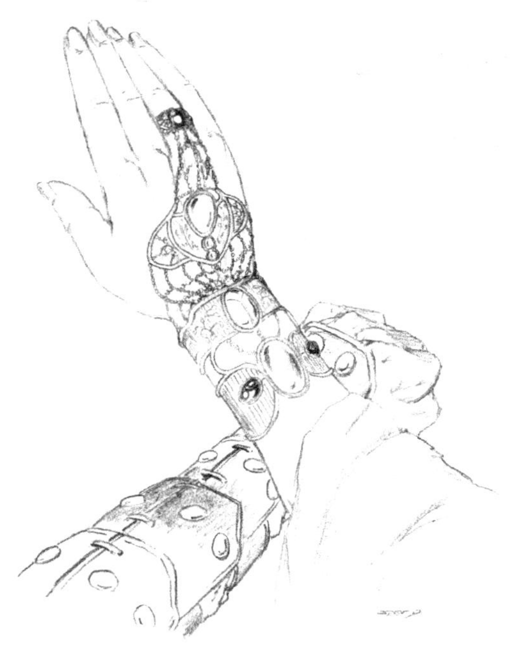

The Yunna Minthra

CHAPTER 14

LESSONS

❧ RUNA-ILLA ❧

RUNA-ILLA SAT DOWN ON A rock in the lengthening shadow of the cliff. Her head was pounding, and it was difficult to think. The sun was setting, and the desert was reflecting back the many shades of the sunset. Rainbows and bright starlight moved up the white stone cliff as the sun descended beyond it. Looking at the light patterns, she let her mind drift as the headache slowly faded. Her hand randomly selected small warm stones to toss.

This desert is amazingly beautiful. Of course, no one risks coming this far into it to discover its beauty. If it wasn't for Lebuin's magic, we would die in a few marks from the heat alone, shade or no shade.

She contemplated all the time she had there. Trying to keep track of time was hard, as the scenery and incessant walking had a mesmerizing effect. *It's been sixteen, no, seventeen days since the surprise attack by those giant predatory arthropods.* Since then, nothing else had bothered the group.

There were signs of other nocturnal creatures, but the Daggers were all sure there were none on the scale of those things. They'd found the shells of shepherd dog-sized adephagans that looked a lot like their smaller cousins the tiger beetles, which she was used to seeing almost everywhere. The fact that the larger ones had been crushed open made her worry about what had done the crushing. They were guessing that the large carabids were the major diet of the arthropods that attacked them earlier.

Though it had been quiet in recent days, they'd all been on high alert. Nothing moved willingly in the daytime, which made that particular attack suspicious and the subject of much debate. Other than overly large insects, the only creatures that managed to survive were small reptiles, a few varieties of more normal-sized insects, and a few species of predatory birds.

The team had stocked up their meat supplies before entering the desert by killing a number of larger game animals, and preparing them for storage in Lebuin's magical pack before they'd crossed the mountains. They'd also fashioned many water skins, which were also in Lebuin's pack. Even with all that preparation, their rations were almost exhausted.

Ditani and Malla had turned out to be an effective team for capturing snakes as they traveled. The last six evening meals were roasted snake. Illa had spied six fresh ones bouncing on Ditani's back earlier, signaling that evening would be more of the same. Every third day, they used a few precious oranges from the pack for the ascorbic acid needed to protect them from the traveler's disease. Vestul had some rather strange things in the pack before Lebuin had come to possess it. But there were too many specific things in there, like the huge quantity of dilotha ointment, two whole barrels of red-peppers, and another pair of oranges. There had even been sixteen empty water bladders.

Vestul was either an extremely organized pack rat, or he expected a trip into a desert. I wonder if they came here before on one of those previous attempts from his time traveling.

Ditani was a great cook, and he spiced up the snake meat with a number of different herbs from the huge selection Vestul had collected in the magical pack. He specifically included the red peppers in a lot of the food, claiming they'd help prevent some health problems. Most of the herbs, he admitted to her, were selected because they didn't taste like the ones from the day before, but were usually enjoyable.

The last of the water had been used two days earlier. Lebuin had pushed his magics, trying to gather some water, without luck. Instead, they had to settle for moving slower, with Lebuin working harder to give everyone a stronger shield against the heat.

None of that was enough. The desert was so dry that just

breathing sucked water out of the body. They needed to find water, but none of the signs Ticca or Persa had mentioned had been found. What they needed was for Ticca or Persa to be there to help them, but neither of them were alive. Persa was dead for sure, and Ticca had no chance of living that long without Lebuin's shields. She might have made it back out to that first cave and water source they'd used, but Lebuin kept searching that area with his magics, trying to find her, and he hadn't seen any sign of her.

Illa would have cried as her thoughts filled with the missing people she'd begun to cherish, except that she was too dehydrated. Ticca, Persa, and Risy had all died in that attack eight days earlier. Sabri, Coedy, and Epton had died in the last attack by the Nhia-Samri, where Illa herself nearly died. And Tuage had died in the Blue Dolphin before they'd even started on the trek.

Ticca and Persa had tried to impart as much desert survival knowledge as they could while the team moved over the mountains, but that wasn't enough. Without them, the chances of finding water in time were dwindling.

As her heart ached for the loss of her friends and the possibility that they might all die, she pulled out the strange carved wooden box. She hadn't had another vision since the one just prior to the creatures' attacking. In fact, most of the group believed the creatures were attracted to them by the shared vision, which could have been the reason for the attack.

As she gazed at the box, Illa felt that she could sense Ticca through it.

I would swear Ticca is still alive. Lebuin refuses to give up on her, too.

She turned the treasure over, inspecting it. There was a catch that would depress in the Imperial sigil on the top, but nothing else happened. She lost track of time as she explored the intricate carving once again with her fingers, trying to find something else that moved or that would move with or without the one catch she'd found. The imagery on the box was almost lifelike. Clever use of shadows and optical illusions made the elven scenes animated as she rotated the box. They were tending to the land, farming, fishing, and some were working in factories. Others were clearly mages, with arcane symbols and books surrounding them. The level of detail was astonishing.

A noise caught her attention, and Illa looked at Lebuin, who was scanning the cliff for a hidden entrance or cave. He had that silver box he'd found in the Nhia-Samri base in his hand, and he was trying to use it to discover anything useful.

He had been playing with it on and off the last week almost constantly. The only time he wasn't playing with it was when he was re-reading the journal, which was now opened. She knew both items confused him and he wanted to talk to her about them. But he kept his distance. Now they stood at the location of the other base they were searching for, but they couldn't find an entrance.

If we don't find that base soon, we're sure to die. Well, at least, the Daggers will. Lebuin seems to be holding up better than most, and I am, too. But I still feel the dehydration and fatigue.

Her thoughts turned to the fact that Lebuin had abandoned them. Anger, unbidden, came rushing back in. Her heart rate jumped, and her jaw clenched tight. She saw Lebuin pause. She turned away from him as he glanced at her. She knew he felt her rush of anger.

Urdu! Why did he have to do that? I would have given my life for him, and in fact, I did that already. I knew he wasn't a normal God. But still, he's a God, so how can he be so diurdu... human?

Nigan landed next to her loudly.

"Phew, it's hot!"

She put the box away and shifted in her seat to get a better look at his profile. He'd pulled down the face shield of his turban, as she had. He had the appearance of a wildly romantic character from one of the steamy books she'd read as a teenager. His face was tanned and colored artistically with the yellow sands. They were all dark, as the sun penetrated even through the layers of cloth they'd worn over their faces to protect themselves from it.

"It's always hot here. That's the problem."

"Yeah, but did you see those heat waves bouncing off the top of the cliff? I mean, seriously, they're playing with the light so much it's like, well, amazing to be here to see it! We might be the first!"

She looked up and saw that the setting sun's light was warped and twisted in the heat, causing a spray of orange, red, and golden beams to radiate out from the top of the cliff. She gasped at the beauty of it.

"From now on, when I say you're more beautiful than the setting sun, you need to remember this."

Her heart jumped at the compliment. But she wanted to keep him on his toes, so she gave his shoulder a friendly punch. "Don't lie."

He twisted around to face her. "I'm not. You are."

She stared at him for a minute in silence, trying to understand how he was still happy, even after losing his lifelong friend Risy. He'd buried Risy with all the same honors and respect as Persa, Sabri, Coedy, and Epton. He'd been quiet for a couple of days after that, but then his joy returned. He was as annoyingly happy as ever. In fact, more so, since without Risy to take some of his jokes and quips, she was getting the full load of his attitude.

Honestly, I'm amazed Risy stayed with him so long. How can anyone be so optimistic, especially under these circumstances? Her face flushed as she realized she really enjoyed it.

"You need to forgive him," Nigan said softly.

She jumped at the unexpected comment. "Forgive HIM?" She started to get up, but Nigan placed his hand on her leg before she could move it. He wasn't applying any pressure, still his touch felt like a steel band holding her in place.

Without raising his voice, he said, "Yes, even Gods make mistakes."

"He was reading fantasies! He was hiding!"

"I've been thinking about it. To be honest, I don't know if I would've come straight back, either."

She couldn't believe Nigan, of all people, was saying that. If Lebuin hadn't been hiding, the Nhia-Samri might not have been able to track them. It was nearly impossible to cover a travois trail.

Nigan continued, "He's here now."

"Only because he feels guilty, and I caught him."

"Are you sure?"

"Of course, I'm sure...." She considered and realized that she wasn't exactly sure. Lebuin was hard to read, even with her connection. She'd felt a lot of conflicting emotions and thoughts from him. She'd tried to ignore them, but they registered.

"You don't sound sure."

"He didn't even check on me! I was stuck in that place a long time, alone with only my thoughts. I was lost. He could have found me any time he wanted to. He didn't want to."

"Did he know you were in trouble?"

She pursed her lips and looked away. *No, he didn't.*

"Did you call for him?"

Her head whipped around to stare at him. Before she'd thought it out, her lips betrayed her. "No."

"So he was sitting in a comfortable chair, drinking some imaginary wine, reading a book that let him escape into some other world where he wasn't under the knife, and where the heroes probably always won and got their loves in the end. We all want to escape reality. There's nothing better than a good fantasy to do that. Why do you think the bards are so popular? Why do people stop everything to listen to your singing? They want to get away to someplace more beautiful."

She folded her arms over her chest and huffed, mostly

because she didn't have anything to say that wouldn't sound childish.

Nigan smiled and leaned in to kiss her on her forehead. "Seriously, I would have spent at least a few weeks there. It sounds wonderful, and with all this speedy time business, why not? Has he gone back there?"

She didn't know for sure, but her gut said *no*, so she shook her head, not trusting her voice just yet.

"Do you know why? I mean, we're sleeping, so what's the harm in popping off to read a few books every night if it doesn't interfere with your sleep?"

"Because that would be escaping again!"

"In your eyes, yes. In mine, not so much. I envy him the ability. So you see, he's trying to please you." Nigan glanced at Lebuin. "Well, you and Ticca, probably. But definitely you. He hasn't run, even after that fight. Did you know he could just go there and say 'to hell' with his body? He'd be safe from everything happening here."

She leaned back. "You don't know that."

"Yes, I do."

"How?"

"I asked."

That caught her by surprise. When did Nigan have enough time alone with Lebuin to ask something like that?

"He said that?" she asked, her voice almost a whisper.

Nigan nodded. "Yes. He learned an important lesson in that library. A lesson about being a Dagger. We all have to learn it. Doing what is right is hard, and almost always, we have a much safer path we could take. But to protect the people we love, we do what is needed."

Nigan lifted his hand from her leg and smiled. "You're hurt, and you won't heal until you forgive him for being a real person. You saw his potential when you committed yourself to his cause. Time for you to learn that being a Dagger, even for a God or his high priestess, means overcoming challenges, and it's a lot easier with a partner."

Did I see only what he could be? I didn't know what was happening. But his goals, his life, his potential were so bright in that moment. I felt so sure that I was born to be with him on his journey.

She looked at Lebuin again, and that time, the anger wasn't as strong. She remembered the shining beacon of power who'd taken her odassi and bent it to his will. Who'd defeated the warlord's attempt to trace him. Who'd come to the rescue of Ticca, whom she thought at the time was his minion, when it wasn't necessary. In that moment, it had been like the whole universe had opened to her, and she could see a line of people going back into her past and forward to her future. All the paths going forward with Lebuin were bright and hopeful. She'd chosen in that moment to serve him.

However, Ticca wasn't his follower. At least, not in that sense. She'd learned he wasn't a powerful God, but a young man surprised and scared by his destiny. And yet he was still trying to grow into that bright beacon she'd first seen. It was clear that the bright and hopeful future would take work, sacrifice, and...forgiveness.

Illa let the wall she'd been holding against Lebuin fall. She was flooded with the feelings and power she'd felt that first moment she'd beheld Lebuin in his true form as a God. Her God. The feelings and power had never really left her. She'd been holding them walled off, pretending they weren't a part of her.

I am Runa-Illa, high priestess of Lord Lebuin, and he needs my help to find his true potential. I serve him, and through him, Lord Argos, the All Father of this universe. I was born for this.

As the thought occurred, she realized it was true. She was born for it in that existence, and in the other she'd glimpsed when she had the experience with Ticca. In that other place, she had long served Lebuin, and he loved and trusted her above all others there, too.

Her mind felt like it was released from a cage, and the power that Lebuin held coursed through her freely once more.

She felt so light, she could almost fly. Her face felt comfortable wearing the smile she had since choosing to follow Lebuin.

I needed to mend myself, too. Forgiving him isn't just for his heart, but to heal me, as well!

Lebuin turned slack faced, his mouth hanging open and his eyes almost tearing.

She walked up to him and gently closed his mouth with her hand.

"My Lord, Gods shouldn't gape."

"Illa?" was all Lebuin could manage. There was a great deal of hope and doubt in his tone.

She'd known his strong desire for her to forgive him, but also his despair in the fear that it would never happen, even with their connection. She could feel his emotions running wild, like a hurricane, confirming all he'd said and not said.

She nodded and smiled, staring into his eyes. "Yes, my Lord. We both had a lesson to learn. I have learned mine. I forgive you. Please forgive me for taking so long to learn this lesson."

She felt the surge of relief and raw joy Lebuin felt. He was so overwhelmed at first that all he could do was holler with joy. Then, faster than she could imagine, he grabbed her in a bear hug, yanking her off her feet. His emotions flooded her, sweeping her away in his elation.

When he finally put her down, Ditani was standing next to them. She looked at Ditani, and he placed his hand on her shoulder and smiled. His emotions then got the better of him, and he wrapped his arms around both of them for a quick embrace.

"I'm glad you two have come around. Now, we might have a better chance of finding the way in."

Lebuin turned back to the cliff face, but Ditani's words bounced around Illa's head.

Find the way in.

She pulled the wooden box out of her pouch.

This was made for me, by someone who knew me.

On it, she found the lady making swords, her mother, the warrior leading a martial practice, her father, the mage surrounded by his tomes, Lebuin, and the singing lady with her head held high and a sword on her belt — herself.

Holding the cube in one hand, two fingers and her thumb could just reach three characters. With her thumb on the forth, she squeezed the four of them together and felt a small click within the box. Smiling, she kept pressure on the figures, and with her finger, manipulated the catch in the Imperial symbol. The top slid free under her hand.

"You got it!" Nigan jumped to look at it with her. The rest of the team gathered round.

Inside the box was a blue silk padded cover. She had to pull hard to lift it straight up, as it was more of a plug. The pad pulled free, revealing a silver filigree-etched manilla, decorated with more diamonds and sapphires than she could count. A set of intertwining chains connected, in a triangle netting, to a matching ring with a massive sapphire, surrounded by diamonds on a twisted vine.

It was so beautiful that Illa sucked in her breath, and her hands trembled. She'd seen many wonders in Hisuru Amajoo, and nothing came close to the treasure she held in raw splendor.

Nigan whistled.

With a broad smile, Lebuin said, "Ticca has really good taste. Try it on."

Illa's stomach fluttered at the thought of wearing such a thing. "Can I?"

Nigan reached into the box, pulling the bracelet out. He handed Lebuin the box and flipped her hand over, sliding the ring on her forefinger. He then slipped the manilla over her wrist and fastened the clasp.

He held her hand, looking into her eyes. "You can, because it's yours."

She held her hand out, showing it to everyone. As she moved it back and forth, it caught the light, reflecting and focusing it, creating sparkling flashes. A few crossed her eyes, blinding her momentarily.

Lebuin's brows tightened. "That looks familiar."

A soft cool breeze brushed past them, holding the lavender scent of the palace's gardens in it. She could feel the moisture of the coming light rain in the atmosphere. It would be a lovely, if chilled night. The morning would be bright and fresh. She thought it would be nice to go for a ride along the seashore.

A laugh came from behind. "Of course it does, my Lord Lebuin."

Illa and Lebuin turned as one to see the princess approaching them. Two of her guards held the library doors open, which was the cause of the sudden breeze, the other two took up positions outside the doorway. She was wearing a beautiful blue dress that matched the silk lining of the box exactly; it even had the same silver piping. As she moved, the silver threads in the dress shimmered. Runa-Illa suppressed a giggle at knowing the resemblance to the box and its treasure was not a coincidence.

Illa curtsied, and Lebuin bowed.

"Your Highness, this is an extraordinary gift. You're most generous," she said to Ticca.

When she stood straight, she noticed that Lebuin was looking at Ticca with narrowed brows. Following his gaze, she saw what had Lebuin concerned. Ticca's face was hollow, and the dress she wore hung loosely on her frame. That was surely not her intention. Ticca had lost a lot of weight recently. This usually indicated a health problem.

Ticca picked up a glass of water and drank it down in quick, successive gulps. She then filled it again, and drank that before she turned to them. "Sorry. It seems unusually hot and dry to me. I find I have an incredible thirst." Ticca pointed at the manilla on Illa's wrist. "Lebuin will soon remember why that looks familiar. I want the rest of the surprise to come in its own way. I enjoyed seeing your face upon opening it."

Illa blushed. "Your Highness! Have you been using the surveillance system improperly?"

Ticca had popped a piece of fruit into her mouth and was chewing it with enthusiasm, so she didn't answer. She made a sweeping gesture, and a short man appeared. He wore a lab coat over a finely tailored blue suit. His black and white hair was cut short, and stood up in tufts at various angles.

Illa laughed. "Oh, Brandon! Are you in on this?"

"Of course I am, your Excellency. Nothing happens here that I don't know about. The princess ruffled a few feathers, taking it away from our research division."

Ticca shushed him. "Brandon, you're horrible at keeping secrets. They still have the Imperial device to study."

Brandon blushed, and turned towards her. "My apologies, Your Highness. I don't think I let too much out."

Lebuin stepped over to stand close to Ticca. "Your Highness, are you okay?"

Brandon's brows tightened, and he, too, stepped towards Ticca. "Your Highness, you are suffering from severe dehydration and starvation." Brandon turned, looking each of them over. "You all are dehydrated. What is happening?"

Amia-Dharo ran into the room. The royal guards snapped to attention, as he slid to a stop and examined each of them. He saw the manilla Illa was wearing, and his eyes nearly jumped out of his head.

Illa recalled that it was a vision, and she was really in the ruins of Elraci, a desert so dangerous no one had dared traverse it in thousands of years.

Ticca had continued to eat and drink even more rapidly. When Amia-Dharo came in, her face went completely slack for a second, and then she started madly stuffing fruits and pastries into her dress. Lebuin ran to another decanter tray, picking it up and running back towards Ticca with it. The panic on his face matched the emotional flood she got from him.

"What is going on?" Brandon asked more urgently.

Amia-Dharo stepped towards Lebuin and Ticca. "I did see you there. You were at Niuni Lol."

Brandon instantly was before Amia-Dharo. "How could they be there?"

"They're caught in a transition wave. Ticca is pulling me into it somehow. Maybe due to my binding to her family."

Brandon shook his head. "That isn't possible. We corrected the fluctuations thousands of years ago."

"It is." Amia-Dharo pulled a beacon key out of his shoulder pouch. "Brandon, make this a key to Kiliun Lol."

"I can't do that without the emperor's consent," he said with a shake of his head.

The far wall wavered as if it was made of liquid. Then it shattered into nothing, and a distortion wave rippled towards them. Amia-Dharo dove to get away from the wave. He was fast, but it was faster. Just as his legs vanished, he threw what he was holding at Lebuin. "This or the Yunna Minthra Ticca ga..." He was gone.

"ACCESS GRANTED!" Brandon yelled as he whirled, pointing at Lebuin and the beacon key as it flew through the air. The wave passed over Brandon, and he was gone.

Lebuin had already handed Illa two large crystal carafes of scented water. "Hold tight and don't drop those, no matter what," he ordered as he took a flying leap to catch the beacon key. He caught it, landing on the floor, his momentum making him slide towards the wave.

Just before the wave washed over Lebuin, he looked at Ticca as if he was watching a friend die. He shouted, "We'll find you!" And then he was gone, too.

The wave touched Ticca, who was desperately hugging three of the large crystal containers full of water. Illa stood in the corner with nowhere to go, so she also gripped the pitchers and closed her eyes, breathing deeply, trying to not sway.

I'll return to my world. I'll be standing. I only need to not fall from the dizziness.

She concentrated on breathing, holding on to the containers, and standing evenly balanced. She was so focused that she missed the feeling of transition.

"Where did you get that?" Nigan's voice came from right next to her.

She sighed and opened her eyes. Lebuin was lying down on a rock a few feet away.

"Lebuin, are you okay?" Malla called as she and Carda ran over to him to help him up.

She looked down, and not only did she still have the bracelet on, but in her hand was a full pitcher of wonderfully fresh fruit-flavored water. She laughed, and she saw Lebuin standing, staring at his empty hand like it was a traitor.

Lebuin turned to her, and his eyes lit up. "If you have that, she might have hers, too!" He jumped around, shouting, "She's alive! She's alive!"

Nigan took the flask and sniffed it. "Orange vanilla water?"

Illa couldn't stop laughing. She grabbed Nigan's arm. "She's alive! I have the jug, so she might have hers too! Don't you see, she's alive! She could have the food, too! She's alive!"

Lebuin heard her and stopped jumping. Then he couldn't contain his joy, and jumped some more. "You have a jug, and she might too!"

Ditani asked, "Ticca? You saw Ticca?"

Illa couldn't speak, she was grinning so wide, so she nodded and held the pitcher high, like a prized trophy.

Nigan snapped his fingers. "They had another one of those weird vision things. Ticca was there, and she took food and water with her like Illa brought back this carafe. Next time, do you think you could bring back a steak dinner platter?"

Illa handed Nigan the pitcher. As soon as he took it, she punched him in the opposite shoulder. It took a while for Lebuin to calm down, but eventually, the whole team was sitting around, sipping the flavored water and listening as Lebuin explained what happened.

"Why did Illa bring back only one pitcher, and where did this beacon key thing go?" Nigan asked.

Lebuin thought about it a couple of minutes. "There has to be a reason."

"Well, I brought back the box, too. Maybe it's a priestess power or something."

"I gave you two pitchers, but only one stayed." Lebuin's eyes lifted to the starry night sky as he scratched his beard and mumbled a lot of stuff, mostly to himself.

Illa tried to ignore that everyone was staring at her. Ditani moved to sit next to her. He pointed at her hand with the manilla. "Was this the hand that held the water you brought back?"

Illa tried to remember, but wasn't sure. She shrugged.

"Yes, it is," Nigan said. "I was on her right side, because I had just put that on her. I took the pitcher from her right hand."

Lebuin leaned in to look closer at the bracelet and ring. "It has a lot of channels. It looks like...." He held up his hand and then shifted to sit behind her. "Hold still for a moment." He placed his right hand next to hers and leaned down, moving his head back and forth, his nose almost touching both his hand and hers.

After the detailed inspection, he grunted and sat back. "That's amazing." He sat there, looking up at the stars.

They all waited, staring at Lebuin. Several minutes passed when, in a single, fluid motion, Ditani leaned over and slugged Lebuin in the shoulder. He jumped and placed his hand over the spot. "Ow! That hurt."

"So does ignorance. We're waiting." Ditani waved, indicating the whole group.

"Oh, sorry. That's an original fae artifact. I mean, elven... well, not exactly. It's older than this world." He sighed and shook his head. Pursing his lips, he paused, looking down. "Let me explain something I've learned. All our peoples originally came from other worlds. Elves, dwarves, and the Gods came from worlds where mana, or magic, was in abundance. Our bodies depend on mana like humans depend on food. We need some foods, too, but not as much or as often.

"Humans came from worlds where there was...well, not exactly none, but practically no mana. They dreamed of magical things, and dreaming made them desire those things. They delved into sciences beyond anything my race knew. And they developed machines and technology that gave them the abilities of magic. When our worlds were threatened, all of the great races worked together to come here. Now, we all live here together."

Lebuin pulled the silver box he'd been playing with out of his pocket. "This is mundane, or non-magical, human technology. Its purpose is to examine things in many ways far beyond just looking at them. It keeps a record of everything it has seen. Those records can be searched, reviewed, and studied in detail. Here...." He opened the small doors on it and pushed some buttons. The thing lit up with many lights. A semitransparent, but almost solid, image of a beautiful glowing machine formed. Placing the silver case down, Lebuin used both hands to move the image, adjusting the angle and size. The image was almost a full meter wide and tall. The machine had what could have been a sun at its core, and around it floated a golden mesh with bright gems of all colors. The machine moved like flowing water, the golden mesh turning, and the crystals glinted as they rotated past.

Lebuin pointed at the image. "That's what was destroyed at the Nhia-Samri base. I'm pretty sure it's a machine that generates energy that's an altered form of mana. It's Elracian technology, a blending of mundane and magical technology. I believe that hundreds of similar machines were here in Elraci." He bent and pushed some more buttons. The likeness of the machine changed colors, and looked like it was in a bank of multi-colored clouds that churned around it. "That's the mana, or magic, it's making."

Lebuin picked up the silver recording box, and yet the image of the machine remained steady. Illa had expected it to bounce and move with the box. But whatever it was doing produced a steady picture.

I suppose that would be a requirement for research. It'd be annoying if it moved when not desired.

Lebuin lifted her hand with the dazzling bracelet, web, and ring. He waved the box over her hand while manipulating the device with his thumb. He gave her a gentle smile, and then produced a second image of the manilla, ring, and connecting silver netting, floating in the air next to the machine. Amazingly, her hand wasn't in it. But the netting and ring moved slightly, as if her hand was there, but was not being shown.

Lebuin manipulated the controls again; the image of the bracelet shifted, and hundreds of glowing yellow to red balls, the size of pebbles, appeared around the manilla. The spheres floated randomly, except those closest to the manilla, which were pulled in, spreading out into a mixed-color layer over the top of the bracelet.

It looked almost like a thin layer of red and yellow water over the bracelet that pulsed, running through and over the webbing, to the ring. The colored liquid went up through the diamonds, which filtered it into narrow beams of clear liquid shooting up from the top of the diamonds, to the large sapphire. It had a series of clear, shimmering, watery rings around it.

Lebuin pointed to the image. "You see, this is filtering the mana." He stuck his finger in the clear rings around the sapphire. "This looks exactly like the kind of mana the Nhia-Samri tried to kill us with when they destroyed that base. Argos said the Nhia-Samri are using a Loehesh Pattern for their mana. This artifact is a Loehesh Pattern filter for mana, and possibly even a storage device. You can use it to collect mana for me faster than you could before. Also, this mana is, well, concentrated and purified. You might even be able to use that mana for yourself if I train you."

Lebuin pushed something on the silver recorder, and the images vanished.

"So it manipulates magic?" Ditani asked.

"Yes. And I think that's why it came through. Those are more than just visions. I think this thing, once it was close to Illa, started collecting and filtering magic. A strong magical wave is pushing us in and out of these visions or other world. This artifact probably drained the wave around it."

"Why me?"

"Because you're a power collector. Even when you were mad at me and blocking me, you were still feeding me some power. This thing was made for you, or at least someone like you."

Lebuin turned to the cliff face. "And I think we can break into this place now."

Everyone stood and turned towards where Lebuin was looking.

"Into what place?" Nigan asked.

Lebuin pointed, and a blast of golden fire flew from his hand. It slammed into something a meter and half in front of the cliff face and spread out, revealing a six-meter-wide bubble, or shield, over a section of the cliff face and into the ground.

"That place."

Everyone gasped. Lebuin stopped his magic, and the bubble faded back into invisibility.

Nigan jumped up, his face tight. "Wait a minute! You're proposing she stick her hand into that?"

"Kind of," Lebuin said, shrugging. "I've been trying to figure out how to get through. It's a lot stronger than any other shield I know of. Also, I'm worried about attacking it outright. I'm not sure what might happen if I manage to break it with sheer force. The backlash might be more than we expect. This filter is a way to drain it, instead of breaking it.

She can try to touch it with that filter. I'm betting it can pull enough power out of the shield to let us pass."

"How much magic can this hold?" Illa asked.

"I don't know. Why don't you try opening it to me? Let's see if we can channel the power. I can send it to the Argos collector. That can hold a lot more than anything we have encountered."

Ditani grabbed Lebuin's arm. "Lebuin, these artifacts are extremely powerful. How do you know you can take the energy from that thing?"

Lebuin pulled out the silver box and wiggled it in front of Ditani. "Because it's putting out 1,733 rellums of mana. The power I filtered off that base was a thousand times more than that, at least."

Illa and Lebuin had to experiment and try many combinations before they figured out how she could channel the power from the bracelet to Lebuin. He'd already figured out how to send the power to the Argos artifact, which was why he'd stopped glowing a few days back. It was almost morning before they were ready to try.

Her stomach was threatening to jump out of her throat at any moment as she stood, staring in the direction of the shield. She approached it. Lebuin touched her shoulder and stood next to her. He connected and shared his magical vision with her. It was strange, looking over her own shoulder at her hand, but the angle was close enough to normal that she was able to adjust for it.

In his magical sight, the shield glowed and pulsed. The small nodules of mana that floated everywhere in Elraci ether bounced off of it or popped on contact. She was distracted by the sensation of moving her hand through floating bubbles that she couldn't see or feel normally. As her hand moved closer, the bracelet continued to absorb the magical nodules.

She opened the channel to Lebuin, and he held his left hand out as a steady stream of clear mana shot, in a solid line, from the sapphire in the ring to his hand. He absorbed the power and channeled it off to the Argos artifact, back in the Argos Guildhouse in Llino.

She started to reach out for the shield, as her hand got within a few centimeters she could feel a pulsing tingle over her fingers. Her hand shook so badly, she made a fist and pulled it back. Lebuin gave her an encouraging squeeze with his right hand on her shoulder. She reached out again, and just before she touched it, she saw power in it begin to swirl. She could feel it too. A slight acrid odor came to her too, as if the air was burning because of the interactions. An arc of mana sparked off of it, to the bracelet. It was absorbed and filtered just like the nodules. Her confidence grew, and she concentrated on keeping the channels open to Lebuin.

The hairs on the back of her hand stood up, and the tingling sensation began tickling up her arm. With her open palm, she touched the shield. It buzzed angrily, and in Lebuin's shared vision, it turned a dark blue. The physical sensation was odd. It felt like she was about to touch boiling water, and tingled like she'd just got a static shock on it. It took all of her self-control to hold steady. She pushed forward until her hand was halfway through the bubble. Its energies parted like water, and with her hand inside it, the device was filtering a lot of mana. The stream to Lebuin's hand from the sapphire became as thick as a tree branch.

They stood like that for several minutes. Aside from the power Lebuin was collecting, nothing changed.

"Pull your hand out. This isn't working," he finally said, his voice full of defeat.

No! We can do this.

She knew she could get through. She grabbed Lebuin's left forearm and pulled him with her as she stepped through the shield.

He squeaked and stumbled after her.

It buzzed and went red, yet it still parted for them. They ended up standing together before a doorway that had been made invisible by the shield. The door was pure white and set back into the cliff face about half a meter, giving them plenty of space to stand between it and the edge of the shield. The ground there was tiled with a blue and white marble with black trim.

She let go of Lebuin and turned to face him. "Gods don't squeak, my Lord."

"The hell they don't! What made you do this?"

"I felt we could do it. I realized that this," she said, holding up the bracelet, "is the Yunna Minthra Amia-Dharo tried to tell us about."

A motion drew their attention back to the shield. The others had stood up and rushed to where it was. She could see them clearly, but they couldn't see her. They were talking to each other in surprise, pointing. Nigan pulled out a dagger and prodded the bubble. A bright spark flashed over his dagger, and he jumped back, dropping the dagger and shaking his hand like he'd been stung.

"Stay here," Illa said. Holding her hand before her, she stepped up to the shield and pushed through it.

Instantly, she could hear the others. They stopped shouting as soon as they saw her.

"What happened?" Nigan demanded.

"We couldn't take it down, but it seems I can walk through it with this. I pulled Lebuin with me. Come." She held out her hand. They looked at each other, and Nigan volunteered to go second. She had no trouble pulling all of them inside. For each person, she fed the built-up energy to Lebuin before crossing it again, just in case there was some limit to how much the Yunna Minthra could hold. They all looked at the door and marble tiles.

"Well, this is interesting," Malla said as she tapped the tiles with her dagger. "Not even a speck of dust, and these aren't glazed ceramic. They look like it, but they're stronger."

Lebuin had the silver box out and was holding it up to the door.

"This isn't magical, but it is pretty complicated. Almost

like a vault door. It has a lot of non-magical technologies in it."

"You know, this reminds me of the doors at the Dolphin and Vestul's tower. I wonder...." He placed his hand in the upper right corner where Duke had touched Vestul's tower door. A square section under his hand flashed green and they slid open with a hiss, causing Lebuin to jump back.

Ditani asked, "Why would it recognize you?"

Lebuin shook his head. They all drew their weapons. Lebuin went first. As he stepped in, lights came on, revealing a large room with chairs and benches. There were small round tables, and at the far end was a tall desk with boxes on top.

Lying on one of the benches was a dried husk of a woman. She was perfectly preserved. Her skin was tanned brown, and her hair was dark black with grey streaks.

"This looks like a reception area," Lebuin commented.

Ditani went over and examined the woman. "She's an elf."

The others approached. Ditani was searching her, lifting her white jacket and checking her pockets. She had a device strapped to her wrist and gold rings on four of five fingers. Her ears were pierced, with a pair of blue topaz earrings dangling down.

Ditani said, "She didn't die of any attack or injury." He held up a small silver box, similar to what Lebuin held.

Lebuin was standing next to him, pushing buttons on his. Floating in the air before them, an image of a female elf appeared. She was smiling.

"Incredible. That thing can show us what she looked like when she was alive," Ditani said.

Lebuin's face was blank, and his eyes revealed his amazement. "No, I asked it to identify her. This is a stored image in the recorder."

Ditani looked over. "Who was she?"

Lebuin pushed some buttons, and text flowed around her likeness. 'Vikta-Kulkian, Scientific Director Kiliun Lol,

Elracian Senate Scientific Council Chair.' Along with that came a series of awards, schools, and accomplishments.

Illa's heart felt heavier than ever and tears blurred her vision. Illa bent down and touched the dead woman. "I'm so sorry, Vikta-Kulkian, we're too late to rescue you. You were waiting for rescue, weren't you?"

Ditani handed the silver box to Lebuin. He put his away and opened the one Ditani handed him. He examined it and opened its controls. After experimenting, something came up on one of the small displays on the device.

"It's a scanner recorder, too, but it's different. I'd say it's more advanced. There's a message. The title is 'Play for the Senate'."

Lebuin pushed a button, and a new image of Vikta-Kulkian appeared but she looked horribly thin compared to the one Lebuin had shown earlier.

When she started talking, everyone jumped back. She remained steady in the center of the group.

"My deepest regrets, I cannot make this report in person. The record will show it has been forty-three years since the destruction of Elraci. My logs will provide all the data needed. Only five of us are left. Although we can make enough food and water for as long as needed, we're dying of a form of mana poisoning. We do not have the magical skills or knowledge necessary to stop it. At this point, we have given up all hope of being rescued. No communications, magical or mundane, can penetrate the energy clouds surrounding us. We fear the whole world is gone. I pray we're wrong and that someday our records will be recovered."

The projection of Vikta-Kulkian bent over, coughing up green bile. She wiped her mouth with a cloth, which she put into a pocket before forcing herself to stand upright to continue.

"My chief physicist has been working on a theory. His proofs, formulas, and experiments of the last forty years are in the logs. He suggests that a surge of at least 10,210 gigarellums Loeheshian-Mana was directed back into a set of void system generators. Such an event could have caused a cascade backlash through the power systems. Using the last sensor data we trust, his calculations show this happened at the experimental system at Dalpha's labs in Brinhi Nik. Brandon had suspected Dalpha was doing something dangerous, but he wouldn't tell me what it was. He swore me to secrecy and set up a secret data feed between her research institute and our systems. The data feed from there was cut off moments before the first wave of destruction hit us. I've kept my oath and not shared this with my team."

With the wave of her hand, Vikta-Kulkian's image was replaced with a different scene in which a number of people moved around a pair of machines similar to the one Lebuin had shown earlier. They were setting up a series of prisms between two machines and a large golden egg.

A beautiful woman walked into the area, and one of the elves stepped over, bowing to her.

"All is ready for the focused feed. This might backfire, and we can lose years of work."

"Will the collector be damaged?"

The elf laughed. "I doubt all of Elraci could generate enough power to threaten the collector."

The woman nodded. "Very well. Evacuate the area. I must have more power than Argos if I am to take lead."

Ditani was standing with his mouth hanging open.

Lebuin sputtered, "She wanted to take control of the Circle!"

Illa remembered the laws of the Gods. The Circle was the ruling group of the Gods. It never had more than seven members, and the head of the Circle was chosen by the simple test of magical might and control. Whoever could control the greatest amount of magic was the ruler of the Gods. It took them thousands of years to build up power, and in that time, the other Gods made sure those with potential were well-vetted for temperament and wisdom. In their long history, a few possible leaders had been cut short, because they were found lacking of the empathy and lawfulness needed to lead.

There was a God trying to gain enough power to surprise the Circle and take control, but in order to do that, she had to exceed Argos in control. He was the strongest God in history and physically enhanced to control the powers of the new universe.

In the image, the room was vacated, and a sudden flash of light wiped it away entirely. Vikta-Kulkian reappeared. She was crying.

"Three seconds later, the world around this institute was ripped apart. There can be no other explanation. The calculations and this data are undeniable proof this was the cause. Dalpha was trying to regain control of the Circle. We don't know why. Soon the magical poisoning will kill me. We've confirmed there are none alive within 600 kilometers. My husband is already dead, and our children were at our house in the capital only a short distance away. I'm sure most of the country is destroyed. I pray not the world, and I pray this message will be found. I go now to join my ancestors. *Vivant et imperii decus est famuli tui Duianna Elraci.*"

Her image vanished.

DALPHA! That was Lady Dalpha. She has all those temples, and they do all that work to heal people. My Lords!

Illa felt her knees wobbling. No one said anything for a long time.

Lebuin went and sat down in one of the chairs. Ditani started looking through some cupboards on the side of the room.

Illa sat down next to Lebuin on a small sofa, and Nigan joined her. The warm smell of arit filled her nostrils. She turned around, and Ditani was walking over with a tray of steaming cups.

"Dalpha," Lebuin said.

Ditani said, "Apparently. Cup of arit?"

Malla took one, as Lebuin did, and drank it down. "That's amazing. Where did you get it?"

Ditani pointed at a tall square sideboard he'd been exploring. The center of the sideboard had a couple of displays showing rows of small pictures of food items. Next to the displays were a set of glass doors that revealed large empty compartments. "There's a machine like one that Vestul had. It makes drinks and foods. It's somewhat different, but it only took me a little effort to figure out how to ask what I needed of it. But we can eat and drink all we need now."

Lebuin turned to the dead researcher. "She said *mana* poisoning. What is that?"

Ditani shrugged. "Don't know. Never heard of it."

Lebuin pulled at his beard staring at the dead husk. "We need to stock up and get out of here. I think it might be something like a sickness I read about called radiation poisoning. It's very dangerous. It changes the body, and if it doesn't kill you outright, it causes you to die of terrible sicknesses. We need to find Ticca and get out of here. We have what we came for."

Carda's eyebrows went up. "What exactly do we have? Aren't we looking for something to stop the Nhia-Samri?"

"Lebuin, you broke the last golden thread on Vestul's journal a couple of days ago. Did it explain anything else that's now clear to you?" Ditani asked.

Lebuin shook his head. "Vestul's journal is no help for this." He looked off into the distance. "Elraci burnt because Dalpha was trying to generate enough power to take control of the Circle from Argos, using their magic generators passing the mana through Loehesh filters. The Nhia-Samri have fifty, or maybe 100, of these generators now, and the Gods, through us, just found this out. Except the Nhia-Samri generators are producing Loeheshian-Mana or something close to it, possibly making them more compatible with the collectors, or whatever Dalpha was up to. That means Dalpha might be trying again.

"We're trying to prevent a catastrophe of which no one was able to discover the cause. What if it was that Dalpha found out about the new and more powerful generators the Nhia-Samri built and secretly tried again? She could already be making preparations, thinking she has solved whatever went wrong the first time or that the new generators are compatible. We have to get out of Elraci and warn Duke. Worse, I just tried to send a message to Argos to warn the Gods, but I'm blocked right now. I think this place has some rather potent shields, which means we need to get away from here, so I can warn the Gods. I must tell them of what Dalbha did and might be doing again."

They took time to refill all their water containers. Ditani figured out how to get a number of foods out of the machine like jerky, trail bread, and some hard candies to take with them. The machine had an amazing selection of foods, and they all had one of the best meals of their lives. Nigan even got the steak dinner he had asked for.

They stuffed Lebuin's pack with as much food and water as they could without making it impossible to get anything else out. Then they left as they came, except that Lebuin kept the new recorder, giving the one from the Nhia-Samri base to Illa. She put it into her pouch with the precious box.

After exiting the shields, Lebuin stood, looking south. "Ticca is alive, and she knows where we're going. We could wait here or go to the capital." He turned to Ditani and Illa. "What do you think she would do?"

Illa was just about to answer when three Nhia-Samri appeared out of nowhere around Lebuin. One of them was her father. She froze at seeing him again.

Before Lebuin could even make a sound, her father struck Lebuin's head with the base of his odassi, as a female touched him with her glowing hands. The third snapped a golden collar around his neck from behind him. Lebuin crumpled. Illa started to draw her weapons when something hit her hard in the back of the head. The last things she saw were more Nhia-Samri than she could count, swarming the team.

Brandon and Ticca

CHAPTER 15

HIDDEN AGENDAS

THE DESERT RETURNED TO TICCA'S vision. The heat blasted her, and the weakness of her limbs almost made her fall. Through willpower alone she managed to stay on her feet. Looking down at her empty hands, she let out a mournful sigh.

Why can't I bring something back from the vision? Illa brought that box back. The thought of Illa made her feel a little better. *At least I know they're still alive. Lebuin was so happy to see me. They must've thought I died.*

The sunset was turning the crystal desert sands into bright tones of orange and red, like a raging fire.

Her belly was rumbling and digesting. She felt full for the first time in eight days. *The water and food I had in me came back, so that's good.*

She knew it wasn't enough. She would need generous amounts of water for a couple of days to get herself to a healthy level of hydration again, but she knew she'd bought herself another day. Her routine was keeping her alive longer than anyone in recorded history had managed.

Of course, I have to live long enough to tell someone. I can see the tales now: 'Ticca, the Dagger who beat the desert.'

She was courting deadly heat exhaustion and dehydration. Her head pounded, and she felt as if her arms and legs were weighted down with heavy irons. It took fierce effort to keep moving.

The routine was standard: Wake up early, try to eat as many bugs as she could catch, suck water from the dew trap she made the night before, follow the road till the sun is a quarter up, find any scrub brush, dig a shallow rut under it, lie in it, nap through the height of the day's heat, drink the little water collected in the canteen the night before, eat anything she can find, follow the road from early evening till the moons come out, find a gully with some scrub, build a dew trap collector, build a fire if possible, visit with Kliasa while sleeping, and repeat. The only reason she wasn't dead was because of the potent healing of Kliasa's magical boots.

The road she was following had scattered remains of different kinds of carriages. She'd torn open a few of them and salvaged a number of items that were giving her the needed tools to stay alive. The most important was the cloth of the seat coverings. She'd used them to help make the dew collector and a fire bundle. Finding enough scrub to keep the bundle going was another matter.

As she walked, she tried to recall every bit of survival knowledge she had. Even Daggers who were experts in desert survival had died in the Circumveni Desert. It was the deadliest place in the entire world. Still, it was beautiful. If she had Lebuin's temperature shielding, she would be a lot better off. But even with the shielding, the desert would suck the moisture out of the body at a rate most wouldn't believe. She worried that the rest of the team might discount its effects.

She kept walking. The horizon was changing for the first time in eight days. There was something that rose up, making an irregular series of peaks with jagged edges.

I'm heading due west, so it can't be a mountain range. Besides, it doesn't span the whole horizon, just a section directly in line with this road.

She resumed her routine. Two more days passed as the topography of the area ahead continued to change. She knew she was approaching her destination, as she was finding more of those enclosed carriages. Most had fallen apart as whatever held them together had deteriorated over the years, but the metal bodies were preserved and sandblasted almost to a mirror shine.

She spent most of her time trying to think of what to do when she got to the city. She hoped her team would be able to find her there. If not, she'd have to turn north and hope to find them or make it to the mountains.

The morning of the third day after seeing Lebuin and Illa in the vision, she woke and began hunting bugs before she realized what was before her. She was on a small rise that sloped down into a valley. The southern portion of the valley was open to a canyon. Not a simple one, but a large one that spread out to the south of the road. She could not make out the far side of it, but only a few miles away, in the center of the valley, were the walls of a great city. They looked brand new, yet the city beyond was ruins. The alabaster walls that drew her attention looked like the cream white walls of Ll_no.

The city was built on the edge of a cliff, with a drop-off to a ledge some hundred feet down that gave way to another cliff into the canyon proper. Many cream white pillars rose up from the ledge, to small walkways that jutted out of the city like raised trellises.

Piers! Those are piers! This isn't a canyon. It used to be the inland sea that connected to rivers with a commercial waterway to the west that connected to the oceans. I've made it! I've found Imridu-Nam!

She decided to risk not having enough fluids by the end of the day in favor of having a bit more of her wits with her as she entered the city. She drank all the water collected in her canteen overnight and sucked on the dew-soaked rocks from the trap. She spent an extra mark hunting down the grasshoppers she'd subsisted on. They were larger than normal, but not hard to catch.

With her belly not full, but fed, and after drinking all the water she could find, she felt a lot more alert. She then followed the road to the city, which took most of the day.

The city was larger than she'd thought and as a result much farther away. Still, by late afternoon, she stood in the shadow of the gateway. She looked at the six-foot-wide steel plate in the road that was the gate. She knew it was the top of a solid chunk of metal designed to rise up in the slots of the walls, making a perfectly impenetrable barrier. She also knew she could control it.

"Imridu-Nam, close the east gate," she said.

Nothing happened. Smiling, she shrugged.

I don't want to cuss it closed. Might be dangerous, as I don't know how to open it again.

She turned back to the city. It was at least four times larger than Llino. The main street led to her right and appeared to loop inward. There were narrow alleys that might connect to another street. She didn't see any side streets. Almost all the buildings were crushed or crumbling. She had no desire to climb into one, for fear it might collapse onto her.

The three tiered city stood at least four hundred feet from the base to the top. The top tier held only a leaning mountain of rubble, which she was sure had once been the palace.

If that was the blue marble palace, I can't tell from here.

The streets and winding roads provided a lot of shade, and it was noticeably cooler there. She followed the main road as it led past a market and to the docks.

She saw signs of a once-thriving city everywhere she looked. Pottery, steel hoops, window shutters. As she peered into windows, she even found some places with dishes still on the tables.

Reaching the docks, she stepped out onto the stone piers to look at the canyon that used to be a sea. A flash on the ridge below caught her attention. Testing each step, she moved out to the end of the pier and looked down. She saw two shiny silver crabs moving slowly. One appeared to be pushing something that shoved a lot of sand before it. As she watched, it pushed the sand over the edge of the ridge, into the canyon, and then it lifted the steel tool and started back towards the city.

The other crab was walking around the pillars of the pier, tapping them with one claw. Occasionally, it would stop and pull something from its mouth and put it on one of the columns. Then it went back to tapping them.

As she watched her foot shifted and a few pebbles fell. She watched them curiously as they fell. They bounced off the shell of the crab creature below her pier. It stopped what it was doing to back up and tilt upwards. After a minute it went back to whatever it was doing.

Strange things to be sure.

Turning around, Ticca saw a man standing only two feet away from her. She squeaked and pulled her dagger. It took every bit of her willpower to not jump backwards as that would send her falling hundreds of feet, off the end of the pier.

The man gazed at her calmly. He looked like he had in her vision. Not a single thing was different. He was shorter than her, standing only five feet tall. He was wearing a white lab coat, with stuffed pockets, over a blue three-piece suit, pin-striped with light grey threads. His hair was the definition of salt and pepper, cut semi-short, and it looked like it had never met a comb or brush.

"Brandon?"

"Your Highness." He bowed and stayed that way.

After a moment, he glanced up at her, raising an eyebrow.

Ticca felt her face burning. *Oh, that's right. I have to acknowledge him first.* "Sorry, yes. Um, please just stand up. You can't know how happy I am to meet you. Seriously, I need help! Is anyone else here?"

Brandon straightened and looked her over critically. "You're nearly dead. Please follow me. We can talk in a more comfortable location. This heat must be horrible."

He motioned, and she started walking. He led her through open alleys, towards the center of the city.

"To answer your question... No, Your Highness. I'm the only survivor. I have managed to adapt some of the maintenance units to the new conditions. But there are unpredictable magical surges that have destroyed or mutated the genome of your servants."

The road continued upwards, and Brandon was setting

a fast pace. She knew she needed to conserve energy in the desert, and what little water she had in her body was starting to sweat out. She held up her hand.

"I'm sorry. I'm too tired. I can't go this fast."

Brandon stopped and looked at her, frowning. "Of course, Your Highness. I don't have the means to bring you any refreshments here. But it's only another fifteen minutes' walk from here. There's AC, food, water, bathrooms, and showers."

"What's AC?"

"You don't...? The air is cooled and moisturized for your comfort."

"That sounds wonderful."

At the promise of food and water, she was tempted to push, but she knew if she went too fast, heat stroke could knock her out in seconds. "If I pass out, you'll have to carry me." She started walking again at the original pace.

Brandon moved in front of her, holding up his hands for her to stop.

"Your Highness, you know I can't do that. It would take marks for one of the crabs to get here. You'd be dead by then."

She raised an eyebrow at him. "Bad back? I don't understand. Do you mean you'd actually try to bring one of those things I saw down there to me? Wouldn't it eat me?"

Brandon's mouth dropped open. "You don't know." It was a statement. "I thought perhaps the entire continent was destroyed. Maybe I wasn't too far off. Are none of the other AIs still alive?"

"I don't know what you mean. Look, I might drop any minute without food and water. Can you go get me some water?"

Brandon shook his head. "Pardon me, Your Highness, but may I have your hand?" he asked, holding out his hand to her.

She didn't see anything wrong with it, so she reached out to put her hand in his, but it went right through. Nothing was there. As hot as it was, she felt suddenly chilled, and the hair on her arms and the nape of her neck stood on end. She backstepped away from him. "What are you? Are you a ghost?"

She drew her dagger, but then she thought that was stupid, since a knife couldn't hurt a ghost. Still, it made her feel better. She started looking for other apparitions or creatures.

Brandon started to laugh, but he caught himself. He moved back away from her, giving her even more space. She appreciated the gesture.

"No, I'm not a ghost. I'm real. But I'm not human. It will take some explaining." He put his hands together. "Please, Your Highness, believe me. I am your servant, and I will do everything I can to protect and help you. But I'm not what I once was, either." Glancing around at the city, he said, "I can't even fix my home. In fact, I'm not really here, either. I'm using the nanobots in your system to project myself into your consciousness."

"You're using the what in my system? You mean my body?"

"Well, yes. In your body are small machines that help keep you alive, prevent you from getting sick, and many other tasks."

"Like making me hallucinate?"

"Uh...yes. But in a good way. You have very few left now. They've done a lot to keep you alive."

He seemed sincere. And she did see him in the vision, and there, he was a longtime friend. She spun her dagger, sheathing it.

"Okay, this must be one of the things Duke didn't want to teach me. Let's keep walking, and you can explain what you are."

"Duke? Well, naturally, he's still alive. Why didn't he train you? He used to love training the emperor's children."

"Things have changed."

"They always do."

"Can you tell me what happened here?"

Brandon looked down with a frown on his face as he walked next to her. "No, I really don't know exactly what happened. In an instant, my city was gone. I was nearly killed, too. I have protections. They were almost not fast enough. I was heavily damaged. I've been working to repair myself for five thousand years now. No one else has come. You're the first new person I've seen in all that time."

"Well, you look fine for a ghost."

"I'm not a ghost. I'm a.... Well, I'm not sure how to explain it to you."

Ticca was busy concentrating on walking, so she didn't answer as Brandon contemplated his lack of ghostliness.

"Why...?" he began. She jumped at the sudden sound. They'd been walking in silence for a while, and she'd drifted off to a mild doze, following Brandon automatically. She wasn't even sure how many streets they'd walked through or the path.

Great. Now, I'm lost. If this ghost is dangerous, I'm in it up to my neck.

She looked at Brandon, who had stopped when his voice startled her. As she was blinking slowly, he decided she'd recovered. "Why don't you tell me about your world, yourself, and your life? That would give me an understanding of how to explain things to you."

She'd never heard of a ghost wanting a story, so she decided it was probably safe. She started telling him about her life. She named her father and uncle, told of how her uncle was a famous Dagger from the war, and how her father had tried to make her a farmer like her mother and himself. She told about how much training she had from her uncle after her father's death. She talked about the cycles working as a Dagger in Llino. She then spoke of Lebuin, but kept most of the details back. In the end, she explained how all the nations were in a war with the Nhia-Samri.

Brandon was a good listener. He made affirmative sounds at just the right time and prompted her for details, showing her he was paying attention. He asked simple questions and never complained when she kept some things vague.

The sun was set, and the moons were out when they came to a stone bridge over a dark ravine. She recognized the bridge.

"The blue palace!"

Brandon smiled. "Yes. It was the traditional vacation home of the Duianna Emperors and their guests."

She glanced around, but she wasn't sure where they were. "Are we still in the city?"

"We're in the far southern quarter. This section was mostly large estates nestled into a twenty-square-kilometer wooded park."

She walked across the bridge and gazed at the palace as she approached it. In the moonlight, it glistened like new.

"Why does it look like my visions? Shouldn't it be in ruins?"

"It was protected by its own independent shields, much older than the ones for the city. Also, most of the power from the main blasts was blocked by large structures farther in." Brandon turned back towards the direction from which they'd come. "My friends are buried in those ruins. This was mostly empty at the time. The few servants that survived died within a few years of some kind of blood poisoning."

"Blood poisoning?"

"Yes. There was so much power in the area, it changed healthy blood into bad blood. The real medical equipment was lost. I couldn't stop it."

Ticca noticed Brandon was looking at her with sadness around his eyes. "Am I going to die of this poisoning?"

Brandon didn't answer. Instead, he motioned for her to continue towards the blue palace and started walking again.

MARU-ASHUA

Warlord Maru-Ashua ignored most of the people he encountered as he moved through the great halls of the fortress. His path took him to the stairs leading down deep into the mountain. He recalled the stories that Hisuru Amajoo had as much space beneath the mountain as it had above. He'd recently decided the stories were wrong. Hisuru Amajoo extended farther under the mountain than even the most grandiose tale dared to claim.

He'd spent marks jogging through tunnels, finding hundreds of mammoth chambers. There were open areas that could hold entire towns, complete with stone streets, buildings, and crystals that provided light like the daytime sun. He'd found vast storerooms with acres below vaulted ceilings, filled and used regularly by the staff and armies, while others had been stocked with seeds, farm equipment, and basic supplies and left alone for years, or perhaps centuries.

He moved down the spiral stone stairs, worn smooth by the thousands of feet that had used them over the years. Moving through doors large enough for covered wagons to pass through, and then descending farther, he came to the chamber he sought.

The stairs ended in a huge archway that opened to the stone room. Thirty guards had their weapons out and ready to fight as he stepped in. He stood tall, looking at the ten warriors directly in front of him. The other twenty were on the far side of the thirty-foot-long room in front of the massive iron doors, securely locked with a heavy iron chain inlaid with silver and gold.

"The moons shall guide."

The lead warrior in the group closest to him answered. "Tis a cloudy night."

Maru-Ashua drew one of his odassi, holding it so the bands showed to the lead warrior.

He willed his odassi to show its power. "Clouds cannot block my sight."

The warriors didn't move, and their blades remained ready. The lead warrior cautiously crossed swords with Maru-

Ashua in salute. The other blade glowed momentarily after coming in contact with his ancient odassi.

As one, the other warriors straightened, sheathed their odassi, and bowed.

He motioned with his hands for them to step aside. They formed ranks on both sides of the chamber. He walked over and tapped the chains with his odassi, willing the locks to be released. The filigreed inlays glowed, and the hinges creaked as the chains loosened.

"Open the doors," he ordered, sheathing his odassi.

Four warriors from each side rushed to pull the heavy chains apart, hanging them on the side hooks that were there for that purpose. Once they were stored, the warriors pulled the releases and strained against the weight of the doors, which opened without so much as a squeak.

"Close them behind me."

He stepped inside and examined the room in detail, while he waited for the sound of the latches being locked.

Lady Lothia was sitting at a desk. Her back had been to him, but she shifted on the chair and stood, turning to face him. He was pleased to see she looked strong and healthy, at last. On the desk was a pile of papers with neat patterns in vertical rows. Two small brushes were in a cup of water, and a bowl of ink was visible.

Fully restored, Lothia was a striking creature. He reminded himself she was not human, nor did she look anything like one in her natural form. The prison collar prevented her from taking a different shape or form, so she was locked into the shell of a woman as much as that body was locked inside the chamber. He knew that the collar, as well as many special shields built into the chamber, prevented her from speaking spiritually with others of her kind.

I'm sure the immortals know where to look for her. I'm surprised they haven't made an attempt for her yet.

"First Warlord Maru-Ashua. It has been some time since your last visit."

He kept control of his body. Pulling energy from his odassi, he sped his reactions up, so he could be sure to stay ahead of her in the conversation. He knew that since she was recovered, collar or no, she was incalculably intelligent, experienced, and knew every minor nuance of human reactions. Even in that form, he was sure she would be able to hear and smell better than any wolf and see sharper than any hawk.

He bowed as an equal to an equal. "Lady Lothia. I apologize. I have been consumed with my duties."

"I'm sure the administration of your new province and the casualty losses in the north are keeping you very busy."

He stopped the adrenaline surge and forced his heart rate to remain steady.

How can she know of these things? His thoughts spun rapidly as he tried to figure out how, in this total isolation, she could know what was going on. Then he realized the door had a slot for letting food and drink in, as well as to remove waste. The guards must be talking. *I need to order this to be a silent guard station.*

"Yes, the Alliance believes it's winning."

Her eyes narrowed slightly. "And Duke, has he recovered yet?"

"Your pet is eating far more bacon than the locals can provide. I'm afraid it's having a detrimental effect on morale. You should teach him to share."

Lothia laughed. "He was never my pet or anyone else's. I'm pleased and sorry. Sorry for what will happen when he gets here." She shrugged. "Even my husband couldn't control him as a child."

"That is our concern, Lady."

She stepped closer to him. She was only five feet tall, and he was forced to look down to watch her moves. She motioned to the only chair. "Please, First Warlord, do sit. May I offer you some of Lord Shar-Lumen's most excellent sharre?"

He watched her in his peripheral vision. He noted her

right hand momentarily vibrated. Her pupils contracted, and she spread her fingers of her right hand.

She tried something, and the collar stopped her.

He stepped at an angle around her, closer to the desk, to see the papers. They were beautifully drawn in a series of pictographs. He recognized the language of the immortals; there were samples of it in the library. Only a few of the more basic symbols had been translated. None of those were symbols he knew. The stack of papers was at least 400 pages tall.

"I'm not here for a social visit. What are you working on?"

She sat down on her bed, her legs neatly pulled to the edge. Her body was straight as a board, and her hands were folded in her lap. She could have been posing for a picture, demonstrating the demure noble woman's posture. He was sure she was doing it on purpose. She was trying to get him to relax his guard.

She tilted her head down to look up at him, which widened her eyes, giving her a submissive and attractive appearance.

"It's a list of things to do when I get out."

He couldn't help it. He snorted. "That's a rather extensive list."

She smiled, still peering up at him. "I'll have time to do it. If not, I need to be able to pass it to someone else. Tell me, why are you here?"

Maru-Ashua pulled one of the silver boxes from his pocket. Keeping his hand closed over it, he held it out to her.

"I've been told to bring this to you."

Since he did not move to her, she was forced to stand and step closer. He placed the silver box in her hand.

Her eyebrows went up a notch at seeing the device.

"I'm told you know what it is and how to use it."

She didn't answer him. She'd already opened a small panel and was manipulating the controls. A flat, glowing square with lines of text that flowed across it like a scroll rolling had come to life on the device. She pushed the buttons even quicker, and the words scrolled too fast for him to follow. He pulled more power from the odassi and managed to read some of it. The letters were a long series of names and dates, with some kind of glyph code.

The more she saw, the more her eyes narrowed. She was completely absorbed and sat down, her back not quite as straight as before. Still, her posture was enviable. She did something, and the lines stopped scrolling.

"Where did you get this?"

"Grand Warlord Shar-Lumen gave it to me."

"Where did he get it?"

"That I do not know, Lady."

She pouted. Her pupils contracted further.

She's really upset by this. Perhaps....

"Lady, I do not know this device."

Her pupils dilated back to normal. "You don't know what this means?"

He put his hands behind his back and raised an eyebrow. "I have been good to you. As I already know enough about Elraci to be killed by the Gods, there should be no harm in further sharing with me."

She pressed her lips together, turning away from him.

He waited, keeping his affect perfectly neutral and his heart rate even.

Pushing her shoulders back, she looked around and said, "This is a recorder. It's not Elracian. It's ancient Imperial technology. This one is unique. I believe you need only to see some of what it contains to understand."

She lifted the device, manipulating the controls. The lines of text scrolled, and she stopped it and then pointed the device at the table and pushed a button.

A miniature person appeared, facing Maru-Ashua, holding a device.

He drew and sliced through the figure before Lothia could blink, meeting no resistance.

I cannot let her escape!

Fearing what would come, he went for Lothia. She dropped the box and rolled backwards, off the bed, dodging his thrust.

"Stop! It isn't real!" she cried out, fear filling her voice, making it quiver. She whimpered in pain, her body wracked with tremors.

He held his position, one sword defending against Lothia, and the other pointing to the figure on the table that had not moved.

Lothia recovered and pushed herself up from the floor. Her arms vibrated under the strain.

She tried to use a significant amount of magic. Was it instinctive, to shield herself, or was she trying to attack me again?

She whispered something he couldn't make out. She slowly stood, using the bed post for support. He stepped into a position where he could watch her and the person on the table.

After a moment, Lothia straightened and held her hands down and out. Her shoulders slumped, and she was doing everything she could to appear docile and submissive.

"It's an image, a memory, nothing more. It cannot harm you or do anything other than exist."

Her tone had been calm, but with a hint of fear.

I can kill her, and she cannot stop me. She likely hasn't been this afraid before, or at least, in a long time.

Knowing Shar-Lumen wouldn't give her something dangerous, he decided to trust what she said. Sheathing his blades, he examined the small figure closely.

He looked like an elf, but not like any elf he'd ever seen. Instead of silver, his skin was darker, with a greenish tint. He was bent, as if very old, and he was dressed strangely. He was wearing a green shirt and pants. A string or rope ran through the waistline of the pants and was tied. The clothing was loose and stained. He also wore a long white coat, with large pockets, that hung open in the front. The shirt had breast pockets with something tucked into them. The coat pockets appeared to be stuffed with items, too.

He noted there were lesions on the back of the exposed hands. And the person had long matted and thick hair.

He slowly walked around the image, examining it. Lothia stood still, waiting.

The elf looked like he was in pain. A grimace twisted the face, and one eye was pure white with a cataract.

Maru-Ashua moved his hand through the image. There was no resistance. Only a tingle on his skin.

"How is this done?"

"It's mundane technology from before this world."

"Mundane. You mean this is human technology? My people could do this?"

Lothia licked her lips and blinked. "Yes, this is human technology. However, don't assume mundane technology is humanity's right. There are more mundane races than just humans. They were part of the Duianna Imperial Union."

We have lost far more than I ever dreamed. I knew much knowledge had been lost, but this is incredible. If it truly works without magic, what more could we do without magic?

He ground his teeth, and he felt his pulse slip from his control as he contemplated how much the Gods had really taken from the world.

Pointing at it, he nodded. "Proceed."

Lothia slowly stepped around the bed and picked up the device. She pressed a button with a small triangle, and the figure animated and spoke. He wriggled as if fighting severe internal pain while maintaining his posture as upright as possible.

"My Lady, I can't last much longer. I don't know how I got infected. But I am. Your collector has been recovered from the remains of Brinhi Nik. As I told you, it was not damaged. It didn't get as much energy as we thought. I don't know why, but it's getting hard to think clearly." The elf's body moved of its own accord. "It will be in Gracia in a few days. On the new virus. We confirmed it's a compound strain with magical properties we've never even dreamed of. It's airborne, hardy and 100 percent infectious. The only lorcasians not infected are the ones not exposed. Every expedition into Elraci, no matter how well protected, has come back infected. Isolation is the only hope."

The figure disappeared. Lothia pushed some more buttons, and the elf reappeared, except that he was more bent, and his skin was like thick, abused leather with many wart-like bumps. His hair had become thicker, tangled, and wiry. His hands were swollen, and his teeth and jaw had changed, too. He looked almost like a brutish monster.

"Lady." His voice was deep and guttural. "Failed. Your fault! Your fault! We not forget!" Then he roared violently, throwing a small silver box, and the image vanished.

Maru-Ashua's mind raced. Virus, a sickness, from Elraci. Something that infected everyone on contact. The pieces fell into place. "Lorcasians, orcs? The orcs were elves infected with a magical virus from Elraci?"

Lothia was staring at the ground, her shoulders slumped. She was crying. Her posture said it all.

"You knew."

Her head snapped up as she stared him in the eyes. "Of course, I knew! We all knew!"

She turned away, wiping her eyes with her hands. Looking at the wall, she sighed. "*All* of the rulers of *all* the kingdoms were informed. We declared Niya-Yur quarantined and cut off access. The borders were closed, and we tried to save the lorcasians. But what we didn't find out until too late was that humans could carry the disease. There was no hope for those already infected. That's why we didn't stop the slaughter when Shar-Lumen lost his mind and went after them. After four thousand years, so few were left, and we still couldn't find a cure. But this." Her voice faltered with anguish. "I knew him!

We thought he died in Elraci. He was a great man. A devout follower of Lady Dalpha."

"Dalpha! He said, 'My Lady,' and he said it was her fault! What was her fault?"

Lothia fell on the bed and cried hiding her face.

Maru-Ashua continued, "The temples, all the healers, all the training, thousands of years of healing people for free.... Lady Dalpha wasn't being altruistic. She was trying to make up for something. Could she have been the cause?"

Lothia didn't answer.

He thought through the whole of history he knew, trying to add the new knowledge into it. *Orcs were an unknown, no, intentionally forgotten race of elves afflicted with a disease. A disease humans could carry. Every major city had temples to Dalpha, built with gifts from all the Gods. Temples of healing and...something more. Eradicating the disease. Cleansing the world.* "Is this disease gone?"

Lothia raised her head enough to shake it. "Not entirely. We keep finding it. And sometimes...." She couldn't continue.

He stepped over, grabbing her and pulling her up. Nose to nose with her, he asked, "Sometimes what?"

"Sometimes, it starts...affecting other races."

He let go of her, letting her fall back into her pillows, sobbing.

He went to the doors and pounded on one. Without a word, he walked out, resealed the doors, and climbed the stairs back to the main floor. His mind worked around the knowledge. He tried to put it together with what he knew before. There had been wars, fires, and natural disasters that had wiped whole towns out of existence. There were even towns the Nhia-Samri had visited total destruction upon, supposedly for harboring the Traitor or some other slight. He concluded some of those might not have been as random as everyone thought.

At some point, Shar-Lumen had discovered the disease.

Was it before or after he started eradicating the orcs from the world?

Pausing in his path, he leaned on a wall for support. Lady Lothia's words played in a loop in his mind. *'Sometimes it starts affecting other races.' It was an elven disease. The elves are the most likely to get it. Shar-Lumen has always said the mission of the Nhia-Samri was first and foremost to protect his own.*

He stepped up to the prison suite that housed Magus Cune and Lady Sula. She'd recovered physically, but was still grieving. He didn't want to add to that grief, but he didn't see a way around it.

He knocked on the door and walked in without waiting for an answer. Lady Sula was sitting at a table, staring at an untouched, cold plate of food. The glass of sharre before her might have been tasted. Magus Cune sat across from her with an empty plate, reading a book.

Upon seeing him enter, Magus Cune stood. "First Warlord." Cune must have seen something in Maru-Ashua's stance. Cune's lips tightened, and he glanced at Lady Sula. "Perhaps you would consider some other time?" His tone was pleading for his Lady.

He shook his head. "I do not desire to deliver more sorrow. However, it's something Lady Sula should know, if she doesn't already."

Sula looked up. "What can be worse than losing my mother?"

He stepped over to her, taking out the recording device. "From Lothia's reaction to this, I would say *much*." He placed it on the table in front of her.

Sula stared at it, but did not reach for it.

Magus Cune raised an eyebrow. "What is that?"

He turned and walked to the door before he answered. "Truth. For the future." With that, he left.

In the corridor, he set aside the past.

The future indeed. I should have gone to Building 9 first.

I've always wanted to get in there. It might have been better to give myself that before.

Then he considered what he'd learned. *Then again, it might even be worse than what I know.*

With a sigh, he decided it was time. He moved through the complex, leaving the fort and walking out to see the bright blue skies and sunshine. By the time he got to Building 9, his heart rate was out of control. Everyone knew it was sealed, but no one knew exactly when, so for hundreds of years, it had been the subject of much speculation over campfires and barroom tables.

Standing before the building, he found his hands were quivering with excitement. Knowing it was over 100 meters tall was different from looking up at the roof high above. The structure dominated the area, but not just in height. It was twenty-one meters wide and 110 meters long. There was a four-meter door set into a pair of barn doors almost as tall as the building on the long side. It had hundreds of windows, all of them shuttered from the inside.

He stepped forward and could feel the buzz of the magic shield that sealed the building, which was a fraction of an inch off the surface, including the door.

A number of warriors went by, carrying supplies from one of the storage areas. They kept their eyes in front but he knew they were looking. How could they not? The structure was one of the most interesting mysteries of the place.

Shar-Lumen did not mention the shield, so it must not be expected to be a hindrance.

He moved the key towards the lock, and it passed through the shield. The handle was long enough for the key to fit into the lock without his hand touching the shield, so he put it in and twisted it. The buzz vanished, and a series of bolts slid open. The door was unlocked, and the shield was down.

He put the key back in his pocket. Taking a breath, he went inside and started to close the door behind him. He froze at the thunderous percussion and the loud clanking of dozens of heavy chains under great strain. His stomach clenched, his heart skipping at least two full beats, and for the first time in ages, he felt unsteady.

The building was hollow. The sun streamed in through the cracks in the windows, glistening off the alabaster white, glossy hull of a ship. He recognized it instantly, as anyone would. It was the *Emerald Heart*. It was a sleek schooner-like vessel with a series of four masts above deck and three outrigger masts swept back and down, like the wings of a bird of prey, from just below the midpoint of the hull. On the bottom of the ship were more rigging masts that swept back and down.

The loud thunder had been caused by the lateen-like outrigger sails on the sides of the ship being deployed in the blink of an eye. The outrigger masts bent, and the roach edges of the sails moved in a ballet of rhythm. The outrigger sail boltropes visibly stretched under the strain. The ship had been sitting on a series of padded holders, but with the side outrigger sails deployed, it floated a full foot off those holders. Six massive chains, like those holding Lothia's cell closed, were looped over the ship, directly over the railing, so tight to the hull that they rubbed the washboards and were set into anchoring hoops in the floor of the building. More chains looped over the bowsprit and quarterdeck, as well as another set of four running under it, connected high on the walls to solid stone pillars that also held the roof up. The ship was unable to move more than a foot in any direction.

A wondrous series of musical tones filled the air. They sounded like a perfect crystal set of wind chimes that played together in harmony. It was coming from the blue and green crystals that were part of the material that the sails were made of. He stood there and watched as the outrigger sails shifted. The craft tilted right, then left, and moved forward and backward, but was held in place by the chains.

The hairs on his neck stood on end, and he had the

impression the ship was staring at him with cold, anger-fueled hatred.

Looking up, he could see that the roof was designed to open.

This building was made for the Emerald Heart. *Or perhaps it was built around it. But how did this come to be here?*

Finally getting control of his emotions, he finished closing the door. He moved around, gazing at the ship, as the feeling of being stared at never waned. Along the sides of the building, like a museum, were over fifty glass cases. He moved to one and looked in. It held a series of books sealed with golden clasps, and all had the Duianna Imperial sigil on the front.

As the ship continued to strain against the chains, he walked on. The next case had a rather plain-looking, long sword in a leather sheath. After that, he saw a silver key in a small case, which was unusual in that it had two rows of teeth going down and a third going up. It also had a hollow tip. He knew what it was. A key to one of the famous Blue Dolphin Inn Dagger room doors in Llino.

The ship sank back down to the soft supports with a groan. He turned to look at it. The sails slowly folded back, until they were furled. The outrigger spars drooped, making the ship appear forlorn.

He shook his head and continued to inspect the items around the edge of the building. Many of them seemed ordinary, but then he saw a beautiful bound book in a special case. Its leather cover was elegant, and on the front, it had the sigil of Aelargo. He stared at it, knowing it was the royal archive for the Kingdom of Aelargo.

How did we get this? It should be in the throne room of Llino, under continuous guard. Every nation has one. Why would we want it, anyway? It can only be opened by the regents or ruler of Aelargo.

There were some silver boxes of different types, which he recognized as recorders. Their variety made him think there might be other types of mundane devices that had a similar appearance. One of them far older than the rest. It had even begun to rust.

After he'd examined all the artifacts, he climbed the stairs to board the ship. Stopping at the top, on a small landing, he looked over the ship. The deck, a highly polished oak, was amazing. The rails all had inlaid rubies on the inner edge. The ship appeared to be perfectly maintained. Everything shone with a coat of wax, the woods were all oiled, and every rope was neatly coiled. The gunwale in front of him had the boarding hatches latched open. The three white masts rose up out of the centerline with a swept-back look. He placed his hand on the railing, and stepped on to the deck.

The reaction was swift and unexpected. The thunderclap of the outrigger sails came, and the ship jumped up a foot, launching Maru-Ashua into the air, before it was snapped to a stop by the chains. The railing creaked under the strain, but it did not give. The ship dropped, landing on the supports with a loud boom.

He quickly adjusted and twisted, ready to land on the deck without breaking anything. Another thunderclap came from the right side of the ship only, and the deck he was about to land on rolled, suddenly and hard, to the left. The unexpected movement hit him with a tremendous force. Pain shot through his legs as he was thrown into the air, over the edge of the railing.

He pulled on the power of his odassi to increase his speed and strength as he tried to adjust. Fortunately, it was over fifteen meters to the ground, and he had enough time to twist into position. He landed and rolled, slamming into a display case, knocking it over. The glass shattered, and he slammed his head into the edge. Blood poured down his forehead as he stood up, disentangling himself from the wreckage of the case.

He used his odassi to heal himself and wiped the blood from his face, staring at the ship.

"That wasn't an accident."

A ruffle that sounded like someone huffing came from some of the sails.

It's alive...and it's mad.

"Can you talk? How did you get here?"

The set of chimes sounded. He didn't understand them, but they left the distinct impression of anger.

"Sorry, I don't understand."

A ship's bell rang evenly twice, paused, then rang twice repeatedly, until it had rung eight times.

He tried to remember what that could mean. Unfortunately, he didn't have a lot of naval experience.

"You need eight? Eight what?"

The bell repeated the eight-ring pattern.

He walked around to the display case that housed the recorders. The one unique recorder was the rusty one. It had a sigil he didn't recognize etched on the case, which he opened and examined closer. It was similar to the one he'd given to Lothia. He opened it and pushed the buttons, like he saw Lothia do.

The small print appeared and rolled through a series of names and dates, which were in standard Imperial. The text stopped scrolling with the bottom half of the screen empty. The last entry shown was titled 'Martidi, 14801-Innadyt-12, Hilth-Na tribe'. He pointed the device at the top of the case and pushed the button with a small triangle on it, as Lothia had.

A man appeared. He was dressed as a warrior, with a red cotton shirt, a steel breast plate, and leather shoulder armor. An orc held a sword to his neck. It had to belong to the man, as his scabbard was empty. He was tied to something not shown. He was brutally beaten, with a bloody face, swollen left eye, and split lips.

"I'm taking you there," the man said defiantly.

Above Maru-Ashua, the ship's bell rang fast and loud. He recognized that signal as the alarm.

"Quiet. I'm trying to watch this."

The bell went silent.

He'd missed some of what was said, but another orc was beating the man. The ship creaked behind Maru-Ashua, but the bell remained quiet.

The orc with the sword held up a hand. "Where is Sandeep? We know he's there!"

The second one cut the breast plate off. "We'll go there ourselves. Our people built this ship. Do you think we have forgotten everything?"

Another orc came into the scene. "We can't get to the heart."

The first one hit the new one hard enough that he went down. "Use more force, you idiot. You have the tools!"

Puncher orc laughed until the first glared at him.

The other one crawled away as the first one turned back to the man. "We can take it with this ship. He won't be able to defend against it. Tell us where!"

The punching orc said something in a language Maru-Ashua didn't recognize. The two got into a heated argument.

Maru-Ashua noticed the man was holding a silver box. He then looked down at the one in his own hands.

That isn't rust. It's blood. His blood.

In the image, all the figures bounced, as if the ship had been hit by a wave.

"Ah, they've gotten to the heart. Soon we won't need you. The ship knows where it is, too." The first orc gloated.

The man whispered, *"Indurat terram, ledo."*

The first orc leapt at him, punching him in the mouth. "Damega, you fool!" And as the deck started to pitch, he thrust the sword through Damega's chest. "Helm, pull up! Pull up!"

Damega sighed, looking at the sword. As his head fell, he whispered, *"Conabamur. Dic ducis ille erat rectum."*

The second orc had rolled out of the scene. The first was

hanging onto something in a wall as his legs floated behind him. He kept screaming, "Pull up! Pull up!"

A loud crash came, and the first was thrown out of the scene, screaming. Damega's body was slammed around, and the little silver box bounced out of his hand as the scene vanished.

Above and behind Maru-Ashua, the *Emerald Heart* slowly rang twelve bells and creaked.

Closing the recorder's cover, he placed the blood-stained device back into the display case and walked around the ship, to the door. Passing the display cases, he recognized many of the artifacts as what Damega had been wearing.

As he headed for the door, the ship rang eight bells.

He stopped and looked back. "I still don't know what that means. But I promise, I'll be back. I do understand why you threw me off. But I am not your captor, nor am I your enemy."

The ship's bell rang eight times.

As he closed the door, the bell rang a simple pattern of three bells, evenly spaced, close together, followed by a single gong that reverberated around the area. Closing the door behind him, he heard the three-bell pattern again. The shield came back as he engaged the locks, which wasn't a surprise. The sound of the gong was cut off when the shield came back up.

He stepped back and stared at the building.

The Emerald Heart *crashed, and Damega died to stop the orcs from getting to Sandeep. I know the legends that Damega found the invisible city that was the home of ship builders and ship yards of the old Empire. If the* Emerald Heart *crashed, how did it get here, and who repaired it? It's obviously being held here. But how could even Shar-Lumen move it here? That was over 500 years ago.*

Pocketing the key, he headed for the library.

First, he found a few merchant marine operation guides, but those didn't have any bell signals that matched what the ship had been doing, except for the alarm bell, which he already knew. Finally, he found an Imperial Navy officer's manual. In that, he found that eight bells communicated the end of the watch, meaning a time for a new officer to take command. The three bells and a gong were under the ship-to-ship signals. It meant the ship was aground and there were hidden dangers for any rescue effort. He thumbed around, looking for the twelve-bells signal. He'd almost given up when he found it in the back, under optional honors. It was to be used only to mark the passing of a war hero, or major officer, who died with honors.

He hunted down the few reference books on Sandeep. That took some time, as Sandeep was a matter for much speculation. There were only two actual exploration references. One was by Lord Buroullen in 11677, and another was by Ogier Spucci in 9203. The librarians scoffed at Lord Buroullen, who'd been proven after his death to have lied about some of his travels. That left only Ogier Spucci as an acceptable account of Sandeep.

Maru-Ashua was surprised when the librarians were able to produce a complete copy of Ogier Spucci's manuscript on Sandeep. Sitting comfortably, he spent a few marks reading the ancient tome. It was amazing to read Spucci's own words on the subject. He stated that Sandeep was the only remaining pre-migration nation wholly intact as a city-state. All eighteen survivors of Spucci's fifth voyage of 9203 signed the record which stated they left New Yurithum for six cycles at western Skogen Huit. Spucci's group then traveled farther east, staying at Sandeep for three years before returning home.

According to Spucci, the city-state of Sandeep was hidden in a crescent-shaped valley spanning fifty miles. It was a peaceful city with no standing military and only limited guards. It had a defense system capable of rendering the entire valley invisible. While it was a semi-democratic state, it had a ruler who would remain supreme until age prevented effective governing, at which point a new ruler would be chosen. Spucci's manuscript detailed the social and economic structure of a society more than a little familiar. It was identical to the Nhia-Samri society, with the exception that the civilians had a governing council with a chief governor who answered to Shar-Lumen.

Putting the book down, he tried to think it through. Legends held that Sandeep was the home of the master ship builders of the great Duianna Empire. It was well known that something had happened around 10300, causing Sandeep to disappear. Every expedition sent to find it vanished. Even before it had disappeared, legends said the precise location of the city had been intentionally hidden, known only to a few. The *Emerald Heart* was supposedly the last and greatest of the ships Sandeep built. It was a prototype, one of a kind. It had been part of the legends until Damega flew into Llino, claiming to have recovered it. Damega had never explained where or how he came to have the ship.

Had Shar-Lumen adopted the Sandeep society blueprint from the manuscripts? Or.... His mind twisted at the possibility. Was the original civilian population of Hisuru Amajoo the remains of the Sandeep society?

How had Shar-Lumen built the fortress? Rumors were that it had been built by a race of giants he befriended, who lived in the mountains, but no Nhia-Samri patrol had ever encountered them. If the Nhia-Samri were a blending of Shar-Lumen's mercenary troops, their families, and a population base from Sandeep, then maybe someone there still knew how to work on ships like the *Emerald Heart*. Also, with that kind of knowledge, many of the things that the Nhia-Samri had done suddenly made sense.

We have magical generators of enormous potential. We have a shield that's capable of repelling attacks of a magnitude I cannot imagine, and the magical gates, which, according to every mage outside of the Nhia-Samri, are impossible to create. We have the new odassi, which are altered copies of the more ancient blades that tap into our own magical resources. The prison collars hold a God or mage captive. Mage power channels allow our mages to use our magical resources, regardless of the local mana lines. Unbreakable chains made of more than simple metals. Sher-Lumen was a powerful mage, an unbeatable warrior, but even he couldn't have done so much in so short a time without help.

As he thought, his eyes focused on the murals in the ceiling. They showed a garden-like city with wondrous terraces. It spanned one whole side of the domed ceiling. The opposite side of the dome exhibited a series of people dressed in robes, with their hands interlocked, smiling, not down, but across. From the center, the sun blazed, and golden roped chains hung down, breaking apart into a series of chandeliers in stylized, glowing stars.

For the first time, he realized the chandeliers were engraved. Pulling on the power of his odassi, he enhanced his vision and stood with his jaw hanging open. The blood drained from his head momentarily as he stood, dumbfounded that he'd never noticed the library's chandeliers before. The stars were interconnected with bands of golden threads, and thousands of strange ship silhouettes were all throughout the chandeliers.

That isn't just a city scene! It's a crescent-shaped city!

His eyes dropped, and the vast library filled his vision. The size, the knowledge, and the history were greater than any library he'd even heard of. He realized he had to help protect the store of knowledge, no matter the cost. The world was no longer safe for some of the knowledge. It had to be preserved until the world was ready, and then shared. That was the secret of the Nhia-Samri.

Giants indeed. The Nhia-Samri are the legacy of a great people. We must protect it for the future of all. Damega was coming here. He died protecting Hisuru Amajoo! The orcs wanted revenge for the Nhia-Samri hunting them down.

With the world changing around him as his understanding of events past and present came clear, he felt he needed to translate Damega's words. It took the rest of the day, digging around, but he finally figured out a rough translation of what Damega had said.

He ordered the ship to crash. That was somewhat obvious. That he did that meant he believed the Emerald Heart *could be used against us. Could the orcs really have taken control of it? And if orcs came from Elraci, and Sandeep was in the north, how could the orcs have made the* Emerald Heart? *Unless.... Elraci was founded by or part of Sandeep.*

Maru-Ashua had hoped it would be explained by Damega's final words, but those didn't make any sense. Still, they kept repeating in his head as he left Hisuru Amajoo for the newly renamed city of Lumendaria.

What did he mean? *'We tried. Tell General he was correct.'*

Broken Plans

CHAPTER 16

THE SACRIFICE

TICCA AWOKE TO THE BRIGHT sun streaming down through her window. Standing up, she stretched. It was the day she'd been anticipating for cycles. The air was filled with the many fragrant perfumes from the flower gardens below her window. She took time to stand in the morning sunlight enjoying its warmth.

She rang for her servants, and with their help, she ate, bathed, groomed, and dressed for the official ceremony. In only two marks, she was walking down the open corridors of the palace, heading for the throne room. Her four guards, in their ceremonial finest, followed at a discrete distance.

As she entered the throne room, she smiled when she saw her father was there, speaking with Brandon and the chairperson of the Elracian Senate. He saw her and dismissed the others. The room was quickly vacated, which was unexpected. She felt butterflies dancing in her stomach as the last door was closed. When she turned back, he'd climbed the dais and sat in the Imperial throne.

Oh, oh, this cannot be good.

"Ticca, approach."

Her palms started sweating as she stepped up in front of her father.

She curtsied, looking up at him with her head still down. "My Lord, Father."

He waved his hand at her. "Don't."

She stood and said, "What do you command of me, then?"

Sighing, he put his head in his right hand. After a moment, his shoulders straightened, and he scowled at her. His eyes held a deep sadness, like whenever he spoke of her grandfather. "I've heard the reports. I forbid you to make any announcements or formal requests at the ceremony. You cannot now, nor ever, marry Lord Lebuin. The Gods will not allow it, nor shall I."

She wanted to stamp her foot, but she knew it wouldn't work. It hadn't since she was much younger. Still, she had to try.

"I won't go through with the binding ritual, then. I'll abdicate. They can't stop us then!"

Her father stood and pointed at her. His voice, the deep commanding one that had held the Empire together in peace her whole life, said, "You have been named heir. Elraci is the last nation for your binding. It will be a serious insult if you refuse their fealty."

She stood as tall as she could, holding back the tears. She was trapped, and she knew it. "Father, please. I love him more than you can know. I don't know why. But I desire no other. I could never desire another."

The emperor persona faded, and he stepped down, grasping her shoulders. "Ticca, you will love another. It might take many years, but believe me. Somewhere out there is someone as grand for you as your mother is for me. Lebuin is an immortal, a God, and the Empire cannot ever be allowed to have a Lord God Emperor. The combined powers, mundane, magical, and political are too great to entrust to one individual, even if that individual is my own grandchild, or perhaps, great grandchild. We have learned this lesson over and over. Power corrupts, unless we're very careful. Our family is designed to rule with trust, dignity, honor, wisdom, and most importantly, empathy. Our genetic behaviors, being, and hereditary memories are woven into our cells with mundane and magical methods. Those traits will not breed true with a deity child."

Deep inside, she knew all those things. Still, it hurt. Her heart ached more than she thought possible.

How could this be? We're so right for each other. The same magics that shaped my early genetic growth tell me so strongly

Lebuin is the one. I don't understand how something so perfect and pure could be forbidden. Why would the Gods give me such a deep love for Lebuin, only to prevent us from being together? It doesn't make sense.

Her father, the 462nd Emperor of Duianna, hugged her. She knew he was right and that even though it broke her heart, she would comply. Even when she became empress, she would have to honor his wisdom.

He kissed her on the forehead. "Now, shall we proceed?"

She wiped her eyes and nose and then nodded. She tried to smile, though her red face and bloodshot eyes were evidence of her true emotions.

"Ticca, I know you're hurting, but you're my daughter. You will be empress. You must show your strength even through your pain. Always."

"I understand."

Ticca took a deep breath. She fanned her face with her hand as they left the throne room for the Elracian Senate chamber. On arriving, he escorted her to the center of the beautiful wood-paneled room. She noticed Lebuin wasn't present, even though he'd come for it. Illa was sitting in the front row of the balcony seats, and next to her was Lady Lothia.

Her father noticed where she looked. For her ears only, he whispered, "Lord Argos called Lebuin to Miniath-Tur to discuss the issue."

Well, that will end it most assuredly. If Lord Argos is going to give Lebuin a direct order, we'll both be up for execution if we try to sidestep the laws.

The aching in her heart was a crushing sensation. She sniffled and blinked rapidly in an attempt to dry the tears that fought to spill over her lids. It took all her strength not to burst into wailing sobs. She continued to fan her face, trying to clear the tears and redness, to no avail.

The Senate chairperson in her ceremonial robes of green and blue held up the golden cup of Elracian nanobot-saturated water. The Elracian nanobots were unique in that they were both magical and mundane. All other nations were still using the old mundane ones, but plans were underway to provide the radiant power lines and enhanced machinery to all the nations. The new power systems were safer for the mundane races, especially humans, and provided almost double the mana for the creatures of magic. They'd taken thousands of years of research to figure out, but the engineers finally found the balance.

"All of Elraci rejoices in your ascension to be heir of the Duianna Empire. Our nation has always been a proud supporter of the Empire and a member nation of the Duianna Union. Your Royal Highness, Lady Ticca of Aelargo, please accept this in binding our nation to your reign. Long live the emperor, long stand the Empire."

Everyone in the room stood solemnly as Ticca plastered on a fake smile, which never made it to her eyes, and accepted the cup. Holding it high, she looked over the entire room slowly. "Citizens of Elraci, the Empire has long been proud of your nation's fealty. You're truly one of the brightest jewels of the Duianna Union. It is with deep humility and pride that I accept your binding to the throne of the Duianna Empire." She drank the metallic-tasting water as quickly as she could, careful to not let a single drop spill.

Handing the cup back to the senator, she forced the corners of her lips to curl upwards as she acknowledged the applause. Her eyes landed on her personal guard and lifelong friend, the captain of the Elracian Royal Guard, Amia-Dharo. He'd been the royal guard captain for over 5,000 years. He was bound to her family by the special magics and technologies Elraci had been researching. That he achieved a form of immortality from it was a surprising side effect and one still under investigation, when he was in a good enough mood to provide more samples. Seeing Amia-Dharo reminded her of marks of training, fighting, and of being...a Dagger.

She turned and looked at her father with tears welling in

her eyes as her throat choked up. Memories of him playing with her as she grew up in the palace in Gracia clashed with memories of him teaching her how to plant fields and care for animals on a farm in southern Aelargo. She leapt at him, hugging him. It was against protocol, but everyone loved it. Cheers went up, and instead of peeling her off, he hugged her back.

"Dad, I love you, no matter what. I promise I won't let you down."

He whispered in her ear, "You never have. I'm proud of you, Ticca. You would've made a great marine, like in Duke's stories you love so much."

She grasped his hand and wouldn't let go. They walked together out of the Senate chamber. Waving at the gathered citizens, they got in an open carriage and started down the spiral streets, heading for the southern park, where a festival had been planned and staged in the wide yards of the Imperial vacation home.

It happened as they rode. Ticca knew it was coming and gave her father another kiss on his cheek. She squeezed his hand so tightly, her father looked at her as the wave passed over him, and he vanished.

Dizziness caused her to fall. Fortunately, it was a soft landing. The thick carpet cushioned her. Ticca cried covering her head with her arms. She was in the blue marble palace, but it was her reality. Elraci had burnt and the huge amounts of magic in the desert had sterilized her. If she didn't escape soon the mana radiation would soon overwhelm her remaining nanobots, causing permanent cellular damage and eventually killing her.

Brandon had explained that magic sterilized humans, which was why no woman over the age of twenty-eight became pregnant. By entering Elraci, she'd ended any hope she had of having a child. She had no brothers, sisters, or cousins Her uncle was too old and childless.

"Father, I miss you. I'm so sorry. If I had listened, I wouldn't be the last."

She'd known farming wasn't for her, and she still knew it, but to know she could never have children.... That was too much.

Brandon appeared. She knew he was a machine or a person who was made by humans. Still, he had feelings, and for all purposes, was an intelligent being with rights and privileges. Brandon was a shadow of his former self without the resources to repair himself, let alone try to deal with the Elraci cleanup.

"What has happened?" he asked.

She sniffled and motioned for him to go away and leave her in her misery.

"Your Highness. What have you done? How did you do this?"

Brandon's tone was one of disbelief. She sniffed, wiping her nose on her sleeve as she lifted an arm to peer at him. "What are you talking about?"

Brandon was bending down over her, staring at her belly as if she wasn't there.

"Brandon, stop that. What are you talking about?"

Brandon straightened up. "You're filled with billions of highly advanced Elracian nanobots of an order that would take hundreds, maybe thousands, of years of research to construct."

Her hands dropped to her stomach. "Uh, I just came back from one of those transition wave visions. While I was there, I performed the binding ceremony before the Elracian Senate."

Brandon started pacing, running his hands through his unkempt hair, mumbling to himself. "I wasn't sure if I could believe you. But this. This is a miracle. Do you know what this means?"

Ticca sniffled and sat up. Rubbing her nose with her sleeves, she shook her head. Brandon was too focused to notice.

"It means I can get you out of here safely. And with your

permission, I might be able to restore all my systems to begin trying to clean up Elraci."

That got her attention. Putting her legs under herself, she stood and waved her hand directly in Brandon's way. He stopped and looked at her.

"Try explaining."

"You have far more bots than you need. They're already transforming themselves to Imperial bots per the instructions in your genome. But if you command them, they will obey me. If you grant me…" He looked up, and his head shifted from left to right a couple of times as he seemed to have a heavy thought that was rolling around inside his head. "…three hundred million bots, I can fix one of the repair units. After that, it can fix more repair units, and eventually, I'll be able to get a factory operating again. It will take a few years at least, but I can be fully restored, and the city can be put right. When I get the shields back up over the city, I can begin rebuilding the research systems here. Elraci might yet be restored!"

"And I'm just going to sit here while you do this?"

"No. With only a few hundred thousand bots, we can make one of the evacuation jets operational. I can program it to take you out of the desert and land safely. I'll give you a device we can use to talk to each other. It won't work until I get the city's communication systems repaired and figure out how to pierce through the high levels of magic that are blanketing the city. I should be able to build a relay system to the mountains in eight or so years. That would let me check in with you, maybe even help. But when I do, we can talk. Maybe you can find out what happened to the other AIs in that time."

"Lebuin and the rest of the team should have been here by now, which means they likely had a real problem and had to head north. Can you get me to them?"

Brandon nodded. "I can program the escape jet to land close to any group of people it finds. If they're coming here, it'll be a short trip. From what you have told me, the only possible group of people here will be your friends. If they're heading north, it will be longer. The jet might be able to move along the mountains to look for them. But it doesn't have that much range."

Only a few marks later, Ticca was sitting in a cupped chair, staring at dozens of controls she had only a vague idea about how to use. In one of the five alternate dimension pockets of her belt pouch, she had Brandon's communication device, which he called a comrec, which stood for communicator recorder. It was actually a mini library of data with recording abilities and a type of technology that allowed for nearly instantaneous communication over long ranges. It looked like a mini cigar case to her. She'd also loaded the cockpit up with as many containers of water as she could, and she had a nice new backpack filled with foods and some fresh clothes.

"You're sure about this?" She smiled at the image of Brandon standing next to the hatch.

"It's all programmed. All you have to do is hit that big red button, and it will do the rest."

"Thank you, Brandon. I'm glad I met you and that I was able to help. Don't take any risks. Go slow and do it right. If I don't hear from you in nine years, I'll come back."

Brandon smiled and bowed. "Your will, my empress. I shall endeavor to work tirelessly on getting things corrected here." Then he stood tall. "*Vivant et imperii decus est famuli tui Duianna Elraci!*"

"What does that mean?"

"It's an ancient promise from the pre-migration Duianna Empire. It loosely translates as *By the glory of its Elracian servants, long may the Duianna Empire live.* The name of the nation is, of course, substituted for the current location."

"Until we meet again," Ticca said with joy in her eyes. She waved and pressed the red button. An alarm sounded, and the panels before her lit up. The canopy door slammed closed, and she was thrust back into the seat. Moments later, the bright sands of the desert were shooting past below her. The speed she was moving was inconceivable in her mind. She was too shocked to be afraid. Brandon had shown her how to read the displays, and everything on the panels looked just like he said it would.

This would be great to get anywhere! I wish I could fly all the time.

The craft weaved and flew in a zig-zag pattern, capable of sensing humans fifty miles away. In order to track her team and Lebuin, it only had to fly for fifteen minutes to cover 500 square miles. The air was comfortable, and she enjoyed eating the last meal Brandon had gotten the food machines to give her, which was something he called a *peat-sah*. She'd had something similar, but this was uniquely good. It was nice, because it was cut up into easy-to-hold slices and put into little containers. Sipping the water, she waited for Lebuin to appear on the scanners.

I can't figure out how he can make peat taste so good. But dang, I like it. Guess this is one of the cases like my uncle used to say about traveling. 'If it tastes good, just go with it. Sometimes it's best to not ask too many questions.'

A couple of marks later, she was approaching the mountains when the alarm went off, indicating that the ship found a group of people. The craft turned and moved towards the location. Ticca sat up and looked out the window. She was near the mountains when the group came into view. They turned towards her as she approached.

She giggled at the spectacle she was about to become. *Now, this is going to be a gloriously impressive entrance!*

Her stomach flipped and her heart began to pound as she realized her entire team was being held captive by a group of Nhia-Samri. The jet, on the program set by Brandon, slowed and banked to fly around the group, giving her a clear view down, while it searched for a safe landing spot.

One of the Nhia-Samri gestured and pointed to Ticca. Lightning flew from her and hit the craft. Half of the panel in front of Ticca went red as klaxons and alarm buzzers sounded. She grabbed for the controls. Brandon had given her a quick lesson on how to fly it, but said it was *really* best if she left the flying to the jet.

She hit the buttons that would give her control, and she turned it away from the group. She was trying to figure out how to make it go faster when a second strike hit. She heard something explode in the rear as more alarms went off. She was slammed into her seat as the jet spun wildly. It started tumbling, and she was thrown back and forth in every direction possible.

Light flashed in her eyes as the sun swung past the windows, replaced by the ground, then sky, then sun. Ticca realized the ground was way too close. She screamed for help just as the ship slammed into the ground. Blackness took her.

Rough hands moved over her body. "She's alive. She's strapped into this thing." She was pulled left, then right. Hands ran across her chest, then waist. "I don't see how to release it. She isn't wounded, and nothing is broken."

"It looks like a type of cloth. Cut the straps. Make sure to cut a sample to take with us. I want to get away from this thing. The smoke back here doesn't smell right. It might burn any moment."

"Sir," said another voice, "she has a large supply of food and water tucked back here."

"Take it. We can certainly use more water."

She opened her eyes when she heard the sound of a sword being drawn. A strong young male Nhia-Samri was bending into the cockpit over her, one odassi drawn. He was wearing full armor and gloves. He nodded to her with a smile as he cut her out of the seatbelts. He cut a length of one of the belts and put it in his pouch as he sheathed his sword.

"Sir, she's awake."

Another Nhia-Samri, a woman, stepped next to the first. "Hello, Ticca. I'm very pleased you caught up with us. I was wondering how I was going to invite you to Lumendaria with your friends." She slowly looked around. "It seems you're full of surprises."

Still feeling dizzy and not entirely sure if she was awake or dreaming, Ticca said, "I'm very pleased I could make it myself. One small favor. I'd appreciate it if you don't forget my peat-sah. I was enjoying it."

They glanced at each other, puzzled. Ticca had to fight not to laugh. She considered not explaining, but the peat-sah really was good, so she pointed to the scattered containers.

The female picked one up and examined it. She nodded, and the other warriors, who'd been taking all the water and food out, also grabbed the half-dozen containers of peat-sah slices.

The lady motioned back away from the jet with her head and said, "Mark this location. We'll want to come back for this craft if any of it remains. We have to get over the mountains before we can open a gate. We don't want to be late."

MARU-ASHUA

Maru-Ashua stalked the halls of what should have been his palace. People scattered out of his way, and guards leapt to open doors. He'd taken the city, land, and people fairly. They'd been surrendered to him, and Shar-Lumen had not amended the documents establishing that he was His Lordship Duke Maru-Ashua, First Warlord of the Nhia-Samri. His family would reign for many generations, if he could hold on to it against the approaching armies of the Alliance, yet he felt alien there.

The walls had unseen eyes the same as his outpost. He knew these eyes did not serve him. Not yet. His outpost was built for the Nhia-Samri and answered to them. The palace and city were built for the Duianna Empire and did not honor treaties of men. If he was to gain control of the region in total, he must wrest it from the Alliance. He must hold it and force them to acknowledge the Nhia-Samri claim to those lands and his status as the overlord there.

He'd mistakenly thought that such an acknowledgment by an official representative of the prior lords of the land would suffice. It did for the population, but not for the ancient systems there. Whatever magic, guardian spirit, or mechanism that controlled the ancient defenses and powers refused to acknowledge Maru-Ashua as the rightful ruler.

That, and the approaching armies, were why he had not yet brought his wife and children there. He knew his son would love to run around the castle, tiring all but the hardiest of watchers. His daughter was older and would spend a lot of time pestering him to let her join the warriors.

His feet had brought him to the balcony where he'd forced the surrender of Princess Sheila, heir to Laeusia. She'd done everything required, according to the historical texts and transcripts, to turn rule over to him. He'd studied the ceremonies used at the formation of the Alliance 5,000 years before. Those had been well documented.

The Duianna Emperor had sliced up his empire, giving it over to the dukes, duchesses, countesses, and barons, making them kings, queens, and rulers. The emperor had traveled to all the new national capitals, and used the exact same ceremony in all the locations, naming the new rulers. It had both diminished the Empire and strengthened it beyond its original limits. It had been a brilliant stroke, breaking the Empire up into more manageable portions and then forming the Alliance to pull all those nations back under the control of the emperor.

The new nations continued to swear fealty to the Empire, even after the last emperor had vanished mysteriously without an heir. The regents had taken control as they were supposed to. The world had continued well enough without an emperor on the throne in Gracia.

The fertile green fields were being tended, and he could hear the industrious sounds of his city. The reconstruction of damaged property was almost finished. With the influx of citizens evacuated from the northern lands, around Nhia-

Samri holdings, ahead of the Alliance attacks, the land was thriving.

The northern cities they'd taken had provided even more civilians with needed skills and hardy backs. Many of the newest citizens taken there had moved out into the open lands, carving homesteads. By all reports, most were happy. He'd given his various honorable officers land grants throughout the areas. A functioning government had formed, one that honored all the normal Nhia-Samri laws and morals.

Dotting the city were the new water towers. To fill them, special aqueducts had been erected through small mage-gates back to Hisuru Amajoo's vast water reservoir. Many of the civilian population had been forced to fetch fresh water from far upstream from the city to comply with the Nhia-Samri code of never drinking or using city water. Several of the locals had wondered at the new requirement to not use their own wells. It was taking a lot of work to keep down the rumors that the wells had been poisoned by one side or the other. With the fresh water supply restored, things had finally settled down.

With Shar-Lumen's most recent order to relocate all the outposts from the southern hemisphere to those lands, there would be a Nhia-Samri outpost within a day's ride of any location. In less than a cycle, it had gone from a sparsely occupied remote area on the southern edge of Laeusia, to a thriving nation with military outposts located throughout the land.

Small towns and cities were already popping up, and trade routes were being established through the mountains to the east, between Hisuru Amajoo and Hopu Rinyaru. Even more trade routes were being established westerly to the southern port city of Ithiliunna, which was a major trade port for goods from Yalthum, Karakia, and Dulgrium.

If we can hold to this new land, we can even establish trade with Aelargo and Nasur to the east.

He breathed deeply, feeling some of the promise of the

air. Throughout his whole life, he'd been a natural leader. Still, that was more than he ever dreamed of. He'd been a strong son. He learned all the drills and won all the games. The only thing he'd never managed to master was the use of mana. He was stronger than most mages, but only because of the blades he wore at his side. Those magnificent ancient blades had chosen him when he'd been sent as a new first lieutenant to Outpost One.

He allowed a smile at the memory. He'd been assigned to clean, repair, and oil every weapon in that armory for speaking out of turn to a superior. In taking that job seriously, he also decided to repair all the ancient shelves and weapon racks. He'd worked day and night to sand, oil, and repair the racks. He hadn't known why at the time, but that included cleaning and recaulking the walls. That was when he found the secret compartment that held the blades. He was sure they'd influenced him to step up and do the extra work. They'd chosen him, perhaps on that very day, after witnessing him work for some time. They never said anything directly to him, only vague feelings and nudges. The power they had was beyond any other blades he'd encountered.

He'd done such good work that the officer he'd offended had publicly acknowledged that Maru-Ashua was a worthy and dedicated officer to be emulated. His rise through the ranks was fast. He slowly learned to control his emotions and tongue. He'd also learned the value of always doing a job to the best of one's abilities. That single lesson had been a defining moment.

His introspection was halted by someone drawing near from the hall behind him. The person stopped to wait for permission to approach. He was alone on the balcony, and his personal guards were in positions around the doorways in the hall, ensuring it remained as he desired. Since his guards didn't react, it had to be one of his generals or an adviser.

"You may approach." As he turned around, he was surprised to see his chief mage.

"Your Grace, the Alliance forces are three days from our borders. We cannot locate Duke or Lord Dohma. The forces have at least a thousand mages. They're maintaining shielding for all three divisions."

"Are you sure they're full divisions?"

The mage nodded. "Yes. Although we cannot see them clearly with magic, we have used gates to move scouts near their locations. We have confirmed division numbers roughly: 1,500,000 warriors, 200,000 Dagger officers, and 300,000 non-combatant support personnel."

The numbers were far more than he anticipated. It was an almost unbelievable number. The Alliance had pulled everyone who could carry a blade. Most had been involved with a battle or two against a Nhia-Samri outpost on the march south, making them seasoned veterans. All of them were being trained by Daggers.

The Nhia-Samri might be able to defeat them if they could fight as mercenaries, but not as a nation. Their tactics of hit and run did not allow for holding and defending land. In that battle, they could easily lose due to attrition.

The fact that the Alliance would field three million warriors against them meant they were serious and scared

"What of the eastern fronts?"

"We have confirmed reports of a similar number of divisions landing in Nasur and western Aelargo. There are no more Nhia-Samri outposts or strongholds remaining in the northern Alliance territories. The last, in Oslald, fell yesterday."

"Duke has kept his word. He's moving for Hisuru Amajoo. Alliance forces will box us in completely from east and west. I need a report on the defenses being built on the northern borders, both east and west of the mountains. Begin preparations. We might need to evacuate all the civilians to Hisuru Amajoo. I don't want to miss even a lone trapper on a circuit."

The mage bowed and left.

Maru-Ashua turned back to look out over the city with one burning question. *Why? Why go through all this effort? Shar-Lumen has had us gather civilian tradesmen from around the world. We have turned no one away that desired to join our people. We have boosted our civilian population with those from the north and south. We have gathered and moved whole families, giving them more freedom and land than they could have hoped for. Evacuating all the outposts to these lands has provided a strong military to police and protect the nation. He even had a name ready. That wasn't something he just thought of. This has been planned out years, maybe even hundreds of years, ago. Why do all of this if the Alliance armies will just destroy all of it before it even started?*

He tried to find some clue in everything Shar-Lumen had said or done, but his mind kept returning to the night the Gods had attacked Hisuru Amajoo. Shar-Lumen had calmly watched as their might was turned aside by a shield he'd built 600 years earlier. Shar-Lumen had said with deep conviction, "I protect my own."

You've been working on this for over 600 years. You said things were not going as you desired, but you're clever. How can you stop the Alliance?

A communication channel opened to Maru-Ashua directly. He touched his odassi. It was Hiri-Rula. Her strike team had managed to get far enough away from Elraci to communicate and gate safely.

He allowed the connection. "Report."

"First Warlord, we have succeeded with a surprising bonus."

"Explain."

"Sir, Lebuin is a God. He had Magus Vestul's journal, and he has broken the seals. We have secured him, Ticca, Ditani, and the rest of their team. They're healthy. I'm opening the gate to Lumendaria."

"Wait. I'll have a terminus established in the throne room

in one mark. I want you to gate through to there directly. Stand by for a link to the terminus mage."

"Sir!"

He closed the connection and moved into the hall. "Get a gate terminus mage to the throne room now. I want a gate to General Hiri-Rula, due south from here on the edge of the Circumveni Desert, established immediately."

One of his guards saluted and ran down the hall. Maru-Ashua went the opposite direction, to his quarters, where he changed into his full ceremonial armor and then jogged to the throne room. He arrived just as the gate mage was completing the assembly of the rods that would provide the focus point for a magic gateway. The room was being prepared. Twenty guards had been brought in, just in case. He noted that a few heads of houses that had relocated from Hisuru Amajoo to Lumendaria were there, too. They didn't seem surprised at his arrival in full ceremonial gear. They nodded and chatted amongst themselves as they took up positions on the sidelines.

He pointed to the center of the room. "Place the terminus there and proceed."

He climbed the stairs to sit in the throne. Moments later, the gateway flashed, revealing a dry mountain path of broken granite and lava rock. Standing back from the gate was General Hiri-Rula, her mage necklace glowing like a bright star. Her armor was spotless, as was all the armor and clothing of the people around her.

She extended all the clasp's abilities to the entire group. At least they'll all be immaculately presentable.

Three at a time, the group proceeded through the gateway. Each triad consisted of a pair of Nhia-Samri one hand holding the arm of a Dagger prisoner who was stripped of weapons and forced to wear a pair of arm bindings. Only four Daggers remained out of the original nine. They were followed by Colonel Runa-Emry, personally escorting his own daughter, Runa-Illa, who once was a shining jewel of the Nhia-Samri, with every chance of eventually becoming a warlord. She too was weaponless and shackled.

Four Nhia-Samri escorted a Karakian he recognized from reports as the ancient warrior, Kiotiaditani, son of Lady Lothia, the Raven. Ditani looked around and smiled, walking where he was told, not docilely, but with a dignity impossible to impersonate.

Kiotiaditani was with them! The Gods have been very busy.

General Hiri-Rula stepped through the gate with one hand holding the arm of Lebuin. Behind Hiri-Rula, six more Nhia-Samri followed, watching Lebuin closely. He had on a collar like those worn by Magus Cune, Lady Sula, and Lady Lothia. Hiri-Rula had taken it as a means to subdue a powerful mage. She was lucky it could hold a God, as well.

Behind those, the last four started to come through. At their center was the young girl he'd met in Algan, the mysterious Ticca of Rhini wood.

General Hiri-Rula had walked up the base of the dais with Lebuin. "First Warlord, I present...." She was cut off by a grand trumpeting that filled the throne room.

A shimmering column of light flowered up from the floor, forming into a sphere, like a fountain, around the gate. Ticca, who'd just come through, stopped, seeming just as surprised as everyone else. Below her, the inlaid seal of Laeusia split and fell away, making it look like the group stood on nothing, over a bottomless chasm that had once been the floor.

From the depths, a shimmering silver seal rose precisely under Ticca. It was in the shape of a square shield. A blazing sun was at its center, the Imperial panther profile at the top, and the dagger of justice in a wreath of olive leaves at the bottom. The shield was topped with the Imperial crown.

All of the house heads present dropped to one knee, their heads down, saying together, *"Vivant et imperii decus est famuli tui Duianna Hopu Rinyaru!"*

The lights intensified around Ticca until her clothes were a luminous, sparkling gold. Her four Nhia-Samri guards were pushed away by the expanding, sparkling sphere.

Ticca held her hands up before her, looking at her glowing sleeves, eyes wide. The shackles melted off her arms, turning into glowing dust that vanished before striking the floor. The trumpeting reached a crescendo.

As the sound of the horns faded, a woman's voice came from nowhere and everywhere. "*Ave, imperatrix Duianna. Ut et illustris, nobilem Duianna, vivere per te imperii. Vivat regiam.*"

Ditani shook free of the shocked warriors holding him and stepped out, eyeing Maru-Ashua.

"Warlord Maru-Ashua, Nhia-Samri all, please recognize me, Kiotiaditani, speaker of the tribes of Kiliua-ona, and allow me to present to you Her Royal Majesty, Empress Ticca Ethulin Duianna, the one true daughter of Duianna. May the honorable and glorious Duianna Empire live through you. Long live the Empire."

Kiotiaditani dropped to one knee.

The warriors looked at Maru-Ashua for guidance. All he could do was stare at Ticca. His mind had frozen harder than the high lakes in winter.

The ice broke with an almost audible cracking, and hundreds of thoughts raced around his head, demanding immediate attention.

Empress! She is the Duianna Empress. A Dagger! No wonder Duke obeyed her. He knew! I can't hold her. She's more precious than Lady Lothia or Lady Sula!

He glanced around the throne room. Aside from the floor, and the shimmering golden globe of lights around Ticca, nothing else had changed. But he knew the city's invisible guardian who'd just spoken in the ancient Imperial formal language recognizing Ticca. It was the same language Damega used to command the *Emerald Heart*, and which the old emperors had used to control their artifacts for hundreds of generations. The city was watching and would not hesitate to protect Ticca with all its might.

He had no illusions about the sudden reversal of the situation.

I sit on the throne, but she commands here. Worse, even if we can hold her, if any of the assembly even suspect we're holding her prisoner here, all of the nations will descend upon us with everything they have. They'll level everything to get to her. There won't be even a speck of usable soil left. Did Shar-Lumen know this? It would explain his order that she be captured unharmed.

He stood and slowly stepped down the dais.

Shar-Lumen's words echoed out of his memory, reverberating around his mind, calming his thoughts. *'I protect my own!'* A plan formed, and he knew what he had to do.

LEBUIN

The spectacle was done. Lebuin squeezed his fists so hard that he felt his nails digging into his skin. His mind raced, trying to find a way out of the mess.

There go all of our secrets. Bad enough we come into an Imperial throne room, but why did Ditani just expose Ticca's full identity? I know that mage commander Hiri-Rula knows I'm a god. If only that meant something! A full Magus would be better suited to deal with this than I am.

The guards were so confused that they let Lebuin pull his arms out of their grip. He took advantage of the situation to shift the collar and scratch under it. Every time he tried to use some magic, it sent a painful shock into his nerves, and worse, it siphoned off the power.

I bet this thing is channeling that power straight to a Nhia-Samri power station. I hope it doesn't figure out how to tap into the connection to my collector.

Everyone in the room was focused on Ticca and the amazing light show she was producing. Ticca was radiant, literally. Her clothes and gear hadn't changed shape, yet everything on her looked as if it was made from some silky substance that flowed and sparkled. She was also surrounded by a shield, but it wasn't like any Lebuin had seen before.

It hummed, and small waves flowed across it, distorting his vision.

He tried to shift to magical sight, only to feel the power sucked away and a painful shock vibrating down his spine.

I wish I could look at the incantation channels making that shield. I bet it's unique. We've learned so much, and yet we've still lost more than we've gained.

The last few weeks had changed everything, but the world was still the same, more or less. The Gods were still living somewhere on the world, and flitting around in the *between* realm, interacting with each other and their followers. Argos still sat, or lay, or whatever he did, in Miniath-Tur, at the center of the universe, watching over not only that world, but hundreds of others.

And yet everything was different. The gods were just another magical race, no better than elves, dwarves, or humans. Lady Dalpha had proven the race that called themselves gods, and acted as if they were truly superior, had all the same problems and issues as those who lived shorter lives. In fact, Dalpha was so greedy that she risked others for her own gain. Because of her greed, an entire race of elves had been destroyed.

Still, Lebuin knew most of the gods blamed others, unwilling to see themselves as a possible cause. But if not for Dalpha's actions, how would things have gone? The visions he, Ticca, and Illa had experienced in the Elracian wastelands had shown a bright and wonderful future gone.

Pay attention to the now! As the Daggers say, 'What we do today can improve all our tomorrows.'

He turned his attention back to the scene playing out before him, looking for any opportunity to help. There were a number of people dressed uniquely, in a style using wrapped robes with pins and leather belts. They were obviously nobles, but they all reacted to Ticca together. They were all on bended knee to Ticca. The only ones not on one knee were the Nhia-Samri warriors, Ticca, Lebuin's team, and of course, the warlord.

He didn't miss that the uniquely dressed nobles had said something in the ancient language used by the Duianna Empire for its rituals.

The warlord descended from the throne to stand just at the edge of Ticca's shields, and bowed rigidly. Lebuin got a surge of concern from Illa.

My connection to Illa is still working!

Bracing for a shock from the collar, he relaxed and opened himself to her. *'Illa, can you hear me?'* No shock came; the collar didn't react.

'Yes, my Lord, I can.'

'Why are you so worried?'

'I think he might....'

"Your Royal Highness. I am pleased you could join us here in Lumendaria."

"You mean Allornia!"

"No, Your Highness. These lands were granted fairly to me by the voice of King of Laeusia. The treaty was signed in accordance with all *your* laws."

Ticca shook her head. "No, you took them by force, and if I'm not mistaken, the Alliance is about to take them back. That's why these warriors were in a hurry to get back here. Am I right?"

"You're correct that Alliance forces are approaching. However, they're led by Duke, and I believe he's more interested in Hisuru Amajoo than Lumendaria."

Standing straight and tall, Ticca said, "I will not allow you to steal these or anyone else's lands."

The warlord stepped back and placed his hands on the hilts of his blades. "You can try to take them back."

Ticca held out her hand to the warrior holding her weapons. "I accept!"

Lebuin's heart sank, and his stomach lurched. He wanted to say something, but he knew it was of no use. *Oh, Lords, please protect her!*

Six people, including Ditani, screamed, "NO, YOU MUST NOT!"

The warlord turned on the robed nobles who'd called out. "You stay out of this! I rule here, and I know what I must do."

The eldest of the nobles, an ancient thin woman in flowing blue and green silk robes, stepped forward, placing her hand on the warlord's hand that gripped his sword. "No, Maru-Ashua, you do not. You are one of her royal guard, and you cannot attack her. It would be treason, and you would be dead before you could harm her. We cannot allow this."

Ticca and the warlord simultaneously said, "What?"

The elder noble pulled the warlord's hand off the blade and then drew it with her other so fast that the motion was a blur. The blade glowed, reflecting Ticca's shimmering, and there was another sound that came from it like a distant, sustained chime.

Holding the blade before the warlord, she said, "Do you not recognize the Duianna panther on this blade?"

Lebuin saw that the bronze bands at the base of the sword had a stylized cat silhouette in profile, over an oblong oval that looked like an egg. It was easy to see, as it was glowing as brightly as Ticca. The cat silhouette matched the Imperial panther in the Duianna coat of arms under Ticca's feet perfectly.

Why would they use an egg on a sword? It must mean something.

He recalled the golden egg artifact at Dalpha's temple and the one at the Argos Guildhouse in Llino that belonged to him. *Not an egg. A mana collector! Could it be? The Empire has THE LOST COLLECTOR! That sword must be Elracian technology connected to one of the most powerful devices ever made by my people. But how could they channel mana to it? I doubt they have mages constantly feeding it, especially for 15,000 years.*

Lebuin remembered the visions. Ticca had given Illa the fae mana filter, and Brandon had said she'd caused a serious stir over taking it away from the researchers, to which Ticca had implied there was an Imperial version.

That must be what Dalpha was trying to replicate! She got the idea from what was done by the first emperor of this world. So what went wrong? Maybe the Elracian generators were too much at once or were somehow not compatible.

"These were made as a gift to the Duianna Empire, which saved us all, and were to keep the emperor and his line safe from all harm. Only the most loyal, dedicated, and honorable warriors were selected by these to protect the Empire. They connect you to the emperor's line, and give you power to protect the Empire. Each one holds the knowledge and personality of a dedicated warrior carefully selected for the honor of eternal vigilance."

The elder noble let the blade drop sideways, catching it in both hands, and held it up to the warlord. "Take your blade and know yourself."

The warlord's back was to Lebuin, so he couldn't see what his initial reaction was. He stood there for a long period.

"This is Imperial technology? This is mundane? Our people made it?"

"No. It is entirely magical, made by the elves and dwarves as a gift shortly after coming to these lands. Only one pair was made that combine mundane and magical technologies. I haven't seen those blades since I was a young woman."

"Did they not work?"

"They worked better than any could dream. The knowledge and key resources were destroyed before more could be made. It's a great tragedy."

The warlord took the blade. Turning back to Ticca, his face was stone neutral. He sheathed his sword and stepped back in front of her. He stood tall and stared at Ticca, who also stood silently, gazing back at him. Finally, Ticca's eyebrow went up, and her lips smirked.

"Not exactly going to plan, is it?" she asked.

The warlord shook his head. "No. You?"

"Nope," Ticca said. "Completely lost. Now what?"

Maru-Ashua gestured around the room. "We have built a strong nation, one that will make you proud. Will you help me preserve it?"

Ticca looked Lebuin in the eyes, holding his gaze.

She wants my opinion. His heart rate leapt up a notch. *She believes in me again. What should we do?*

'*Illa, can he be trusted?*'

'*Yes, my Lord. He will never break his word. But he is clever and dangerous.*'

'*Then we need him with us.*'

Lebuin nodded to Ticca. She smiled warmly at him, and then looked back to the warlord.

Ticca's eyes touched Lebuin's soul. He felt a small tremor throughout his body as his mind still focused on that sweet smile. She'd left a warm feeling that was swelling in him.

Oh, I feel like dancing! If I wasn't in shackles with this collar on, of course.

"Tell me about Hopu Rinyaru," Ticca said.

The warlord explained the war casualties, the outposts, the citizens, the new farms, the trade routes forming, and small towns that might someday become cities. He gushed over the farms and other settlements. Lebuin was shocked that a Nhia-Samri warlord could be so passionate over farming settlers. Ticca, on the other hand, chewed her lower lip thoughtfully and followed every word intently, leaning forward towards the warlord nodding at key points. When he finished, everyone looked at Ticca.

"You're right. I'm proud of this, of you, and of what has been done in such a short time. Laeusia did not use this land well. It's no real loss to them, and if this stands, it would be a strong nation."

She looked up, holding her hands wide, calling out, "Allornia, hear me and obey."

She looked back to the warlord. "Lord Maru-Ashua, I accept the treaty and your rule here. Allornia is now Hopu

Rinyaru, this is the city of Lumendaria, and you are the ruler. But the ends do not justify the means. Shar-Lumen still has much to pay for."

"*In nomine imperatoris, Maru-Ashua. Maru-Ashua vivat rex Hopu Rinyaru,*" said the same loud husky female voice from before, from all around them.

The warlord glanced around and, for the first time, his face showed a sign of awe.

"Did the city guardian just accept me?"

A fountain rose up out of the floor next to the warlord. On it stood a golden cup, and it appeared to be filled with some kind of silver liquid.

The warlord considered the small fountain. Then, with care, he picked up the cup.

Ticca pointed. "You're supposed to fill the cup and offer it to me."

"Yes, I know the binding ceremony. I just didn't expect the cup to actually be gold and the water to really be silver. I thought those were just metaphors."

He scooped the cup full of the silver liquid, and with two hands holding the cup before him, approached Ticca. The shield around her vanished.

"Your Royal Highness, Empress Ticca Duianna, please accept this in binding our nation to your reign. Long live the Empress, long stand the Empire."

How do they know what to do?

Ticca took the cup and then slowly looked around the room, taking time to give each person present a significant amount of eye contact and her gentle smile. "Lord Maru-Ashua and citizens of Hopu Rinyaru, I am pleased to accept you into the Duianna Empire. It is with deep humility and pride that I accept your binding to the throne of the Duianna Empire."

The elder noble covertly dabbed the corners of her eyes.

Ticca then drank the entire cupful down in one go.

She handed the cup back to the warlord, who called out "*Vivant et imperii decus est famuli tui Duianna Hopu Rinyaru.*"

He dropped to one knee.

The Nhia-Samri all dropped to their knees. Most of the warriors drew their blades and held them forward, forming a cross. Lebuin spotted the glowing Imperial panther on the blades.

The Nhia-Samri are Ticca's royal guards and didn't know it! He noted that not all of the blades had the glowing panther, so it wasn't 100 percent.

Hiri-Rula was still standing and holding her drawn blades, staring at the glowing panther on them. Her eyes lifted to Ticca, and she knelt, crossing her blades before her. She shouted, "LONG LIVE THE EMPRESS, LONG STAND DUIANNA!"

The call was echoed by the other warriors.

Ticca went red, but smiled so wide her dimples came out. She looked magnificent. Finally, she made lifting signs with her hands. "Everyone up, this is a bit much."

The nobles stood and stepped forward. The elder took the lead. "Thank you, Your Majesty, for accepting our nation. With your permission, we shall now return to our duties.'

Holding up a finger, Ticca said, "First, I'm going to swear everyone here to secrecy. I do not want to go sit on a throne in Gracia. I'm a Dagger, and that is my calling. So all this, and who I am, is not to be revealed." She looked around, meeting the eyes of all there.

The elder nodded. "And so it has been for many generations, since the time of Aphren Duianna the 34th. Our ancestors made a similar promise to him, to keep his progeny's status within our borders. As it has been since before this world was born, your will, my Empress. We shall all do as you command."

Looking down at herself, Ticca asked, "You wouldn't happen to know how to stop this show, would you?"

"Your will, Empress."

After a little laugh, she said, "Yes, of course. Uh, City

of Lumendaria, please stop this shimmering and coat of arms display."

The Imperial coat of arms sank away as the city seal closed under their feet. The shimmering effect washed away from Ticca, leaving her with a normal appearance.

"Ah, that's better," Ticca said with a small bounce.

The eldest gazed at Ticca, tilting her head to the side. "You weren't trained in the command language? Your family promised to keep the line true in all things."

Sadness crept into Ticca's eyes. "My father died when I was very young. I'm sure my uncle plans on teaching me more. I sort of insisted on Daggering."

"Is he in Rhini Wood with your family's lands?"

"Yes."

"Then he must be the guardian. With your permission, I shall communicate with him on this. Also, we must seek his permission to train another."

Ticca held her hands out to the warrior holding her weapons.

The warlord held up a hand. "Uh...before we give you all your possessions back, we need to consider what to do about the coming war. I have to present you and your team to Shar-Lumen in Hisuru Amajoo."

"By your leave, Your Majesties, we shall continue our work," the elder woman said and bowed to both, Ticca first. The other nobles did the same, and they left.

"Are you going to tell him?" Ticca asked, returning to the subject at hand.

The team and warriors gathered closer together.

"Shar-Lumen knows who you are. But not about Lebuin."

"And?" Ticca prompted.

"I'm unsure. I cannot betray Shar-Lumen, but I cannot allow you to be taken prisoner, either." The warlord sighed and held his hands up.

"Give us a moment?" Ticca asked.

The warlord nodded. "Come join me in the rest lounge

through there." He pointed to some doors and then motioned for the manacles to be removed. He and all of the Nhia-Samri left, closing the doors behind them. Ticca and her team were alone in the throne room.

"Should we make a break for it and join Duke?" Nigan asked.

Ticca grabbed a chair from the side and sat down in it, leaning back against the wall, her eyes closed.

Carda said, "It wouldn't necessarily be making a break for it. We can probably ask for horses and provisions, and then simply ride out."

"Ticca...." Lebuin started.

She opened her eyes and looked at him.

"I'm really glad you made it. We thought we'd lost you, and I...." *I love you.*

He couldn't say it, and it burnt. She raised a brow at him, and all eyes were on him. "I...I need to tell the other Gods about Dalpha. This collar has me locked in tight."

Illa put a hand on his shoulder. He knew she felt some of his angst.

"Thanks," Ticca said. "Me too. What do you mean about Dalpha? What did you learn?"

Lebuin summed up everything they found. Ticca sighed, leaning her head back, and closed her eyes again. Tears ran down her cheeks.

"She stole more than you know. All our lives could have been so very different."

Illa shoved him forward. He looked at her, and she pointed with her chin to Ticca, giving him a *do-something* look.

A realization came to him. *She saw far more than we did of that alternate path. She must've learned that ceremony and Imperial protocol there. She knows clearly what could have been.*

He stepped forward and knelt down in front of Ticca, putting a hand on her shoulder. "I'm with you." His mouth betrayed him. He should have said, "We're with you."

Ticca sobbed and grabbed him, pulling him into a strong hug and burying her face in his shoulder. She cried, mumbling something about her father, Illa, and him. He couldn't understand what she was trying to say.

Ditani moved beside her and placed his hands on their backs. Illa did the same on the opposite side. Nigan, Carda, and Malla all stepped up and put their hands on Ticca's back.

"We're all here for you both," Ditani said.

They held the embrace for several minutes before Ticca pulled away. She stopped, her face inches from his. As their eyes met, his soul melted for her. He felt an energy between them that was much larger than they were. It was larger than life. In that moment, consequences ceased to matter.

"Lebuin, I care for you far more than you can imagine. You must understand what I'm about to tell you here and now. Something happened to us in that flood of power when all that magic was directed to destroy us at that Nhia-Samri base. I think a part of our potential came out of that other realm and changed us. But I promised my father...." Tears flowed freely down her cheek as she choked to a stop. After swallowing, she continued, forcing the words out. "If that other possibility had come, we had a shared destiny. I will not be controlled by another's desires, even if that person is myself from another realm. I know your feelings, and I admit we might yet have a shared destiny in this realm. But here and now, neither of us can be sure of our feelings. I need time, probably a lot of time. All I can offer you is my friendship, and if you want, you're welcome to put your dagger out with me."

His heart pounded and tears pooled in his eyes. He knew that was the most important turning point. Lebuin swore to himself that he would earn Ticca's true trust and love. Abandoning her was never an option. Even if she never came to love him as he loved her, he would stand by her and never let her doubt his support again.

He took a breath, and in as firm a tone as he could hold,

as much as it hurt he said the right thing. "I know I have a lot to learn. And to prove to everyone. I'd be proud to call you my friend and to be part of your team."

Ticca let her breath out. She'd been holding it, afraid of his reaction. He knew he'd won points, and the tally was finally going positive. She smiled, and his heart leapt at that.

He let her pull him to her for a solid hug, before she leaned back and wiped her eyes.

He'd completely forgotten about where they were, or who was there. Someone coughed, reminding him that he and Ticca weren't alone. His face and ears burnt as he glanced around. The rest of the team was standing around, looking at them with smiles. Illa even nodded once to him.

Nigan patted his back. "Now that you two have worked that out, perhaps we can get back to saving the world."

Ticca stood, and offered her hand to help him back up off his knees. He took her warm hand, and it was as if he felt lighter standing.

"Nigan's right. Now is the time for work," she said, sniffling and wiping her face on her sleeves.

"Now what?" Ditani asked.

"Right," she said, putting her hands on her hips. She looked like a commanding officer should. The transformation was amazing. "I want to preserve this land. This new nation will be good for its people. We have to find a way to stop the slaughter that's coming. That means both Duke and Shar-Lumen have to be stopped."

Ditani said, "So now we fight both sides with Warlord Maru-Ashua at our side? He won't raise a sword against Shar-Lumen. I'm sure they'll back us against Duke."

"Tactically," Carda said, "we should deal with one side. Take the easiest one down and then deal with the other. Duke is more likely to listen to us. So I suggest we get Duke in on this plan, and then we can all head for Hisuru Amajoo in force."

Ticca looked doubtful. "If I do this, do you think Shar-

Lumen will surrender? Or listen with all those troops with us?"

"So we attack Shar-Lumen first?" Ditani asked.

Ticca said, "No. We let Maru-Ashua takes us there as prisoners, and we try to talk him down."

Lebuin laughed. "Talk Shar-Lumen down? We'll be thrown in his deepest dungeon. Probably tortured."

Nigan and Illa nodded agreement.

"No, it won't happen. Don't forget, we'll have fifty or so of my personal guard along for the ride. That might change things a bit."

With a frown, Illa said, "They'll be viewed as traitors and killed. We couldn't stand against Hisuru Amajoo's numbers."

Ticca motioned for them to move and started for the doors, where the warlord was waiting. "I have an idea."

A Solution

CHAPTER 17

JOURNEY'S BEGINNING

Sweat poured down Ticca's back. She'd never been so scared.

This was my idea. Stand tall, make it work.

'Preparation with boldness overcomes many obstacles,' said the voice of her trainer, Amia-Dharo, from her memory.

Dharo, I hope you're right. There's no maneuvering room for mistakes.

Warlord Maru-Ashua, flanked by General Hiri-Rula and Colonel Runa-Emry, walked in front of their group. Fifty Nhia-Samri warriors surrounded them. The arms of Lebuin, Ditani, Illa, Nigan, and Ticca were bound behind them. Lebuin had the bonus of leg shackles, and the magic prison collar.

I hope nothing goes wrong with Malla and Carda. They should get to the front line in two days and deliver my message to Duke. At least two of my team will survive my first big command.

The magic gate was just like the last. There was a slight pressure, like pushing through the surface of water, a mild shock, and then she was someplace else.

Ticca was struck by the implications. At twenty years old, not even a full year into her Dagger career, she was standing in Hisuru Amajoo, the fate of the world resting on the next few marks.

Everyone knew Hisuru Amajoo was big, but nothing prepared her for the scale. They stood before a pair of doors taller than the walls of Llino. The exterior fortress towers stood almost 1,000 feet tall and were 200 feet wide, with arched walkways between, hanging in the air.

Dozens of such towers surrounded a central one, which was 300 feet wide and extended into the sky well above the others.

Turning, she could see the valley, which was over fifteen miles wide. A single town was nestled in the center, encompassed by lush green farms and forests. Around the entire area, a heavy grey wall stood.

Ticca was pushed forward by the guards and marched into the fortress. Once through the main doors, they proceeded across the front lawn and up a set of polished stairs flanked by massive statues of panthers with growling open mouths showing full fangs. Each had a paw extended with claws out, ready to leap and kill.

The entry foyer was over fifty feet tall, with arched ceilings and patterns inlaid into the stone floor. Hundreds of Nhia-Samri officers collected around them as they were pushed into the throne room.

I never imagined the numbers. We could never fight free. I wonder if all the armies of the Alliance even have a chance of taking this place. Even if they did, the cost in lives would be too much. I can't let this war continue.

She was brought before the throne, in which a man she knew well sat. Shar-Lumen hadn't changed one bit from her visions with Kliasa. As she thought about the fact that he'd once been such a wonderful being, tears came to her eyes. He was twisted and lost. Even if he could be brought back to sanity, he'd never submit to being tended by the elves. He was so handsome, it was hard to imagine the atrocities he'd personally committed.

She almost laughed when her eyes dropped to his boots.

How did he manage to make those last 700 years? They look just a little more ragged than I remember, but that is serious stubbornness. If only Kliasa had managed to steal them and destroy them, he might be wearing the boots she made for him. Then he would've known she was waiting and might have been saved.

Shar-Lumen leaned forward in his throne. "So this is the Dagger General of Duke's, who was supposed to find a clue to stop us in the ancient ruins of a dead land?"

His eyes traced over every person with them. The warlord had continued to step up onto the dais to stand at Shar-Lumen's right side.

"Grand Warlord, I present Ticca of Rhini Wood, general of Lord Lebuin and a commander of the Duianna Armies. Lord Lebuin, of unknown origin, a Journeyman Mage in service to Lord Argos, and a deity. Runa-Illa, once Nhia-Samri, now first priestess of Lord Lebuin. Nigan of Eppen, Dagger in service to Lord Lebuin. And finally, Kiotiaditani, speaker of the tribes of Kiliua-ona, son of Lothia, the Raven and Lord Argos, servant of Magus Vestul."

Shar-Lumen listened to Warlord Maru-Ashla's introductions. He then stood and bowed. Every Nhia-Samri present also bowed.

Ticca looked at Lebuin, and he shrugged. So they waited.

Shar-Lumen flowed down the stairs. "You failed to mention one thing, Warlord. However, I forgive the oversight. I know she wishes to remain..." Shar-Lumen approached Ticca and stepped behind her, removing her shackles. He whispered into her ear, "...undiscovered. However, that will not do here, Your Majesty."

He picked his voice up. "Remove their shackles. They are our guests." He stepped before Lebuin as the guards removed all the chains. "Lord Lebuin, you're truly a mystery. And..." He stepped over to Illa and lifted her chin to gaze into her eyes. "...very persuasive. I had great expectations for Runa-Illa. It seems her potential is appreciated by you, as well."

He held out his hand to one of the warriors, who produced Runa-Illa's odassi blades. Shar-Lumen drew both and held them before Runa-Illa.

Oh, no! What have I done?

Ticca and Lebuin moved together. Four Nhia-Samri grabbed them and held them back.

"Don't harm her!" Ticca shouted.

Shar-Lumen paused his inspection to look at Ticca. He spun the blades expertly in front of Runa-Illa and stopped. Lebuin's color left him.

He's tapping their power!

Shar-Lumen smiled, sheathed her blades, and then put them into Runa-Illa's belt, in their proper place, with the air of a proud father.

"She has chosen freely." He placed his hands on her shoulders. "I release you from all your Nhia-Samri vows. You're not the traitor we thought, nor the corpse we feared." He leaned over her, and whispered something in her ear before returning to the throne.

"I believe it's time for all our guests to come together. We have much to decide before the Alliance's war can be finished."

Shar-Lumen motioned towards a pair of doors that opened by themselves. Through them was a ballroom chamber as impressive as the throne room. Ticca gasped when she saw Lady Lothia standing next to Sula and Magus Cune. All three of them wore collars similar to the one on Lebuin. With them stood another lady, and a man she didn't recognize. The man looked thin and tired, and his clothes appeared to have been slept in. The lady was young and attractive. She had the olive complexion of a Gracian. Just behind her, dressed as a servant, was a short, stalky woman who moved more like a warrior than a servant.

Ticca took a closer look at the short woman's face and put a name to it. *Mandy, you're a Dagger from the Dolphin. Probably assigned to guard the regent. Very well done, sticking to him.*

The unknown lady's mouth dropped open when she saw Ticca. Her eyes teared up, and her face went pale. She quickly recovered, drying her eyes with her index fingers.

I've never seen her before. I'm sure I'd recall someone like her, even if she was disguised. But she's really shocked and happy to see me.

The guards pushed the three into the throne room. Shar-Lumen frowned. "Lord Regent Bayion, you could have availed yourself of the accommodations. There is no reason for this appearance."

The man stood tall. "It's to remind you that we're your prisoners, not your guests. I shall not pretend otherwise."

Shar-Lumen regarded the Aelargian regent briefly before ignoring him.

Shar-Lumen said, "And now, at last, I will have that which will change all. General Hiri-Rula, you reported that you recovered Magus Vestul's journal from Lebuin's possessions. Give it to me." One of the guards produced it from a sack.

From all her experiences with Kliasa's memories of Shar-Lumen, Ticca could see past the statue-like mask he wore. His eyes told her all she needed of his thoughts. They sharpened, locking onto the small book handed up to him. She'd never seen anyone long for something as Shar-Lumen did for that journal.

Sula jumped at it. "YOU'VE UNLOCKED IT! NO!"

A Nhia-Samri guard grabbed her and yanked her back to her spot, lifting a hand to strike her. Magus Cune body-slammed him out of the way. Two guards jumped Magus Cune, and three more drew their blades, racing for Sula.

"STOP!" Shar-Lumen ordered.

Taking advantage of the distraction, Ticca leaned to Lebuin, whispering, "You should've told me you finally opened that. What's in it?"

He whispered back, "I didn't mention it because I opened it a couple of days after we lost you. And there hasn't exactly been a moment to discuss it since then. But there is nothing really important in it. It's mostly a lot of details about making those soul image statues. There are also some maps of an island chain far to the west, a little north of the equator. The rest of it is about scrying and shielding from scrying."

"Is that valuable?"

"Not that I could think of."

"Another distraction?"

"Possibly."

Once everyone was back in position, Shar-Lumen sat down in the throne and began to read the journal. At first, he had a happy smirk on his face, but soon that smirk vanished. As he read, his eyebrows got narrower. His face started to distort into a hard grimace. He flipped through it rapidly. He then stood and jumped down the stairs. He punched Lebuin, who flew backwards and landed with a grunt.

Ticca screamed, "NO!" but was ignored. Her heart pounded, and her mind raced, as she tried to figure out a way to help her partner.

"WHERE IS MAGUS VESTUL'S REAL JOURNAL?" Shar-Lumen's violet eyes glowed in anger. "THIS IS NOT WHAT HE CARRIED TO LLINO!" He shook the journal violently, and threw it away.

Stamping towards Lebuin, Shar-Lumen drew his blades. He spun his blades around him in a pattern with such force and speed that they sang a high-pitched tune.

"STOP!" Ticca cried.

Lothia threw herself over Lebuin. "You cannot attack a child. If you want to fight, fight me."

Magus Cune stepped forward. "No, fight me!"

Ditani called out, "Fight me!"

Illa was already in motion. She drew her odassi swords and spun to stand between Lebuin and Shar-Lumen. Their blades met with a series of explosive rings.

Sula stepped next to Ticca. She tapped Magus Vestul's pouch, which the Nhia-Samri had emptied, but left hanging on her belt. "Do you still have the vanedicha?" she whispered to Ticca.

Why would she want the poison I got off the Knife? There's no way to get him to drink it, let alone sniff it.

"Yes," she whispered.

"Quick, give it to me."

Ticca unlocked the dial on her pouch and rotated the control. She slipped her hand into the pouch, feeling for the vial on the end. Pulling it out, she glanced around. Everyone's attention was on the fight. She slipped the vial to Sula.

Sula whispered, "You're Damega's progeny. You can hold

your own against him. Embrace the chaos. Challenge him to a duel to end the war."

She moved back next to Cune. Ticca reset the dial to the empty compartment and locked its position, just in case they went to search her pouch again.

Is she insane? If I lose, he knows who I am. That will give him the rights to take the Empire.

Illa was good, but no match for Shar-Lumen. As fast as the fight had started, it ended. With a rapid series of cuts, Shar-Lumen disarmed Illa and kicked her back. She fell over, smacking her head on the hard floor. She was clearly dazed. Shar-Lumen advanced over her, and raised his swords.

"I had such plans for you," he growled.

Ticca's gut wrenched sideways.

He's going to kill her! Lords and Ladies, help me!

"LEAVE HER ALONE!"

Shar-Lumen turned to face her.

"Leave her. Fight me," Ticca said.

"Why?"

"To end this war."

Shar-Lumen smiled and lowered his swords. "Empress, is that a formal challenge? By the ancient right of the Empire, between two peers?"

Lord Bayion gasped, and turned to look at Ticca. A fraction of a second later, the lady next to him also gasped and did the same.

She stood tall and faced Shar-Lumen. "Yes. Let us spare our peoples. Let this be between us."

Shar-Lumen scrutinized the room. "If your guards interfere, so shall mine."

He knew! We never had a chance. This is playing right into what he wanted all along.

"They won't." She could feel the pulse in her neck as her heart pounded. She fought to hold the tears back as she realized how the scene had been arranged. Turning to each, Ticca acknowledged the participants. "Lady Lothia, you are witness for the Gods. Ditani, you are witness for the nations. Sula, you are witness for the temples. Nigan, you are witness for the Daggers. Magus Cune, you are witness for the mages. Lord Bayion, you are witness for the Alliance."

Lebuin stood. "Ticca, if he wins, he can claim the Duianna Empire."

Shar-Lumen bowed. "Yes, that's an added bonus. No one sane, or insane, wants deaths on the scale that would occur should the Alliance armies reach Hisuru Amajoo. This was supposed to be between the Alliance champion, in the form of Lord Dohma, and me. However, Ticca is a far better candidate."

Shar-Lumen squared off with Ticca and stood tall. "Empress Ticca, I...."

Ticca held up her hand to stop him. "One condition."

Shar-Lumen closed his mouth and raised an eyebrow.

"I require this to be a fair competition. You will fight me in the boots Kliasa made for you. Win or lose, those boots you have on now are mine."

Shar-Lumen took a step backwards. His mouth dropped open, and his face went even paler. "How...?"

Ticca lifted her leg and slammed her foot down on the hard floor. Not even a whisper of a sound came from the action.

Shar-Lumen dropped to his knees and gaped at Ticca's boots. "You.... Those.... How...?"

"I'll wait while you fetch yours from your bedchamber."

Shar-Lumen's eyes locked onto hers. She could see the tumbling thoughts behind them.

I might have unnerved him enough to at least make this look good. Dear Kliasa, you saved my life numerous times over. I return the favor and give you a chance at your love, should I fail.

As Shar-Lumen's stone face returned, he stood and stepped towards her, vanishing without a trace. The entire room gasped.

The warlord was by her side instantly. "Your Majesty...

Ticca, you take a tremendous risk. You cannot beat him. No one can."

"I've been trained for this. I might not know the royal protocols, nor the ancient language, but this is something I *do* know."

Lord Bayion came over, followed by the red-haired woman. "Can it be true? Are you really of the royal line?"

Before she could answer, Shar-Lumen reappeared. He wore an elegant pair of boots etched in silver that mirrored the inlays of his armor. In his hands were the old, scraggy boots he'd just been wearing. He held them out to Ticca.

She took them and then handed them to Hiri-Rula. "Burn these to ash now."

Hiri-Rula had raised eyebrows, but she didn't comment. She walked over to one of the large braziers and dropped the boots in. Lifting her hands, she said something as her necklace shined. The boots went up in flames.

Shar-Lumen was staring at the boots, but his eyes were looking through them, to something beyond.

"Kliasa's will serve you better. Keep those on always."

Shar-Lumen's brows were tight. "Why should you care?"

"That's my business. Shall we?"

He bowed and stepped back to the middle of the room. "Give Ticca her weapons."

Sula moved out from the side with a silver tray. On it were two glasses. She stepped to the center of the floor. "What are the terms?"

Shar-Lumen said, "To end the declared war between the Duianna Alliance and the Nhia-Samri. Between the acknowledged rulers of both nations. Till one combatant cannot continue."

Sula asked Ticca, "Do you agree to the terms, Empress Ticca Duianna?"

"I agree," Ticca said.

Sula looked at Shar-Lumen. "You are the challenged. Name the weapons of choice."

"Odassi, sword, and dagger."

Sula asked Ticca, "Do you accept?"

"Yes."

"Empress Ticca Duianna, choose your glass."

So that's why she wanted the vanedicha and the formal challenge. Is this right? Should I warn him? Her instincts warred within her. The glasses looked identical. There was no way to tell and no indication from Sula which she should pick.

I'm a Dagger. I must do what is right. But poisoning Shar-Lumen? Is that right? The answer depends on whether or not I can beat him in a fair fight. If I get lucky, yes. But really, no. Not yet. I might be able to beat him in a few more years, after I've fought dozens of better warriors and gotten less 'wooden'. As my trainer always said, 'Be thankful when luck happens, but don't count on it.' All right, it isn't fair, but it is the right thing to do for the Empire. I have to stop this war somehow.

She calmly reached up, and just as her hand came level, she saw the sign she knew had to be there. The crystal glasses were etched with the Nhia-Samri symbol of the growling panther against the sun. The glass closest to her was turned so that the panther was almost in profile, leaving only a portion of the circular sun, while the glass closer to Shar-Lumen was facing her squarely, showing the entire Nhia-Samri panther symbol.

The one almost in silhouette against the eclipse is as close to the Duianna seal as she could get with these glasses. That one is mine.

She took the glass closest to her. Sula didn't blink, flinch, or react. She simply turned to Shar-Lumen.

"Grand Warlord Shar-Lumen, take your glass."

He picked up his glass and raised it high. "To an end that brings our people a bright future."

Ticca raised hers, as well. "To a peaceful future."

They both drank the wine down. It was sweet, and it burnt all the way down, but it didn't stop there. For a moment, Ticca thought she'd picked the wrong glass. The burning rushed out through her body and down every limb. But instead of cold numbness, it brought a feeling of renewal and energy.

They put the glasses back down on the tray, and Sula moved away.

Shar-Lumen drew his blades. "Empress, these are not from your royal guard. I hope you weren't counting on them stopping me."

She pulled her dagger and sword. An unexpected flare of power surged down her arms. The black sword she'd taken from the Knife didn't react, but her uncle's dagger did. The blade flared with a golden light, and the hounds on the hilt shimmered with glowing, silver eyes.

Shar-Lumen raised an eyebrow at the dagger. "I thought that was just a copy. This will be interesting indeed."

He didn't give her time to ask what he meant. He lunged in, his leading blade shooting for her chest. She twisted out of the way and brought her sword up, parrying his second. The clash sent shivers down the blade and into her bones.

Before she could change her parry to an attack, he stepped in closer, swinging his back foot under her as his blades screamed with the speed of his cut.

She pushed herself backwards, under the blades' path, and leapt, floating between the two attacks. As she started to fall, she twisted to the left, chopping down towards the floor with the sword, while thrusting at him with her dagger.

A howl of rage came from her dagger as it rocketed towards Shar-Lumen. He twisted sideways, and the dagger slid past, scraping her knuckles on his armor.

She pushed up with the hand on the floor with a strength she didn't know she had, causing her to fly up, cartwheeling in the opposite direction.

Shar-Lumen dropped one hand back to catch the floor and snapped to standing, bringing a blade forward and thrusting at her. She saw it coming and snapped her head to the side, letting the sword brush past, cutting some of her hair.

She finished the cartwheel and brought the sword along the same path, adding to its spinning momentum, to bring it back across. Shar-Lumen was forced to parry it with the edge of his sword.

She took advantage of her size and brought her leg up, kicking him backwards. He recovered and danced around her. Ticca kept her stance open and balanced.

Shar-Lumen attacked, slashing his blades downward. She brought her own blades together in a cross block. The strike was as light as a feather. Shar-Lumen's blades only touched the edges of hers before he pulled them back up and swung them around, spinning them in a circle, slashing up. Caught off-guard by the feint, she leapt backwards, barely managing to dodge.

Shar-Lumen didn't give her time to recover. He lunged in. Years of training reflexes saved her. Her sword dipped, parrying his blade enough to let her dodge sideways.

She snapped back, realigning her feet. As her balance recovered, she slashed at him with the sword while holding the dagger back defensively.

Shar-Lumen popped back to guard and easily parried her attack with the back of his blade. He brought his other blade up, slicing for her neck.

Ticca leaned the opposite way of his slice, avoiding the strike. She stepped around, and she kicked him in the shin. He moved away, eliminating the force of her kick.

As he came back to face her, his arm was slightly behind. He used the momentum of the spin, adding to his strength, bringing one of his blades in a downward strike.

She had nowhere to go. Ticca tensed up and brought her blades up in a cross. That time, it was not a feint. Their blades rang, and sparks flew. The force slammed her down to her knees.

Both her arms screamed in pain. She was in trouble. Shar-Lumen didn't give her pause. He slashed at her with his other blade. Ticca bent backwards, going flat on the floor with her knees under her. Shar-Lumen's blades shrieked as they cut the air over her.

As soon as his blade had passed, she slapped the floor with both elbows and jumped up to get her feet back under her. Shar-Lumen turned the failed attack into a spinning kick that hit her in the chest. She felt her feet leave the ground as she flew.

She arched herself backwards, in line with her momentum, bringing her hands over her head. Gripping her sword and dagger, she used the knuckles of a couple of her fingers to control the reverse somersault. She landed with her rear foot on the first step of the dais.

She quickly stepped back to Shar-Lumen as he stepped into her range. She sliced with her sword. He lifted one of his blades up, blocking the attack with the back of it.

He spun his blade, entangling hers, forcing it up, and bringing his other blade in for a thrust to her exposed chest.

Ticca twisted to the left, bringing her dagger up. Sparks flew as her blade engaged his, knocking it just far enough out of alignment to pass by her safely.

He was overextended, and she whipped her dagger back at him, reversing it in motion. It connected, with her dagger sinking an inch through his shoulder armor, stabbing him.

Gasps came from all around.

Shar-Lumen jerked backwards, pulling himself free of her blade. Bright yellow liquid, which turned sullen orange, oozed from the wound.

He grimaced as he went en garde. Ticca knew he wasn't done and quickly brought herself en garde, too. Shar-Lumen's eyes bore into her.

Ticca heard her trainer's voice. *Steady, calm, wait for the right moment.*

Shar-Lumen glanced at his shoulder. He stepped in, swinging his blades in a pattern she knew instantly. She countered as fast as he moved. They exchanged several nicks as they went through variations of the fighting patterns. It was as if he was testing her.

He moved in and out. Every time she was too slow, his blades cut into her skin. Their arms, necks, and legs were covered in a mix of her red blood and his sullen orange.

His attacks were sticking stringently to the fighting patterns taught to Daggers. However, Ticca had to use a mix of elven tactics, as well as several others she knew, to hold him off because of his raw speed and power.

Then he changed. He no longer followed any pattern. His blades sang in and out in a ballet of motion. Ticca parried everything. Her strength was reaching her limits, and they both knew it. Still, she fought on.

I have to relax like I did before. Release, calm, find my center.

She controlled her breathing, and she felt a core of power form at her center. She rotated, spun, and leapt, using it as a balance. Her swords began riposting against his attacks.

You forgot one of the best Dagger rules. 'Don't waste time in a fight. End it as fast as possible, or else you might lose by example.'

Shar-Lumen had been testing her, wasting time, letting her learn from him. That's when she realized what her trainer had always complained about. She had been *wooden*, stuck in the patterns. But she saw the balance, the core, and at her center was a mass of energy she could push off of, pull herself to, and use to control herself.

She shifted her stances and moved up and down. Taking advantage of her smaller size, lower mass, and female flexibility, she fought. Shar-Lumen was put on the defensive.

The chance came, and she didn't hesitate. She allowed one of his thrusts to cut her side deeply. The pain shot through her, but it wasn't a critical strike. By not parrying, her dagger was left clear to slam into his chest. The hounds howled a hunting cry as the dagger flared with power, slicing through his armor, digging deeply into his chest.

Shar-Lumen fell backwards, his grip ripping his one sword back out of her side painfully. His arms spread as he fell, dropping his swords. He brought his empty hands to his chest to cover the wound. Yellow and orange blood flowed from his chest spilling on the floor quickly turning dark orange. His hands started to glow, but they faded. He coughed more blood covering his lips and chin.

He motioned for her to come closer. Cautiously, she leaned down. He grabbed the back of her head and pulled her down, so he could whisper in her ear.

"I'm too weak. Honor the treaty, and let our nation stand. Protect our people." His mouth was so close to her that his blood rubbed off his chin onto her cheek. The strong salty sweet smell of his blood filled her nose.

Tears burst forth, and she sobbed as she wiped his mouth clean. "I'm so sorry. Kliasa waits for you. Go to her. We dreamed you could have used the soul statue of her in Llino to bring her back. And I wished for that so hard for her."

He stared at Ticca, and his brows furrowed. His eyes moved back and forth rapidly as he thought through something. His coughing continued as he said, "I name... First Warlord... Maru-Ashua... my successor. ...Make Ashua...." His coughing became uncontrollable as more blood surged out of his mouth.

Ticca put his head in her lap and cried over him. Everyone gathered, encircling them. Shar-Lumen stopped coughing, looking up at her, as if he was trying to control his dying body. His breathing became shallow, and he closed his eyes.

Just when she thought he was gone, Shar-Lumen spit some bright yellow blood out, reached up, and pulled her down again. He whispered, "Make Ashua...drink the water. He's...true son of Duianna...like you.... I can feel her... I can see her. Thank you, my Empress. I...."

Then he breathed no more.

After carefully placing Shar-Lumen's head on the ground, she stood. "Open the doors and summon all the officers."

Dozens of Nhia-Samri ran to obey.

Ticca walked up to the throne and sat in it. "Remove all their restraints. Our guests are allowed to leave or stay as they wish. Fetch an appropriate coffin for Shar-Lumen. I want his body placed on the right side of the dais. Warlord Maru-Ashua, you are to stand here on my right."

Sula approached and bowed. "May I provide healing for you, Your Majesty?"

"No, not yet."

Lady Lothia was talking to Lebuin, and they turned to Sula.

Before they said a word, Sula nodded. "Yes, I was given similar information. I'm aware of my mother's actions."

"Lebuin has proofs Dalpha was responsible for Elraci. Shar-Lumen was well within his rights to execute her," Lady Lothia said.

Nhia-Samri officers were flooding into the vast throne room, as were a number of people dressed in fine robes, but with no weapons.

Warlord Maru-Ashua bent to Ticca, looking at Lothia, Sula, and Lebuin. "Empress. The gods will execute all of us for our knowledge of Elraci."

She put her head in her hands and leaned sideways in the chair. She was weak and tired, and hadn't even finished clearing one problem up, and already more issues were climbing onto her back.

I do not want this. I am a Dagger. I can do more good as a Dagger.

"Lord Lebuin. Please approach."

Lebuin left his conferral with the other gods and walked up to her and the warlord.

Ticca said to Maru-Ashua, "Now is not the time for secrets. Tell Lebuin what the Nhia-Samri know of Elraci, and he might be able to prevent any punitive actions."

Maru-Ashua bowed to her. "I obey, Grand Warlord." Turning to Lebuin, he said, "I beg this does not go far. The Nhia-Samri are what remains of the Elracian society. We have lost much in knowledge and skills. Seven hundred years ago, Shar-Lumen discovered, or was approached by, those who remained. Together they built this fortress and brought their knowledge here. Shar-Lumen was attempting to preserve that nation. The whole society predates this world. And now, once again, we are a nation with a voice. However, we desire to quietly bring our gifts and knowledge back."

Ticca felt as if the floor had just dropped out from beneath her.

That explains a lot.

"Do you have proofs of this?" Lebuin asked.

"We do."

"I believe you. You cannot share your knowledge outside of your nation. I require safeguards to allow trade with the other nations. But Ticca and I have seen the possibility of letting your nation thrive, and I want to see that future. I will so inform the gods, and I will ensure the Circle puts protections to prevent tampering with your society."

With creased brows, the warlord asked, "Who are you?"

"No secrets," Lebuin said, smiling. "I am the grandson of Lord Argos and Lady Lothia. I am the keeper of Elraci. I alone dictate the gods' laws on Elracian knowledge. This knowledge you will protect as much as you protect the secrets of your origins."

Maru-Ashua's jaw dropped.

Ticca giggled and said, "Get control. We still have to convince the Alliance and Duke. But first, we have to find Duke and get to him."

The fifty officers who came with Ticca from Lumendaria stood as honor guard to the sides of the throne. They all looked fiercely at the Nhia-Samri officers who filled the throne room.

To the side was Lady Lothia, who once again floated above the floor. Lady Sula stood regally with Magus Cure to her right. Lebuin stood to Ticca's left, next to the throne. And Lord Bayion stood with the red-haired woman, whom no one had bothered to introduce in all the excitement.

Shar-Lumen's body rested on a panther's fur with his

blades crossed in his hands. His head was on a silver pillow. Someone had wiped most of the orange blood away, but a little had oozed out since and was turning even darker orange.

Ticca stood. "By the ancient Imperial right of formal challenge of peers, witnessed by the gods, the mages, the Alliance, and the Nhia-Samri," she said, gesturing to the body, "I have bested Grand Warlord Shar-Lumen. The Nhia-Samri nation now belongs to me, Empress Ticca Ethulin, true daughter of Duianna, and through me, owes allegiance to the Duianna Empire. Swear it!"

A thousand odassi blades came out, ringing together as they were crossed. All of the officers dropped to their knees, blades crossed before them. "I am yours to command! Command me!" they called out, causing the entire room to reverberate in the echoes.

Ignoring the pang in her side, Ticca drew her dagger, spinning it around her hand dramatically, and held it high. The blade bloomed with a golden flare, and the call of hunting hounds could be heard.

"From this day forward, the Nhia-Samri shall be the guardians of the Duianna Empire. You shall not take any commission or action that would harm the Empire or the Alliance."

The room remained on their knees, but they shouted as one. "Yes, sir!"

Ticca pointed to the Nhia-Samri around her. "These are your generals now. Only someone selected to hold an ancient blade of the Nhia-Samri may hold the rank of general. Do you understand?"

"Yes, sir!"

"Unless my family decrees it, you are to never reveal who we truly are. Outside of Hisuru Amajoo and Lumendaria, we're to be treated as ordinary Duianna citizens. Do you understand?"

"Yes, sir!"

"I declare Hisuru Amajoo to be part of Hopu Rinyaru,

and I name Maru-Ashua Grand Warlord of all of Hopu Rinyaru."

She stepped aside and motioned for Maru-Ashua to come forward. He looked frozen in place, but then approached the throne.

The room cried out, "I am yours to command! Command me!"

She smiled as she detected a lot more enthusiasm behind that cry than when she stood there.

Grand Warlord Maru-Ashua stood rock still for a time and then drew his blades. "Stand." The room snapped to attention.

He turned to Ticca. "Long Live Empress Ticca Ethulin. Long stand the Empire. *Vivant et imperii decus est famuli tui Duianna Hopu Rinyaru.*" He dropped to one knee.

The room followed to one knee.

Ticca motioned for Maru-Ashua to stand, and he obeyed. Turning to those in the room, he said, "Continue your duties until new orders and assignments come. Dismissed."

The room reverberated as everyone stood as one, snapping to attention. The room then began to empty.

Ticca and Maru-Ashua descended from the dais to stand with the others.

"Now, what?" Nigan asked.

Ticca said, "Just the impossible. Find Duke and convince him to stop the Alliance troops. Get the Alliance Assembly to agree to the end of war treaty. Then we have to get those orders to all the divisions coming in before any more battles start."

"I can stop Lord Dohma," said the red-haired lady.

"Who are you?" Ticca asked.

She blushed, and Lord Bayion coughed. "Very sorry, Your Majesty. Allow me to introduce the Right Honorable Lady Electra Neyon, Countess of Waylisia, Deputy Secretary of the Duianna Alliance, and Lord Dohma's unofficial intended."

Lord Dohma's intended! Shar-Lumen really planned on forcing this issue on Lord Dohma.

Electra reached behind her and pulled the short woman forward. "And this, Your Majesty, is Mandy, captain of my personal Dagger guard. She has served with great distinction."

Ticca nodded to Mandy, who stood proudly by Electra. *Not assigned to the regent, but to Electra. I wonder if Duke had something to do with that assignment.*

"Your Majesty," Mandy said as she attempted a curtsy.

Ticca nodded and held out her hands. "Your service honors Duianna, and yourself."

Mandy took her arms. "You have done more than any of us. I'd be proud to serve with you, but I'm under life coin to Countess Electra Neyon."

Electra gave a quick smile to that pronouncement, but didn't protest.

Maru-Ashua said, "Your Majesty, I think I know how to deal with this. Please, everyone, gather your gear and follow me. General Hiri-Rula with me."

"One moment, Grand Warlord," Ticca said. She turned to Lady Sula. "I'll take that healing now, please."

Sula smiled and stepped up to her, touching her shoulders and closed her eyes. A feeling similar to a gentle hot shower ran over her body, and with its passing, the aches, pains, and wounds healed. The feeling reminded her of one other thing. As she worked Sula's face tightened and her brows moved down.

"I'm glad I spotted your signal," Ticca whispered to Sula once Sula's eyes opened.

"What signal?" Sula asked as her brows furrowed.

"The Duianna coat of arms in the glasses to tell me which glass was safe."

Sula grimaced slightly and stared into Ticca's eyes for a split-second before smiling. "Oh...yes.... I'm just glad you won and are safe now."

She lied. Why would she lie? Sula stepped back, and Ticca decided to look into it later. There were more important things to deal with first. Ticca looked at Lebuin. "Can you do that magic you did in the desert?"

Lebuin looked at her and then laughed, stepping up and touching her shoulders. The blood and gore fell from her, turning to dust, and she felt clean again.

"Now we can go."

Maru-Ashua nodded and started walking out of the room. They took their gear back from the guards and followed him to a gigantic building on the same scale as the rest of Hisuru Amajoo.

He pulled out a key and unlocked the door. They all followed him inside and stopped, gaping at the white ship.

Ticca's mind spun out of control. *Lords and Ladies, the Emerald Heart! She's real!*

One joyful bell rang out from the ship.

Ticca stepped forward and placed her hand on the glossy hull. A steady, welcoming beat thrummed on her palm. A series of chimes filled the air in wondrous song.

Nigan coughed. "Um, maybe we should leave them alone."

Ticca came back to her senses, and realized she'd spread her arms wide and pressed herself against the hull. Reluctantly, she pushed herself away.

Smiling, Lothia said, "It has been too long since she graced our skies. We thought she'd been destroyed."

Maru-Ashua explained, "She was almost destroyed when the orcs tried to take control and attack Hisuru Amajoo. Damega ordered her to crash. I think we repaired her."

Lebuin called out, "What is this?" He was looking at a display case.

"Most of these items are Damega's personal property," Maru-Ashua said.

As she eyed another case, Electra said, "This belongs to Llino!"

"You may take anything you desire. I give all this to you," Maru-Ashua said.

Electra pushed open a case and pulled a large golden-bound leather book from it. "I'm returning this to my Lord."

Lebuin opened another case and took out a silver key. "Ticca, look at this."

"That looks like the key Vestul left for you."

Lebuin nodded. "It's an exact match."

Maru-Ashua pointed to the set of stairs that led up to the deck. "I'm hoping you don't get thrown off like I was. I think the ship likes you, Ticca."

"How are we going to fly it? We don't know how," she said.

"It has a helm, which I presume has some control. But according to the records, it flies itself just fine and accepts commands from its captain."

"And who is its captain?"

He smiled. "I believe you can command her. Want to try?"

Her heart raced, and she didn't even bother to answer. She ran up the stairs two and three at a time. At the top, she looked out onto the shining oak deck. Everything was so neat and tidy, so perfect. It was as it had looked in her dreams when she was growing up, listening to the tales of Damega and his flying ship.

"May I?" she asked.

The others followed her up the stairs, but stopped as a series of chimes floated through the air. It was a welcoming sound, so Ticca stepped out onto the deck. As her foot hit, a whistle was blown. It went up and back down an octave, and then a single bell rang out.

Maru-Ashua stood on the platform behind her. "According to the naval book I read, that piping was announcing the captain had come on board, and the bell signaled the beginning of the watch."

Ticca moved around the deck, touching the ropes and railings. It was magnificent.

Maru-Ashua stood firm in front of everyone else, holding his arm up, preventing them from coming onto the ship. Ticca roamed to the quarterdeck and found a chair before a series of controls with a rudder wheel. She walked back and looked down at the warlord.

"Why aren't you coming aboard?"

Smiling, he said, "Just want to be sure we're safe. Even chained, this ship is very potent. Permission to board?"

Ticca laughed. "Permission granted."

Maru-Ashua cautiously put his foot on the deck. Ticca felt a thrum through the deck under her feet, as well as in the railing. It almost felt like a chuckle.

Guess they encountered each other differently last time.

The rest of the group came aboard and walked around, marveling at everything about the ship. Lebuin and Lothia joined Ticca at the helm.

"Now what?" she asked.

Maru-Ashua moved to the first chain. "Now we find out if she can fly for you." He pulled his blade, and a gong rang out. He moved from the front to back. As his blade touched a chain, a light flared through both, and the chains fell away.

He then pointed to some levers. "Hiri-Rula, pull the locks and push the roof open."

Hiri-Rula concentrated, and moments later, the roof lifted, opening to the sky. The ship didn't hesitate; with a loud crash of thunder, it launched into the sky. Everyone grabbed for a rail or rope, hanging on as it flew upwards.

Ticca was pushed back into the braced seat. The ship vibrated under her feet. She could sense the power in the sails. She laughed with uncontrolled joy as they rushed into the blue sky.

With a snap, some of the main sails unfurled, and the wind rushed by as the ship rocketed forward. Rainbows danced across the blue crystal sails.

Maru-Ashua climbed up to the forecastle with a wide grin on his face. "This is everything I ever dreamed of! Isn't she magnificent?"

Ticca was too lost in the experience. She took hold of the rudder wheel and turned it, and the ship tilted and moved in that direction. She turned it the other way, and the craft responded. There were some levers next to the wheel that had shifted when the ship started flying. She grabbed one and pulled back, and it slowed. She pushed it forward, and the schooner sped up. More sails unfurled. Just as the wind became too much, it suddenly stopped, and an almost clear dome appeared over the decks. Occasionally, a rainbow danced across it.

These are a lot like the controls of that jet that took me out of Elraci.

Slowing the ship, she circled back over Hisuru Amajoo. The warlord appeared to be concerned.

"What?"

"You left Hisuru Amajoo and circled back without a problem. I see why Damega crashed it now."

"Why?"

"Our shields allow the *Emerald Heart* to pass unhindered."

"So how do we find Duke?"

He gestured to Hiri-Rula, standing on the forecastle, looking at the ground far below. He called out, "General, locate Duke and Dohma and give us a course."

Hiri-Rula went back to the quarterdeck and pulled a book out of her pouch. From that, she produced a mirror and began to concentrate on it. Moments later, she pointed. "That way."

Ticca laughed and spun the wheel. As the ship finished turning, she straightened the rudder and pushed the controls for more speed. It accelerated, deploying more sails.

This is so much better than that jet!

DOHMA

Lord Dohma rode on his horse next to Duke at the head of their division. The cavalry of a thousand warriors rode, arrayed to his left and right. Behind them marched the well-seasoned veteran soldiers who'd seen many battles with the

Nhia-Samri. They were only a day and a half away from the city of Allornia. Duke intended to take it back before closing on Hisuru Amajoo.

Behind him, Cundia, his privy councilor and Dagger guard, was speaking in low tones with Orahda, who nodded and said, "It could be the red rage."

Dohma pulled his horse short to let them come even. "What are you two talking about?"

"Cundia was attempting to discount the twenty years of weapons training I gave you. She believes your exceptional fighting skills are because of the legendary red rage of the Duianna Royal Guards."

"Well, I do get pretty mad."

Orahda harrumphed. "I've never seen evidence the condition exists. Don't discount your own abilities, my Lord. I've been training warriors for a lot longer than the forty years I've been Aelargo's weapons master, and you're the best student I have ever trained, except for a select few which have...well, an unfair advantage."

Laughing, Cundia asked, "Still keeping secrets?"

Orahda said, "I keep my promises."

As they went over a rise, the expected resistance finally appeared. He stared at the thousands of Nhia-Samri waiting on the far end of the valley between hills.

Duke's ears picked up, and he laughed. "That can't be all they brought to this fight. We'll crush them."

Dohma scanned the horizon to the left and right. "This isn't a bottleneck. They could have more forces out of sight, waiting to flank us."

Elades said, "If they do, we can have the divisions close ranks and squeeze them from both sides."

Duke called a halt and sat down, looking over the force before them.

"They're not stupid. And neither am I. Send out some fast scouts and order the other two divisions to close ranks."

The mages began relaying the orders.

Elades pointed. A lone Nhia-Samri warrior in red armor was riding out.

Duke said, "That's the warlord you fought at the base they blew up. Shall we see what she has to say? Maybe they're surrendering."

Laughing, Dohma spurred his horse. "Form ranks and hold."

Duke jogged along beside Dohma.

The warlord stopped a short distance from them and held up a hand.

Dohma stopped, and Duke stepped another pace closer.

"Warlord," Duke said.

"Supreme Commander, I'm ordered to cease hostilities and hold."

"Oh, but we were so looking forward to a good fight," Duke said, his tone dripping with anger. "I owe you one."

The warlord dismounted and took two steps towards Duke. "You may kill me. My warriors will not fight." She stood with her hands spread apart and open.

Duke growled. "This is a new tactic. Why shouldn't I kill you? You killed almost a hundred thousand with that stunt."

The warlord didn't move. "We were at war. You have killed almost as many."

Dohma felt his blood pressure rising. Dropping off his horse, he drew his sword. "You captured Lady Lothia. Release her and surrender, or I'll kill you myself, unless you have a mage hiding someplace to yank you to safety again."

He advanced. Still, the warlord did not move.

"I have been ordered to cease hostilities and hold here."

Rage boiled, and Dohma lunged at her as a primal scream ripped out of him. She didn't move, and he barely stopped in time. He stood with his sword tip touching her chest armor.

"My Lords, Duke, she isn't lying."

The warlord stared into his eyes. She didn't flinch or move. "I am ordered to hold."

Duke walked around her, growling. "Why? What do you hold for?"

"The Grand Warlord is coming here to parlay with you."

Duke stepped back and sat down. "Well, that will certainly speed things up. Why isn't he here already? You have that marvelous magic gate technology that was used to attack Llino."

"I don't know."

"And how long do you propose we wait?" Duke's ears swiveled. He turned and looked up. "I don't believe it."

Dohma stepped back, keeping his sword ready, and then glanced upwards. A black spot was in the sky.

"What is that?"

"Something I thought I'd never see again. What do you know, warlord?" Duke asked, still staring at the flying object.

"I know only that I am ordered to cease hostilities and hold." She sounded resigned.

The thing dropped below the horizon. "It's attacking our other divisions!" Dohma yelled and rushed back to his horse.

Duke shook his head. "No, I think we should cease hostilities and hold."

Dohma stopped and looked at Duke.

In the distance, a sound like an orchestra of wind chimes grew louder. Over the rise, fifty feet above the ground, an alabaster white schooner of impossible design, with outrigger sails on both sides horizontally and another set pointing down, with lateen sails that spread out and swooped back, came into view. Above the deck were four masts flying a set of mainsails.

"LORDS, THAT IS THE *EMERALD HEART!*" Dohma shouted as his heart leapt into the sky to be on that magnificent ship of his boyhood dreams.

"Yep, it is," Duke said as it flew past so fast that Dohma was almost thrown to the ground by its jet stream.

People were visible on the deck. Dohma didn't get a clear look at them, but he heard their screams of joy and triumph.

A jubilant cry went up from the army, and many swords and spears were shaking in the air.

The ship hugged the ground, and it continued over the next hill.

As he sat down, Duke said, "So, warlord. Uh, what is your name?"

She slowly lowered her hands. "I'm First Warlord Eshra-Zunia."

"First Warlord? What happened to Warlord Maru-Ashua?"

"The Grand Warlord will explain. I am only ordered...."

Duke cut her off. "Yes, yes, urd. You sound a lot like a broken record. I get it. Fine, we'll wait. Did you know about that?" Duke motioned with his head in the direction of the *Emerald Heart*'s passing.

She looked at the crest of the hill. "No."

"Good. I hate being the last to know."

The *Emerald Heart* came back over the hill and slowed. Duke stood up. "Warlord Maru-Ashua is on that ship!" Its top sails all furled, and it dropped to float ten feet off the ground. But then it started to drift.

A girl leaned over the quarter deck railing. "How do we get this thing to hold still?"

Duke laughed.

"Duke, this isn't funny! I know you know!"

He rolled on his back, laughing even harder.

Lady Lothia floated down from the ship. Dohma sheathed his sword and ran to meet her.

"My Lady! Are you all right?"

She smiled at him, and his heart lifted. "Yes, Lord Dohma, we shall all be fine." She moved towards Duke and pulled him up. "Duke, please. This is supposed to be dignified."

That only made him laugh harder. "You found the *Emerald Heart*...." he said, coughing, "... but... can't stop it! Oh, this is going to make for such fun!"

A loud twang came from the forecastle, and a harpoon-like device slammed into the ground. Three spring-loaded hooks snapped out from it, digging into the dirt. A male voice called out, "That's what this thing does. See if there's another one aft."

Another twang came from the rear, and an identical anchor dug in. The ship stopped moving as the lines tightened. Two men were shouting at each other, trying to coordinate the activity of tying off the lines.

Once it was anchored, a group of four floated down. One of them was clearly a Nhia-Samri mage, with her necklace glowing. The other was the largest Nhia-Samri Dohma had ever seen in full battle armor. The other two were dressed as Daggers: a tall, strong-looking man and a fit woman. She was the one who'd been asking Duke for help.

Elades came riding out of the line, whooping. He climbed off his horse and ran to them, grabbing the woman Dagger. "Ticca! Thank the Lords and Ladies, you're back!"

Elades put her down and looked over the group. "Is this all that remains?" His tone was saddened.

Ticca shook her head. "Nigan, Ditani, and Illa are still aboard." She put a hand on Elades' shoulder. "Carda and Malla are on their way here. We can pick them up before we head to Nae-Rea. But that's all."

That got Duke's attention. He stopped laughing. "What do you mean, we're going to Nae-Rea? With the *Emerald Heart*, we can take Hisuru Amajoo down to dust."

Dohma thought, *Ticca? This is the team that went south, that Duke said was following a long shot to stop the coming disaster.*

He scanned over the others and identified the remaining members of the team, leaving only the Nhia-Samri a mystery.

Ticca held up a hand. "Duke, allow me to present Grand Warlord Maru-Ashua. You should listen."

Maru-Ashua stepped forward and bowed. "I'm pleased to be able to meet you again, Duke. We have much to discuss, and we must present all this to the assembly for a vote. If we're fast, we can prevent unnecessary loss of life and any further animosity between our nations."

Dohma felt the floor drop out from beneath him. "Are you surrendering?"

The Grand Warlord said, "Not exactly. But it will take some time to explain. If you will order your divisions to hold here, we can proceed."

Lord Dohma started to draw his sword. "What makes you think I'm going to go aboard that ship?"

Maru-Ashua smiled and pointed up. Dohma's eyes followed the gesture, and his heart skipped a beat. Standing on the forecastle, his brother and Electra waved at him, smiling.

Duke looked back and forth and then growled. "Where is Shar-Lumen?"

Lebuin said, "Well...uh, Ticca killed him in a duel."

Slapping Ticca on her shoulder, Orahda said, "Oh, you're so going to explain that to me! Along with some other things that have been bothering me of late."

All the Nhia-Samri did a double take, as did Dohma. *When did he get here?*

Ticca's reaction was even more of a surprise; she let out a soft squeal of joy and jumped up, giving Orahda a bear hug.

"Amia-Dharo!" Maru-Ashua and Eshra-Zunia said together.

Orahda bowed. "I'm no longer in hiding, and you will stop hunting me. Yes?"

"Yes," Ticca said enthusiastically. "*Right, Grand Warlord?*" She added with a strong undertone.

Maru-Ashua said, "Uh, yes. One moment, while I issue the order."

Cundia slapped Dohma so hard from behind that he stepped forward. "We get to fly on that! I knew you were going places, but back to Nae-Rae on the *Emerald Heart* is beyond words."

Dohma coughed and then asked, "Where did you two come from?"

Laughing, Orahda said, "My Lord, you need to stop staring at Lady Neyon to see others approaching."

Duke shook his head. "Ticca," he growled.

"Yes."

"Will you please stop killing people I want to torture to death?"

"I'll try. Shall we go?"

VESTA

Vesta sat back, humming to herself. She activated the playback. On the walls, thirty displays shifted to show her Ticca and Lebuin's return to the Duianna Alliance territories via the Lumendaria throne room.

"You've watched all that at least twenty times before," Arkady said.

She looked over her shoulder at him. "Actually this is the forty-eighth viewing. I'm just so happy we were wrong."

"Well, now we have a tenth kingdom again."

"True. But I think it'll work out."

She finished going through the whole scene again. The displays returned to all the restoration reports.

"I just wish we had more satellites. I'm still upset we couldn't keep up with the diurdin prototype royal frigate she sailed out of Hisuru Amajoo on. I told them not to build it." Arkady griped. "Last I heard it was just a set of blueprints. I can't believe they had the time to finish it."

"Do you think the Nhia-Samri have more of those?"

"The emperor help us, I sure as hell hope not. Did you see the proposed specifications on that thing I sent?"

"Yes, a sentient ship with blended technology does sound like it might be a problem."

"The good news is that there's just that one building that's big enough to house it. None of our other scans show shipyard-like activities. And Sandeep itself is still silent. If there's anything active there, it's well-shielded. I want to send in some spies, but if the defenses are still in place we won't even get close enough for a visual scan."

"How are things on your end?"

"Well, Thilis isn't Gracia. But I doubt Duke will come looking here. I've set up a mimic set in Gracia in case anyone tries to check up on me. You'll note we have a full grid established between Aelargo and Nasur now."

"Yes, I did notice you're a lot chattier now with the extra bandwidth. I'm building a secondary grid link to Stegen."

"Oh, nice. It will be good to have access to the deep space sensors in Oslald's systems."

"Once Electra is back, we can start making some plans for how we're going to go about our work of helping society grow back up."

The city proximity alarms went off.

"Oh, urdu, now what?"

She focused her sensors on the detected flying craft heading for Llino.

"Arkady, you'll love this. Tie into my sensors." Vesta said as she flipped her concentration to the sensor inputs.

A heavy gust of wind blew down the street as the sound of chimes filled the air. People stopped what they were doing, grabbing their hats and cloaks to keep them from being blown off. A rolling cry of awe came as the people identified where the sounds originated.

Above, a ship with graceful curves flew over the roofs in an arc, heading for the docks. Eight Daggers manned the ship, maneuvering around the rigging, using the lines to furl the sails.

Someone yelled, "It's the *Emerald Heart*!"

Tasks forgotten, hundreds of people ran, following the ship's flight, some screaming and others wiping tears, all with wide smiles. Just as legends told, it slowed as it approached the three-story Blue Dolphin Inn with the four-story tall stone central boat dock platform. Two warriors stood on the forecastle calling out distances.

With a twang, a three-pronged hook attached to a thick rope shot through the six-foot wide chrome hoop that was at the northwestern corner of the stone platform. Warriors on the ship's deck began winding a large toothed winch and the craft swung around as the anchor line tightened. More sails furled as the ship was pulled down level with the platform four stories in the air. A pair of women wearing leather armor jumped down and turned to catch ropes thrown by their comrades, tying them to the horn cleats.

A plank lowered from the docked air ship, and the warriors made a formal line, coming to attention and saluting as Ticca proudly walked down the plank, to the landing platform. She stepped over to the edge and drew her dagger, spinning it around her hand before holding it high.

The crowd silenced.

Ticca called out loudly, "THE WAR IS OVER! SHAR-LUMEN IS DEAD! THE REMAINING NHIA-SAMRI HAVE SURRENDERED AND ARE UNDER ALLIANCE CONTROL!"

The crowd screamed as one. Lebuin with Runa-illa stepped up beside Ticca, and behind them, Lord Dohma stood as tall and straight as he could. The crowd once again became silent after hearing cries of, "It's Lord Dohma, Lady Electra, and Lord Bayion!"

Lord Dohma smiled and waved. "CITIZENS OF AELARGO, PEACE IS RESTORED." He turned and gestured as the remaining members of Ticca's team stepped up to the edge of the platform. Lord Dohma waved for silence. Behind them, Duke sauntered off the ship to sit behind the seven on the front line.

Dohma continued, "THESE SEVEN HEROES SAVED THOUSANDS OF LIVES AND HELPED END THE WAR. I GIVE YOU TICCA OF RHINI WOOD, DAGGER GENERAL OF THE ALLIANCE; LORD LEBUIN, DAGGER JOURNEYMAN MAGE OF THE GUILD OF ARGOS; ILLA OF CAWLI, DAGGER COMMANDER; DITANI OF KARAKIA, SPEAKER OF THE TRIBES; NIGAN OF EPPON, DAGGER COMMANDER; CARDA

OF ARFORD, DAGGER COMMANDER; AND MALLA OF LLINO, DAGGER COMMANDER. THREE CHEERS FOR THE HEROES OF AELARGO! HIP-HIP!" Dust came off the walls and roofs as the crowd screamed for the heroes.

Lord Dohma smiled and waited for the crowd to calm somewhat before he held up his hand. "I DECLARE A WEEK OF CELEBRATIONS IN HONOR OF OUR HEROES AND TO CELEBRATE THE END OF THE WAR!"

After the crowd began to calm, they smiled and waved one last time before turning to descend into the Blue Dolphin, followed by Lord Dohma and Duke.

Arkady appeared in the Llino control room next to her. "You know, you should move out of Llino. Duke looks like he's planning on settling back down there."

Vesta glared at him. "Never. This is my city. Don't worry so much, I won't let him find me. Right now, we need to get our workforce back. If a ship runs aground or a baby leviathan gets stuck in the Loren Sound, Duke will come looking for the reason."

TICCA

Lords and Ladies! That was thrilling!

Ticca let her dagger flip around her hand before sheathing it. As they descended, she saw the old sign warning about clearing the platform if the *Emerald Heart* appeared. From deep down inside her, laughter boiled out uncontrollably. Lebuin looked at her, raising his eyebrow.

She pointed. "That sign! I used to laugh at it, because I thought it would never happen again."

Lebuin turned and read the sign. He laughed, too. "I see what you mean. But now the *Emerald Heart* is yours, so I guess it will be coming here often."

She wagged a finger at him. "It's ours. You have as much claim to it as I."

Lebuin stepped closer to her, but didn't say anything.

Be strong Lebuin, you may yet earn my heart.

Ditani cleared his throat, and they looked at him. "I thought I might take it for a while. After all, you got the property in Algan. I need to travel a lot between Karakia and Gracia for the next few years."

Illa pouted. "Nigan and I wanted to use it for a little side trip."

They all turned to see a red-faced Nigan. "Uh, yeah. Well, um. I...well, I...."

Illa punched him hard, making him wince and cough. "Don't be so silly." She said to Lebuin, "Nigan asked me to marry him, and I agreed."

Ticca's heart practically exploded with excitement, and she squealed, jumping to Illa to give her a hug. "Oh, I'm so happy for you two!"

Lebuin went a bit pale and his mouth started to open, but he closed it fast.

This can't be that big a surprise.

She lifted her eyebrow to him, trying to get him to congratulate them by sheer thought projection. But, like most men, he just stood there slack faced.

"OYE! YA KNOW, DER'S A FEE FER DOCKING DAT BLASTED THING HERE!"

They all turned to see Genne standing at the top of the stairs. Ticca let go of Illa and bounced over to give him a bear hug. "I'm so glad to see you! There were more than a few times I thought I wasn't going to come home."

Genne patted her back. "Yeah, well, ya done good. A lil over da top, but yer one fer drama. Oh, and Damega paid da docking fee clear for anoder hundred years. After dat, you'll have to pay!"

Ticca laughed, and as she let go and looked around, she noticed a hint of jealousy in Lebuin's eyes.

Nigan also saw the jealousy on Lebuin's face. He pulled him aside while Duke, Genne, and the others chatted. Ticca pretended she couldn't hear, but, she strained to catch every word.

"What are you waiting for? You need to say things aloud to the woman. They might be able to read your mind, but they insist on clear, audible pronouncements."

"It's complicated, and you know it."

Nigan harrumphed. "Anything that takes a lot of hard work is usually worth it. Don't give up, and remember to do stuff."

"It may never be allowed, anyway."

"What do you mean?"

"The laws forbid it. Ticca and I can never be together."

"I don't understand. Why?"

"Our offspring would have too much power. It's to avoid corruption. It's the law."

"Ouch. I had no idea. But, to be honest, if it was me, I wouldn't give up so easily. Look at what we've gotten away with already." Nigan gave Lebuin a quick embrace, with a pat on the shoulder. "What are you going to do?"

"There's nothing I can do...now. But, I'm patient."

Nigan pounded him on the back. "There you go. That's a Dagger's attitude. You'll do just fine if you hang in there."

Genne and the others started down the stairs. They all went down to the main room, where a party had already started. People continued to stream in with congratulations and warm wishes.

Ticca headed for her table and saw it was heavily laden with food and drink. She looked around to see if someone else was sitting at her table. No one seemed to be trying to claim it. The food was still steaming. She pulled some extra chairs over, and pointed Nigan and Illa to them. Just as the five of them sat down, Ellar came bounding out of the kitchen with a platter full of milk glasses. He stepped over and put the first in front of Ticca.

She leaned over and gave him a peck on the cheek.

"Now, I know where this food came from. Thank you, Ellar."

He made a gurgling sound that rather resembled, "My pleasure, Lady."

He put the other glasses down, and bolted for the kitchen.

Suddenly, the main doors snapped open hard, making a loud bang. All went dead quiet and stared. In the doorway, panting, stood a woman dressed in royal robes that were askew, escorted by four Dagger guards who were so red faced and panting that Ticca was worried they were about to have heart attacks. The woman scanned the room and spotted Dohma.

"YOU THREE STARTED TO PARTY WITHOUT COMING TO SEE ME FIRST?"

Dohma coughed, appearing to be embarrassed.

The woman stalked over to him like a lioness ready to kill. Dohma had the strangest look of shock on his face, and Bayion was trying to get behind Dohma. Before Dohma decided, or perhaps he'd decided and wisely stood still, she grabbed the front of his tunic and pulled him in for a huge embrace.

"Thank the Lords and Ladies, you rescued Electra from that place!"

Oh, that's Ellua, Dohma's sister.

Bayion cleared his throat. Ellua looked over Dohma's shoulder. "Oh, and thanks for bringing our brother home, too! There's a pile of paperwork that needs to be done."

Lord Bayion blanched and sputtered as Ellua laughed. She shoved Dohma out of the way to give Electra a hug, and then she wrapped her arms around Bayion.

Ellua whisper to Bayion, "I was worried about you." She then said, "Now, we have a party and then a wedding to plan."

"I need help planning mine, too." Illa said.

Ellua glanced at the group. "Any other weddings?"

Dohma shrugged, "Sorry sis. Only two weddings to plan at the moment. But," he paused to look at Lebuin, "maybe another one in a few years."

Duke yelled out, "THIS PARTY IS ON ME! MUSIC, FOOD, WINE!"

As the evening wore on, nobles, guards, dock workers...

everyone came and went. The party spread to consume the streets around the Dolphin. Some of the Daggers took select people up to see the *Emerald Heart* firsthand. Duke had his table moved outside, and was laughing and drinking with the rest.

Ticca giggled as they all listened to Duke talking about everything that happened. When Duke took a break to get a drink, Ticca turned to Lebuin, who sat next to her.

Lebuin was smiling. "So what do we do?" he asked.

Ticca pulled out her dagger and spun it, dropping it into the holder. "Just wait. It'll come looking for us."

They sat back, enjoying the food and drink that never ended, thanks to Ellar's attentive service.

Later that night, the minstrels were playing some new songs when a call went out for Illa, who unwound herself from Nigan and joined the musicians. She took a dulcimer from one of them and strummed it. Then they struck up the tune Illa had helped write. All the dock workers quieted down to better hear the music. The tune floated around, bouncing off the buildings on the street. Then Illa started to sing, and everyone was mesmerized by her voice and the hope of her song.

> There's a time to learn who you are,
>
> A time to create who you'll be,
>
> Learn from the past; look to the stars,
>
> And build a home for you and me.
>
> Show me an honest blade,
>
> Show me where magic starts,
>
> Help the children to be strong,
>
> To live with courage in their hearts....
>
> There's a time to learn who you are,
>
> A time to create who you'll be,
>
> Learn from the past; look to the stars,

And build a home for you and me.

Teach the children to believe

Show them how to conquer fear

Help the children to have hope

To find the path where dreams appear....

There's a time to learn who you are,

A time to create who you'll be,

Learn from the past; look to the stars,

And build a home for you and me.

Learn from the past; look to the stars,

And build a home for you and me.

Duke's ears locked onto Illa, and his eyes narrowed. "Where the hell did that come from?"

Safe Piloting

EPILOGUE

OUR FUTURE

TICCA PRAYED SHE WOULDN'T TRIP, slip, or mess it up. She'd rarely felt this nervous. But there she was, out of her element. She was wearing a formal gown, much like the red one she remembered from her first vision in Elraci. She felt self-conscious in it. On her head was a diamond and ruby crown, with the Duianna coat of arms on the front, provided at the last minute by her uncle. She knew he'd intentionally not told her about it to keep her from refusing to wear it.

Behind her were her friends, Ditani, Lebuin, Illa, and Hiri-Rula. Also present were representatives of all the great powers of the world: Lord Dohma, Lady Electra, Lady Sula, Magus Cune, and Lady Lothia representing Lord Argos. Before her stood Grand Warlord Maru-Ashua, and behind him were the seven heads of state known as the council for the new nation of Hopu Rinyaru. They were all there to bear witness to the event. Her only consolation was that the ceremony was short and not public.

Keeping her head from tilting too far was problematic. Still, she managed to pick up the golden cup and fill it with the silvery liquid from the palace fountain without losing her crown. Turning, she walked to Maru-Ashua, who wore the crimson and silver colors of the Duianna Imperial Family. She looked him in the eye as she held the cup up to him in offering.

Maru-Ashua took the cup in both hands and looked at the people behind Ticca. He acknowledged each person directly, going down the line, squaring off with each and bowing slightly to Ditani, Lebuin, Illa, Hiri-Rula, Lord Dohma, Lady Electra, Lady Sula, his wife Lady Maru-Zanni, and finally Ticca's uncle, Faltla of Rhini Wood. He then turned to the seven council members who ruled over the civilian population of Hopu Rinyaru, acknowledging them.

Turning back to Ticca, he glanced at the silver liquid a bit nervously and licked his lips. With only a slight blanching of his face, he drank the liquid down in a single swallow and handed the cup back to Ticca.

She gave him a warm smile, remembering how metallic the silver water tasted.

Ticca placed the cup on the fountain, which descended silently into the floor.

Don't mess this up, girl! After all that practice, you can do it.

Ticca took a breath. "*Nomino Maru-Ashua nomine heredem regni Duianna. Et nunc cedo ad successionem in sempiternum.*"

She stole a glance at the council elder, who smiled at her and nodded.

A female voice came from all around. "*Agnoscitur, adversus Maru-Ashua Duianna appareat.*"

Everyone applauded. Maru-Ashua smiled, and against all protocol, gave Ticca a friendly hug. "It's so strange to know we're cousins and the progeny of Damega."

Ticca nodded. "I'm just glad I can go back to being an ordinary Dagger soon." She pulled on the dress, shifting it somewhat. "I feel like a fish out of water in this getup."

He laughed, and shook hands with all who approached and congratulated him for being named the next heir to the throne of the Duianna Empire. Ticca was glad she wasn't going to be the last of her family.

Her uncle stepped up to her. "Sorry I didn't prepare you for this. I thought I would teach you all about it in a few more years."

"Yeah, well, I was a bit rushed."

He patted her back. "And that isn't any different than any other part of your life."

"Can I take this thing off my head now?"

Laughing, he took the crown from her and put it back in

its storage box. "I'll put it back with the archives for the next time it's needed."

"So what else is in these family archives?"

He looked at her. "Sorry. That's on a need-to-know basis. Only the next Imperial guardian will learn all the details. To be honest, I'm still studying, even after holding this position for thirty years."

"Can I take over the position?"

"Only if you abdicate the crown." He quickly pointed a finger at her nose. "Which isn't an option at the moment. Of course, now that we have Maru-Ashua, it is a possibility later. But I was thinking of training his son."

"Why not his daughter?"

Faltla smiled. "I caught her twirling a knife, trying to do that trick you do with yours. I suspect she's going to turn out more like you, especially in the 'wandering feet' area."

Outside, a series of warning cries came, followed by a loud screech and the sound of dozens of screams.

All ran for the main doors. Ticca, even in the dress, managed to get there before everyone else. Guards were running everywhere, pointing up. She stepped out from the palace to look.

The rest of the group gathered around her to look where the guards were pointing, which turned out to be one of the palace towers. The cause of the alarm was apparent.

Racing around the tower, at a breakneck speed, the top mast only inches away from the tower, was the *Emerald Heart*. On the deck, dozens of children were hanging onto the foredeck railings, dangling their heads over the side. They were moving so fast that even the shortest hair was being blown back. At the helm was Maru-Ashua's son, Maru-Follo, apparently tied into the helmsman's chair on some books to boost him high enough to see clearly. He was grinning so wide every tooth was showing.

Tied into a position just behind Maru-Pollo was Nigan, who was hanging onto the back of the helmsman's chair with white knuckles and a massive smile. Hanging over the forecastle, both front paws wrapped around the bowsprit, was Duke, his mouth open, screaming right along with the kids. Riding on Duke's back, with her head between his two ears, was Maru-Sonna, Maru-Ashua's daughter. She was apparently laughing and screaming, her eyes bright with excitement.

As the ship passed, Nigan and Duke spotted the group in front of the palace. Duke howled as Nigan waved and whooped. The *Emerald Heart* dipped and swung back in the other direction, its keel going almost horizontal as the ship barely cleared the next tower, accompanied by more kids' screams. After banking around the tower, the ship's bow lifted, and it rocketed into the sky as the screams faded with distance.

"I'm not so sure it was a good idea, letting him fly that," Maru-Ashua said. He stood next to Ticca, his head craned back, using his hand to block the sun as he watched the ship finish its climb and tilt back, towards the ground.

Ticca tried to reassure him, in spite of the obvious visual evidence against it being a sane and safe ride on the *Emerald Heart*. "I'm sure your kids are safe. Uh…Duke knows what he's doing."

"I was referring to Duke."

Don't Interrupt

EPILOGUE

TIMELY KNOWLEDGE

OLMANA-YILLION

Olmana-Yillion stepped through the mage-gate and walked into Llino, the guards oblivious to her passing. She glided through the city as one who knew every corner and every street.

The late-night moons were up as she entered the Night Market. She paused for a moment to look around. Spotting the Hand she wanted, she moved towards him. He was with another client, but he noticed her coming and quickly shooed his current client away.

The client was dressed in expensive silks, and had six overly bulky bodyguards orbiting him. He looked at Olmana-Yillion and snuffed. "You can complete your business when I'm done."

"Lord, you really shouldn't. She doesn't like to wait."

Olmana-Yillion motioned. "I'll only be a moment. Be a good lad and entertain yourself over there."

The client pointed. "I'll not be spoken to like that. This is the Night Market, and you shouldn't have meddled with me! Take her!"

The six bodyguards started to move towards Olmana-Yillion, when they all fell backwards, shivering and screaming in pain.

"Come now, silly boys. Such drama. Don't be such ninnies. It doesn't hurt that bad. You'll be fine."

The client bolted for the exit at a dead run.

Olmanna-Yillion turned back to the Hand. "So sorry. I do hate demonstrations like that. You have what I want?"

The Hand stepped away from the still-vibrating bodies, turning his back so he wouldn't have to look at them. ' Yes, of course. I did everything you asked. I gave the substitute to the agents who forced it out of me. You didn't mention they'd try to poison me."

She laughed. "I didn't tell you to set a poison trap on the wrapping."

He blanched, visible even in the dark. "You knew...."

She patted his cheek. "Of course I did. But that just made it more convincing. You've been a good boy. I'm giving you a bonus for it."

He smiled and produced the leather journal he'd bribed the Knife to bring to him instead of the Nhia-Samri. The mysterious and impossible to break golden threads tied it shut.

"It took you a long time to come and get this."

She took it and placed it in her pouch, pulling out a small felt purse. "Yes. Well, it has been rather inconvenient to get into Llino the last six cycles, hasn't it? And I knew you'd take care of it. Here you go."

"One question. Why did you trust me to keep it?" he asked, taking the purse.

"Because you couldn't open it, could you, dear?"

He laughed, shaking the purse. "No, it would've cost fifty times this small fortune you're paying me for it. I'd be interested in knowing how those golden threads are made. For a fair price, of course."

Olmanna-Yillion didn't reply; she simply patted his cheek one last time, then walked out of the city and back through the mage-gate to Hisuru Amajoo. She proceeded to her library, passing the main corridor, into the long halls and chambers that housed the library's vast collection.

She smiled as she moved through the halls under the mountain. She knew every inch and every volume stored in the miles of archives. She hadn't been made the chief librarian of Hisuru Amajoo for no reason. She loved the passages, and she loved every volume there. She'd been keeping track of them for over 3,000 years.

She knew someday the potent rejuvenating spells and custom nanobots would lose their fight to time. But she still had at least a thousand years before she needed to start seeking a new chief librarian. She kept careful track of her estimated time left. It was her duty to make sure a new librarian was found, trained, and fully installed before she retired.

Various gates and wards needed to be passed. She held the ancient key ring in one hand, selecting each key as needed It took a long time to reach the special vault she sought.

The silver key that opened the door was unique. There were only three. She had one, the other had been passed on to Lebuin, and the new Grand Warlord had gifted the last one to Empress Ticca for safekeeping. But Lebuin and Ticca didn't know there were two doors that the key could open.

As she set the sliders, the keyhole popped open. The key slid in, and the massive three-foot-thick door swung open without even a hint of a sound. She stepped into the small library room, and lights came on automatically. The room was cozy and comfortable. There were six reading chairs, a pair of work desks, and one large conference or project table. The circular room was three stories tall. Every inch of the walls was covered with shelves holding the most precious scrolls and tomes of many worlds and two universes, and unique works by the greatest minds she had the pleasure to know.

She stepped over to the correct section, pulling a rolling ladder along with her. Climbing up halfway, she found the section labeled 'Temporal Sciences'. She rearranged the dozen books, making room. Opening her satchel, she pulled out a leather-bound journal, wrapped tightly in golden threads, and slipped it into the new open space.

She patted the journal. "Don't you worry. Duchess Yillion will let you out when they're ready. Now, if you'll excuse me, I need to plan a tea party in that quaint little town on the northern coast for the new Magus there." She winked at the journal. "He really does like my pastries."

Climbing back down, she closed the door and made sure it locked before making her way back out, locking every gate and resetting every ward.

Recovering

EPILOGUE

PATIENCE'S PRIZE

RICIO NATHER BRUSHED SOME DUST from his grey embroidered silk doublet as Adulir, the emissary for the Baroness of Tenby, made for the exit.

Silly nobles will always be doing something, causing them to need me to locate and fix their mistakes.

He felt the weight of his purse under his armored cloak.

I will need to get Muccini onto this one. It seems rather delicate, and with Duke setting up for a long stay, it will have to be done with more than the usual finesse.

Ricio scanned the area. His guards were still moving around him like planets orbiting their star.

I'm surprised no one has made an attempt on my life in over a cycle now.

He recalled the first several attempts on his life, when he initially started working the Night Market.

It took a lot of effort to set myself up here. But ever since that diurdin Magus pinned me and forced me to call on some favors, I'm not being seen as the most dangerous Hand. I think I'll have to arrange some demonstrations that I'm still a force to be reckoned with here. Well, at least my reputation outside of the Night Market remains intact for now. I'm not going to lose five years of effort to one Magus!

As he moved through the market area, looking for any possible clients, he thought about it.

There are those rumors that that Dagger, Ticca of Rhini Wood, spied on the Night Market for a time as part of that whole Nhia-Samri business. A lot of people would like to take her down for the affront. Now that she has returned to Llino in the flying ship, she'd make an even better signal.

He smiled at the idea of taking out a senior Dagger in a Dagger Home. He then shook his head, thinking better of it.

No, that would just bring Duke and all those Daggers down on the market like a swarm of locusts. However, she still goes shopping. I'll have to think about this a while. Maybe it will blow over on its own. Just need to have a few plans in place if this gets any worse or doesn't make some improvement.

It was getting close to morning, and most of the customers had left, along with a good number of lesser Hands.

Looks like nothing else to do tonight. I think I'll go get a nice meal, a hot bath, and some sleep. Then I'll start looking into the baroness's little problem.

Plans made, Ricio pulled his cloak tighter around him, concealing himself, and started heading for the exit.

As he came around one of the wooden stalls of a Day Market vendor close to the exit, a wave of air blew down hard on him and the surrounding area. Many people, including Ricio, grabbed their cloaks to keep them from blowing off. The gust of wind stopped, and there was a slight buzzing feeling on his skin. Knowing full well that anything unusual in the Night Market was best met with not being discovered as a witness, Ricio wedged himself into a dark shadow and made sure his cloak was fully covering him.

The twang of a large bow came from above. Ricio looked up in time to see a heavy bolt appear from nowhere and slam into the ground. As it hit, a series of springs released, causing three hooks to flower out of the shaft, digging into the dirt.

Connected to the end of the bolt were three cables threaded through a ship pulley and a smaller rope tied to an eyelet. The cables went tight, and the clicking sound of a toothed winch could be heard. The cables tightened as the clock-like *tick, tick, tick* of the winch continued. The lines swung around the end of the shaft, showing the pulley was mounted on an integrated swivel. The taut cables' motion, and that they ended in sharp points, reminded him of the needles of a clock.

The ticks of the winch stopped with the cables pointing directly above him. Even though nothing was there, he could feel the weight of something above him. A strange musical sound, like soft wind chimes singing an ancient melody, floated on the air.

That's the same sound I heard when I was directly under the Emerald Heart, *which is described in legend as the sound all flying ship sails make.*

The feeling that something was over him passed as the cable attached to the bolt swung away. The odd music also moved away in the same direction.

There's an invisible flying ship up there! My Lords and Ladies, how many of these things are there? More importantly, where can I get one?

Silence had descended on the entire market. No one moved, and everyone had taken to a hiding place, awaiting what would happen next. They didn't have to wait long. The sound of rope pulleys preceded the platform that came into view. As it lowered, more of its single occupant was revealed.

First, a part of a cloak behind a pair of expensive boots, shiny even in the darkness, was followed by grey pants tucked into the boots. Then his waist appeared, with two very expensive-looking swords there, as well as three pouches of fine grain leather, all marked with some inlay that was not completely visible. Finally, he saw the man's shoulders and head. His cloak was thrown back over his wide armored shoulders. His head was fully covered, and he wore gloves on his hands.

The stance, and rolling bicep muscles, declared the stranger was a warrior. He worked quickly, but with a clear purpose. His hands worked the ropes, lowering the platform. On it was an empty padded seat, decorated with glinting silver threads. When the platform touched the ground, the warrior stepped off it and walked boldly towards the market entrance. That was an invitation for attack. Two thieves rushed him with knives.

Ricio smiled at their stupidity.

Seriously? You would rush a warrior that made that kind of entrance?

Without looking, the warrior kicked out at the first thief, hitting him in the throat with enough force to guarantee death by suffocation. At the same instant, he drew both of his blades, performing a twisting maneuver, swinging the blades around behind and over his head, scissoring the other thief's head off instantly. The warrior paused to clean his blades, using the cloak of the headless thief, before sheathing them. He looked around as if to say, 'Bother me again, and all will die.' He then turned and walked to the Night Market's entrance.

From his pouches, he dug out a series of items and a leather booklet. He consulted the booklet regularly, as he placed the items slowly and with great care around the entry statue. Ricio caught flashes of light from the torches and street lanterns, reflecting from the stones the stranger was placing on the pedestal.

Those are jewels. My Lords, look at the size of those stones! One of them is worth more than the baroness's entire pouch of jewels!

He had to stifle his curiosity to keep from moving closer.

Finally, the warrior produced something made of gold that fit over his right hand. With a last glance at the booklet, he put it away. He gestured, and a beam of golden light sprang from the device over his hand at one of the jewels. The light hit it, causing it to glow bright red. It fractured the beam of light, which jumped towards the other jewels, until all of them were connected by the light.

The jewels lifted and began to move, with the bands of light between them, forming a beautiful filigreed web work around the entire statue. The warrior stepped close and reached up his hand with the golden artifact on it. He sang something, which vibrated through the ground, and through Ricio's body. Ricio could feel the powers being used, and his heart raced, knowing he was witnessing an act of a magnitude only the Gods could match.

The lights flared as the warrior's melodic voice reached

a crescendo. The jewels stopped their orbiting of the statue, glowing brighter as it changed from its marble white, to a polished silver, and then to the natural hues of life. But the maiden's skin was silvery grey. Her bright green summer dress moved in the wind. The wicker basket was brown with red, purple, and yellow flowers sticking out from under a red gingham cloth tucked into the basket. The sound of shattering crystal split the air as the jewels all fell to the ground, each turning into a sparkling cloud of dust.

The maiden of the statue fell forward into the arms of the warrior, who caught her. Holding the unconscious woman close to his chest, he bent down at the knees and picked up her basket. He then walked back to the plank. He placed the woman, who was clearly an elven maiden, into the padded chair. He placed her basket next to the chair. Reaching up he grabbed the loose ropes and pulled the full plank back up into invisibility. The last thing Ricio saw was that basket sitting next to a pair of beautiful maiden's feet and the shiny boots of the warrior.

After a few minutes of the sounds of movement above, the loose rope attached to the eyelet of the anchoring bolt pulled tight, causing a spring lock to release, and a set of hammers sprang out, hitting the hooks up out of the ground. With a quick yank, the bolt and its three hooks jumped into the air, vanishing.

A moment later, the song of hundreds of soft wind chimes floated through the air as a gust of wind blew dust around the area. Then all was quiet as the remaining denizens of the Night Market contemplated the possible meaning of the two dead bodies, and an empty pedestal that marked the entrance to the Night Market.

The next evening, when he came back to the market, there was a new statue on the pedestal. It was a rather odd modern art rendition of what might be a person. It incorporated many elements with spurs and textured surfaces. A small plaque read, 'Enemy of the State'. At first, Ricio didn't like it. As he entered the market a week later, he stopped to contemplate it for a moment, as had become his habit.

Strange as it is, the new statue is better for this place. It's appropriate. I wonder who made it. No one is willing to admit they know where it came from.

A PERSONAL NOTE FROM LEELAND...

As promised, no cliff-hanger this time.

If you liked the series, please, please take a few minutes to write a review at the eBook retailer where you purchased it. Here's a link to Amazon's "Leave a Review" page for this book: lartra.com/leave-review/thread-skein

I'd like to thank you for reading through the entire Golden Threads Trilogy. I hope you enjoyed reading these books. By now you should be familiar with the complex world history I spent twenty years slowly working through. If you write a blog review about it, please send me a link. The more positive feedback I get, the more energy I have for writing the next story! I love interacting with my readers, so if you feel like chatting with me about this story or others, please visit me. You can find me at:

www.LArtra.com
www.Facebook.com/Leeland.Artra

Sign up for my mailing list at http://bit.ly/artranews and get updates, special giveaway items, and be the first to know when I release something new.

LEBUIN'S LEXICON

Aelargo: A human kingdom that extends from the northern realm of the Halias-Ne Mountains along the eastern edge of Bear Foot Sea north to the Dorn hills northeast to the Alorn Mountain and all lands east to the Darian Ocean. Aelargo is unique as it is held a separate country from the Duianna Empire, yet it is to be ruled jointly by all the direct heirs to the Duianna Throne. Llino, the capital of Aelargo, was built by Duke as an Imperial military fort at the creation of Niya-Yur, and predates all other cities except for Gracia which was built at the same time. Capital: Llino. Ruler: All direct heirs to the Duianna throne jointly, however the royal line is lost leaving it ruled by the regents Chief Regent Lord Dohma Gerani-Uriosal and his family. Abbreviation: AL.

Algan: Inland farming city on the western border of the Kingdom of Aelargo.

Alorn Mountain: An ancient volcano, now dormant, on the northwestern point of the Kingdom of Aelargo.

Amia-Dharo: The second-in-command Nhia-Samri who betrayed the Nhia-Samri in a great war and helped the Alliance Nations end hostilities. Considered the second most deadly warrior in the world. Personal trainer for Ticca of Rhini Wood. Known aliases: The Traitor, Orahda Ima.

Ankidyt: The eleventh month of the Imperial year considered the second month of winter. *See Lebuin's Lexicon: Time*

Apprentice: Any tradesman under training for a guild (Mages' Guild included).

Argos Guild of Mages Sigil: A stylized gold dragon with the five silver waves behind it.

Argos: The All Father God of the Universe is considered the chief deity who oversees the magicians in all lands.

Arit: A strong, bitter drink made from roasted beans of the aritia tree, which only grows in tropical climates.

Avenarius: The chief officer of the stables of a king, and the officer in charge of obtaining positions for horses belonging to the king. This position has existed since before the Duianna Empire and is sometimes shortened to avener.

Blade: A professional soldier, mercenary fighter, sword master

Blood compass: A magical artifact, made with blood, which is capable of retracing a person's life. Its construction is taboo in many lands and illegal in a few. It is effective for as long as the subject lives and for many hours after death.

Blue Dolphin Inn: Dagger Home and merchant's inn that has a huge stainless steel hoop mounted on the roof, with a platform, which the owners and legends claim was the main port of call for the *Emerald Heart*.

Boadua of Mostill Valley: A senior priestess of Dalpha in Llino. Boadua left the temple to take up Daggering again being made the chief of medicine for the Imperial armies under Duke. Later she returned to Llino, but chose not to serve Lady Sula. She continues to Dagger out of the Blue Dolphin Inn.

Breorchy: Onasa Channel port city on the northwestern border of the Kingdom of Aelargo.

Brinhi Nik: An advanced magic and science research lab run under the direct command of Lady Dalpha.

Burga Mountains: A blue mountain range which cuts east-west across the southern part of the North Duianna Continent from the Darain Ocean to the Onasa Channel.

Burga Spine Mountains: A blue mountain range which cuts north-south from the Onasa Channel to the Windy Pass.

Carmine: A spice out of Rhonia used to flavor fish or poultry in cooking. It also has the unusual property of burning out the nasal receptors, causing temporary loss of smell if burnt and the fumes inhaled through the nose.

Circumveni Desert: A vast wasteland of unforgiving desert, which spans the entire Duianna continent, from east to west, along the southern edge of the Halias-Ne Mountains. No known safe path exists across this desert, and it is plagued with strange, deadly creatures.

Councilor: A member of Leading Council of the Argos Guild of Mages.

Cycle: A unit of time corresponding approximately to one cycle of the moon's phases, or about thirty days or four weeks. *See Lebuin's Lexicon: Time*

Cycle: One complete cycle of the moon Tempa. Each year has twelve lunar cycles divided into the four seasons: winter (Samag, Noelag, Foilleg), spring (Gearra, Marta, Abra), summer (Sealen, Ogmen, Luchen), and autumn (Lunas, Sultas, Fomas).

Dagger table: Various inns and taverns allow mercenaries to hire out from them. A Dagger table is reserved for only Daggers. Daggers signal they are open for hire by placing their dagger into the table standing up. Senior Dagger tables have a Dagger holder mounted on the table and, in Dagger Homes, can be owned exclusively.

Dagger: Professional warrior specialists for hire that hold to a strong set of ideals based on commitment, courage, and honor.

Dalpha: Lady of Light, Goddess of healing, woods, and the elves, represented by large temples in almost every major city on Niya-Yur. Her symbol is an oak tree with eight rays of light forming a circle. Legends state she was the right-hand maiden of Uialua, dwelling with her in Aridu-Veni-Kussi. Dalpha is believed to hold the secrets of life itself. Dalpha is married to Larak, the Lion Lord. Dalpha was killed by Shar-Lumen in the Assembly Hall in 15292 and her daughter Lady Sula took control of the temples.

Damega Drakeruin: Legendary warrior who started many of the Dagger traditions. Although very mercenary, he's always portrayed in a 'Robin Hood' fashion. A good-hearted rogue, who refused any offer to settle down. Supposedly stole or was gifted the *Emerald Heart*, a flying ship by the guardian of Sandeep.

Day: The 24-hour period during which Niya-Yur completes one rotation on its axis. *See Lebuin's Lexicon: Time*

Delivery Channel: A waterway system of all ancient port cities, which connects one or more rivers together to flow under the city, creating a simple, smooth-flowing, barge-friendly means of transporting large loads.

Demi-God: A son or daughter of the race of Gods, who was conceived on purpose with enough magical energy to allow them to one day join the ranks of the Gods. Primary attributes are nearly immortal with the ability to control tremendous amounts of magic.

Dilothalai: A medicinal herb once known as aloe-vera, that comes from a flower which grows in Karakia called dilotha, or Lothia's Light. Many Karakians, mostly women, also use the cream regularly to keep their skin soft and youthful.

Ditani (aka Kiotiaditani, Speaker of the Tribes of Kiliua-ona): A Karakian servant to Magus Vestul. Hero son of Lothia and Argos, and Lebuin's Uncle.

Diurdin: (adjective) Used for emphasis, especially to express anger or frustration. "It's none of your diurdin business." (synonyms) darn, diurdu, drat, shoot, blast, rats, urd, urdu.

Diurdu: (adjective, adverb, & noun) Used for emphasis, especially to express anger or frustration. "I'm really tired of the diurdu tariffs." (synonyms) darn, diurdin, drat, shoot, blast, rats, urd, urdu.

Dohma Gerani-Uriosal: Born and raised in Aelargo, rose to captain of the city and palace guards in Llino. In 15292, at the age of 37 Dohma, along with his sister Ellua, and brother Bayion were discovered to be of the regent's blood line and was restored as regent rulers of the Kingdom of Aelargo by Duke. Lord Dohma proposed to Countess Electra Neyon of Waylisia and they were married on Patredyt 21, 15293.

Dolphin dagger doors: Unique doors which are considered unbreakable and thief proof, that require a combination and a special key to open, and are used only at the Blue Dolphin Inn in Llino for Dagger and special guest rooms.

Dorn Hills: A large range of hills on the northern edge of the border between the kingdoms of Aelargo and Nasur.

Duianna: The central lands of the North Duianna continent, under direct control of the Duianna Empire. A human imperial nation. No claim to the imperial throne has been recognized since Prince Aphren Duianna disappeared in 10485 shortly before Emperor Covos Duianna died. Ruler: Imperial Regent Lord Aphastes Menthran. Capital: Gracia. Abbreviation: DE.

Dulgruim: A dwarven kingdom on the southern tip of the Duianna continent, bordered on the north by Karakia. Capital: Or-Ani-Thi-Umta in Mount Arm-Im-Trest-

Un. Ruler: Chief Queen Ninki Paha, heir Prince Amizin Paha. Abbreviation: DU.

Elades of Stegea: A long experienced highly capable dagger with a prime table at the Dolphin indicating that Genne too judged him worthy of high ranking. Elades served as the Dagger Lieutenant General under Ticca for Duke in the War of Hope of 15292.

Electra Neyon of Waylisia: The ancestor of Countess Muriel Neyon-Banaschel, the last chief systems engineer for the Duianna Empire. Born and raised in Waylisia, an Imperial province on the eastern border of the Imperial capital of Gracia. Countess Electra Neyon of Waylisia, the youngest Chief Deputy Secretary of the Duianna Alliance to an Alliance state. Electra married Lord Dohma Gerani-Uriosal the Chief Regent of the Kingdom of Aelargo on Patredyt 21, 15293 after the War of Hope.

Elraci: A lost human and elf nation located in the central Duianna continent. It once spanned the entire Duianna continent, from east to west, along the southern edge of the Halias-Ne Mountains. Elraci is legendary in its sciences and magics. Capital: Imridu-Nam. Ruler: An elected Senate of representatives, the Senate would name a Chairperson.

Emerald Heart: Legendary flying ship of Damega Drakerzin. Legend has it that it flies faster than any creature and is home-ported in a secret place far in the north.

Eri hish: (vulgar slang) (phrasal verb of hish) (of a person) Go away.

Faltla of Rhini Wood: Ticca's uncle, a retired tactics Dagger, who served in the Realms' War and trained Ticca from birth.

Gadriel: God of the dwarves.

Garduan-ka-Gadriel: The dwarven name for the world (more commonly known by the elven name Niya-Yur or just Yur.) Loosely translated, it means Gadriel's Flesh.

Genne: The current owner of the Blue Dolphin Inn, the original Dagger House in Llino.

Greyrhan: A province of the Duianna Empire in the far north, just south of the great ice fields.

Guard: City soldiers, general police force.

Halias-Ne Mountains: A thick, rocky mountain and volcano range, which cuts the entire Duianna Continent in half, spanning from the Darain Ocean on the east, to the Occiduis Ocean on the west.

Hand: Broker or facilitator for trade in various goods or services, usually illegal.

Hero: A son or daughter of the race of Gods, who was conceived on purpose or by accident with only enough magical energy to allow a live birth. Primary attributes are a strong constitution, high strength, no magical abilities at all, and with an expected life span of nine to eleven thousand years.

High Councilor: Chairman of the Leading Council of the Argos Guild of Mages.

Hish: (vulgar slang) (verb: hish; 3rd person present: hishes; past tense: hished; past participle: hished; gerund or present participle: hishing) 1. have sexual intercourse with (someone). 2. ruin or damage (something).
(noun) an act of sexual intercourse.
(exclamation) used alone or as a noun the hish or a verb in various phrases to express anger, annoyance, contempt, impatience, or surprise, or simply for emphasis.

Hisuru Amajoo: The city fortress home of the Nhia-Samri.

Situated in a hidden location in the mountains west of Nasur.

Hopu Rinyaru: A unified kingdom of displaced Duianna citizens and the remains of the Nhia-Samri city-state of Hisuru Amajoo. Established by treaty accepted in the Duianna Assembly in the War of Hope of 15292. Hopu Rinyaru was originally the southern portion of Laeusia, taken over by the Nhia-Samri. Its borders were ratified in 15293 as being from the eastern border of Yalthum to the western border of Nasur spanning between the latitudes of 8° north and 2° south. Capital: Lumendaria. Ruler: King Maru-Ashua, Grand Warlord of the Nhia-Samri. Abbreviation: HR.

Hyly: A semi-sweet liquor made from honey.

Innadyt: the sixth month of the Imperial year considered the third and final month of summer. *See Lebuin's Lexicon: Time*

Journeyman Mage: Title of a mid-level magician for the Argos Guild of Mages; carries a unique badge of office and is seen as a direct representative of Argos.

Karakia: A mixed nation of tribes spanning the central part of the South Duianna continent, from the Darain Ocean on the east, to the Occiduis Ocean on the west. The northern border is the Circumveni Desert, and on the south, the Dulgrium Nation. Capital: None. Primary gathering: Summer solstice in Wakiza Valley. Ruler: None, however each year a speaker for the tribes is named at the Wakiza Valley gathering of tribes. Also, there is a deadly warrior competition to be the speaker's companion, adviser, and guard known as Honor Warrior Guide. Speaker for the tribes: Great Chief Otoahhastis. Honored Warrior Guide: Eyota. Abbreviation: KA.

Khab: (vulgar slang) (verb: khab; 3rd person present: khabes; past tense: khabed; past participle: khabed; gerund or present participle: khabing) express displeasure; grumble. (synonyms: complain, whine, grumble, grouse)

(noun) 1. a spiteful or unpleasant woman. 2. a difficult or unpleasant situation or thing. 3. a complaint.

Kiliun Lol: Primary research station for advanced secret Elracian research. Conducted dangerous experiments using secondary facility called Niuni Lol.

Kiotiaditani: see Ditani.

Kishadyt: The eighth month of the Imperial year considered the second month of fall. *See Lebuin's Lexicon: Time*

Kliasa: The daughter of House Elaeus of Rea-Na-Rey.

Knife: An assassin or hired killer, strongly controlled by a secretive guild.

Laeusia: A human kingdom that lies between the Duianna Empire and the Kingdom of Yalthum. Laeusia was originally a Duianna Empire barony that was made into its own kingdom by the Duianna Covenant of 5231. Capital: Pentegull. Ruler: King Brinus Laeusia, Heir Apparent Princess Sheila Laeusia. Regent Lord Madiyaa Isran. Privy Councilor: Lord Anduelo. Abbreviation: LA.

Lahmudyt: The ninth month of the Imperial year considered the third and final month of fall. *See Lebuin's Lexicon: Time*

Larak: The Lion Lord, God of Archery, Healing, and Guards. Larak is said to guard all cities that pay tribute to his wife Dalpha. His symbol of a winged lion can be found in every city of the Duianna Empire on the guard offices. A statue of a roaring, winged lion stands watch over the arched entry of the palace in Gracia, as well as any major government building throughout the Duianna realms. Legends state Larak was the commander of the Meassatoni Army, charged with protecting all of the cities of the Gods. Although he traveled often, he lived and spent much time in Aridu-Veni-Kussi with Dalpha.

Lebuin of House Caerni: Born 15268 in Llino and raised in Llino. Son of Waylen and Alia, Grandson of All Father Lord Argos and Lady Lothia. Although a God, Lord Lebuin lives as a Dagger working with Ticca of Rhini Wood.

Llino: The Sea Princes' stronghold and capital. Notable places: Blue Dolphin Inn, the Night Market.

Lodi: The day of the week before Vendi and following Merdi. *See Lebuin's Lexicon: Time*

Loehesh Pattern: A specialized magical filter that alters the state of mana. Once mana has been transformed by the filter it gains a surface tension like ability and can be held by mages almost like a physical ball, while still being usable as a power source for incantations.

Lords and Ladies: Also Lords or Ladies. A polite expression used to indicate surprise or give emphasis. Also, used as a euphemism for any deity.

Loren Sound: An inlet of the Darian Ocean bordering the southeastern part of the north Duianna Continent.

Lothia: The Raven. Primary Goddess of Karakia and wife of Argos. She often takes the form of a large raven.

LUMED: Light-Unit-Microbot-Emitter-Displays.

Lumendaria: Capital city of Hopu Rinyaru. See Hopu Rinyaru.

Lundi: The day of the week before Martidi and following Solidi. *See Lebuin's Lexicon: Time*

Mage (pl. mages): The common informal term for wizards, or sorcerers, or magicians. The term may be used to refer to female or male.

Magus (pl. Magi): A higher magician who has achieved the rank of master in the Guild.

Magus Andros: A fifty-year master mage of the Argos Guild of Mages and Lebuin's mentor at the Llino Guildhouse.

Magus Cune: A twenty-five-year master mage of the Argos Guild of Mages and Lebuin's nemesis for all of Lebuin's twenty years at the Llino Guildhouse.

Magus Gezu: A seventy-year master of the Argos Guild of Mages that died in the summer of 15348.

Magus Nillo: High councilor and a sixty-year master mage of the Argos Guild of Mages and Lebuin's mentor at the Llino Guildhouse.

Magus Seriel of Elraci: An ancient mage who wrote the secret tombs of magic Lebuin acquired and studied.

Magus Vestul: An immortal master mage who predates the Argos Guild of Mages. Close friend of Duke. Lives in Algan.

Mana: The energies of magic which travel through and around the worlds of Yur's Universe. Mana takes on the influences of the materials it passes through and is also used or generated by living creatures. Mana is a form of energy which can be controlled and made to do work as well as be converted to matter. Mana measured in ancient times in units of *rellum*.

Mark: A period of time equal to a twenty-fourth part of a day and night and divided into 60 minutes. The name 'mark' is based on the tick marks used on all clocks. (see Lebuin's Lexicon–TIME)

Martidi: The day of the week before Merdi and following Lundi. *See Lebuin's Lexicon: Time*

Menadyt: The first month of the Imperial year considered the first month of spring. *See Lebuin's Lexicon: Time*

Merdi: The day of the week before Lodi and following Martidi. *See Lebuin's Lexicon: Time*

Miniath-Tur: A great fortress complex at the center of the universe where the All Father Lord Argos sits on His throne constantly overseeing all things and keeping magic flowing for all.

Minute: A period of time equal to 60 seconds or a 60th of a mark. *See Lebuin's Lexicon: Time*

Miumi: Port trade city on the Loren Sound on the eastern border of Oslald.

Muriel Neyon-Banaschel: Countess Muriel Neyon-Banaschel born in 10289 in Waylisia, an Imperial province on the eastern border of the Imperial capital of Gracia. She was also the last chief systems engineer for the Duianna Empire. See Electra.

Nabudyt: The seventh month of the Imperial year considered the first month of fall. *See Lebuin's Lexicon: Time*

Nae-Rae: An elven kingdom spanning the eastern third of the North Duianna continent, bordered on the north by the White Ocean, the south by the Burga Mountains, the east by the Darain Ocean, and the west by the Duianna Empire. Nae-Rae is a member of the Duianna Alliance, but is not part of the Duianna Empire. Capital: Rea-Na-Rey. Ruler: Lady Saba-Arrur, High Lady of Nae-Rey. Abbreviation: NR.

Nanadyt: The third month of the Imperial year considered the third and final month of spring. *See Lebuin's Lexicon: Time*

Nasur: A human kingdom on the southeastern edge of the North Duianna continent, bordered on the north by the Onasa Channel, the south by the Halias-Ne Mountains, the east by the Sea Princes' Kingdom of Aelargo, and the west by the Western Burga Spine Mountains. Oslald was originally the Duianna Empire province of Megea. It was renamed the Kingdom of Nasur after, and granted to, Imperial Cousin Lord Sesitak Nasur by the Duianna Covenant in 5231 for his heroic conduct with Lord Oslald preventing war with the Rhonian Empire in the Reislen Bay Kidnapping of 5230. Nasur supports the Duianna Covenant but is known to be friendly with the Nhia-Samri. Capital: Thilis. Ruler: King Helman Nasur with Regent Lady Adurh Chena. Abbreviation: NA.

Newton: The scientific unit of force used in the original non-magical universe. It is equal to the force that would give a mass of one-thirteenth of a stone (originally known as a kilogram) an acceleration of one meter per second.

Nhia-Samri: A shadowy, ruthless mercenary group of warriors of unknown size, who fight with inhuman speed and agility.

Nigan of Eppon: A combat specialist Dagger who works out of the Blue Dolphin Inn in Llino. Partners with Risy and is called "Hairy" by Ticca.

Night Market: A unique black market in Llino, in which any service or goods may be purchased through brokers known as Hands. The market opens every day at sunset and closes at sunrise.

Ninurdyt: The twelfth month of the Imperial year considered the third and final month of winter. *See Lebuin's Lexicon: Time*

Niuni Lol: Secondary research station for Kiliun Lol. One of a pair of secret advanced Elracian research labs built for dangerous experiments.

Niya-Yur (Yur): The world. The elves called the world Nhia in ancient times. The dwarves called the world Garduan-ka-Gadriel (Loosely translated, it means Gadriel's Flesh).

Niya-Ziel (Ziel): is one of the seventeen Duianna Imperial worlds built at the founding of the universe. It is home for three Duianna Union citizen species, the Zielats, Urganthiats, and Bratinians. Niya Ziel is named after the dominant humanoids' home world. The Juntiath House immortals have adopted Niya-Ziel as their symbiotic-protectorate.

Odassi: Single-edged magical weapons of the shadowy faction of warrior mercenaries called the Nhia-Samri.

Onasa Channel: Inlet of the Loren sound, which traverses through hundreds of miles of canyons northerly, to the great Empire Lakes, generally salt water transitioning to fresh water near the Empire Lake outlets. Also known as the Onasa River.

Orahda Ima: Weapons master for the Kingdom of Aelargo, personal trainer for Lord Dohma Gerani-Uriosal, current regent ruler of the Kingdom of Aelargo. Orahda Ima is an alias for Amia-Dharo adopted to hide from the Nhia-Samri during the 40 years he was hunted for betraying Shar-Lumen. See also: Terms: Amia-Dharo.

Oslald: A human kingdom on the southeastern edge of the North Duianna continent, bordered on the north by the Burga Mountains, the south by the Sea Princes' Kingdom of Aelargo, the east by the Onasa Channel, and the west by the Darain Ocean. Oslald was originally the Duianna Empire province of Steosae. It was renamed the Kingdom of Oslald after, and granted to, Imperial Cousin Lord Nimri Oslald by the Duianna Covenant in 5231 for his heroic conduct with Lord Nasur preventing war with the Rhonian Empire in the Reislen Bay Kidnapping of 5230. Oslald has remained a strong supporter of the Duianna Covenant. Capital: Stegen. Abbreviation: OS.

Patredyt: The fifth month of the Imperial year considered the second month of summer. *See Lebuin's Lexicon: Time*

Poalua: Lord of Air and Yur, twin of Uialua, chief God of the Circle, and according to legends, was once ruler of all the Gods. Poalua is the God of Laeusia, although he does not ban temples to other Gods. His symbol is a feather-robed and turbaned archer figure, seated in a throne and superimposed on a sun disk with fire around the edges. Legends also say he created a crystal city at the center of heaven, which was visible to all the realms of the heavens, called Thi-Illi-Veni (literally Brightest Star City), which touched no lands or seas and floated over all of creation, giving light.

Red Door: A high-class brothel.

Rellum: A scientific unit of measure for mana, abbreviated RL. The scale the RL unit of work or energy, equal to the work done by a force of one Newton, when its point of application moves one meter in the direction of action of the force. When used in physical construct equations, one rellum is the necessary energy to produce one-thousandth of an ounce of carbon.

Rhini Wood: The old-growth forest along the northwestern edge of Bear Foot Sea in the Kingdom of Aelargo. Also the name of the village and farming lands in the same location.

Rhonia: The largest main continent six hundred leagues east of the Duianna Empire eastern coastline. Home of the Rhonian Empire. Also, used to refer to any of the hundred plus islands that are part of the Rhonian Empire.

Rhonian Empire: A vast empire of eastern islands founded by Rhonias III after 834 p.m. and brought to the height of its power and glory by his daughter, Ruth I, and her sons, Amizin and Eluar, from 974 to 1024 p.m. The empire extends over three thousand leagues, and the waterways between the islands are fiercely patrolled.

Risy of Eppon: A combat specialist Dagger who works out of the Blue Dolphin Inn in Llino. Partners with Nigan and is called "Frumpy" by Ticca.

Runa-Illa: A converted Nhia-Samri warrior who is now the high priestess and first disciple of Lord Lebuin. Runa-Illa lives and works out of the Blue Dolphin Inn with Lord Lebuin and Ticca.

Samudyt: The fourth month of the Imperial year considered the first month of summer. *See Lebuin's Lexicon: Time*

Saturdi: The day of the week before Solidi and following Vendi, and (together with Solidi) forming part of the weekend. *See Lebuin's Lexicon: Time*

Sayscia: The high priestess or the great lady of Dalpha in Llino.

Sea Princes' Kingdom of Aelargo: A human kingdom on the southeastern edge of the North Duianna continent, bordering on the northern edge of the Halias-Ne Mountains, between the Darain Ocean and the Kingdom of Nasur. Capital: Llino. Abbreviation: AE. Commands the largest known navy and tightly controls all sea trade.

Second: Is the smallest unit of time measurable by available clocks and is of time equal to one-sixtieth of a minute. *See Lebuin's Lexicon: Time*

Sencial (aka Sentient): An artificial life form that lives in the ancient machines and technologies. Sentients are not machines but life forms created by the non-magical races before coming to Niya-Yur. When Niya-Yur was settled, Sentients were considered alive, with all the same rights as any other intelligent race. They were voluntarily put to sleep as the old societies fell, by an act of the assembly, to wait for the time of the races' re-ascension.

Sharludyt: The tenth month of the Imperial year considered the first month of winter. *See Lebuin's Lexicon: Time*

Shar-Lumen: (14223-15292) The Grand Warlord of the Nhia-Samri. Born 14223 in Nae-Rae to the Shar clan. He left Nae-Rae in 14523 with the brothers of the red robes to study their ancient tomes and learn their ways. Kishadyt-14537 Shar-Lumen starts the Nhia-Samri mercenary band based on the ancient descriptions he has learned and mixes a number of tactical and historical references together for the foundation of the group. Shar-Lumen was killed in a royal duel with Ticca ending the War of Hope late in 15292.

Sharre: A sweet wine made by the elves from unknown ingredients. If kept properly, it grows more potent over time. Five to fifty-year-old sharre is very robust and gives a little energy, as well as making people drunk extremely fast. Sharre over one hundred years old can heal wounds, revive tiredness, and sharpen the mind dramatically. Sharre over five hundred years old is thought to restore youth.

Skeed: (vulgar slang) (verb: skeed; 3rd person present: skeeds; past tense: skeeded; past participle: skeeded; past tense: skeed; gerund or present participle: skeeding) expel feces from the body. 2. soil one's clothes as a result of expelling feces accidentally.
(noun) 1. feces. 2. something worthless; garbage; nonsense. 3. unpleasant experiences or treatment. 4. personal belongings; stuff.
(exclamation) used alone or as a noun the hish or a verb in various phrases to express anger, annoyance, contempt, impatience, or surprise, or simply for emphasis.

Solidi: The day of the week before Lundi and following Saturdi, and (together with Saturdi) forming part of the weekend.

Sula: With the death of Lady Dalpha in the War of Hope of 15292 Lady Sula took up her mother's mantle of Lady of Light, Goddess of healing, woods, and the elves, represented by large temples in almost every major city on Niya-Yur. Her symbol is an oak tree with eight rays of light forming a circle.

Tarudyt: The second month of the Imperial year considered the second month of spring. *See Lebuin's Lexicon: Time*

The Traitor (Amia-Dharo): See Terms:Amia-Dharo.

Ticca of Rhini Wood: Born in Rhini Wood, a farming and trapping community in the southern section of Aelargo, Ticca trained as a Dagger. She has worked for Gods, and served as the Senior General of the Imperial Armies under the direct command of Duke for the War of Hope of 15292. Ticca maintains a permanent Dagger table in the Blue Dolphin Inn in Llino.

Uialua: The Great Queen, Lady of Birth. Twin of Poalua. Uialua is worshiped in all nations of Duianna. Her symbol resembles the Greek letter omega (Ω), which should always be placed on the upper tier of any structure, indicating her importance. The Duianna Empire uses her symbol on all of its boundary markers in the top border. Legends state she once was queen of the greatest of heavenly realms, known as Meassatoni, where she ruled from the great city of Aridu-Veni-Kussi (literally Greatest City of Beauty), which she built. It was the birthplace of Argos long before the great migration.

Urd: (verb) To be condemned by the deities to suffer eternal punishment. "Lord Argos urd you."
(exclamation) Expressing anger, surprise, or frustration. "Urd! I completely forgot!"
(adjective) used for emphasis, especially to express anger or frustration. "Close the urd door!"
(synonyms) blast, darn, diurdu, diurdin, drat, shoot, rats, urdu.

Urdu: (exclamation) Expressing anger, surprise, or frustration. "Urdu! The horse broke its leg!"

(synonyms) darn, diurdu, diurdin, drat, shoot, blast, rats, urd.

Vanedicha: A poison which induces a trance if a small amount is inhaled, and kills in less than a minute in larger doses. Victims are unusually truthful when revived from a vanedicha-induced trance.

Vendi: The day of the week before Saturdi and following Lodi. *See Lebuin's Lexicon: Time*

Week: A period of seven days. The Imperial names for the days are Solidi, Lundi, Martidi, Merdi, Lodi, Vendi, and Saturdi. *See Lebuin's Lexicon: Time*

Windy Pass: A series of hills and valleys which separate the Burga Spine Mountains from the Halias-Ne Mountain Range, bordering Nasur on the east and Laeusia on the west.

Yalthum: A human kingdom spanning the entire west coast of the North Duianna continent, from the Halias-Ne Mountains on the south, to the northern ice fields. Yalthum is as old as the Duianna Empire and has never attempted to expand its borders, but has bitterly defended its borders and western sea lanes. Yalthum is a member state of the Duianna Empire. Capital: Kayseler. Ruler: King Deorgra Yalthum, with Heiress Apparent Jawayi Yalthum. Abbreviation: YA

Year: The period of time during which Niya-Yur completes a single revolution. The Imperial calendar is broken into four seasons starting with spring. The month names for each season are spring Menadyt, Tarudyt, Nanadyt; summer Samudyt, Patredyt, Innadyt; fall Nabudyt, Kishadyt, Lahmudyt; and winter Sharludyt, Ankidyt, Ninurdyt. *See Lebuin's Lexicon: Time*

Yunna Minthra: An original fae Loehesh Pattern filter artifact that predates Niya-Yur. Only one exists somewhere in Elraci, Runa-Illa acquired it when it was given to her as a gift by Ticca in an alternate reality and then transported here by accident.

Yur: See Niya-Yur.

Ziel: See Niya-Ziel.

Zielat: a native or inhabitant of Niya-Ziel. A near human race of beings distinguished by their large size and potent magical abilities. Zielats are usually 20% to 30% larger than the average human with an average of 250% magical potential.

ABOUT THE AUTHOR

Leeland Artra lives in the Emerald City (Seattle, Washington) with his wonderful wife and idea-inspiring kids. He spent the first half of his life as an avid science-fiction/fantasy reader, while becoming a US Navy-trained computer scientist and self-taught table-top gamer. After twenty years of thinking he should publish, he finally got serious, pulling out all the notes and ideas he had stored, and sat down to learn how to be a professional writer. He soon discovered he got as much joy from writing fiction as he did from reading it. His goal is to transition to full-time writing someday. In the meantime, he works as a software engineer and architect at Expedia. In short, by day, he helps people take fabulous vacations, and at night, he helps people take even more fantastic trips of the imagination, which he finds to be symmetric.

OTHER WORKS BY LEELAND ARTRA

LIST OF PUBLISHED BOOKS
http://lartra.com/books

GOLDEN THREADS TRILOGY
Book One : Thread Slivers (January 2013)
http://lartra.com/books/thread-slivers

Book Two : Thread Strands (August 2013)
http://lartra.com/books/thread-strands

Book Three : Thread Skein (July 2015)
http://lartra.com/books/thread-skein